THE VOICE INSIDE

THE VOICE INSIDE

John FARNHAM
WITH POPPY STOCKELL

hachette
AUSTRALIA

JILLIE'S SONG Words and Music by JOHN PETER FARNHAM and GRAEHAM GEORGE GOBLE © 1980 WARNER CHAPPELL PTY LTD (APRA) All Rights Administered by WARNER-TAMERLANE PUBLISHING CORP. All Rights Reserved. Used by Permission of ALFRED MUSIC.

hachette
AUSTRALIA

Published in Australia and New Zealand in 2024
by Hachette Australia
(an imprint of Hachette Australia Pty Limited)
Gadigal Country, Level 17, 207 Kent Street, Sydney, NSW 2000
www.hachette.com.au

Hachette Australia acknowledges and pays our respects to the past, present and future Traditional Owners and Custodians of Country throughout Australia and recognises the continuation of cultural, spiritual and educational practices of Aboriginal and Torres Strait Islander peoples. Our head office is located on the lands of the Gadigal people of the Eora Nation.

Copyright © Sirius Nominees Pty Ltd 2024

This book is copyright. Apart from any fair dealing for the purposes of private study, research, criticism or review permitted under the *Copyright Act 1968*, no part may be stored or reproduced by any process without prior written permission. Enquiries should be made to the publisher.

A catalogue record for this book is available from the National Library of Australia

ISBN: 978 0 7336 5274 5 (hardback)
ISBN: 978 0 7336 5303 2 (paperback)

Cover and picture section design by Christa Moffitt
Front and back cover photographs (hardback) © Jimmy Pozarik OAM
Front cover photograph (paperback) © Jimmy Pozarik OAM
Author photo of Poppy Stockell by Georgia Blake
All other photos from Farnham/Wheatley collections unless otherwise credited
Text design by Christa Moffitt
Typeset in 12/22 pt Sabon LT Pro by Bookhouse, Sydney
Printed and bound in Australia by McPherson's Printing Group

The paper this book is printed on is certified against the Forest Stewardship Council® Standards. McPherson's Printing Group holds FSC® chain of custody certification SA-COC-005379. FSC® promotes environmentally responsible, socially beneficial and economically viable management of the world's forests.

To Jill, Rob and James, you are the best thing that ever happened to me – John

CONTENTS

Prologue ix

1	Opportunity knocks	1
2	'I'm the singer with Strings Unlimited'	27
3	'Give it a good go, son'	51
4	Dear old Sadie	67
5	The learning curve	73
6	A piece of meat	85
7	'I've got something in my eye'	105
8	He's cute. Very cute *A word from Jillian Farnham*	125
9	The hard way	139
10	Johnny to John	155
11	Boom-tish	161
12	Please, please help me	169
13	The Farnhams and the Wheatleys	177
14	I saw you in Red Rocks	195
15	Whispering Jack Phantom	209
16	Johnny Peter Farnham	227
17	Burn for you	251
18	The good, the bad and goodbyes	269

19	You only live once	293
	A word from Jill	
20	Thank you	303
Acknowledgements		317
The story of *The Voice Inside*		322
Select discography		325
Gigs, tours and events		337
Photo captions		353

PROLOGUE

I don't enjoy talking about myself, I really don't. Don't get me wrong, I'm an egomaniac, but dredging up the past and picking through what has and hasn't been, it's just not something I've ever really enjoyed. I'll try to share as much as I can, but it's not easy because I've never really been that open. I guess there are reasons for that, reasons for my reluctance. I was just a kid when 'Sadie, the Cleaning Lady' came out in November 1967. A kid dreaming of making a career as a singer, but working as a plumber's apprentice. I'd never spoken to a journalist before and there I was with people suddenly interested in me and asking me lots of questions. There were a couple of journalists around at that time, I'm not going to name and shame or anything like that, because that's not something I want to do, but a couple of people who were around then were looking for anything they could get, in any way, shape or form. They were relentless. When you think about it, trying to trick a teenager into being a bigger fool than he already is, because you're a fool when you're that age, well, it's not sport. It was their trickery more than what they wrote that affected me at the time. Still hurts me to think about it now. Back then I didn't know people were like that, had no idea they could be so cruel or manipulative. I was 'Chirpy Johnny', a naive, pretty, young boy and I was ripe for the picking. So there are things I don't want to remember. But now I'm sitting down to tell my story, it's all rushing back. The good and the bad. It's like my life is flashing before my eyes. I've got so much going through my head it's like *flick, flick, flick, flick*. It's a bit disconcerting actually. It's a very strange feeling sitting here looking back on my life. There are things I could tell you that would make your toes curl. I just need to make sure I get the balance right, because though there are things that have happened that are hard to talk about, I know I've been lucky, so very lucky, to be able to do what I do. And from all the wonderful things that have happened to me over the years,

PROLOGUE

from all over the world, I couldn't imagine my life in any place other than Australia. I wouldn't live anywhere else on Earth. This country has given me and my family so much. And this book? I don't know whether remembering my life and putting it down on paper is going to be cathartic or not; I think it might be helpful, somehow. It certainly brings some memories back, geez, my mind is going a million miles an hour . . .

CHAPTER 1

OPPORTUNITY KNOCKS

Picture post-war London, East End. Half of the area was bombed in the war, actually more than half. Absolutely flattened. Tens of thousands of houses and buildings were destroyed and thousands of people killed by the German blitzkrieg bombings. Whenever you see pictures of the East End of London from that time, all the people look dusty and everyone looks poor. I was born four years after World War II ended and though in our household there wasn't much money to go around, I never felt poor, quite the opposite. We knew we didn't have the stuff some of the other kids had, but we were never made to feel anything other than happy. Most people I knew were in the same boat, and there was so much life to catch up on after years of war, disruption and loss, so people were just getting on with it, living optimistically. It felt like all the people I knew were filled with happiness.

My parents, Rose and John Snr, were young when they got married, but not as young as Jill and I were when we married. My mum was a year older than my dad and the war years had interrupted her education, so she could barely read or write, but she was a bright spark and a sweetheart. She was one of three sisters and everyone called her Rosie. There's a good chance she was already pregnant with me when they married, and she was twenty-three when I was born.

My dad had been in active service peacekeeping in India after the partition and he met my mum not long after he returned to England. He never enjoyed talking about his time in India, it troubled him, but years later when he got older, a lot older, we were sitting down having a couple of beers, and I asked how it was for him in those times.

The silence went on for a while and then Dad finally said that when a woman's husband was killed, part of his job was to stop the woman from throwing herself on the funeral pyre and going up in flames.

I've never been short of words but I didn't know what to say to him after that because I saw the distress on his face. We never talked about it again.

After Rosie and John were married, they lived with my nan and grandad, Dad's parents, in a small house in Dagenham, London. That's where they were when they had me, and we stayed there until my sister Jean was born, when I was two. My other sister, Jacqueline, was born when I was eight and my brother, Stephen, is thirteen years younger than me, but he was born in Australia. Anyway, when a council flat came up, one of those massive tower blocks, the four of us moved onto the thirteenth floor. The flat was high in the sky and tiny. I can remember sitting around a gas stove with the door open in the winter to get warm before going to school. My mother never showed us she was worried about money or where she lived, she was always bright and optimistic. Like I said earlier, she was a sweetheart. I always knew I was in trouble if my mum called me Johnny. I'd hear, 'Johnny!' And I'd think, *Oh shit, I'm in trouble now.* I can never remember an actual walloping. Many were threatened, but they never eventuated.

'I'll smack your bleedin' arse!'

'Go on, get off you little sod!'

I can remember Mum sliding cardboard into my shoes because the soles had holes in them. I know this sounds like a 'poor me' moment, but honestly they are wonderful memories of Mum looking out for me. There she was carefully putting cardboard in my shoes to stop my feet getting cold. I would rush around outside and my feet would always get wet anyway.

My dad was a good man. He was a fitter and turner and he used to have this bicycle he rode to work at the Ford Engine Plant in Dagenham. It had a little motor on it and I thought it was the best thing in the world. Every Friday night, without fail, Dad would come home from work with a treat for us. Friday was payday and he would bring home Rolos, the chocolates. If my sister Jean – Jeanie Jam Roll is what we called her – was out, I'd eat hers too. If she came home and there was only one chocolate left, I'd quickly eat half and hand her the other half, which of course used to piss her off something shocking. Yes, her older brother was a ratbag! I was terrible.

Jeanie and I used to fight quite a bit as kids, which is probably not surprising since we had to share a bed. Head to toe, which was the done thing back then if space was tight. I regret fighting with Jeanie now, we lost her to cancer a couple of years ago. I came across a photo of her the other day that I hadn't seen for forty or fifty years. There's Jeanie standing next to me, a head shorter and she's got a frilly dress on that absolutely typified her girly nature. Later on in life she became agoraphobic, she couldn't leave the house at all, which was very limiting for her. On top of that, she took on the role of carer for my father after he had a massive stroke. She looked after him and my mother, too, which was a lot of work. I didn't know all that was to come, so I just used to rile up my sister whenever I could.

But my sister got her revenge for my chocolate transgressions. She got me back real good. Jeanie always had a better sense of direction than me. I'd walk around with Mum and Dad or other family and not really pay attention to where we were going. I was rarely on my own so there was no need. We went down to a local park one day and I was on the swing enjoying myself when Jeanie said, 'Come on, I want to go home!'

I didn't want to leave and I told her so, but Jeanie wasn't going to wait. 'Well, I'm going.' And off she went.

I kept swinging and hanging about but when I was ready to go home I got hopelessly lost. It was only a short walk to the flat but I got completely bloody lost. I'm still the same, I can get lost in a corridor, I kid you not. I wandered around trying to find our place and I must have looked very troubled because finally this man came up to me and said, 'Are you alright, son?'

I blinked, looked up at him and replied, 'I'm lost.' He took me to the local police station and the first thing the copper asked me was, 'Did he touch you? What happened?'

I told them no, and they grilled me for a little while. I was able to give them enough of a description of where I lived that they could work out where it was. I was so relieved as this copper walked me up the stairs. My mum was frantic with worry. Jeanie was happily playing with her doll in the bedroom.

When I think back on my childhood, most of my earliest memories are filled with music. My dad was very musical. He would whistle or sing constantly. Around the house, reading the paper, whatever he was doing, music radiated from him. It's the same with me. I love to whistle. Well, I can't now because of all the surgery I've had on my mouth, but when I could I whistled constantly. I was the same as a kid, I would whistle, hum or sing wherever I went, totally unawares, completely in my own world. One of my teachers obviously got sick of it, because one day he stopped in the middle of class: 'Right, that's it, I've had enough of that, stick your head out of that window and sing "He's Got the Whole World in His Hands".' So I did. I stuck my head out of the window and broke into song, singing at the top of my voice.

I guess I can't blame that teacher; even Jill loses her patience with my whistling and humming from time to time. One day when my career had finally started to take off again and we were flying a lot, we were walking down the aisle of a plane to our seats and suddenly she'd had enough.

OPPORTUNITY KNOCKS

'John! *Shut up!*'

'Oh, sorry,' I mumbled and closed my lips.

I had no idea I was even whistling. It's a family trait: when happy, whistle. I'm just like my father and my grandad.

Grandad's name was John but everyone called him Jack, which is where I got my nickname from. He was a sprightly old bastard. He was little but very agile, which helped him in the boxing ring. He fought under the name 'Kid Johnny Farnham' in the local pubs. Publicans would set up a ring to draw in the punters and away they'd go. When he wasn't boxing inside the pub, Grandad was busking outside of it. He'd start singing and people would spill out, surround Jack and all sing along with him. It was the same story at home. He could play the piano by ear and someone, my dad or grandad, would be whistling or singing and then an uncle or aunty would catch on and break into harmony and, before you knew it, the whole family would be singing in three- or four-part harmonies. I'm sure it sounds like a scene out of a musical but that's what it was like. It was wonderful. At every 'knees up', which is not a piss-up but just a party, someone, either my mum or Aunty Mary or Aunty Grace or even Nan, would stick a lampshade on her head and kick off into the Cockney classic 'Knees Up Mother Brown'. Then we'd all join in.

Knees up Mother Brown
Knees up Mother Brown
Under the table you must go
Ee-aye, Ee-aye, Ee-aye-oh
If I catch you bending
I'll saw your legs right off
Knees up, knees up
Never get the breeze up
Knees up Mother Brown

My Uncle Christopher, Dad's brother, was also a bit of a musician. He was in a trio with another couple of local lads and they would perform around the place. One day they even got themselves on the British talent show *Opportunity Knocks*. It was so exciting, we all huddled around Nan's television because she was the only one who owned one, and we watched Uncle Chris perform.

Stupidly enough, I did a version of *Opportunity Knocks* years later in Australia, not as a singer but as the compere and it was the worst. I was working on another show, a pilot program for a drama series and the director of Channel 7 literally blackmailed me into doing it. He cornered me in the studio one day and said, 'I want you to do *Opportunity Knocks*.'

I said, 'No, I don't want to do that.' He said, 'Well if you don't do it, you won't go on the drama series.' It was pretty clear he wasn't going to take no for an answer so I said, 'Oh okay. I'll do it.' (When you put it like that . . .)

The creator and host of the show, Hughie Green, came over from London for the taping of the program. It was a nightmare and he wasn't much fun at all. He had this particular way of saying 'opportunity knocks' that really drew out the syllables and he combined that with an over-egged North American accent. He didn't like the way I said the words at all.

'No, you're doing it wrong!' he kept telling me. He didn't give me any advice or direction other than, 'When you talk about the show, say Op-por-tun-i-ty Knocks!'

I tried it, over and over, but I could never get it how he wanted.

I never would have dreamed, at eight or nine years old huddled around the TV at Nan's, that one day I would be on the other side of the screen. But all that was years away and all that mattered at that moment was that Uncle Chris was amazing. He had beautiful bright red hair, not that you could see that on the black and white telly, and a good singing voice, but his band didn't win.

So much of our family life revolved around music. My Uncle Alf had a record player and I used to listen to Tommy Steele, the Everly Brothers and Paul Anka over and over when I was a kid. I loved them all. Years later I went to see Tommy Steele at Her Majesty's Theatre in Melbourne with my nan. After the show we waited at the stage door to catch a glimpse of him. Eventually Tommy emerged. There were about ten or fifteen other people there with us and Nan mustered up her thickest Cockney accent and shouted over the crowd, 'Tommy! Can we have your autograph? We've come all the way from England to see you!'

That wasn't why we'd moved to Australia so I nearly died hearing that, but it worked and we got his autograph.

I'd never really thought about Australia, or the possibility of moving here until one day my family went to South End, to the beach. It's hard to call it a beach when there's no sand but at the time it was the only beach I knew of. My Uncle Alan, who was like an older brother to me, had bought this army surplus life raft, a big circular thing, about twelve foot in diameter and we launched it off the pebbles into the sea. We were all sitting in it – me, my Uncle Alf, Uncle Alan, Uncle George, Uncle Christopher, Dad and Grandad – rocking on the tide and Grandad, because he was always the life of the party, stood up shakily and barked out to no-one and everyone, 'Why don't we paddle all the way to Australia?!'

OPPORTUNITY KNOCKS

We did no such thing that day of course but the joke lingered, then morphed into an actual question. That was perhaps the first time I heard of the possibility of immigrating.

Next thing I remember I was watching an advertisement on the telly at Nan's place. It must have been a call-out for the ten-pound Pom scheme but all I remember were sparrows landing on someone's knee and then eating out of someone's open palm. 'Immigrate to Australia where you can have birds sitting on your knee!'

Some of the extended family had already made the trip, and then it was happening for us. We were moving to the other side of the world as assisted passage migrants – yes, ten-pound Poms, but kids travelled free. I can remember lying in bed at night listening to my dad and my Uncle Alf nailing tea chests closed. They were packing up all our gear, and that packing continued right up until the day before we left. Even the morning we set sail they were still stuffing clothes into suitcases. We left England from Southampton in early 1959 on the SS *Orsova*, bound for a different life.

We were the second wave of Farnhams to leave England. There was me, Mum, Dad, Jeanie, Jacqueline, Nan and Grandad, two uncles and 1500 other passengers. I was nine, Jean was seven and Jacqueline was one.

It took us about six weeks of sailing to make it to Australia. Luckily I found my sea legs quickly, but Nan and Grandad were sick the entire voyage. We'd be up on deck and I'd turn to Mum and ask her where Nan and Grandad were, but I didn't think much more about them because there was always something to keep me busy onboard. I only found out years later that they spent most of the trip vomiting their guts up in the cabin.

Us kids had our moments on the ship. Jacqueline was a pretty little thing, and it turned out there was a man onboard who was rumoured to be an Arab prince or dignitary, or perhaps he was just very wealthy. Anyway, he took a shine to Jackie and offered to buy her from my parents. My father was beside himself. He was furious, but he didn't seek any punishment for the fellow's inappropriate request. He and my mother were far too English, they just gave a polite smile, spun around and walked off, with Jackie in their arms, in the opposite direction. Of course they wouldn't sell Jackie or even consider it, but I am sure they kept a close eye on her for the rest of the trip.

No-one tried to buy me, but I did nearly fall overboard. I never told Mum or Dad, not at the time; actually, not ever. I had a little tomahawk, a toy one not a real one, which I loved. One day I left it in the kids' area. It was much later in the day when I got back to our cabin and realised I'd left it behind. I went to get it but the access doors to the area were closed. I could see the tomahawk on the other side of the glass gate so I decided to get up on the outside rail and climb around. Not exactly a good idea, and it got worse as I climbed. It turned out there was a partition in my way. As I was manoeuvring around it my foot slipped. I somehow just managed to hold on, my feet dangling down with the ocean beneath me. I regained my footing and made it around the partition and into the kids' area. Safely back on deck, I picked up the tomahawk, took one look at it and tossed it overboard. Better it than me.

It seemed like those weeks went quickly, though not quickly enough for my seasick grandparents. We stopped at Fremantle first, and then the next thing I knew we were coming into Melbourne. I remember the ship felt like it was tilting because everyone had rushed to the one side to wave to their relatives ashore. All the relatives were waving madly back. We arrived in Melbourne on 15 May 1959.

Because half the family on my dad's side were already settled here, we managed to dodge the transit hostel and we all moved straight into Aunty Mary's weatherboard house at Lot 13, Joan Court, Noble Park. The first wave of Farnhams, uncles Stephen and George and aunties Grace and Mary, had stayed in one of the hostels when they first arrived and they told us it was dismal. There were maggots in the rice and all sorts of depressing things like that, but they coped and eventually did quite well for themselves. We were lucky to skip all that when we moved straight in with family.

Thankfully, nobody could ever accuse us of being whingeing Poms. We weren't anyway, but soon after we arrived, Mum, Nan and Aunty Mary pooled their money and bought a lottery ticket, or Tatts ticket as they were known. They bloody won! They won £10,000, can you believe? That was a lot of money back then. They were beside themselves, jumping up and down, carrying on. Of course, Jeanie and I had no idea what was happening. Eventually they calmed down, then they sat us down and told us (Jacqueline was still too young for a sit-down like that). I couldn't believe it. The prize was divvied up and the money allowed them to each put a deposit down on a house or land. Mum and Dad bought a block and built our house at number 10 Doonbrae Avenue, Noble Park. Aunty Mary, Nan and Grandad bought houses just around the corner.

From day one I embraced living in Australia. I was so happy and grateful to be here. But I didn't like school. I didn't like it anytime, anywhere, England or Australia. When I arrived in Noble Park they put me into a grade below my age group because I'd missed out on so much schooling on the voyage, so that wasn't a good start. Then, on my first day of school, I got six of the best. The teacher lashed me three across each hand and the strap was about an eighth of an inch thick. It hurt!

I'd been sitting in class and the kid next to me farted. He dropped his guts and when the smell hit I blurted out, 'Yuck!' The teacher was not impressed and he strapped me for it. There I was, standing up the front getting lashed and trying not to cry in front of my new schoolmates. What a brute that Mr Baddley was. Mind you, I can still remember some of the lessons he taught me.

'Now, when you talk, don't talk through your nose like that, talk through your throat and your mouth.'

I remember that lesson vividly. And when you think about it and actually start listening to people, a lot of Australians, English too, they speak very nasally, they talk through their noses. That made such an impression on me. Ever since that day, I've always tried to talk through my throat and mouth rather than my nose.

I got through primary school okay and then started high school at Lyndale High. Australia is a sporty nation and Lyndale High School was a sporty school, but unfortunately I wasn't sporty at all. I was a fat kid. I was good at tunnel ball and that's about it. Everyone was Australian Rules mad and I tried my best at the game, but my best wasn't near good enough.

One time we were playing against a neighbouring school and I took this terrific mark. I was thrilled. I caught the ball and held it tight against my chest. I started running like buggery toward the goal but my head was faster than my legs and I went arse over. Somehow, I picked myself up and retrieved the ball. A teammate standing in front of goal was yelling madly for the ball so I kicked it as hard as I could. It went straight up, then came straight back down again. In a matter of moments I had ballsed it up twice. First with the stack, then the kick.

Cricket was worse. It nearly knocked me out. They had me fielding in silly mid-on, which, if you don't know, is fielding dangerously close to the batter. No helmet back in those days. This kid hit the ball and it got me right in the eye. Geez, it hurt. Gave me the best black eye though. That was it for me and cricket.

Being a fat kid, in those days, made me a prime target for bullies. There was one boy who used to give me hell. He was in the grade above me and wherever I went, he'd be there. He had it in for me. Do you remember the Three Stooges? They were a vaudeville comedy trio all us kids would watch on television. They had this signature slapstick joke which was the 'V' finger eye poke. One of the Stooges would go to poke the other in the eye but before he could, the other Stooge would block the fingers just in the nick of time. Well, this older boy came up and did that move to me and, of course, I didn't have time to block him and he actually scratched my eyeballs. It was awful.

I didn't fare much better in class. I was a terrible student. I was forever daydreaming out the window. I'd rather be out doing something, anything, than sitting in a stuffy classroom. One particular maths class I was sitting there daydreaming as usual. The maths teacher was a big man, huge even, he was well over six foot tall with a barrel chest. Out of nowhere he suddenly bellowed, 'Farnham! What are you doing?'

I must have been thinking about how I was going to sort out the boys who were bullying me because I blurted back to this teacher, 'Do you want a fat lip?' I honestly don't know where it came from. I mean, it's the last thing I would say to a teacher, let alone to a giant. *Do you want a fat lip?* Blimey. He gave me a detention and I was relieved that I wasn't getting the strap.

One day I tried to get my own back, I tried bullying someone else. I thought, if I'm getting bullied, I'm going to give it to someone else. I went out into the schoolyard and found this skinny little kid who was minding his own business, hunched over playing marbles. I walked straight up to him and gave him a big push in the back. Quick as a flash, the kid regained his balance, swung around and gave me one in the nose. Smack!

His punch was so quick and so strong it took me by absolute surprise.

'Piss off!' he said.

I ran away crying. I wanted to crawl under some rocks. I knew I'd done wrong and I knew I deserved that punch. It was a valuable lesson. If you don't know pain then you never understand it in others.

Thankfully the story at home couldn't have been more different. My home life was very loving. I never heard my mum and dad have a harsh word between them. I'm sure they did, because that's just the way it is, but in front of us kids they never fought. I can remember when Jill and I first got married, I had in my head that we would never argue. I wanted to model our marriage on my parents', and not arguing was what I'd grown up with.

Something would happen between Jilly and me and if it was going to escalate into an argument, I would just hold up my hand, drop my head and walk away. Then, later, I'd gloss over it like nothing had ever happened. That must have been really frustrating, being married to someone who wouldn't react. I mean, everyone wants a reaction.

One day, Jill came to me and she said, 'I want to ask you to do something. When we are having a disagreement, I want you to argue back!'

'But I don't argue.'

'I *need* you to argue with me. Argue back!'

And so I try to do what Jill asked, but I've never really mastered it. I try to react and give Jill something to bounce off. It costs me nothing to say I'm sorry or to say it's my fault. And if I don't believe it's my fault, I'll still say sorry. Because I value my relationship with Jill and I've got no qualms owning up to whatever it is to make her happy. I guess that's the influence of my love for Jill. We've been married for over fifty years now. So it's working!

Family is important to me. All of my dad's side of the family immigrated to Australia and settled in or around Noble Park, so we got on with being the same tight family unit we'd been back in England. I can't ever remember an unpleasant time when we were all together. We were all so happy to be in Australia and we wanted to make the most of it. So we did. We'd go fishing up at Eildon Weir or camping on the Goulburn River, about two and a half hours from home. Everyone was invited – uncles, aunts, cousins, Nan and Grandad and Mum and Dad – the whole lot of us. We always had a ball. Sometimes

Uncle Alf would bring his guitar, he'd strum away and we'd all have a sing. I thought it was the best thing ever, that guitar.

Uncle Alf had bought it not long after we got off the ship and he taught himself to play it. He'd be strumming away and I'd hang around and badger him for a go. Then, completely out of the blue, Uncle Alf gave me this guitar. I was absolutely rapt. I couldn't believe it, my very own guitar! Before I ran off with this incredible gift, Uncle Alf taught me three chords: C, G and F.

With this guitar and my new-found musical confidence, I decided to perform at one of the school concerts. Instead of singing 'He's Got the Whole World in His Hands' with my head stuck out the window, I sang it onstage to the whole school. I got through the performance and it felt okay. After that, I started getting invited to a lot of parties. Kids would come up to me and say, 'Hey Johnny, we're having a party. It's Jonesy's birthday, Friday night. Bring your guitar.'

So I'd go to the party and I'd take my guitar along and end up having a sing. I had to pick very simple songs, because I was very limited in my chord selection, but it was fun. I loved to sing. I would've been singing at home anyway so it was nice to be sharing music with these new friends at their parties. Song by song, party by party, I became a little more accepted by my peers, and I got to like that taste of appreciation.

OPPORTUNITY KNOCKS

As my reputation as a musician grew, so did my circle of friends. There were a couple of guys at school who also knew how to play C, G and F, so we formed a group and called ourselves The Mavericks. Neither of the other guys cared to sing, so that made me the singer. With our very limited repertoire of 'Love Potion Number 9', 'Wooden Heart' and 'Dizzy Miss Lizzy', we'd play at school dances and parties, wherever they'd have us.

The music scene in Melbourne in the mid-1960s was absolutely thriving. If The Mavericks weren't playing at a friend's party, we'd head out to see live music. Every Friday and Saturday either at the Lyndale, Noble Park or the Dandenong dances there'd be a band or a DJ playing. It was great. There was this disc jockey and performer, Grantley Dee, who used to regularly work the dances. He was a great singer but blind as a bat, so to stop him falling they'd put a piano wire a couple of feet back from the edge of the stage so he knew how far he could go. Grantley was talented and he also had a great sense of humour. A couple of years later, on a dirt track in South Australia, I taught him how to drive a car. We were both in Adelaide for gigs and we somehow managed to convince someone to lend us their car. I drove us out to the bush and then let Grantley take the wheel. The extent of the lesson was me saying, '. . . a little bit more to the left! Little bit . . . right

. . . Right . . . RIGHT!' It was the most exhilarating five minutes of my life up to that point.

From a young age I was mad about music, cars and . . . cigarettes. Both my parents smoked, but neither of them had a car or a licence. Mum and Dad would catch the bus or train everywhere. Unfortunately, Dad left his bicycle with the motor back in England, so he was reliant on public transport. They both were. Desperate to get behind the wheel of a car, a couple of mates and I pooled our money and bought an old Studebaker. It was a complete bomb. I think we paid £10 for it from some local bloke, which was probably £10 too much.

Where I lived in Noble Park was still semi-rural, so there were a lot of empty paddocks around. Because the car was far from roadworthy and none of us had a licence, we decided to turn it into a paddock bomb, fanging around on the grass rather than the road. It was around that time that I started smoking in earnest, and I was forever pinching a fag out of Mum's pack. It was either pinch fags or buy them. Mum or Dad would give us twenty cents pocket money for doing odd jobs around the house and, back in those days, twenty cents was a lot. You could buy a packet of ten cigarettes for that. One weekend we went to play with the paddock bomb but the battery was flat. We managed to get the darn thing out, it was one of those long, heavy-as-buggery batteries. We were runty little kids, only fourteen or fifteen years old, and I remember lugging that heavy battery up this bloody great hill then down the road to the service station. We put it on the ground to go and talk to the mechanic and out of nowhere I heard, 'Put that fag out!'

It was my dad, he'd caught me! I'd been standing there, catching my breath with a cigarette sticking out of my mouth. I thought, *Oh shit!*

As a child in England, I got pretty bad pneumonia and I've still got quite a bit of damage to my lungs because of it. Smoking a hundred cigarettes a day didn't help either. I'd be in the studio puffing away while I laid down vocals. It's just crazy to think back, absolutely stupid, but we never knew how bad it was for us. Anyway, Dad never said another word to me about smoking after that day, and I never let him see me smoke again until I was much older.

So, I had made friends, was playing in a band and getting out and about. Strings Unlimited were a local band, a whole band complete with guitars, drums, keys, and they were good. I'd seen them perform at the Lyndale Dance and I was impressed. They were definitely playing a wider repertoire than C, G and F. Because they were good and there were tonnes of music venues at the time, they were getting a lot of paid gigs, but mostly as a backing band because they were missing a lead singer.

One Saturday I was at my friend's brother's twenty-first birthday. The party was fun and The Mavericks were performing our songs. A local songwriter and singer, Hans Poulsen, was also at the party. He knew the guys from Strings Unlimited and he also knew they needed a singer. Hans must have been impressed with me because at the end of the night he introduced himself and encouraged me to audition for the band. It was an exciting suggestion, but I didn't have much time to think about it because early the next morning, Sunday morning, the keyboard player from Strings phoned with an invitation to audition. I was more than excited. I turned up at his house that afternoon feeling very, very nervous. I'd never auditioned or even played with a full band before. The guys asked me what I wanted to sing and I opted for 'House of the Rising Sun' by The Animals, which was a big hit at the time. The guys all knew it. The drummer clicked his drumsticks a couple of times and then they launched right into playing. I went to sing the first note . . . but my voice was completely shot. I'd been singing close to five hours at the twenty-first the night before and my voice was too hoarse. I was mortified. Luckily the guys were really relaxed, they told me not to worry and to come back for a second audition when my voice had recovered.

A couple of days later I auditioned for Strings Unlimited properly. I decided to try 'House of the Rising Sun' again.

Thankfully, I sang it in tune, which is good because I love singing that song. The guys were great, they said, 'Yeah you're in, you've got the job.' So I became the lead singer of the semi-professional Strings Unlimited. At fifteen, I was the youngest member of the band. I was ready and eager to build my musical repertoire and experience.

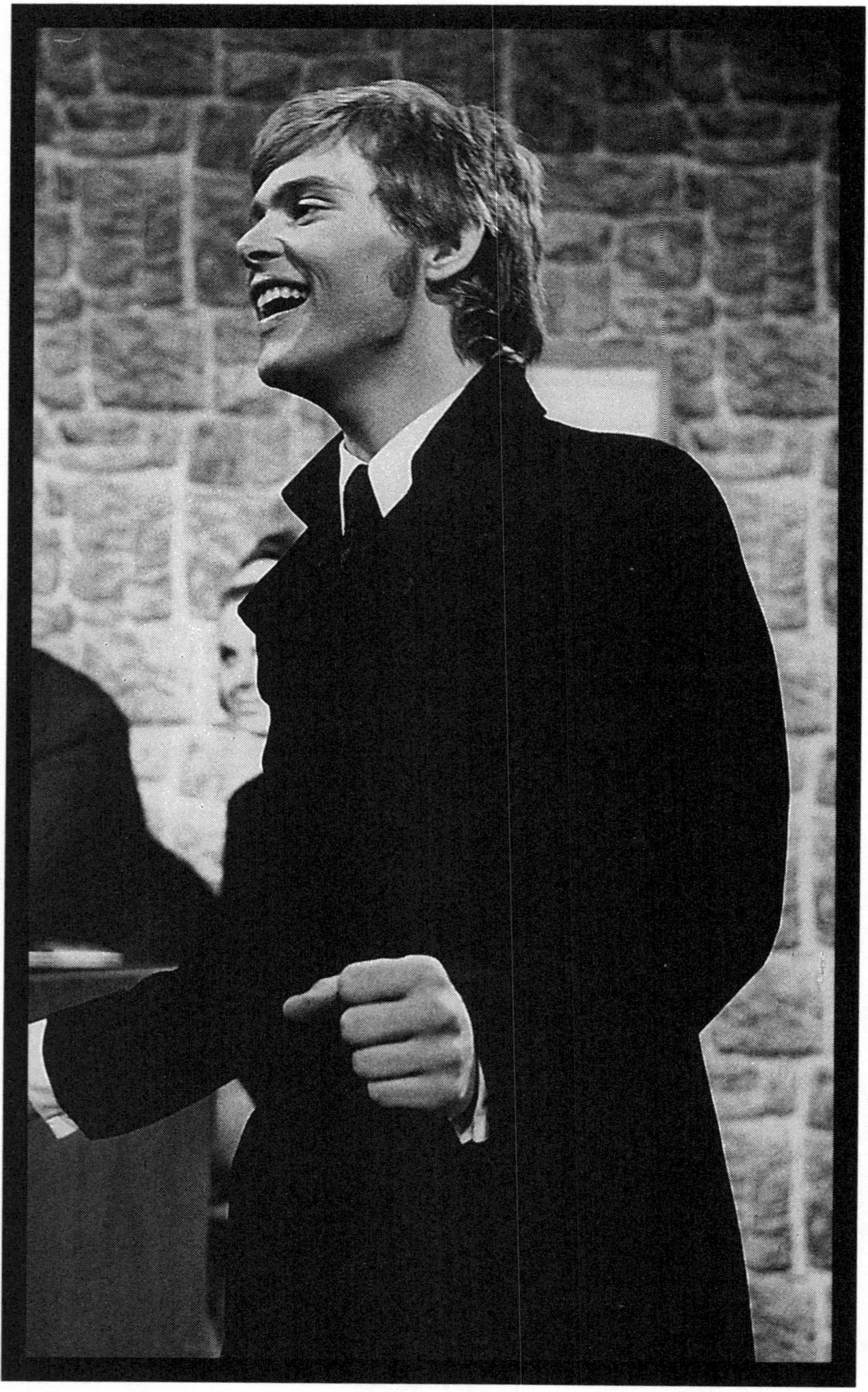

CHAPTER 2

'I'M THE SINGER WITH STRINGS UNLIMITED'

There I was in June 1964, just shy of fifteen years old, standing in a crowd of 250,000 people on Bourke Street, waiting for the Beatles to arrive during their one and only tour of Australia. I listened to their records on my uncle's record player over and over and over again. I thought they were absolutely fantastic. So, when the foursome came to Melbourne, I made sure I was there. They had a police escort as they made their way to their accommodation at the Southern Cross Hotel. Mounted police, police on motorbikes and police in cars were trying to part the crowd. I'd never seen anything like it. I still remember the sound and the energy of all those people. People were being trampled, girls were fainting. Luckily for the band, all those police turned out to be a diversion, enabling them to enter the back door of the hotel safely. There was no way they would have made it through the front.

When John, Paul, George and Ringo came out onto the roof of the hotel a bit later to acknowledge everyone, the sound went up to a level I didn't think was humanly possible. I don't think anyone in Australia had ever heard a crowd like that. I sure hadn't. Here was a band that made music that worked so well. Yes, they sang about love and girls, but their lyrics also explored human experience, social commentary and politics, which made their songs relatable to everybody, me included. I just loved them, they were the best.

The Beatles were playing Adelaide then Melbourne then Sydney, flying to New Zealand for shows in Wellington, Auckland, Dunedin and Christchurch and then flying back to Brisbane to finish the Australian leg of their world tour. Somehow, I managed to get myself a ticket to one of their shows at Festival Hall. Seeing them onstage blew my head off. Of course, I couldn't hear them much during the whole concert because there were 5000 screaming girls filling the hall. You could barely hear a single note they played over the screams. In

'I'M THE SINGER WITH STRINGS UNLIMITED'

those days, there were no big sound stages or speakers, not in the music business anyway. So, it was more of an event than a concert, but that didn't bother me one bit because I knew most of the Beatles' songs forward and backward. I idolised them. Even though I was already playing in a band and wanted to sing rock'n'roll, I didn't dare think one day I could be onstage singing to this many people. No way.

Strangely enough, nearly ten years after that tour, the promoter who brought the Beatles to Australia, Kenn Brodziak, became my manager. They called Kenn 'Mr Show Business' because he was a canny producer, manager and entrepreneur. Of course, when I realised he had worked with the Beatles I had to quiz him about them. One day I started interrogating him about how he'd convinced them to come to Australia at the height of Beatlemania. He looked at me and said, 'I've still got their contract.'

What?!

Kenn reached across his desk into a filing cabinet beside him. After a few moments of rummaging, he pulled out a single piece of paper and handed it to me. He then passed me a few more sheets and I looked at them. The band were paid the equivalent of £2500 a week for the tour. I looked closer. Brian Epstein had signed the contract on behalf of the band.

On one itemised hotel bill, Paul McCartney was written down as Paul McCarthy. Someone, probably Kenn, had spelled Paul's name wrong then corrected it. This single piece of paper felt sacred.

I was spellbound. I asked Kenn if he would leave the contract and papers to me in his will.

'No. But you can buy them off me,' he said. So, I did.

I'd heard someone once say Kenn was 'tight as a fish's arse', and I couldn't argue about that. When he was managing me, he used to charge me for postage. He would send me receipts for two and three dollars and when I'd ask what they were for he'd say, 'Stamps. Stamps and envelopes. I have to reply to some letters.'

'Okay, Kenn.' I handed over the money for stamps and envelopes.

School, for me, was going nowhere. Performing at friends' parties had improved my social life, but it hadn't improved my grades. My father had worked his trade as a fitter and turner all his life, so he suggested I drop out of school and get an apprenticeship. During school holidays I had been working with a family acquaintance and fellow Cockney, Stan Foster, in his plumbing business, Caulfield Heating and Cooling. I enjoyed

'I'M THE SINGER WITH STRINGS UNLIMITED'

the work and was more than keen to get out of school, so I took Dad's advice and asked Stan if I could come on as a full-time apprentice. Stan agreed, but to get officially signed on I needed to get approval from the Apprenticeship Commission of Victoria.

I turned up at the Commission office and my career as a plumber was nearly all over before it began. I didn't know it, but to become an apprentice you needed a pass in maths. Oh no! The man behind the counter asked me for a copy of my school records. I sheepishly handed them over, knowing they included my latest maths results: thirty-seven out of a hundred. A fail.

The man at the Commission surveyed the papers then squared me up.

'Do you really want to be a plumber, son?'

'Yes, I do, sir.'

He dropped his eyes back down to my results and, without a word or even a sideward glance, he changed the three to a five, bumping my maths score to fifty-seven and bumping me over the eligibility line. Out of the goodness of his heart this man, who didn't know me or anything about me other than that I wanted to be a plumber, changed the course of my life.

If you're still out there, thank you!

It was official, I was a plumber's apprentice with Caulfield Heating and Cooling. I was proud as punch, and it was a huge relief to be out of school. There were a few of us apprentices when I started, and each week we alternated what we'd do – one week air-conditioning, the next plumbing. I learned quickly, I enjoyed the work and I was good at it. I recently came across a sheet metal pot that I'd made way back then, it was an oil pot that I had soldered together. My mum and dad must have kept it and it turned up at my son James's house. I was looking at it just the other day and I was pleased with it. It was quite handy work.

I liked the work, but I was still a young kid so not always looking for the hardest job or wanting to charge people a lot of money for not much effort. Another apprentice and I would get the work sheet, survey the jobs and we'd pick the easy ones. For example: *Mrs Smith, South Melbourne, leaky garden tap.* To get a plumber to turn up to your house to fix a leaky tap wasn't cheap, but we'd go to Mrs Smith's house in South Melbourne and we'd fix her leaky tap, no charge. When we got back to the office we'd tell the boss, 'We got there and she hadn't turned the tap off properly.' We'd do all these little jobs for people for no charge, it was nice to be able to help people out. I don't think the bosses ever twigged because I still did enough paying jobs to bring money in for them.

Even though there were a few apprentices, I was definitely the butt of most of the gags. The qualified plumbers would pull every last trick on me. They weren't mean-spirited, just rite-of-passage stuff that most apprentices copped at one time or another. It was all good-natured fun for a laugh. And, of course, I had to do all the running around. 'Get this, Johnny.' 'Can you take this over there, Johnny?' 'Johnny, get lunch!'

Getting lunch was definitely not a chore. I'd take everyone's orders and go down to the sandwich shop. I used to love running this errand because there were a couple of pretty girls who worked in there. I'd walk into the place in my overalls, strutting my stuff and we'd flirt. Nothing major, just a look and a wink as they handed over the salad rolls. I'd always find the perks. I learned five or six different ways to sit on a shovel. Ten minutes into digging a ditch someone would yell, 'Let's take a break. Okay, take five.'

We'd all lean against our shovels and have a fag. The camaraderie among the guys was good.

Stan, the big boss, was a nice man, too. I was earning $22 a week, which was more money than I'd ever had before but it wasn't a huge amount. Because of my terrible sense of direction, I used to hate taking public transport to work. I'd get lost even catching the train, and I knew if I was late too often, I'd be history. It really worried me, so to avoid being late and lost I started catching a taxi to work. Can you imagine, a young plumber's apprentice turning up to work every day in a taxi?

One morning Stan saw me arrive and yelled, 'Oi! What are you doing?'

'I'm coming to work,' I said, acting like taking a taxi to work wasn't unusual.

Stan wasn't having any of it. He knew where I lived and he said, 'If you want to stand on that corner near your place, I'll give you a lift in every day.'

See, Stan was a good bloke!

I used to walk down to the shops from my house and stand on the corner and Stan would come pick me up in his car and take me to work. If he was late, I was late, which didn't matter because he was the big boss.

I was working as a plumber's apprentice during the day and singing with Strings Unlimited at night. It was fantastic – they were a good band, they could play and they were good people. I was the youngest in the band, but the drummer, Peter Foggie, was only older than me by a couple of days. The other guys, keyboard player Mick Foenander, lead guitarist Stewart Male and rhythm guitarist Joe Cincotta, were only four and five years older but they felt like adults to me. I was incredibly nervous about joining the band. Sure, I'd mastered C, G and F

'I'M THE SINGER WITH STRINGS UNLIMITED'

with The Mavericks, but now there was an A minor and a D in there to remember, too. The guys in Strings Unlimited were accomplished musicians and I was a dribbling mess. Actually, nothing has changed, I'm still a dribbling mess, and not just because of the surgery on my mouth. Before every performance I get extremely toey. I get very, very nervous and then, once I walk out there and I'm doing it, when I start to sing, I'm fine. When I sing, if I can't hear the note in my head I won't go for it, but if I do hear it, I'll think, oh I'll have a go at that and then I'll hit it. Hearing or not hearing the note started with Strings, and it's become a bit of a habit of mine. It gave me confidence to go to those harder notes, being able to hear them in my head beforehand. It meant I knew how far I could go.

When I joined, the band already had several permanent weekly bookings, so I'd do one set, then the band would do an instrumental set without me, then I'd come back on and do another set and then they'd finish up with a final instrumental set. The band members figured because I was only doing half the work, I would only get paid half the fee. That was fine with me. Before Strings I had no idea about performance and now, suddenly, I was performing five or six nights a week, week in week out. That felt like enough reward in itself.

We used to work the dances, local pubs and clubs. Our regular gigs included the Havana Coffee Lounge in Dandenong, the Surfrider at Black Rock, The Rendezvous in Mitcham and the Hibiscus Room in the Hampton Hotel. I was too young to drink, but that didn't stop me having the occasional beer. The older boys had promised my mum they'd take care of me. They did their best to honour that promise and keep me out of trouble, but occasionally trouble found us.

The gigs varied a lot. Sometimes there would be hardly anyone in the crowd, while at other times it was packed. One night we were onstage at the end of a show, packing our gear up and two separate groups of men started taunting us. The only way to get out of the venue was to walk down the stairs at either end of the stage, and that's exactly where these two groups of guys were standing.

'Come on, ya faggots!'

'You bunch of girls!'

By their threats, it was easy to think they were ready to beat the shit out of us. I was terrified. Luckily, a fellow named Bob McConnell, who was our manager at the time, talked them down. We seized the moment, grabbed our gear and got out of there as quick as we could.

A young kid at a gig at Lyndale Hall wasn't so lucky. I still have nightmares about it. We were working a regular Friday night dance like any other and, as usual, it was packed with teenagers and young people. It was the era of the Mods and the

Sharpies, two rival Melbourne subcultures who took umbrage with each other in the mid-1960s. They took any chance they could to battle it out. That night when it was time for our set we went out onstage and started playing. I was singing our first song when I noticed a fight break out in the far-left corner of the hall. I kept singing, the band kept playing, but the kids kept fighting. This fight got bigger and bigger and bigger until all of a sudden the whole crowd seemed to be circulating around this one poor guy who was being pummelled. From my vantage point up on the stage, I watched this kid cop punch after punch after punch. He got pasted, and I mean pasted. The old adage is the band *has* to play on. Don't stop playing – if you stop playing then that's it, it gets worse and everyone joins in. That night we kept playing, but it did nothing to stop the beating. I often think about that poor bugger, because they could have killed him. They might have killed him, for all I knew. It was a horrible night, and something I never wanted to witness again. The strangest thing is, it was supposed to be the Sharpies and the Mods against each other, and I'm fairly certain this kid wasn't one or the other.

I'd catch a lift with Stan to get to and from work during the day, and at night one of the older boys in Strings would pick me up and drive me to our gig. I didn't have a licence because my parents couldn't afford a car and neither could I – at least, not one that was roadworthy. The boys in Strings had a couple of cars and a van between them. When we travelled in the van, which was loaded with all the gear, I'd lie across an amp to catch a few hours of sleep while one of the older boys drove.

I was so tired most of the time I hardly knew what was going on. Plumbing all day then a quick stop at home for an APC – armpits and crotch – wash. Next minute I'd be onstage performing in Dandenong. We'd finish the set then whip across the city for another gig in Geelong or somewhere else. We were never the headline act, we were part of the filler, so the performance pressure wasn't too intense. For a teenage boy it was tiring, but also really, really exciting. But it took a toll. We were driving home late one night after a post-gig spotlighting rabbit-shooting session. There were three of us across the bench seat of the ute when we all fell asleep, the driver included. Dead to the world, we were. The ute drove across a bridge then veered off, became airborne then crashed into a bank. It was the crash that woke me up. Miraculously, nobody was hurt, not even a scratch. The local police who attended the crash couldn't believe we were all alive. I'm not a man of faith, but after crawling out of the wreck, I had to agree it was a miracle.

The constant stream of gigs allowed me to gain more and more confidence onstage. The feeling of standing up there

'I'M THE SINGER WITH STRINGS UNLIMITED'

with people watching your every move was both strange and amazing. I started to think about how to better engage an audience. When I wasn't performing, I'd go to gigs and study other musicians to see how they worked the crowd. I'll never forget, I went to see MPD Limited at the Dande, the Dandenong Town Hall. Mike Brady (M) was on vocals and guitar, Pete Watson (P) on bass guitar and vocals and Danny Finley (D) on drums. Strangely enough, years later Danny Finley managed me for a while, but on that night, watching him play, I was mesmerised by his drumming. I've always wanted to be a drummer, so there I was watching Danny when suddenly he turned and winked at me. I gasped and thought, *I just got winked at by a pop star!* Danny doesn't remember it, of course, doesn't even remember the gig, but that wink really struck me. That I caught his eye, even for a nanosecond, and he acknowledged the connection stuck with me. From that moment, I decided to really make the effort to look people in the eye and connect.

Australian rock'n'roll pioneer Johnny O'Keefe – JOK, as he was known – was brilliant at eyeballing a crowd. JOK was a genius, he could work a crowd like no other. It helped that he had these googly, oogly eyes. He was in a very bad car accident that screwed his eyes up, screwed him up, but the benefit was that one eye would be looking here, the other over there, each looking at someone different. He'd walk onstage, the crowd would boo and carry on and by the third song, JOK would have them right by the short and curlies. He was fantastic, he could eyeball an audience and make everybody think he was singing and sweating just for them.

A few years later, JOK became a mate. He was a funny bastard and a good man. One time, he knocked on my door at about four in the morning. I found him standing there, leaning against the door jamb with a bottle of Scotch under his arm and a joint sticking out of his mouth. I didn't know what it was at the time, no idea. I'd never used any drugs. He said, 'Do you want some of this?' And I said, 'What? What is it?'

'It's a joint.'

In my house a joint was a cut of lamb. Mum would say, 'We're going to have a joint for dinner.' Yum.

I said, 'No. I'll have a drop of your whisky though.'

So I had a swig, and after I gave him the bottle back he handed me the joint and said, 'Take a puff, you smoke don't you?'

'I smoke cigarettes, yeah.'

He said, 'Just take a puff.' I did and oh Jesus! Straight away I wished I hadn't. I had the smallest, smallest puff and I didn't like it at all. All I could think of afterward was chocolate.

JOK was a total nutcase but he was very charismatic, an absolute master of his craft. And boy did I study him. I watched him work the audience and could see he had them in his grip.

I was working hard at my stage presence, trying to hold my own onstage. Mind you, it's not just the singer who has to hold their own, every band member has to perform. If you play the guitar, play the bloody guitar! But my efforts must have paid off because it was during that period, with Strings, that I started getting noticed. Particularly by the girls down in the front. I'd be focusing hard on remembering lyrics and trying my best to perfect my stage presence and I'd look down and there they'd be, smiling, waving and saying hello. It was cute, it was nice, and it was terrifying.

The guys in Strings also started to notice this appreciation from the crowd. Stewie, the guitar player, loved playing music by The Shadows, the instrumental rock band who backed Cliff Richard. Stewie chose the songs I'd sing, and gradually the band started to give me more work – more songs to sing and more time onstage. After one gig, Stew came up, clapped me on the back and said, 'People are enjoying what you are doing. Why don't you stay on longer?'

'Great, I will. Thanks, mate.'

That was fantastic for me, a pat on the back from Stewie was much appreciated.

Mum and Dad were really proud of my singing and the whole family was always enthusiastically on my side. Unfortunately, Nan and Grandad never saw me work because the performances were mostly in youth dances, which weren't really a venue for them. Uncle Alan, on the other hand, loved what I was doing. Being only ten years older than me, he was young enough to appreciate the music in all its sweaty teen glory, and he came to a lot of the gigs.

One of the biggest gigs for any band in the country at that time was Hoadley's Battle of the Sounds, which was a talent quest for unsigned bands. Bands from around Australia entered and the prizes for winning the national final were $1000, a trip to England and a recording contract. Record companies weren't interested in signing up local acts, because the mothership was in England, so the prize was a major drawcard. It was a burgeoning industry at the time, there was so much live music going on, so much excitement in the air. We were up against a whole lot of bands we knew and a whole lot we didn't know. We played our hearts out in our heat and made it through to the Victorian state finals. We had a blast but the fun stopped there, we didn't make the national finals or even place. The Twilights, a South Australian band with Glenn Shorrock as the lead singer, ended up winning the 1966 national finals held at Melbourne's Festival Hall.

Disappointed at losing out on a recording contract, we decided to pool our savings and lay down a demo. One of the only independent recording studios in Melbourne around then was Armstrong Studios, run by the legendary Bill Armstrong. In time, Armstrong's would become the studio of choice for many local and international artists, but at that stage, the studio was still only a small, converted terrace house in South Melbourne.

Going into the recording studio at 100 Albert Road for the first time was amazing. I'd never been in a studio before, had no concept of what it was or what it would be like. I remember being taken aback by the awesomeness of it all. The studio had everything, it was almost overwhelming, but the two engineers, Roger Savage and Ernie Rose, were lovely. They were the pioneers of the Australian recording industry. I subsequently worked with Roger Savage on 'Susan Jones', an advertising jingle that was created for Ansett-ANA airlines. The jingle was released as an EP and got me noticed by the record label EMI, but on that day, we were there as a band intent on breaking into the recording scene.

My status in the band had grown considerably by then and, as a perk, I had a big say in what covers we recorded. Naturally

I voted for the Beatles. We ended up recording three covers, two by the Beatles, 'I Feel Fine' and 'I'm Down', and one by Gerry and the Pacemakers, 'Don't Let the Sun Catch You Crying'. The instrumentalists all recorded their tracks and then it was time to lay down my vocals. Being alone in the booth, with everyone on the other side of the glass was, at first, terrifying. I had never really heard myself sing that clearly before, it kind of threw me a bit – like, *Oh, shit, this is what I sound like?*

After a little bit of encouragement from Roger and from my bandmates, I settled in and started to really enjoy the process. Before we knew it, the session was over, we were done, the money spent. The tracks were eventually pressed on a demo acetate by Rambler, a small label based in Frankston. Five copies were made, one for each band member. I have no idea what happened to mine, and I wonder if any of the Strings boys still have theirs?

In Cohuna, three hundred kilometres north of Melbourne, a local dairy farmer had a side hustle, running a Saturday night dance at the Cohuna Shire Soldiers Memorial Hall for the local kids. He was doing a good job too, convincing big acts from all around the country to play in the otherwise sleepy town. Before my time, the band had played an instrumental set at the dance. They were such a hit they'd been invited back for an encore, and this time I was part of the package. The plan was to do two sets, one with me and the other as a backing band for Bev Harrell.

Bev was a big star. She was one of the best-known Aussie female pop stars of the day, had a powerful, superbly ranged voice and a couple of hits in the top ten. I really liked her song 'What Am I Doing Here With You?'. I'd seen her perform on the television shows *Kommotion* and *Bandstand* as a solo singer, and also with the backing band The Vibrants. Bev was lovely and, of course, I instantly fell in love with her. I think everyone in the band did.

We arrived in Cohuna early; we'd had a gig in Melbourne the night before so we drove through the night to make the early sound check the next day. After sound check I was sitting on the drum kit tinkering around, dreaming I was a drummer, when Bev and this bloke walked in. Bev is this tiny little petite thing and next to her was this tall, skinny guy with long dark hair and a beard, who was dressed in expensive Italian clothes. His name was Darryl Sambell. Darryl looked me up and down, then cocked his head and said, 'I hope you're not the drummer!'

'No sir, I'm Johnny. I'm the singer with Strings Unlimited.'

I thought Darryl was Bev's boyfriend.

I chatted to them both briefly before the gig, but that was that. Teenagers quickly started to fill the hall and it was time for us to go on. My set was before Bev's, as she was headlining. The band did a couple of instrumental numbers to break the ice, then it was time for me. I was typically overwhelmed with nerves, but when I walked out onstage all the nervousness fell away. The hall was packed, the kids were up for a good time. I started singing one of my favourite rock numbers, 'Johnny B. Goode' by Chuck Berry. I pushed it, I really gave it my all, and the crowd gave it right back. Next was 'Unchained Melody' by the Righteous Brothers and during that ballad, out of the corner of my eye, I could see someone standing on the side of the stage watching. It was Darryl Sambell, his eyes locked on me and my performance. The intensity was a bit unnerving, but soon enough my set was over, and I made my way offstage for Bev to step up and take the mic.

At the end of the night, as we were packing away all the gear, Darryl walked up and asked if he could have a word with me. He wanted to know if I had a manager.

I had no real idea what a manager did, I'd never thought about it before. I was just a singer in a band. I found out later that he had already run the idea of managing me past Bev, he had asked her if she thought I was good enough, if I had

'I'M THE SINGER WITH STRINGS UNLIMITED'

what it took to be a star. When she said yes, absolutely, he approached me.

'I'd like to help you,' he said.

He wasn't an ordinary bloke, he was definitely different, but he was interested in what I was doing so that was good enough for me. He asked me for my number. I gave it to him and didn't think much more about it.

Seven weeks later the home phone rang. My mum answered.

'John, it's for you.'

I was on the lounge-room floor mucking around with my baby brother, Stephen, who was only four years old at the time. I remember the conversation went something like this:

'Hello, it's Johnny.'

It was Darryl. After introducing himself he said, 'Look Johnny, I've got some work for you in Adelaide.'

'Adelaide?'

'Yes, Adelaide. I can get you three jobs for $30.'

'Three jobs for $30?!'

'That's right, are you interested?'

I was still a plumber's apprentice and still on $22 a week. The band money wasn't adding much to my wallet, so $30 for one night of work was an incredible proposition. But I had to think about it.

Joining up with Darryl meant leaving Strings Unlimited, it was an either/or situation, and I did think about it quite hard because it was a heavier step and a lot more responsibility. This was me going out alone, doing it for myself. I was apprehensive and, to be honest, a bit frightened.

Not long after, Darryl turned up at our house to talk about it some more. Mum and Dad couldn't believe their eyes, my father in particular. Darryl walked in wearing velvet flares and a chain necklace and he had what many back then would call quite camp mannerisms to match. But he was utterly convinced he could make me a star. Mum and Dad, despite their hesitation were, as always, totally supportive of me and what I wished to pursue.

Ultimately the decision was made for me. I'd just turned eighteen when in July 1967, Stewart Male told us he was leaving the band to get married. In turn, Peter Foggie decided he was going to take a break from performing and then, spurred by these departures, Mick Foenander joined another local band. Joe Cincotta had already quit months earlier. That left me free to go it alone with Darryl as my manager. I never signed a contract with Darryl, it was just a handshake. I never signed a contract with any of my managers – it was all done, or not done, on a handshake.

In late 1967 Darryl and I flew to Adelaide for the promised three jobs for $30. We could have driven, but Darryl insisted we fly. I was petrified because I'd never been on a plane before. We went in an Ansett-ANA–operated Douglas DC-3, a noisy, cluttery, buggery old twin propeller. Once we took off, I couldn't believe it, it felt like being on clouds. I was in heaven.

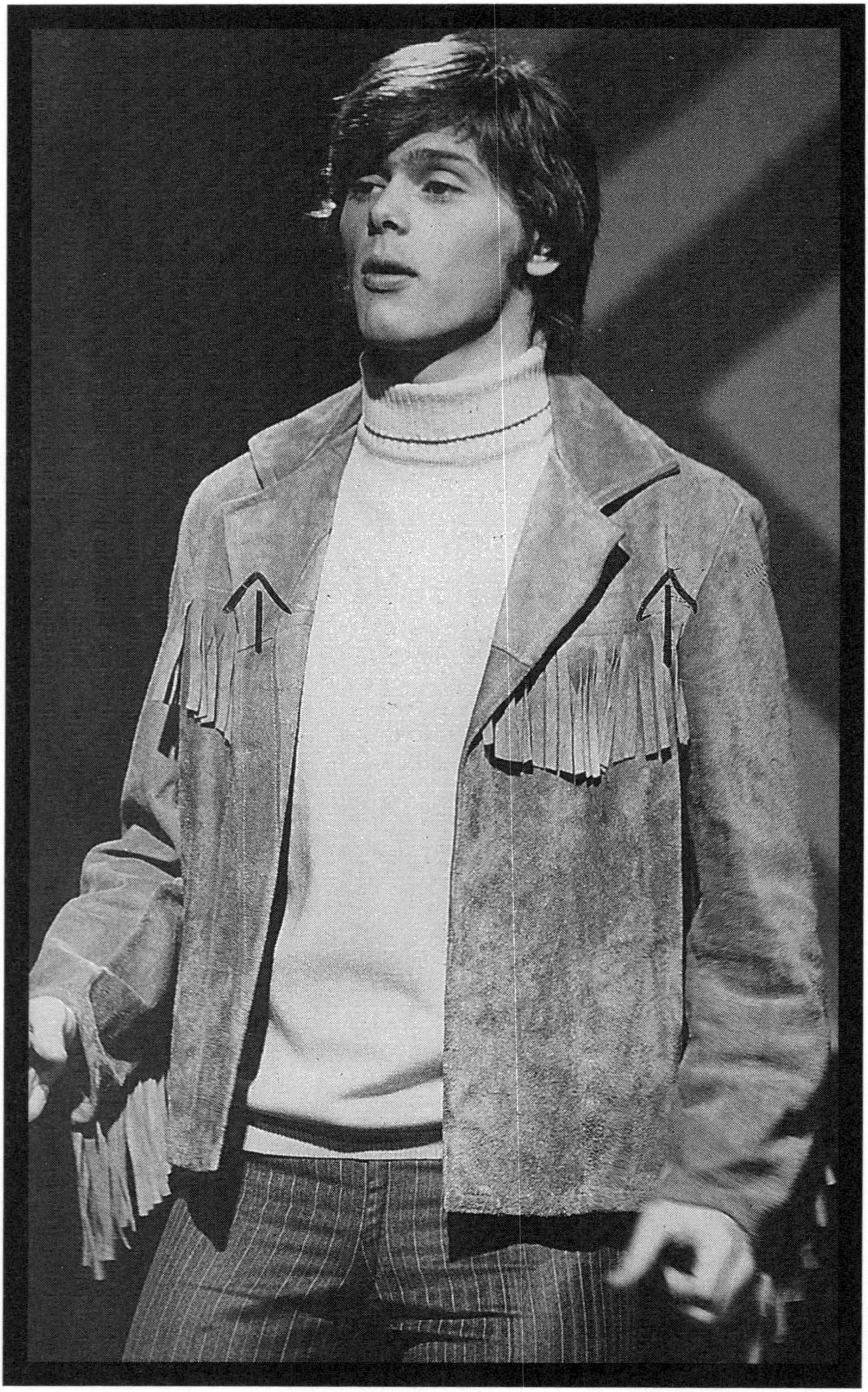

CHAPTER 3

'GIVE IT A GOOD GO, SON'

The truth is, when Darryl Sambell started managing me, I didn't know much about him. Neither my parents nor I thought to ask many questions when he turned up at our house in his fancy clothes, talking up his grand plans. All I knew was that Darryl was going out with Bev Harrell, that he was an experienced manager and that he wanted to make me a pop star. Only the bit about wanting to make me a star was true but, in the end, even that was questionable.

Darryl was from South Australia and because he knew this local circuit much better than he knew the vastly bigger

Melbourne arena, he started heavily promoting me in his home state. The first job I did in Adelaide was at the St Clair Recreation Centre. It was like a huge ballroom, and they held a dance there every Saturday night. They would often get a crowd of about 1000 people, and drew some big-name acts, like the Bee Gees and JOK. And me. I was so nervous that night. I went onstage and somehow managed to sing despite being terrified. During the second verse of my first song, a cover of Gene Pitney's 'Half Heaven, Half Heartache', the girls in the front row started screaming at me. I couldn't believe it. I kept singing and they kept screaming. I'd only ever heard girls scream for the big stars like Normie Rowe, Ross D. Wyllie and JOK, and yet here they were screaming at me. For me? The more I sang, the more they screamed. I couldn't decide at first if it scared me or excited me. I kept singing and soon enough, I settled in to my set and started to really enjoy myself. The girls didn't let up and I thought, *I don't mind this at all!*

From that moment, for some reason, the Adelaide crowds really took to me and gave me a chance and I love the place for that. In the late sixties, Melbourne and Adelaide had extremely healthy live music scenes. Sydney was more the leagues club circuit, which had their particular flavour, but Adelaide and Melbourne had so many live music venues they quickly became my strongest cities to perform in. As a musician, any opportunity to work is terrific. Back then I would have walked across broken glass to get out there and sing, not just for the attention but to be in a professional situation and pursuing a career doing what I loved. Performing up there in front of a crowd felt really good.

After that first weekend in Adelaide, I went home and the next morning I was back on the corner waiting for Stan to drive me to work. Darryl got busy booking more shows. Very quickly, a weekly routine started to take shape. I'd work my plumber's apprenticeship all week then, after knock-off on Friday afternoon, I'd race home, have a shower, put on fresh clothes, pack my gear and wait for Darryl. He'd pull up out the front of Mum and Dad's place late Friday night, after driving from South Australia, have a quick cup of tea and a sandwich, then turn around and make the 850-kilometre trip back to Adelaide with me in the passenger seat. We'd arrive early Saturday morning and get ready for the gigs he'd booked for me. Then, late Sunday night after my final performance, we'd drive through the night back to Noble Park, arriving in time for me to start work on Monday morning. The highway back then wasn't much more than a single lane the entire way, and Darryl drove like a complete maniac. The best I could do was close my eyes and sleep.

With so many performances booked, I was on a steep learning curve. I started working at the St Clair fairly regularly, and every time we worked there I'd get my shirt ripped or my sleeves pulled off, or my trousers clawed at. This happened because the only way to or from the stage was through the audience. One night the staff created a passageway to the stage using fold-up chairs as barricades. It was a busy night and people were there to have a good time. Unbeknownst to me, the crowd had split into two camps, men on one side of the barricades, women on the other. As I made my way through the parted crowd, about forty blokes were trying to hit or kick me from one side and about fifty women were on the other side trying to kiss me. It was the most remarkable experience, and to be honest, to have such extreme responses to what I was doing up onstage frightened the shit out of me.

Darryl was booking gigs and watching me perform and he saw something in me that he thought he could sell. Not just as a singer, and it feels strange to write it like this, but as a product. I thought he was an experienced manager but, in actual fact, he was making it up as he went along. He came from a town in South Australia called Gawler, where he trained as a hairdresser. It was at a gig in Gawler that he met Bev Harrell. Bev was performing with The Vibrants and Darryl quickly became a groupie. As a trained hairdresser, he started fixing Bev's hair before her performances, then he'd position himself right up the front with four or five pretty young girls, who were also hairdressers, to watch the show.

Because of his friendship with Bev, Darryl had met a lot of the promoters and venue managers at the gigs she was playing at. By the time I met him, he was working as a quarry manager during the day and spending his time at clubs and dances at night and on the weekends, trying to make his way in the music industry. When he started managing me, he was counting on those contacts to give him, and me, a foot into the South Australian music industry.

His management style meant he started to oversee far more than booking my gigs – he started to dictate what I wore. He'd dress me up in suits and frilly shirts, he'd put me in these over-the-top outfits with scarves around my neck, bandanas with a knot tied in the end. It wasn't me, but I went along with it because I was a clueless kid. The whole time all I was thinking about was getting onstage to sing, and maybe a little about those screaming girls.

But I wasn't always singing to girls. I didn't know at the time that Darryl was gay. I had no idea of homosexuality at all, no concept of it, it wasn't something I had ever thought about. But it turns out one of the good things about having a gay manager was being booked for all these wonderful underground dances in Adelaide, Sydney and Melbourne. Homosexuality was illegal then, so these dances were not widely advertised. The first one I did, all these men were screaming at me, I mean *really* screaming. I couldn't believe it, they were such an enthusiastic audience. I had no idea that it was a gay audience until I did a block of these dances in a short period. By the third show, I was getting pushed and adored and jostled, and one young guy came up to me in a break and said, 'Excuse me, Johnny. Can I tell my friends that I sleep with you, is that okay?'

In that moment I was as affable as always, and I said, 'You go ahead.' Only later did I grasp what the young lad really meant.

This guy who was a friend of Strings Unlimited had grabbed me a few times and I'd just laughed, pushed him away and said, 'Piss off!' I didn't think about it any further. I never saw it as an advance. I was pretty, I was blond, I was blue-eyed and it turns out most people thought I was gay, or camp as it was described in those days. Darryl did nothing to dispel the myth. I have no problem with homosexuality, I've always believed each to his or her or their own, but as a sheltered teenager I had no idea that it was Darryl who was creating and perpetuating a myth about my sexuality. At that stage I also had no idea that Darryl was infatuated with me. He was sexually aggressive, very aggressive and some of the other people around at that time were also sexually aggressive but I was too caught up in and dazzled by what was happening around me. And those screaming girls!

———

David Mackay, a very respected record producer at EMI Records, had a reputation for working with the best. Hans Poulsen, the singer/songwriter who had hooked me up with Strings Unlimited, gave David a demo of mine and said, 'Take a listen to this guy, you should get him into the studio for something.'

David apparently liked what he heard, so much so that he put me forward to sing the jingle on that Ansett-ANA airline commercial with the hugely successful composer Peter Best. Recording the single 'Susan Jones' back in Armstrong Studios was amazing and intimidating. It was very different from making that demo with the Strings boys.

By the time I got to the studio, the session musicians had already laid down their tracks. All they needed to finish the job were the vocals, which was where I came in. David Mackay, Peter Best, Roger Savage, Bill Armstrong and a number of the campaign's advertising executives were all in the control room, leaving me alone in the booth. They could all hear the feed from the vocal booth, but inside the booth I couldn't hear anything, unless they deliberately pushed the talk button.

Being in the booth can be overwhelming for a singer, or any musician, because any time you see someone in the control room talking and laughing, you think they are talking about and laughing at you. Often it's just paranoia, but it's still very unnerving. We used to call it 'red light fever'. Just before I went into the booth to lay down my vocals for 'Susan Jones', an idea popped into my mind. I thought it might work to sing like Peter Noone, the Scouse lead singer of the band Herman's Hermits, who were so popular in 1965 they outsold the Beatles.

Anyway, Peter Noone sang like he was singing through his nose – exactly the way my old school teacher Mr Baddley warned me against. I went into the booth and sang through my nose, trying my best to emulate Peter's nasally style à la 'Mrs Brown You've Got a Lovely Daughter'. Thankfully, everyone in the control room liked what I was doing and, after several takes, they deemed my vocals a success.

Susan Jones was the name of an air hostess used for the Australian aeroplane advertising campaign, and she was also a real woman who really did work as an air hostess. After I recorded the single, I got to meet the real Susan Jones. She was absolutely gorgeous. She had a boyfriend, who was the director of the television commercial, but that didn't stop me flirting. It was fun meeting her and all the other hostesses. After being a part of the campaign, every time I flew with Ansett the crew really looked after me. It made flying all that more special, and I felt very lucky.

When I was done recording, David Mackay popped his head into the studio wanting to have a chat. He pretty much got straight to the point: 'I want you to sign with EMI.' He wanted me to sign right then and there and I was more than keen, but I was still a minor. I told him I was interested but that he'd have to talk to my mum and dad. Which he said wasn't a problem.

True to his word, the next day David came out to our house at Noble Park to chat with my parents. I was still an apprentice living at home, performing on the weekends. Mum and Dad were pretty shocked to have a record executive in the lounge room and, to be honest, more than sceptical about David's offer. Dad was open about the fact he thought my focus should be squarely on my trade.

We were all sitting in the lounge room mulling it over when David asked me if I wrote my own songs. 'Well, yes, yes I do,' I said. I took out Uncle Alf's old guitar and sang 'In My Room' (which I wrote, as the title suggests, in my room).

In my room there is heartache

In my room there is sorrow

In my room there's no happiness, only pain

Lots of pain, from a broken heart

In my room there are shadows

And on my wall there's a candle

In my room is a candle

That stands for all our love that is dead

Oh, dead and no more

No, you don't want me anymore

Not like you did the day before

I think about the fun we had together

Go to church, feed the pigeons

Come back home and dream about you

And wake up and I'm without you, baby

Just thinking about writing this song, sitting here now thinking of the woman I wrote it about, is giving me tingles. At that stage I had managed a few kisses with girls, nothing serious, but there was one particularly beautiful girl, April Byron, who I was completely and utterly besotted with. I'd never met her but I thought she was absolutely gorgeous. April was a couple of years older than me and was a famous pop star while here I was, an unknown kid with a big crush, writing a song about her in my bedroom. April looked like a young Elizabeth Taylor, so much so that she was sometimes referred to as 'Australia's Liz Taylor'.

A couple of years after I wrote the song I had the opportunity to ask April out on a date. Much to my excitement, she agreed, and out to dinner we went. Not knowing anything about restaurants or even how to book a table, I asked Ron Tremaine for some advice. Ron was part of the same management company as Darryl. I'm not sure why I asked him – I knew Ron had a wicked, wicked sense of humour and was generally a bit of a ratbag, which I mean in the nicest possible way. Ron was very reassuring. 'Leave it to me, Johnny,' was all he said, and he booked me a table at what I thought was one of Adelaide's finest restaurants.

Unbeknownst to me, the restaurant Ron booked us into was famous for being rude to its customers. For example, if you were seen putting too much salt on your food or you asked for extra butter for your bread roll, or did anything that caught the staff's eyes, the chef would come out and abuse you. I had no idea that was the gag. I was blissfully sitting across from this beautiful creature, pinching myself that we were sharing a meal. Then dessert came out. We both tucked in, but April couldn't finish hers. She gave it a good go, there was nothing wrong with it, she just couldn't polish it off. The waiter asked if we were done. *Yes, yes, we were, thanks.* No problem, he cleared away the plates. A few moments later, this huge guy storms out of the kitchen, straight over to our table and starts abusing April, really tearing shreds off her for not finishing her pudding. Of course, I didn't know that it was all a big joke, and I got up and started having a go at this fellow, growling and carrying on, chivalrously springing to April's defence. Anyway, it all calmed down and that's when we realised the bust-up was all part of the show.

The night came to an end and I went to pay. The meal came to $23.50. That might sound cheap now, but it wasn't then. And silly me, I only had $25 in cash. I handed over my money and took the change. On the counter, right at eye level, was a big bowl of delicious-looking apples. Just as we were about to leave, April grabbed an apple. My heart sank – did I have to pay for that? Yes, I did, the apple cost fifty cents. I handed over the coins and was left with a single dollar in my pocket. I was terrified April would want something else and I wouldn't have the money for it, so I quickly bustled her out of the restaurant. On the upside, I got a kiss that night. Only a kiss. Lovely April was just being nice, I was way too young for her. We never went out again, but we stayed friends.

'GIVE IT A GOOD GO, SON'

When I sang that song to David, I had no idea that I would one day meet the gorgeous April. Already impressed with my voice, David was also impressed with my songwriting potential. This, in turn, gave me the confidence to double down on my efforts to convince my parents I had what it took to make a go of it as a singer. I told them I could take this chance to make pop music or I could stay at plumbing and work at that for the rest of my life. I told them I was only going to get one chance in my life to really get stuck into singing and I wanted to focus on that. On top of the once-in-a-lifetime opportunity, I was getting $22 a week as a plumber but I was earning $20 a night as a singer. To my parents' credit, they wanted to support whatever I wanted to do. Mum said, 'Alright, you do that if you want to do it.' Dad was initially reluctant, but he eventually agreed to support me all the way. He said, 'Look, you give it a good go, son. You give it your best shot. You can always come back to plumbing if it doesn't work out.' So I left work and came straight into the music business, which was a bit of a shock, a massive shock, but it didn't shock me quite to death – I'm still here.

So I signed with EMI and all of a sudden I had what very few Australian artists of the day had – a recording contract. Unfortunately, leaving my apprenticeship wasn't as simple as just letting Stan know I was finishing up. In those days, leaving an apprenticeship required approval from the Apprenticeship Commission. Apprentices had to submit their case and attend a hearing, and the wait time for a hearing was around six months. I applied for leave from my apprenticeship and got busy making sure I had what I needed in my new 'tool kit' as a performer ... and that started with singing lessons.

The Jack White Singing School was apparently the place to go for singing lessons in Melbourne. Jack taught Helen Reddy, Peter Allen and Olivia Newton-John. Lucky for me, when I opened the phone book and looked up 'singing lessons' that's who I found. I called the number and made an appointment with the man himself. I was thrilled, but there was a catch. To get to the studio I had to take a train all the way into the city. You know how much I hate trains. Actually, to be fair, once I am on them I love trains; navigating from one place to another is what I hate. Despite my woeful sense of direction I managed to find my way through the platforms, exits and city streets and fronted up for my lesson on time and eager. Jack ran me through a couple of warm-up exercises, then had me sing a few songs to assess my ability. Midway through my warm-up, he stopped me.

'Johnny, you've got the talent to be an opera singer, son.'

He was almost hyperventilating with excitement, and started laying out the training regime I needed to follow to find my voice as a tenor. I was flattered that Jack thought I had the potential to be an opera singer, I really was, but that kind of music was not what I wanted to sing. I mean, opera, that takes some serious training, training that I didn't have the patience for. And besides, opera wasn't in my world, it wasn't in my universe. I was more fish and chip shop than opera.

'I don't want to sing opera, Jack. I want to sing rock'n'roll.'

As quickly as Jack's eyes had lit up when he heard my singing voice, they dulled with my response.

'Okay, fine. Go and see Viola. She'll look after you.'

Viola Ritchie was a teacher at Jack's studio and to my great delight and benefit, she took me on. Thankfully, she liked the sound of my voice. Viola had me doing scales and all sorts of things, but what she really wanted me to focus on was learning how to control my breathing. By learning to control my breath, I could avoid gasping for air during a song. Ultimately, Viola wanted to teach me how to become a stronger singer for longer.

One of the exercises Viola had me doing involved a door frame, a needle and a thread of cotton about a foot long. First, I had to thread the needle, then stick it above the door with the cotton hanging down. Then, using only my breath, I had to blow and make that piece of cotton hang at an angle. The challenge was to keep the cotton at that angle for as long as I could. I went home and straight away asked Mum for a needle and thread. She looked at me strangely, then got up and started rummaging in her sewing kit.

'Any particular colour?'

She was teasing. I gave her a quick peck on the cheek, took the needle and cotton and stuck it above the frame of my bedroom door. I practised and practised, and I got quite good at it actually. I didn't have lessons with Viola for long, but the tuition really helped me. Down the track she used to come to my shows and give me a critique afterward. Viola was a gem, a lovely lady, and I was very lucky to have learned from her.

When you look back on any career, there are people in your life who, in varying degrees, made a difference to the paths you took. Darryl, David and Viola were three of many people who made an impact on me, and because of them, in varying ways, things were starting to happen. I was going to listen to my dad, and give it a good go!

CHAPTER 4

DEAR OLD SADIE

I wanted to sing rock'n'roll and soul. Back then, I might not have had the life experience to sing soul the way it should be sung, but I loved the blues. I'm not a religious man, but I've always had a deep appreciation for the intricate arrangements, soulful choral music and captivating singing in rhythm and blues. As a young teenager, I loved going into Brashs record store, picking out an album, popping on the headphones and getting lost in the music. Listening to the work of Stevie Wonder, Ray Charles, Ella Fitzgerald, Tom Jones and Aretha Franklin, I can hear their hearts – I mean, really hear their hearts. I love those singers and that was the kind of singer I wanted to be, and the kind of music I wanted to sing.

Others had different ideas about what I should be singing, though. They were looking for the next big star, madly searching for the next smash single, whereas I was looking to build a career. I didn't want to record 'Sadie, the Cleaning Lady', I really didn't. But I was talked into it. Many argue that the song gave me a start, that it gave me years of work and it's part of why I'm still around now. All that could be true. I am very lucky for all the success I've had, it's just that 'Sadie' was not the best piece of music I've ever recorded – far from it. 'Sadie' didn't show people my heart. It didn't even hint at what was in my heart.

Although 'Sadie' was a big hit, after it was released my credibility with my peers went through the floor. I guess I put myself out there, so I've got to cop what happened to a certain degree. But it's okay, I can live with the responses I got. I've learned to live with 'Sadie'.

When I signed on the dotted line with EMI, David Mackay immediately started hunting for songs for me to record. Back then, it was really hard to get good songs that hadn't already been recorded. There weren't many local Australian songwriters working in the industry unless they were writing for themselves, and all the publishers in England and the US kept the really good songs for their own local artists. Only the songs that everyone else had passed on made their way to Australia. We were at the bottom of the song selection barrel. 'Sadie' was one of those songs that everyone else had knocked back. It was probably sent to Australia as a last-ditch effort to have someone record it and it fell into my lap. Well, more like placed in my lap.

David was a good record producer, a gentle guy and a motivating force. He really encouraged me to give my best to my vocals. David also knew the kind of songs I wanted to sing. The first time he played me 'Sadie', what I heard was a little ditty, a novelty song. Something my aunts or my nan might have sung loudly at a family gathering (with or without the lampshade on their heads). I listened carefully and then shook my head. *Not for me, thanks.*

The record company didn't take that no for a final answer. They'd decided that this was what they wanted me to record. I held fast, but so did they. It came down to an ultimatum. The executives at EMI made it clear in no uncertain terms that I had to record that song or else lose my contract, and every shot I had. They had me. Of course, I relented.

For me, recording 'Sadie' was not dissimilar to recording the jingle 'Susan Jones'. I was again stepping into Armstrong Studios and when I arrived the team was set up and ready to go. David was producing, Roger Savage was once again the engineer, Bill Armstrong was there. Anne and Johnny Hawker, a married couple who had formed a pop duo, were also in the studio. When they met, Anne was a singer and Johnny had his own band. That day, Johnny was leading the orchestra and he played the ukulele on the beginning of the track. Johnny Hawker also had the idea of putting the vacuum cleaner solo in the middle of the song, which was a bit of fun. If you listen closely to that solo, you can hear me humming the tune of 'In My Room'.

By the time they were ready for me to lay down my vocals, all the instruments had been recorded and all the arrangements done. They were all terrific people, and once again they treated me like I was a professional. They didn't tell me how to sing the song, other than, 'Yep, that's okay.' I just followed my instincts and sang it the way I heard it in my head.

I now know the trick with studio sessions is that you've got to have longevity in your neck and throat. You're going to sing the song all day, well, maybe ten or twelve times, to get the right timbre, the right feel, to get it all sounding right. You have to stay focused and not let yourself tighten up physically or mentally. As I walked into the booth, I decided to sing 'Sadie' with a smile on my face. I sang the song over and over again, grinning from ear to ear. Perhaps you can hear that smile in the recording.

And that's really all I did, I laid down my vocals and that was it.

It was satisfying. When it was finished, I knew it wasn't the greatest song in the world, but I did my version of it and I stand by it. That's all you can do. David, Bill and Roger all gave me encouraging feedback. It was lovely to get that reaction from these guys. I mean, these were people who were right on the cutting edge of the recording industry, so their positive feedback was a great boost. But now I had done my job I just had to wait and see what happened next. I had no idea that this one song, this one day in the studio, would set me on a single path for years.

IN MY ROOM

Words and Music by
JOHNNY FARNHAM

Castle Music Pty. Limited
2ND FLOOR, WHITE HOUSE,
403 GEORGE STREET, SYDNEY, N.S.W. 2000

BELCAS MUSIC LTD.,
408 HUTT ROAD,
LOWER HUTT, NEW ZEALAND

CHAPTER 5

THE LEARNING CURVE

Things were changing, but I was still a plumber's apprentice until the Victorian Apprenticeship Commission released me. Thankfully, my parents accompanied me on the day of the hearing, so there was no danger of me getting lost. The committee representing the Commission heard about the diligence of my work and the high marks I had received at tech school. This all leant in my favour. They also noted I was hardworking and a better-than-average apprentice, and after hearing all this I was granted two years' leave from my indentureship. Honestly, I really think they believed

I'd realise this music industry caper was a waste of time and soon return to my senses and my trade. I was finally released from my apprenticeship and free to pursue a music career but, despite wanting to perform, it was still a very hard decision to leave plumbing. I really appreciated the faith Stan had placed in me, so I kept working for him a while longer.

In November 1967, 'Sadie, the Cleaning Lady' was released as a single seven-inch record. On the B-side of the single was 'In My Room'. The release of the record was absolutely surreal for me. Only two days before, I had finally finished up with Stan, and then the roller-coaster ride began.

A big part of the 'Sadie' marketing plan was for me to go around to all the major radio stations to promote it. Grantley Dee was a disc jockey on 3AK, and Stan 'The Man' Rofe was on 3UZ. I knew both of these guys from the live music scene, but this new radio world was beyond my realm of understanding. I had no idea what to do, I was completely out of my depth. I wish someone had taught me how to deal with the media and given me a heads-up on it all. When you're young and hot – and by 'hot' I mean when everything is working – everybody wants to know you, and the attention can become quite intrusive. A reporter or disc jockey would ask a question and I'd answer it and then they'd stay quiet and I'd start blustering and talking too much to fill the empty space. It's an old journo trick and I had no idea what they were doing. I learned by making mistakes. Some of the interviewers were kind, others not so much.

By early 1968, the song I didn't want to record had gone to number one nationally on the *Go-Set* charts. It would stay there for five weeks and remain in the charts for twenty-four weeks. It was absolutely incredible. It became the highest-selling single of the 1960s and for a while there it was the highest-selling single ever. With the meteoric rise of 'Sadie', my life went completely nuts. Darryl went into overdrive, booking me for everything and anything with what I can now see was little thought about what was best for a long-term career. I performed concerts all over the country, made store appearances and did record signings – I'd be signing autographs for hours and hours. Sometimes I got overwhelmed by the crowds, but mostly I was overwhelmed by the success. I felt a huge responsibility to get out there and thank people for their support. Generally, I had a lot of fun and people were pretty good to me. What's not to like about being loved? But I was flat out like a lizard drinking.

The first time I appeared on Brian Henderson's *Bandstand* was an incredible moment. *Bandstand* was a variety television program that was broadcast live nationally on the Nine network. Hosted by the now legendary news anchor Brian Henderson, it drew a huge audience every week. Some of Australia's best and brightest became regulars on the show, including Col Joye, the Bee Gees, Olivia Newton-John, The Delltones and Helen Reddy. The day I went on I met Patricia 'Little Pattie' Amphlett, who was a huge star. Back then, performers on the show had to mime to a backing track. I'm a terrible mimer. On top of having to mime, I was also given instructions to follow: 'Walk to this spot, then walk to that spot, then turn around and walk over there.' All my moves were choreographed to hit certain marks for the cameras. To add to the degree of difficulty, two Sadies were going to be dancing around me while I was 'singing'. I made it through the rehearsal okay and then, all of a sudden, it was time to go live. My heart started racing as Brian introduced me with a line about being a plumber before he said:

'He started singing with groups around Melbourne and is now being groomed as pop music's young hopeful . . . Ladies and gentlemen, a *Bandstand* start for . . . JOHNNY FARNHAM!'

My heart felt like it was pounding out of my chest. I started to mime but completely forgot all my moves and missed my camera marks. I had to make it up as I went along, trying not to crash into the Sadies as they spun around me with their buckets and brooms. The floor manager wasn't that impressed, but he copped it sweet.

I ended up being on *Bandstand* six times between 1967 and 1968. Each time, I was terrified. After a few appearances, I insisted on singing live because I really hated miming. I was lousy at it. Everybody else mimed and didn't seem to be bothered, but I just had this thing about it. I thought it was awful seeing someone move their lips to the wrong lyric. Requesting to sing live was a pretty big ask for a young bloke starting out. I was going against the way things were done and that is a hard thing to do, but thankfully the producers agreed. I was very relieved, and only used backing tracks for the music.

At home my family couldn't believe all the fuss. Mum thought it was amazing all these people were so interested in me and what I was doing, Dad was plain gobsmacked. Despite the chaos, they were on my side as always. Mind you, they would've been there for me if I was laying bricks. Jeanie Jam Roll loved all the hype and attention. Because she was only two years younger than me, she knew exactly what was going on. I'd come home from a concert or an autograph-signing session and Jeanie would be there with a gaggle of her friends. They'd all be very excited to see me, even Jeanie! Her friends were all so nice, and couldn't believe I still lived at home.

Mum and Dad had to put up with a bit. Because our number was listed in the phone book, young girls would call the house all the time asking for me. I suggested that Mum change our phone number to a silent one and she shrugged and said, 'No, I like it when they ring.' She'd end up chatting to them.

Mum became a sort of Agony Aunt of Noble Park. Soon enough, some of those girls started calling wanting to talk to her, asking for Rosie's advice. They'd tell her all their problems and she'd lend them her ear. Others only wanted to talk to me. They used to cry and say, 'I love Johnny.' Sometimes I'd pick up the phone and say hello. It all felt a bit strange, but it was great fun and I got a kick out of it most of the time.

Technically I still lived at home, but the truth was I was rarely there because I was always out working. When I was home I used to play with my younger brother, Stephen, a lot. There may have been a thirteen-year age gap but that didn't bother me. I used to play with my little sister, Jackie, too. I've always loved kids and I've always been sorry that when Stephen and Jackie were young I was busy doing my plumbing apprenticeship and then off at gigs at night. When 'Sadie' came along I was hardly ever at home, so I missed a lot of their younger days. I made up for it later in life, and we shared a lot as we got older.

It might have been hard to pick the four of us as siblings. Jackie had bright red hair, as did Stephen. Jeanie had blonde hair, like me. Well, I did have blond hair – what little hair

I have left is now grey. But we were a close family. I even wrote a song for Jackie when I was a teenager, but I changed her hair colour.

> *Oh Jacqueline, sweet Jacqueline*
> *She's the cutest girl in town*
> *And her hair is golden brown*
> *Oh I love Jacqueline*

Perhaps not one of my best, but the intention was good!

When everything started to happen after 'Sadie', the learning curve was steep. Really steep. Being a solo performer, I had to work out how to quickly rehearse a band before a show. Many of my bookings meant I was working with a house or backing band that I'd never met, and the musicians didn't necessarily know the music. I'd be booked in somewhere like a shopping centre or some big mall and a couple of hours before my set I'd meet the band members, share a chord chart and rehearse with them. Ironically, I rarely finished performing my set because I'd get pulled off the bloody stage. Quite early in the success of 'Sadie' I'd go on, start to sing, girls would start screaming, then one of the girls in the audience would bolt to the stage and try to grab me. This would encourage more girls to do the same, and before I knew it, I'd be swamped and literally pulled off the stage into the crowd. At least when that happened I knew the audience was engaged and enjoying the show!

Sometimes the response I got from the public wasn't so great. I was on tour with Mike Furber, Christopher Kite and Tony Worsley in rural Queensland when we pulled into a service station to refuel. The station was full of people about to ride off on motorbikes and we arrived in a van that had my face and the words 'Sadie, the Cleaning Lady' painted on it. The bikers mustn't have liked the power ballad 'Sadie' because they all got off their motorcycles and started coming toward us. Mike, who was an interesting fellow, grabbed the mic stand out of the van, got out and stood there ready to use it as a weapon. These guys were enraged by his stance, and they looked even more like they were going to kill us. Our roadie, Jimmy Considine, tried to defuse things and said loudly, 'It's okay, boys, these are just pop stars. They're singers and dancers and stuff.'

The bikers weren't impressed and kept moving toward us, so Jimmy tried another tactic. 'Alright, I'll fight one of you,' he said. Jimmy was a tough little bugger and he followed up with, 'Pick your biggest bloke, I'll take him.'

I was quaking behind the van somewhere. The bikers collectively made a quick decision and out stepped this guy who was built like a brick shithouse. Jimmy fought this bloke. They each got one in the earhole and then that was that. Everyone walked away, job done. We filled up the tank, got back in the Sadie van and went on to our gig. It was pretty scary, and there was a bit of that senseless violence around at the time so it wasn't a one-off.

―

The *TV Week* 'King of Pop' awards were a pretty big deal in those days. Like the Logies, the awards were decided by reader polls and were televised. For the first two years of the awards, 1967 and 1968, Normie Rowe won the King of Pop crown. I had watched Normie on *The Go!! Show* as a kid, and as I sat there on the lounge-room floor watching all those pop stars perform on the show, all that was running through my mind was, *That's what I want to do!* I always knew I wanted to sing but being nominated for the King of Pop award was beyond anything I had ever imagined. And then it happened. It was nice that 'Sadie' was a hit and everything was going well but I didn't expect to be nominated and I never thought I'd win it. But I did.

I can't put into words how I felt that night. I'm a bit of a crier, I cry at *Lassie* movies, I cry at sad stuff, I cry at happy stuff and I cried that night. They announced my name and I bumbled up to the stage and between sobs spluttered into the microphone, 'Oh, thank you very much.' Someone said, 'What are you crying for?' I couldn't respond properly. The emotion of the moment overtook me, I was completely overwhelmed and the tears flowed. I ended up being named King of Pop for five years in a row, and the thrill and the emotion never diminished. And I cried every time. At one of the King of Pop ceremonies, I remember wearing the crown and it fell off. One of the gemstones popped out. I was a bit embarrassed, but thankfully they fixed it really quickly.

It must have been hard for Normie Rowe to see my success. He was a huge star and then, under the compulsory national service scheme where a conscription lottery was put in place based on birthdates, everything changed for him. Normie, born on 1 February 1947, was told his number was picked and he was drafted for national service. Normie's two-year tour of duty in Vietnam during the war effectively ended his King of Pop career. I wasn't looking to squeeze into anybody's space and I didn't feel like I had beaten anyone, because it was never a race, but I could recognise that was a tough break for Normie. I was very grateful for the acknowledgement, and the award definitely gave me a push along to do what I wanted to do.

Fame wasn't something I thought about a great deal. I mean, I was blown away by the responses I'd get about a song or a performance and I'd think, *It's worked! It's a hit! I'm so happy!*, but I didn't think about fame itself per se. I guess I was too absorbed with everything that was going on around me to sit back and assess what was happening and what it meant. I didn't even get a moment to take stock of my finances. I must have been making a lot of money from all the work I was doing, not to mention the royalties, but I really don't know where they went, and at the time I didn't even think to ask Darryl. I was either working or asleep. And when I was awake, my head was like scrambled eggs. I did manage to buy my dad a Holden. He had never owned a car or even had a licence before; he used to catch the train and bus everywhere, including to work. It was a brand-new car that cost $3500, which was a crazy amount of money, but I was so proud that I could do that for him.

After the success of 'Sadie' came the pressure of having to back it up. It was a bit disconcerting because journalists would say, 'You've had success, what are you going to do now?' And I'd think, *What* am *I going to do now?* I'm sure every artist in every art form feels the same pressure at some point. *How am I going to back up that success?*

Of course, the executives at EMI said, 'We need another record.' I stood up for myself and told them I didn't want to do another novelty song, but they'd already picked out the exact kind of song I didn't want to sing: 'Underneath the Arches'. It was a song for my mum and dad and nan and grandad, not a song that appealed to me or my mates. David Mackay had to back up his colleagues, but he knew how I felt and so he helped me search for alternatives. Together we presented 'Friday Kind of Monday' to the executives. This was a song I absolutely loved. When the record company doubled down on their choice I, their highest-selling star, threatened to rebel. I had to hold my ground on this and we reached a compromise, releasing a double A-side single with 'Friday Kind of Monday' on one side and 'Underneath the Arches' on the other.

With that release, EMI had a bob each way, trying to capture both the younger fans and the nans and grandads, too. 'Friday Kind of Monday' was a much better song than 'Sadie' but, unfortunately, it didn't have the same impact. It did okay, but it was hard to match the success of 'Sadie', and even harder for me to get any credibility back as a singer. The tightrope walk of satisfying a record company, developing a career, keeping true to what I wanted to sing and developing as a musical artist was just beginning. But my creative confidence took a hit after that second record, because the song I'd chosen didn't fire like I'd hoped. After that, following my instincts and speaking up for myself became much harder.

CHAPTER 6

A PIECE OF MEAT

After the success of 'Sadie' and the not-so-successful 'Friday Kind of Monday', Darryl Sambell's grip on me tightened. He was managing everything, and the schedule he had me on left little time for a girlfriend or even friends. The only acquaintances I had were people he knew. I was never home, so I hardly had time to see my family, let alone hang out with any old mates. I was too busy to be lonely, or too busy to realise I was lonely. Darryl often organised late-night performances and then followed those up with an early call time the next day. If I was awake, he had me working. It never stopped. I was young and healthy and looking to seize my chance, so I didn't mind the work, and I still had confidence in Darryl. I thought he had it all planned out. Because my parents lived almost an hour's drive out of the centre of Melbourne, Darryl started insisting I stay overnight at his penthouse. I was so tired, it made sense to cut out travelling time, which meant I was sleeping at his place more often than not.

When Darryl quit his job at the quarry in Gawler to manage me full time, he'd moved to Melbourne and into a flat on Beaconsfield Parade, St Kilda, overlooking the Esplanade and the beach. He called it his 'Penthouse'. It was actually just the top floor of this little block of red-brick units and was nothing like a penthouse, but that's how Darryl dressed it up. Since I still didn't have a car, a licence or a sense of direction, I was often stuck there.

Darryl was only four years older than me, and just twenty-three years old when 'Sadie' became a hit, but the combination of his balding head, his beard, his height and a manufactured air of sophistication made him an imposing figure. He drank almost as much as he smoked. He would take a litre bottle of Coca-Cola, pour out most of the cola then top it up with Scotch. Often wearing expensive Italian suits, Darryl was rarely without a Scotch and Coke in one hand and a cigarette in the other.

A PIECE OF MEAT

Since our success, Darryl had worked his way into the Melbourne glitterati and he became entrenched in both the music and theatre scenes. He hand-picked a tight group of people with whom to network, gossip and party. People, mostly gay men, would come to the flat at all hours to drink, smoke, play cards and party with him. Since I was often there between gigs, I was regularly surrounded by aggressive gay men who, thanks to Darryl, thought I was gay.

Around Darryl and his friends, I was seen as young, naive and probably fair game. I was oblivious to much of what was going on at first, but as the months went by, I started getting prodded from all sides, which meant I was on guard most of the time. I like a bit of fun, I'm not a complete prude, but I didn't want to get involved in all that was happening in that penthouse. It was the low end of the stick, if you'll pardon the expression. So I tried to keep out of the way.

The Masters Apprentices were a band from Adelaide. They began life as a four-piece instrumental group called The Mustangs, with Mick Bower, Rick Morrison, Gavin Webb and Brian Vaughton the founding members. After advertising for a lead singer, they joined up with the charismatic Jim Keays and, not long after, changed their name and musical direction. The Masters Apprentices were born. They became one of South Australia's most popular groups and then, like many others, relocated to the bigger scene in Melbourne. They were writing and recording their own material, and their psychedelic rock sounded unique within the Australian music scene. They were fantastic. They had hits with 'Undecided' and 'Living in a Child's Dream' and their debauched antics were widely publicised. They were definitely the bad boys of rock'n'roll and I, by comparison, was the cream cheese of manufactured teen pop. By late 1968, the Masters Apprentices and I shared the same manager, Darryl Sambell.

One weekend, the Masters and I were both working at the same venue and we decided to get together after the show and have a few beers. They were massively popular and I was riding the 'Sadie' wave, so we couldn't go out to a pub or club because we would have been mobbed, so we decided to meet up back at Darryl's apartment. We all got on really well, and that night they taught me how to drink. Their bass player, Glenn Wheatley, and I clicked instantly. I got on with all the guys in the band, but Glenn and I naturally gravitated toward each other. He was only a bit older than me, a good bloke and he had a driver's licence, which was fucking great because I still didn't. With our busy touring schedules, we didn't have much time to hang out but when we did, we'd jump in the Masters van and head out to the bush to shoot rabbits, go fishing, sink a few beers and jam on guitars. It was good fun, and it was a great way to let off a bit of steam, away from the music industry and the spotlight.

The Masters had already enjoyed some outstanding success, but by the time they'd signed Darryl on as their manager, they were flat broke. Darryl arranged for them to rent the flat underneath his 'Penthouse', but the two-bedder wasn't really big enough for the entire band, so Darryl offered Glenn the spare room in his own flat to give him some space. Glenn was reluctant, but too poor to find an alternative. With me so often stuck at Darryl's after gigs and Glenn crashing there, we got to hang out more, and became good mates.

Darryl Sambell lived large. On top of the partying, and his expensive Italian suits, he added cars, racehorses and gambling to his extravagance. I never thought, *Hang on, where's my share?* It's hard to explain, and even harder to understand why I didn't ask more questions and demand more answers, but I just didn't. I was too busy working. Darryl often threw lavish parties and luncheons. One particular time, it was Christmas and I was on a rare visit to see my family while the festivities in his apartment were well underway. In the apartment directly underneath, the broke Masters band members were well on their way to personifying the cliched 'starving artists'. Literally – they were starving. They could hear the drinking and partying above them, so they went up and knocked on Darryl's door.

'What do you want?'

'We don't have any food.'

Apparently, Darryl didn't miss a beat. He threw twenty cents at them and said, 'Go and buy a pie' before slamming the door closed. This was the response from their manager, the person who was booking their tours and performances and controlling their money. Definitely not the way to nurture young, impoverished musicians.

Glenn pretty soon worked out that everybody in the music industry was making money except the artists. One particular gig at Festival Hall in Brisbane solidified his hunch. The Masters were told they'd played to a crowd bigger than for the Beatles. It was the biggest crowd the venue and the band had ever seen, but they ended up losing money that night because they had to replace the clothes that were ripped off them by the fans. After the gig Glenn sat down in his torn clothes and thought to himself, *This isn't right. A bigger crowd than the Beatles and we got paid $200 between us?* He calculated the box office would have grossed somewhere between $30,000 and $35,000 and yet the band was on a fixed fee. Pretty soon after that night, the Masters Apprentices sacked Darryl. From that moment on, Glenn started to manage the band himself.

Like many Australian bands and artists of the time, the Masters decided to try their luck in London. Australia was still an emerging music scene and we all looked to Europe, particularly London, for validation and success. If you could make it in London, you'd made it. But before the Masters left Australia, Glenn decided to throw himself a massive twenty-first birthday party. It was a pretty wild party and everyone was having a great time, most of all Glenn. But then the night tipped over into not-so-fun for him, because he drank too much and had to disappear into the bathroom. I was passing by and heard him heaving in the loo. I knocked and then went in to see how he was doing and found him passed out with his head in the dunny. I mean, his head was right down in the toilet bowl. I did what anyone else would do – I dashed over, grabbed him by the shoulders and pulled him out. I propped him up against a wall and got him a drink of water. Then I sat with him for a little minute while he came to. From that day forth, Glenn and I had a story about how I saved his life by stopping him from drowning in the toilet bowl at his twenty-first.

The time came, and the Masters set sail for England to find their fame and fortune. We farewelled them with yet another party, but this time Glenn was very careful around the booze.

Hi Jim, Glen, Doug, Colin

   Just a note to wish you all the luck (which you won't need) in the world. Wish I could be there but I'm working - But be assured I'll Definately be there in thought and Rooting for you all the way

Kindest Regards
To Four of the Nicest Guys I've ever Met & th Most Talented
Sincerely
Johnny '69

It was hard for me to see them all go, really hard, because aside from them I had no real friends to speak of. I didn't realise it at the time, but looking back I can recognise that I was being isolated. By booking me for three to four spots a night, adding multiple store appearances, photo shoots and then autograph signings slotted into any spare moment around all that, Darryl kept me out of the way of everybody. Aside from work, I didn't get to go anywhere or do very much at all unless it was with people he knew. Very quickly, working all the time became quite normal to me.

Without mates, I took to spending as much of my free time as I could on my little seventeen-footer half-cabin cruiser. I think I paid about as much for that motorboat as I paid for the car I bought my dad. I kept it down at St Kilda marina, which was an easy walk from Darryl's apartment. I'd turn up and one of the deck hands would take it out of storage for me using a forklift. The forklift would drop the little boat gently on the water, I'd hop in and off I'd go. Sometimes I would drop in a fishing line and try to catch a flathead, but mostly I'd just enjoy the quiet and calm of being out on the water. Port Phillip Bay is notorious for turning nasty very quickly, and the sailors down at the marina soon gave me the nickname the 'Temporary Australian', because I would go out in any weather. Black storm clouds would be filling the sky and

I'd be whistling and getting ready to set off. I didn't care about getting wet or knocked about by the wind, I just needed some time away from the life I was living.

Recording in the studio became an in-and-out-as-quickly-as-possible affair. The process for me was laid out, and creatively I didn't have much input. It was basically, get into the studio, quickly learn the lyrics, set the key, lay down the vocals as fast as I could then Darryl would have me running out the door for the next store or shopping mall appearance. I really didn't spend a second more in the studio than was absolutely necessary. I hardly even had time to listen back to what had been recorded before I was rushed out the door. It became mundane, a bit of a blur, and all I took away from a recording session was the record that was released. Nothing more than that. I must admit I smoked like a chimney then, and I can remember getting told off by a producer and asked to put out my cigarette. I'd been singing and smoking, with the cigarette inches from the microphone. Smoking while making a record became a signature of mine. Crazy stuff, so stupid, but in those times I still had no idea how dangerous it was.

Recording 'Raindrops Keep Falling on My Head' was no different. They gave me a copy of the demo, I had a listen and loved the Burt Bacharach and Hal David song straight away. I didn't even know about the Hollywood film and BJ Thomas's version, which was being used on the new Paul Newman and Robert Redford movie, until later. The executives at EMI wanted to rush my version out. They knew if they released it after *Butch Cassidy and the Sundance Kid* was in cinemas, my version would sink without a trace. There was a big thing about cover versions in those days. I recorded a few covers over the years and it's always better as an Australian to be first to release a song. The local industry would take singles from English or American artists, but those markets wouldn't reciprocate. When they tried to release my version of 'Sadie' in England, EMI Abbey Road said, 'No thanks, we can get someone to record and release it here.' They flat-out rejected it. I got my own back with 'Raindrops'. It was released into the Australian market first and was a massive hit. It went to number one on the *Go-Set* charts at the end of January 1970 and stayed there for more than eight weeks.

With the success of 'Raindrops' and another number one single in the bag, Darryl had me believing even more that my success was dependent on him, and him alone. He had me stitched up in all sorts of ways and I had no idea. I was too tired and had barely any time to think. He was wearing the tailored suits, not me. His spending went into overdrive, buying more cars and stuff, and yet every time I needed money, I had to ask him for what felt like a handout. It was demoralising and degrading. I didn't know where the money I was earning was going. I didn't even know how much I got paid, I thought Darryl was taking care of it all. I was working all the time and not seeing much for it. My parents started asking me questions about money and my financial situation, and I couldn't answer them. My dad took it upon himself to help me get control of the situation. He hired a lawyer to get some answers from Darryl. By Dad's and my calculations, I should have been making a lot of money from the record royalties, performances, concerts, tours, all of it.

This lawyer was supposed to help us but, to my absolute horror, it seemed he leaked our request and my financial uncertainty to the tabloid paper *The Truth*. Once that happened, all hell broke loose. The headlines in the newspapers were huge, and I was embarrassed beyond belief. Darryl went absolutely nuts. He was prone to theatrics and tantrums and he went berserk. He was yelling, saying how dare I question him after all the things he'd done for me. He screamed that I should be thanking him after he plucked me from obscurity and turned me into a star. He went on and on. It was too much, I broke down. I wasn't crying for anything other than the fact that I was so embarrassed by the whole situation. Honestly, I felt like such an idiot. I was mortified, and felt shamefully exposed. I told Dad to drop it. I didn't want to investigate what was going on financially, I just wanted the lawyer to shut up and the whole thing to go away. Basically, I stuck my fingers in my ears and sang *la la la* until the public humiliation faded away.

It was ironic that Darryl was so angry at the tabloid attention, because he was forever leaking information about me to newspapers and magazines in order to get publicity. I was so naive, and too busy to put two and two together until much later. My life became a goldmine for the tabloids; they would print the most ridiculous stuff about me, or print things that were almost true but not quite. I had no idea where they were getting their stories, but the forensic attention and publicised half-truths made me incredibly wary of the media. Actually, it's just occurred to me now that it was probably Darryl, not the lawyer, who leaked the story about my finances.

Darryl wasn't a nice man, and he used me like a piece of meat. It was around this time that I discovered he was drugging me. He'd been putting amphetamines in my drink to keep me up working all night. People used to say to me, 'You speak really fast' and 'Jeez, you're dry in the mouth.' I had no idea that I was on drugs. Then he'd put sleeping tablets in my coffee in the morning and I'd be knocked out cold. I could have slept through anything. He drugged me for years and I had no fucking idea. I caught him one day. I was drinking a cup of coffee and there was a pill only half-dissolved in the bottom. When I asked him what it was, Darryl replied, 'That's just something to help you stay awake.' I honestly couldn't remember if it was night or day half the time.

I feel so ashamed of myself for not realising what Darryl was up to or speaking up more often to put him back in his place. I didn't question any of it, I just went along as if nothing was off key. I still don't know why I didn't react more. I put it down to being young, under stress, tired and feeling unsure and insecure about my own instincts. There was a lot of pressure, too – a *lot* of pressure.

I was still a teenager when I realised people were gossiping and that Darryl was fuelling the rumour that led some people to say directly to me, 'Oh, you're a poofter!' My knowledge of the gay community, or the camp community as it was called in those days, was non-existent. I really was so incredibly naive. At my twenty-first birthday I stood up and made a speech, which ended with thanks to my manager.

'I just want to thank Darryl, he's always right behind me.'

Everyone in the room cracked up. I was confused by the cynical laughter from people who were supposed to be my friends. It was like everyone was in on the joke except me.

I may have been exhausted and at times overwhelmed, but I was a resilient young man. I had grown up in a safe home with a very comfortable upbringing, not materialistic, but comfortable and loving. So I was able to shake off the weirdness with Darryl and all the shit that was thrown at me. I got pretty good at ducking. I knew to a certain extent that in entering the music industry there would be interest in me, but I really had no idea how much and the types of interest. From girls, from guys, from the media, from other people in the industry. There were people who talked about me positively and others who were always negative. It's overwhelming, everyone wants a piece of you, everybody wants to know you, everybody wants to look at you, touch you, be seen with you. Everyone has an opinion of you and it's like . . . *Who am I? Which way do I turn?* If anyone reading this book is dealing with attention like this, talk to someone you trust for support.

The party scene at Darryl's was full-on and there were a few people who made me feel very uncomfortable, but I didn't detest all of his friends. One person who often turned up at Darryl's parties was Frank Thring. Frank was the epitome of the saying 'camp as a row of tents', and despite his outrageous behaviour I would end up considering him a close friend. Francis William Thring IV was a great bloke. He'd started his career in theatre productions in Melbourne before moving to London, then on to Hollywood. He starred in several major motion pictures, including *Ben-Hur* and *King of Kings*, both religious blockbusters, which is quite amusing when you think about it.

Like many of the older men I met through Darryl, Frank also tried to seduce me but, unlike many others, he never expected it would ever happen. He never stopped trying it on though, and my rejections seemed to entertain him. He used to hit on me in front of other people, just to embarrass me. I should have realised what would happen the first time I went to Frank's apartment. I was sitting on his couch with a drink when he handed me a stack of photographs. I picked up the first photo and it was a sailor masturbating. I thought, *Oh, Jesus!* I am sure I blushed as I flicked quickly to the next, and then the next. They were all men dressed up in uniforms in pornographic poses. I looked over at Frank and he laughed and said, 'Pornography, Johnny. I want to get you hot.' Not the way to do it, Frank! I said, 'I'm straight.' Frank replied, 'That's okay darling, I love straight men.' Despite Frank's objections, I wasn't going to hang around so I called a cab and told him I'd wait outside. The cab pulled up just as Frank came out, stood next to me and then announced in his loudest voice, 'Well, darling, thank you for coming!' and he kissed me on the forehead in front of the bloody cab driver. The cab driver didn't know what to make of it all, so it was quite an uncomfortable drive home.

A PIECE OF MEAT

Frank was always entertaining company, so I didn't mind going to an occasional show with him. One time we went to see Buddy Greco, the American jazz singer and pianist. We went with a very famous English actor who made it clear he wanted to sleep with me and offered me a pill. 'No thanks, mate!' I was getting used to rebuffing men. Anyway, we got to the door and security stopped us because of Frank's bag. Frank had this big bag he carried with him everywhere. I had no idea what was in it, I never thought to ask. Security were already eyeing me and Frank off and I'm thinking, *Here we go, they think we're a couple.* One of the security men told Frank he couldn't go inside with the bag. Frank pointed his nose down at the man and asked, 'Why not?'

Everyone in the line was looking at Frank Thring and Johnny Farnham, and the guard then asked the obvious question: 'What's in it?'

Frank replied, 'First of all, there's a knife, booze, and money to pay you, you cunt!' Frank delivered his response so regally, and everyone, the whole queue, in fact, the whole ballroom heard, because Frank had the lungs of an elephant and the voice projection of a talented thespian.

(Buddy Greco was great, by the way – really good. Old Frank eventually conceded and left the bag outside and we all went in to watch the show.)

To Frank's credit, he never tried to trick me, he wasn't secretive and he didn't cross my boundaries. He was hilarious, he had a very droll sense of humour and he opened my eyes to a world beyond the little bubble in which I was trapped.

Being around Frank and hearing his stories of working in the theatre in Melbourne and London inspired me. I had starred in a pantomime, *Dick Whittington and His Cat*, which was fun except for the green tights I had to wear. But through that experience I learned to love the theatre. I loved the camaraderie of being in a cast, of having to get your lines right so that everybody else could get theirs right, too. I was also at that stage in my career where I was keen to give everything a go. When I was approached to audition for the Australian production of the West End hit musical *Charlie Girl*, I jumped at the chance. The only snag was I had to audition for the part in front of the director Freddie Carpenter, who was casting in London.

David Mackay, who had produced both 'Sadie' and 'Raindrops', as well as several other singles and albums of mine, had since left Australia for a position with EMI at Abbey Road in London. David was very keen for me to travel to the London office to meet with the EMI executives there. He wanted to see me get a foothold in the UK market so it made sense to combine this with meeting up with Freddie Carpenter.

Of course, Darryl was part of the negotiations, but it was David who was trying to open doors for me in a bigger territory.

That trip to London was horrendous. It was my first trip back to my birth country and so I was looking forward to it, but from the moment we boarded the plane things weren't good. For some reason, Ian 'Molly' Meldrum accompanied Darryl and me, and from the get-go it was a disaster.

One day I was having a quick bath to get ready for meetings and Molly burst into the bathroom, tore off his clothes and jumped into the bath with me. 'What the fuck are you doing, Ian?' I said as I jumped out of the bath and grabbed a towel to cover myself. Ian thought it was hilarious, and mumbled something about me taking too long in the tub.

The whole trip, Molly and Darryl were either bickering or drinking. On the flight over, Darryl drank the whole way, and by the time we reached Heathrow, he was an embarrassing mess. Many years later Australian cricketer David Boon would set a long-haul record for drinking fifty-two beers on a flight to London, and I suspect Darryl was more drunk than him. The meeting with EMI was brief. They weren't interested in me, and Darryl was too pissed to be coherent. It was embarrassing for me and for David Mackay.

Thankfully, the audition for *Charlie Girl* went much better. I was excited and incredibly nervous to meet Freddie Carpenter.

Freddie decided my audition should take place at Drury Lane. Stepping into that theatre was awe-inspiring. It's one of those classic London theatres steeped in history, and as I stood there I felt every bit of that history. Someone gave me a script and Freddie directed me up onto the stage. I was reading the part of Joe Studholme, a Cockney. I was standing there, only twenty-two kilometres from where I was born, and in that moment I decided to use my Cockney accent. Freddie didn't know I was born within the sounds of the Bow Bells, he didn't know my history or upbringing. To him, I was just some Aussie pop star.

I cleared my throat and delivered the lines in the thickest Cockney accent I could muster. Old Freddie did a double take. His mouth dropped open. I kept going. He sat there agog, and after a little while he said, 'You've got the job.' I was beyond happy.

I'd never aspired to be an actor, and if you'd seen my acting you'd understand why. I'm stiff as a board and I'd never done musical theatre before. I knew I had a lot to learn, but I was ready for it. Just learning how to project my voice was going to be a massive challenge. But the feeling I had standing in that theatre, on that stage, was absolutely incredible. Hearing Freddie say I got the job was electrifying. The course of my life was about to change in the best possible way imaginable.

CHAPTER 7

'I'VE GOT SOMETHING IN MY EYE'

I was excited and very nervous when I first set foot inside Her Majesty's Theatre to meet my fellow *Charlie Girl* cast members. To be involved in such a big theatre production was a huge opportunity for me to learn and grow. And grow I did.

Before it all kicked off, I managed to convince Darryl that I needed to rent my own apartment. I argued that the intense rehearsals, let alone the production schedule itself, meant travelling back and forth in taxis to my parents' house, which would be expensive, or crashing at his place, weren't good options. Renting an apartment, I reasoned, would be cheaper and less taxing. Secretly, however, the reason I was pushing so hard was because I couldn't bear to spend another night at Darryl's. Darryl was mad about musical theatre, had pushed me to go after *Charlie Girl*, and he didn't want me to stuff it up so eventually he agreed. I moved into my first flat on Millswyn Street in South Yarra. It was fantastic. I felt like the rope around my neck had loosened ever so slightly.

I was working alongside Dame Anna Neagle and Derek Nimmo, two international stars and both English theatre royalty. Anna and Derek had been part of the original 1965 cast, who opened the show in the West End of London to a hugely successful run. Thankfully, they both embraced me into the fold as a fellow professional from the start. Anna was just a sweetheart. She was sixty-seven years old by the time the show came to Australia and she had already been playing the role of Lady Hadwell for over six years. She was such a talent, and always very generous with me. When I first met her, I introduced myself with the words, 'How do you do, Dame Anna?' She instantly shot back, 'Oh no please, call me Anna.'

Derek Nimmo appeared to be a classic British upper-crust thespian but, interestingly, he was actually a Scouse just like the Beatles. Under his refined English accent he actually spoke like a Liverpudlian, which is where he was from, but he rarely reverted back to his roots. Before joining the cast of *Charlie Girl* as the character Nicholas Wainwright, Derek had made his name in the UK playing an incompetent reverend in the hugely successful television sitcom *All Gas and Gaiters*. I loved that show and thought he was really funny. In it, Derek's character, Reverend Mervyn Noote, had this faux stutter and Derek brought that stutter with him for the part he played in *Charlie Girl*. Derek and I became firm friends and, years later, Jill and I visited him a couple of times in London. He had this beautiful Rolls-Royce, a big old, heavy-arsed bastard of a car, and of course the streets of London, the back streets particularly, where the theatres are located in the West End, are very narrow. Derek didn't care a jot, he'd knock bloody dust bins over and out of the way, he'd just plough through it all with his grand old Rolls. It was a hilariously funny car ride.

Derek's wife Pat was a beautiful woman, she was gorgeous. During one trip, they took Jill and me up to their country house in the Cotswolds. We were joined by friends of theirs, two seriously famous English character actors, Basil Hoskins and Harry Andrews. They were a gay couple, and they were lovely. They have both passed away now, but in their day they were very, very well known characters who starred in lots of the old war movies and theatre productions. Jill and I were suitably impressed. It was autumn when we visited, and the six of us went rambling across the English countryside to take in the colourful autumn leaves, which was something Jill and I had never seen before. They got a kick out of showing us around, and we loved every minute of the trip.

Not everyone in the *Charlie Girl* production was pleased to find out I had been cast in the show. The stage manager, Fiona McKenzie-Geary, was convinced I was a talentless pop star who shouldn't have been given the opportunity over some dedicated and more deserving theatre actor. Fiona was lovely to everyone else, but initially she'd say to me, 'You'll never be an actor. You're not an actor. You'll never be any good in this.' All of this shit-canning and naysaying was before the show even opened and it didn't make me feel good, but I just tried harder to prove her wrong. So, yeah, I thought Fiona was a bit of a cow at first. It took me a while to win her over, but she had definitely mellowed by the last Melbourne show.

The production ran for nearly a year, it was a big hit, but that isn't why it was such a game changer for me. There was somebody in that show who took my breath away, and she changed everything.

It was a bright winter's day and we had just started rehearsals. I saw this young woman in front of Her Majesty's Theatre. She was going one way across the street and I was going the other, and she turned around and looked directly at me. It was just like a lightning strike, and I was history. I swear that was it for me. That girl's name was Jillian Billman.

Jillian remembers that day too, which is lovely. She was on the arm of Lewis Fiander, an actor who was in a different theatre production. I was pleased to discover they weren't actually going out together, they were just hanging out.

Jill walked across the street with these long, long, long, long legs and these beautiful big eyes and it was like . . . *JESUS! She's a knockout. Who is that?* To this day I can still picture Jill crossing that road. I have the image of her in my mind and when I look at her now, more than fifty years later, I see her just like I did when I first saw her.

I didn't know my way around Her Majesty's Theatre at all, but I soon found my way to the Sunroom. The Sunroom was a big open space with floorboards, lots of windows, mirrors and sunlight and it was where the chorus girls rehearsed. I walked up the stairs and into the studio and I saw that same beautiful girl over in the corner with the other dancers. Again, my heart leapt, and my brain went, *Oh, please.* I walked over and introduced myself and as I did, Jill said, 'Oh, I've got something in my eye.' I pulled a clean tissue out of my pocket and said, 'Let me fix it for you.' I got in really close, she giggled and I giggled, and from then on we were inseparable. We started going out and, of course, staying home, which was lots of fun, and we just clicked. The other female dancers were lovely, they were beautiful girls too. Of course, me being a 22-year-old, I didn't know where to look half the time because there were gorgeous girls everywhere, but Jill and I gravitated toward each other and once we got together, we stayed that way.

From the first day, Jillian and I grew up together, too. She was still a teenager when we first met and some people might think the age difference mattered, but to us it didn't. We made a pact not to try and change each other. I mean, there are still things she does that grate on me, and I know for a fact there are things I do that grate upon her, but if we have a real problem we discuss it, we talk about it like grown-ups, and that's done us the world of good. From day one we've worked at our relationship, and it has been a real partnership, one where we have always respected each other.

I was surrounded by people who, ostensibly, wanted to make money from me. Some had good intentions, some bad, and I guess that's just the way it flies. As a teenager, seventeen, eighteen, nineteen years old, and then in my early twenties, to separate some of that stuff was very difficult. So it was good to have Jill to talk things through with, to have her to fall back on. She's always been very strong. Always, always. Jill calls a spade a spade, and from the beginning of our relationship she has always told me honestly what she thinks. And, of course, she's always right.

When we met, Jill was living at home with her parents in Glenroy, which was a hell of a trip for me. I still hadn't got my licence or bought a car, so I used to borrow Dad's and drive without a licence, but no-one could lend me a sense of direction. To get to Jill's house I had to get myself to my parents' place to pick up the car, then drive to Glenroy, which meant driving from one side of outer Melbourne to the other. Of course, I had no idea how to get to Glenroy and I knew if I tried on my own I'd get hopelessly lost. So, I ordered a taxi and I gave the driver Jill's address and said to him, 'Don't lose me, I'll be driving right behind you.' I followed that cab all the way to Jill's house just so I could take her out for a drive. She was onto me pretty quick and, to this day, Jill still gives me instructions on where to go – and also how to drive and how to think and how to walk. She's my navigator on the road and in life.

Jill was my first girlfriend. I mean, I'd had other girlfriends before, but I couldn't really maintain a relationship because I was always on the go. When I met Jill I was still seeing another girl, who I met on a work trip to Queensland. Because this girl lived in Brisbane I didn't see her very often and, unfortunately, when I started with Jill I had to break up with her by phone.

I rang her and said, 'Look, I've met someone and I'm sorry, but I don't want to lead you on anymore, I'm really sorry.' This woman was a little bit older than I was, and she actually took it very well.

I knew pretty quickly I was falling in love with Jill, and at the same time I was falling in love with the professionalism and camaraderie that came with working alongside the same group of highly skilled people night after night. It was such a change after being a solo act since leaving Strings Unlimited at the age of seventeen. Since then, I'd been working with different bands night after night. Before working in the theatre my voice wasn't as strong as it could have been, but the rigour of rehearsal, together with singing alongside the best in the business, helped me improve the strength of my voice. That improvement benefited me for years to come. I also loved the professionalism and the discipline it took to memorise a script, and the way we were all relying on each other to get it right.

The cast of *Charlie Girl* were all good people and they became great friends. We'd spend a lot of time working with each other and then, because everyone got along so well, we spent a lot of time having fun together, too. We would all go out to restaurants or parties or wherever it might have been. I not only met my wife in *Charlie Girl*, I met my best mate, too. Louis Guthrie was working in the male dancers' wardrobe department. All the male dancers were strong, tall and gay – and then there was Louis, who's only five foot five. He's this little Jewish-Italian guy, and straight. But all the dancers adored Louis, they loved him, so you can imagine all the laughs they had. And Louis loved fishing, so he and I used to head off together when we had time. Louis also met his wife, Jenny Tew, during that production. Jenny was Jill's closest friend and they had started dancing together, even before *Charlie Girl*. So Jenny Tew became Jenny Guthrie and Louis and Jen, Jill and I, all became great mates. I went from being very lonely to suddenly having a full and wonderful life.

Louis witnessed Darryl's violence toward me. He was there during one of Darryl's drunken rages, which was probably about something entirely inconsequential because I don't even remember what brought it on. Darryl had always been a big, big drinker and he didn't hold his booze very well. When he'd had too much he became a very nasty drunk. To be fair, he wasn't very nice sober, either. Anyway, he was raging about something and all of a sudden he grabbed a television and hurled it at me. I caught it and threw it back at him. I had never retaliated before, instead I got good at ducking, but I think having Louis there forced my hand. I was sick of copping Darryl's shit but, more than that, I didn't want to look like a pushover in front of my new friend.

Darryl's behaviour got increasingly bad during the run of *Charlie Girl*. He tried all sorts of dirty tricks to break Jill and me up. He told a lot of lies about her, and he even paid other men to try to seduce her. Jill told me about it all. I was obviously glad she hadn't been wooed by these men, but I was also relieved that she didn't hide what Darryl had done from me. Darryl had then threatened to find me work interstate so he could send me away. Jill told him to watch himself. I marvelled at her bravery. Jill wasn't scared of Darryl, she wasn't scared of anyone or anything. She's strong, she always has been, and I really admire that in her. I mean, I got a bit of a caning from her this morning because I didn't do any exercises yesterday, so she let me have it. She's a very powerful force in my life, my wife. Her bravery makes me feel brave. In those early days, I felt like together we could handle anything life threw at us. As it turns out, I was right.

Darryl was determined to get Jill out of my life and so he tried to get her fired from *Charlie Girl*. I don't know what he said about her or me, but Kenn Brodziak, who was producing the musical, called me into his office to try and shut down the relationship. I walked in and Kenn said, 'Now, I hear you're having a relationship with one of the dancing girls?'

I said, 'Yes, Kenn, I am.'

'Well, ah, we want that to stop,' he replied.

'I'VE GOT SOMETHING IN MY EYE'

I wasn't having any of it.

'Kenn, with all due respect, that is not going to happen. We love each other.'

Kenn wasn't finished. 'We'll have her fired if you don't stop seeing her.'

'Go ahead, I'll leave too.'

He pulled out my contract and started going through the clauses and I said, 'I don't care, Kenn. I'll walk. If you fire her, I'm gone.'

He was a good man and he saw that I was serious about Jill. He realised I was committed to the relationship, and he conceded. For a long time, I'd felt like I couldn't trust anyone around me, but I knew I could trust Jill with my life.

Looking back on all that has happened over my life so far, it makes me realise yet again how lucky I am at the good people I have had in my life. I like to focus on them. The other day Louis and I were sitting on the couch talking, reminiscing, his wife Jen was there and Jill was, too. All of a sudden Lou stopped talking, he just shut up. I said to him. 'Are you alright mate?' Lou replied, very slowly, 'I'm having trouble speaking.' He was having a stroke. It was scary. I said to him, 'Don't you fucking die on me because I'll have no one to compare scars with.' Jen got right into action, she whipped him off to the hospital and he had an operation and they discovered a blockage in his neck, in his carotid artery. A bloody stroke! That's how fragile life is, but if you're lucky you don't realise that until you are very old. Thanks to Jen and the doctors, Lou has recovered and is doing okay. Anyway . . . getting back to 1971 . . .

The opening night of *Charlie Girl* was very exciting. It went off without a hitch and I was proud that I held my own alongside Derek and Anna and all the amazing talent on and off stage.

My mum and dad were there, Jeanie Jam Roll was too, and my buddy Frank Thring was also cheering me on. After the show I was chatting with them while still in costume and all rigged up. I had on my mic pack, which was attached to a little microphone on my chest that transmitted through the PA when I spoke and sang. It was a pretty low-fi set up back in those days. Frank, out of the blue, noticed the mic pack. Pointing at it, he asked, 'What's that?' I said, 'That's my microphone and that's the pack that transmits to the PA.' Frank leant in and said, 'Where do they put it?'

Before I could answer him, Frank chirped up, 'I know where I'd like to put it.' Frank never missed an opportunity for a double entendre or a chance to act outrageously, even if my mum was there.

A couple of days after opening night, Kenn called me into his office again.

What now? I thought as I made my way up the stairs.

I knocked on his door. 'Yes, Mr Brodziak?'

KB squared me up, then laid it on the table. 'Derek has a problem. He wants you to stand at the front door each night and ask the girls in your audience not to scream when they see you on the stage.'

We were only a few nights into the run, but every night so far, as soon as I stepped onstage for the first time, all these girls in the audience would scream and carry on. Sure, it was momentarily disruptive to the other performers, but I wasn't sure what I could do about it. They were paying ticket holders after all.

I sighed and said, 'I'll do that, no problem, Mr Brodziak. I'll do that if he stands at the other door each night and asks his audience not to laugh.'

Kenn didn't miss a beat. 'Enough said.'

That night as I stepped onstage, some of the audience screamed as expected and when Derek stepped onstage others cracked up as expected. Derek gave me a wink and we got on with our performances.

It was actually Derek Nimmo who suggested I marry Jill. Not that I needed much encouragement. I must have been driving him mad because I couldn't stop talking about her. I was forever chewing his ear off, 'Oh, Jill this and Jill that . . .' From the second I woke up to the moment I fell asleep at night, all I thought about was Jill. Derek turned around one day and said to me, 'You should marry that girl.'

He was probably saying it to shut me up for a minute, but I thought, *You're right, Derek. You are absolutely right, I should.* 'Thanks Derek, that's a great idea,' I said as I dashed off to find Jill and ask her. I didn't even have a ring, the idea was such a good one I wanted to act on it there and then. I wanted Jill with all my heart. I went downstairs to the girls' dressing room, found Jill and said, 'Will you marry me?' She said, 'Yes.' And the rest is history, as they say.

Well, not quite history. The next day, when the dust had settled, Jill asked me to speak to her dad, Bob. I had to ask for his daughter's hand. I said, 'Yeah, I can do that.'

So off I went to Glenroy. Now Phyllis, Jill's mum, didn't like me very much. She didn't like me because I was getting between her and her daughter. So, I walked into the house and asked Bob straight, 'Can I have your daughter's hand in marriage please, sir?' Before he could say a word, Phyllis cut in and said, 'What do you mean? *Jillian!* Jillian, are you having *sex* with this man?'

Jill, to her credit, said, 'Yes, Mum.' And Phyllis was absolutely outraged. She turned to Bob and said, 'Do you realise this man is having sex with your daughter?'

Bob put his hand forward to shake mine and said, 'Congratulations, son.' I dead-set thought he was going to hit me. And Phyllis just went nuts, she went absolutely bonkers. In the end I won her over, but Bob and I got on really well from the get-go.

When I met Jill, Bob barracked for North Melbourne and I barracked for Geelong. Bob asked me, 'What footy team do you barrack for?' I wasn't stupid and said, 'Ahhhh, what team do you barrack for?' He said, 'North Melbourne.' I said, 'Me too.' And ever since then I've been a North Melbourne supporter with a soft spot for Geelong.

When I told my parents about my plans to marry Jillian, they were true to form in their support, despite the fact that we were so young, so very young. I said to Mum and Dad, 'What do you think of Jillian?' And my father, to his credit, and Mum agreed with him, said, 'We don't have to love her, you do.' He did love her, so did Mum, but that wasn't his point. He continued by saying, 'I'm not marrying her. If you love her, son, then follow that through.' We also had the seal of approval from Jeanie Jam Roll. Jeanie loved Jill, though she did tell me early on that she was always disappointed I didn't marry one of her friends.

Because Jillian was too young to get legally married, we had to have written permission from her parents. We had to work pretty hard to convince Phyllis. Each time we thought she was on board and she'd sign the paperwork, we'd end up having to convince her all over again because she'd tear it up after having a fight with Jill about something or other. In the end we didn't need her permission and we set the date for 11 March 1973, a month after Jillian turned eighteen. I was twenty-three.

Outside of our castmates on *Charlie Girl*, we tried to keep our relationship fairly secret. Darryl had repeatedly warned me not to get married. By his reckoning, the second I got into a relationship my career would be over. Somehow this low-life journalist from *The Truth* got wind of our relationship, and he took it upon himself to show up at Jill's house. He tricked Phyllis into giving all these quotes about us. She had no idea who he was or where he was from, I guess she thought she was just having a chat with a charming young man who knew Jill.

After a year at Her Majesty's the cast of *Charlie Girl* toured the musical to New Zealand. We were appearing at the St James Theatre in Auckland, and opening night was 26 May 1972.

Darryl insisted on travelling with the troupe. Jill and I got to share a room together and I thought that was wonderful because all I wanted was to spend every spare moment with her. We were staying at the White Heron Hotel, and we were given a corner room on the ground floor. One day we were heavily petting on the bed – very heavily petting – and I heard *clink, clink*. I said to Jill, 'What's that? Did you hear that?'

She shrugged and pulled me back to keep kissing her and then it went again. *Clink, clink, clink.* I looked over at the window and the venetian blinds were parted ever so slightly, there were three fingers pulling them open from the outside. I told Jill not to panic, but someone was looking in at us. 'I'm going to get him or her or whoever it is.' So I did. I jumped up and opened the door and this bloke took off like a rocket and nearly, very nearly, got away.

The hotel was on a cliff top, high above the water, and there was a long staircase going down to this black sand beach. The guy ran down these stairs and was hiding somewhere on the beach. As I walked down I was calling out, 'Come out, wherever you are, just come out!'

I wasn't going to give up, I was going to get him. He didn't come out of the shadows so I started searching and I finally found him, grabbed him and walked him up that staircase with his arm three-quarters up his back. He was lucky I didn't throw him back down the stairs. I marched him into the hotel foyer and said to the guy on reception, 'I want to see the manager or the person in charge, now!'

I had this guy with his arm pinned up behind his back, and the guy on reception said, 'What do you want to see the manager for?'

I told him, 'I just caught this guy perving, he was looking through the window into my room.'

The hotel receptionist said, 'Sorry sir, we can't do anything.'

I wouldn't accept that. 'No, I need to see someone.'

And he said, 'We are not going to do anything.'

I was outraged. I wanted him to call the police and he refused. I was young enough and foolish enough to let them get away with it, but it made me acutely aware of how exposed Jill and I were, and even more protective of what we had together. I never saw that man again, but I did give him a bit of a 'tickle' when I let him go, just a little tickle around his ribs.

We had another big invasion of our privacy when Molly Meldrum printed our wedding invitation in the *Go-Set* newspaper. Suddenly, everyone and their dog knew about our special day. We ended up having to change the date. I was very angry with him about that. Molly was never a friend of mine, but he was a close friend of Darryl's who was still, at that point, my manager. Once that ran in the paper, Jill started receiving threats and hate mail. That worried her a little bit. Mum and Dad were also getting girls ringing up and asking what was going on with me. I got all these letters from girls saying they weren't going to love me anymore and that they hated me because I was getting married.

At one point Jill and I talked about having a double wedding with Jillian's sister and her fiancé, as was the fashion in those days, but it all became too much. We realised that our wedding was more than likely going to be bedlam, and it would have taken away from their special day, so we decided to have separate weddings. They ended up getting married two weeks before us.

We were right, our wedding day was nuts. Because it had been leaked by Molly, every tabloid in Melbourne had printed where and when we were getting married. Even the new date, 11 April, didn't remain a secret. When I watch footage of the day, I think, *Jesus Christ, there were a lot of people there.* There was a huge crowd at St Matthew's Anglican church in Glenroy; police had to hold them back so Jilly could get into the church. Jeanie Jam Roll was one of Jill's bridesmaids. Everyone is nervous on their wedding day, but at ours there were thousands of screaming strangers upping the ante. Darryl was the best man. He told me he wanted to be there for me and I let him have it, despite everything. It was just the way it was back then.

A family friend of Jill's made her dress. It was a very demure, plain blue dress with puffy long sleeves edged with lace. Jill described it as smart and comfortable. I'm ashamed to say, I didn't turn around to look when she was walking down the aisle. I only looked at her when she was standing right next to me. I was too scared I'd cry if I watched her walk toward me. There were a lot of people packed in that church and I didn't want them all to see me burst into tears. The rest of the day was a blur. I just wanted to get married and be with Jill and she just wanted to get married and be with me; neither of us cared much about the actual wedding service. We just wanted to get it over with and get on with our lives.

CHAPTER 8

HE'S CUTE. VERY CUTE
A WORD FROM JILLIAN FARNHAM

I didn't know John, or Johnny, as he was known then. I had no idea who he was when I saw him that day on the street. I had no idea because, at that stage of my life, I was all about me.

My parents were very working class. We lived in housing commission in Glenroy. My mother was a stay-at-home mum and she was tough, very tough. My dad stood over six foot four, he was lanky, skinny and very quiet, probably because he was the only man in a household of women. I loved my dad, and although it was an acceptable part of parenting at the time, he never ever smacked us. He just gave us this look. You know that look? Mum smacked us, but Dad never did, he'd just give me his look and, because he was a manual labourer he had huge hands. I'd look at his hands and think, *Oh no, I don't think so*, and I'd stop being cheeky quick smart. He was a really hard worker, my dad. He was a labourer during the day, then he'd go off to his other job printing *The Age* newspaper overnight. Then he'd get home at six o'clock in the morning, have a couple of hours sleep, then get up and go off to his labouring job again. He did that five days a week. And on the weekend, he kept busy too. He'd be up at 7.30 on a Sunday morning mowing the bloody lawns. I think it was partly to keep away from Mum. And us girls.

I was the youngest of four sisters. I was the dainty, cute one with ringlets who did ballet from a young age, whereas my older sisters were all into competitive horseriding. My second-eldest sister moved out when I was young, so there were three of us girls left in the family home by the time I was a teenager. We'd all get our periods at the same time and there would be blues between us all. Poor Dad was as quiet as all get out, but even then we'd tell him to shut up all the time. 'What would you know, Dad?' we'd scream at him. Poor old bugger. No wonder he worked so hard, it gave him an excuse to stay away.

HE'S CUTE. VERY CUTE

All those ballet lessons paid off and I was considered a gifted dancer – so much so that I got written permission to leave school at fourteen to study under the tutelage of prima ballerina Kathleen Gorham. Kathleen had danced in Paris and London and then came home to be a principal dancer with the newly formed Australian Ballet company. I studied under Kathy for more than a year and always wanted to earn my living as a dancer. When I turned fifteen, I auditioned for a production of *Promises, Promises*, starring American actor Orson Bean, which was a musical based on the 1960 film *The Apartment*. I lied at the audition, telling everyone I was sixteen, and I got the job. And that was that – I had realised my childhood dream and become a professional dancer.

I was only a teenager, but I clearly knew what I wanted, and I basically moved out of home when the show started. As far as Mum and Dad were concerned, I was still technically living in Glenroy, but I was never there. I danced six nights a week, twice on a Saturday, and on top of that, many nights after work my castmates and I would go out to a club. Being a dancer in the theatre back then was like joining another family. It was tight-knit, very protective and a lot of fun. We worked hard and we played even harder. You'd finish a two-hour show at 10.30 at night, race back to the dressing room, take your theatre make-up off, put on a fresh 'streetie' (make-up to wear on the street), and go out to the nightclubs for more dancing. The guys in the chorus were all gay and they would take us to these gay clubs, which were illegal in those days. Because they were illegal, the parties had to change venues often, so it was all word of mouth, which made it all the more exciting. The gay clubs always had the best music. We'd go off to these clubs with the guys and there were often these big, round raised pedestals where people would get up and dance. The boys would throw one of us up there and want us to dance for them, so we did. I loved it. We barely slept before going back to work the next day. There were drugs around, but I never got involved with that scene. I didn't even drink. I didn't need to, I was high on the fact that I was dancing professionally. I had trained hard since I was a child and now I was doing exactly what I'd always wanted. It was fantastic. I was young and tall and skinny and beautiful, as we all are when we're bloody sixteen. I really was having the time of my life.

I was in *Promises, Promises* for around ten months, first in Melbourne and then it travelled to Sydney, and then I went straight into dancing in *Casino De Paris*, another musical-cum-Las Vegas type show. I actually started rehearsals for *Casino De Paris* while I was still on *Promises*. There were quite a number of dancers who were doing the same thing. We'd perform at night and then rehearse during the day.

HE'S CUTE. VERY CUTE

When *Promises* closed up in Sydney, we went back to Melbourne and did *Casino De Paris*, at Her Majesty's Theatre. *Casino De Paris* travelled up to Sydney too, and I went with it. When that run finished, I worked as a showgirl at the Chevron in Melbourne. It was a cabaret club and I had to walk around wearing feathers and looking fabulous. I lied about my age again, because I was still a minor.

Then I got cast in *Charlie Girl* and started rehearsals with the leads. I knew who Derek Nimmo and Dame Anna Neagle were, they were both theatre stars from London, but I had no idea who Johnny Farnham was. We were in rehearsals and at the same time, there was a play on at Her Majesty's called *1776* starring an Australian actor by the name of Lewis Fiander. Lewis and I were good pals. One day we grabbed some lunch together and were walking back to Her Majesty's when, just as we got to the stage door, John and Darryl walked out. I looked at John and thought, *He's cute, very cute*. I didn't go into the theatre. Instead, I stopped and watched him walk across the road. When he got halfway across, he turned back to look at me. In that moment, we locked eyes. Then he turned around and kept walking. I thought, *He's got to be gay. He's too handsome and too pretty to be straight*. And then I went inside for the afternoon session of rehearsals.

Ten days later, we were in the middle of rehearsal when John came in. At some point in the afternoon we got chatting. I still thought he was gay. I had been around a lot of gay men, and I thought I knew who was gay and who wasn't. John continued coming to rehearsals and I was aware of him whenever he was in the room. Then one day I went to the toilet and got stuck in there. The door was jammed and wouldn't open. John kicked the door down. He rescued me. After that I saw him in a completely different light. I thought to myself, *Hello, that was very butch!* From that day onward he started wooing me and that wooing turned into us courting. That sounds so old-fashioned, but that's how it was. It took him ages to get a kiss from me. We started with flirting, catching each other's eyes and lingering touches. John started bringing me hot chocolates, then roses. He'd buy a fresh rose at a local florist each day and bring it to me.

When the *Charlie Girl* season opened, I still hadn't given him a kiss. There was eight weeks of courting during rehearsals and then it was three weeks after opening night before we finally kissed. John took me out to dinner once in those early days and it was the first time I'd ever had oysters. And, no, I didn't like them, it was like swallowing snot, but I ate them, thinking I've got to look like I'm sophisticated, like I know what I'm doing.

HE'S CUTE. VERY CUTE

There was this wine back then called Blue Nun. If you ordered a bottle of Blue Nun you were the ant's pants. It was a very sweet German wine and it was ghastly. John ordered a bottle of Blue Nun and I thought, *Oh, no, I've got to be the good little girl and drink it.* It was revolting.

When John and I weren't at work, we'd snatch time together whenever we could. We couldn't be seen in public because we didn't want to start rumours, and we couldn't go to John's apartment because Darryl was always turning up unannounced, so we'd hang out at friends' places. They'd go to work and leave the key out for us. John and I would have our little rendezvous in their houses. Or we'd pack lunches and a flask and go out on his boat. For years to come, if John asked if I wanted to go out on his boat it was code for 'Would you like a kiss and a cuddle?'.

One night, halfway through the performance, John proposed to me. I was downstairs in the girls' dressing room just before the end of interval. There was a knock on the door and one of the girls sang out, 'Jill, John is at the door.' I was half naked, because you never sit around in your costume if you don't have to, so I grabbed a housecoat, raced to the door, opened it and said, 'Yeah?'

John said, 'Will you marry me?'

And I said, 'Yes.'

Then he slammed the door, raced up the stairs and went onstage. It was not at all romantic. I stood there thinking, *What did I just do?* After the show, he asked me again properly in his dressing room. He got down on his knee and I said 'Yes' a second time. I was very young, too young, and I hadn't known John for long, but I just knew. And I was lucky. I mean, it could have been a leg-up, my legs were already up, but it could have gone completely wrong. And you know, today, as I put these memories down, is our wedding anniversary.

Don't get me wrong, we've had our ups and downs – relationships aren't easy. I think the problem with many people today, they go into a marriage and think it's all going to be roses and butterflies, they don't realise you actually have to work at it.

You've got two people living together with two different opinions. Sometimes you're looking at them and thinking, I want to kill you. You know, I want to grab you and smash your face in. That's how irritated you can get. In the beginning John wouldn't argue with me. It was so frustrating. I wanted a reaction and he'd just sit there. The no-reaction thing would make me more angry. I'd want to grab a book or plate or whatever and smash it, to provoke him. Of course, I didn't. In the end I said to John one day, 'Please give me something. I need someone to vent at. And it's you.' So yeah, we work at our relationship.

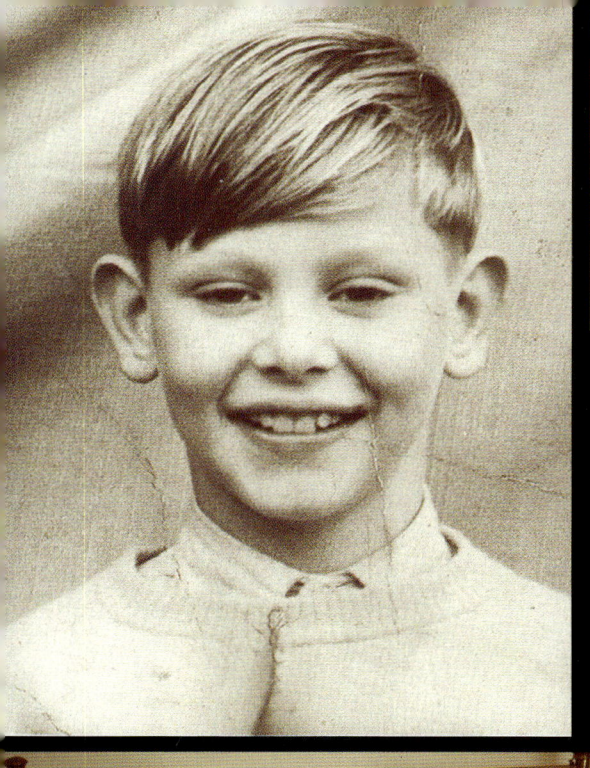

That's me on the right at the back with the Caulfield Heating and Cooling crew. Stan is on the back left. I had no idea of the wonderful life that was to come.

Me and my little brother

Me and my Jilly

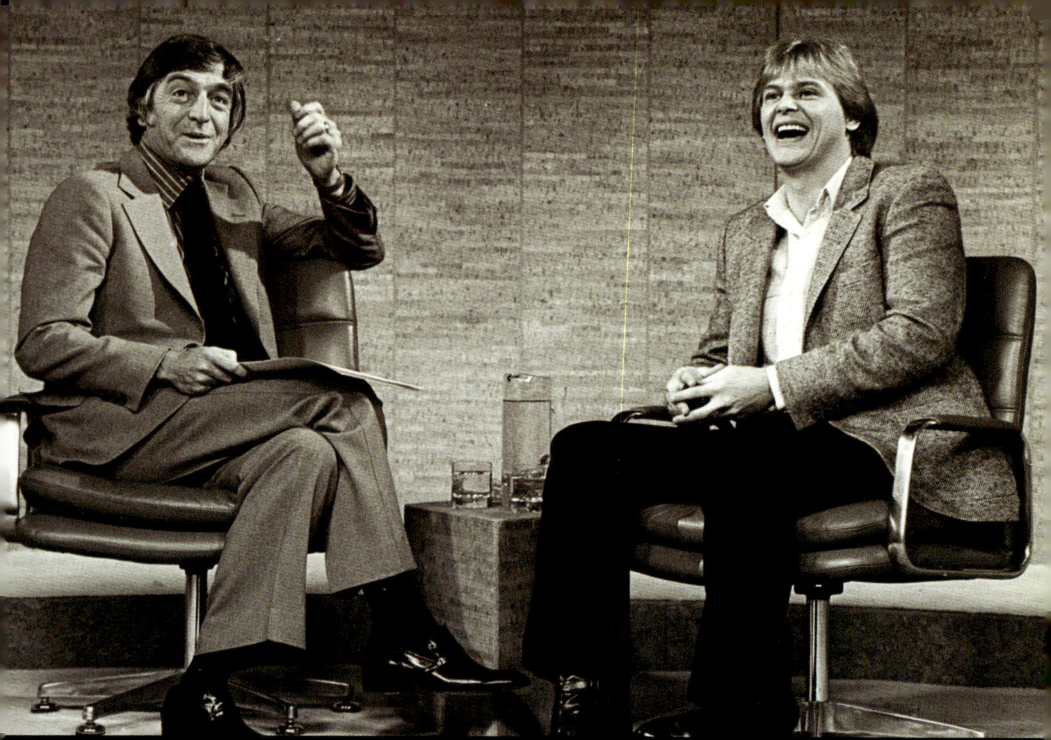

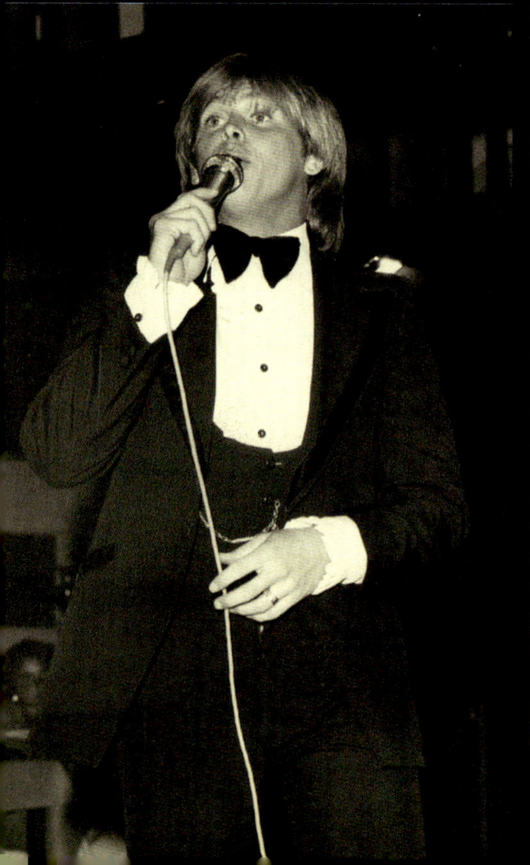

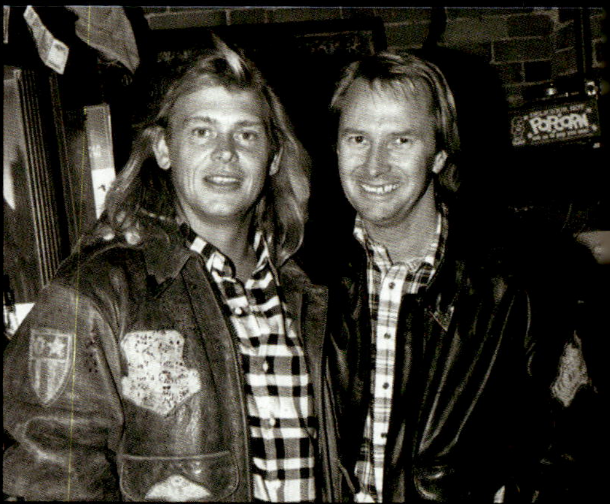
POPCORN

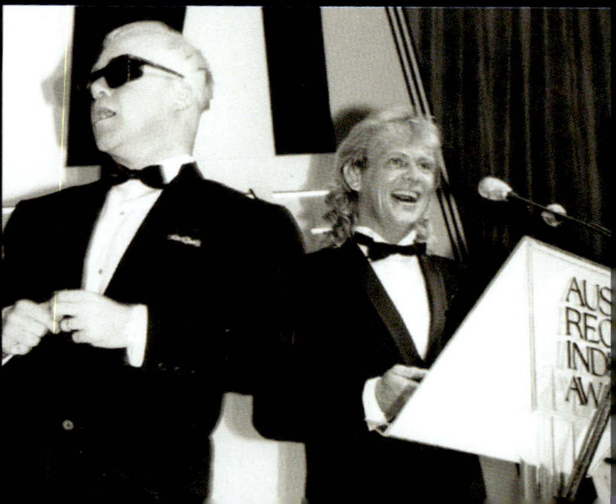

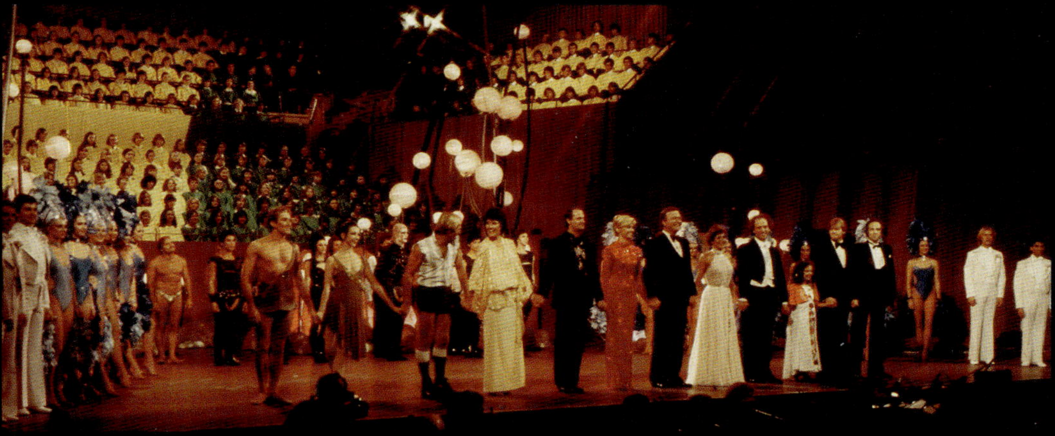

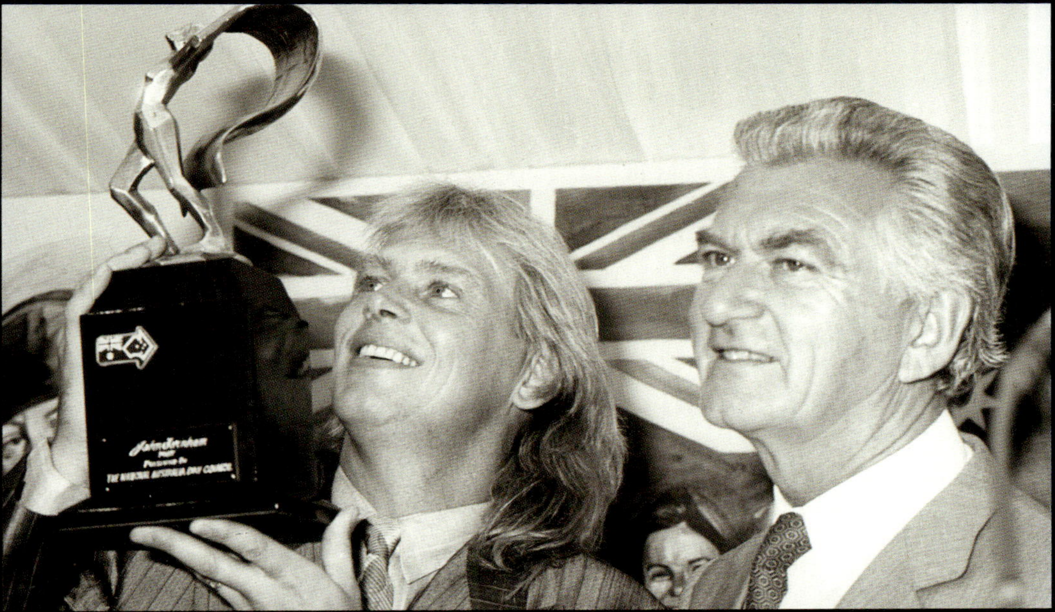

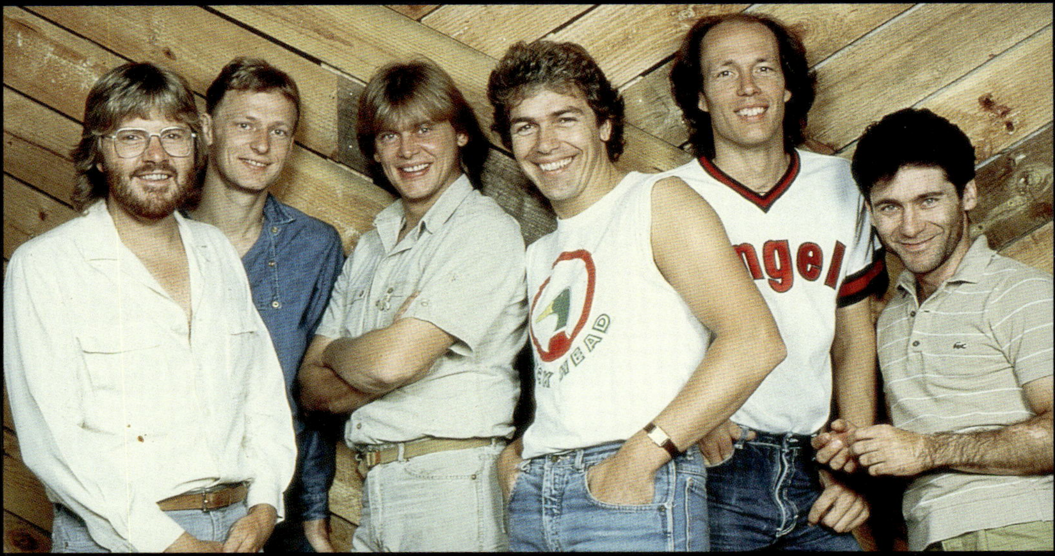

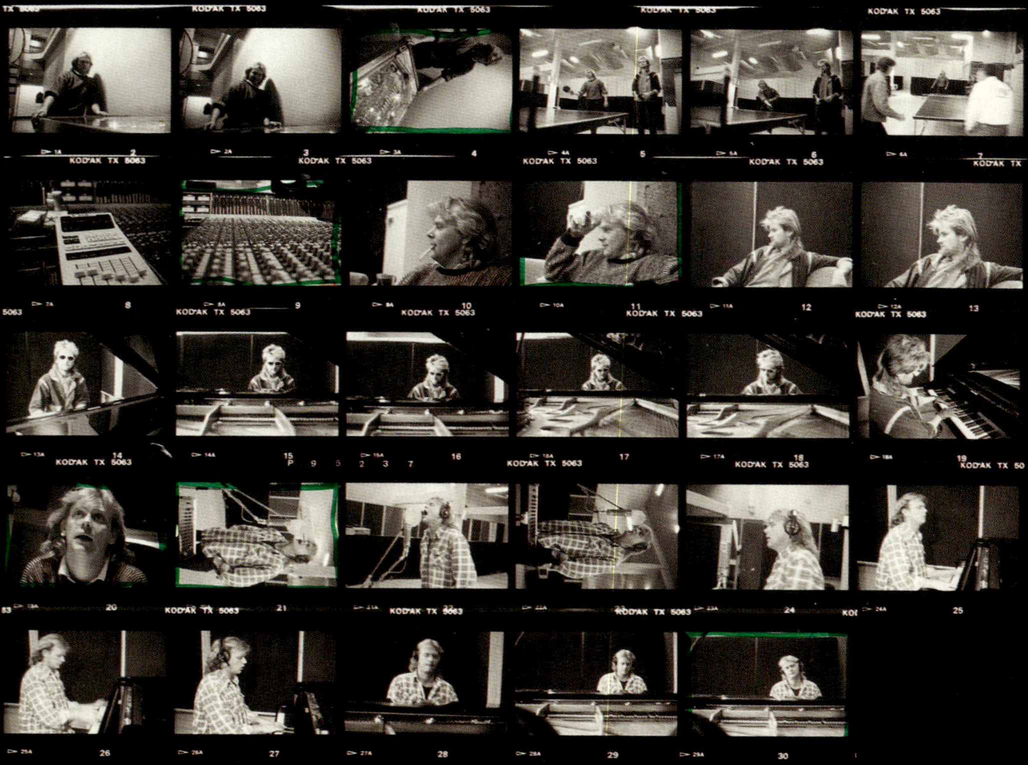
KODAK TX 5063

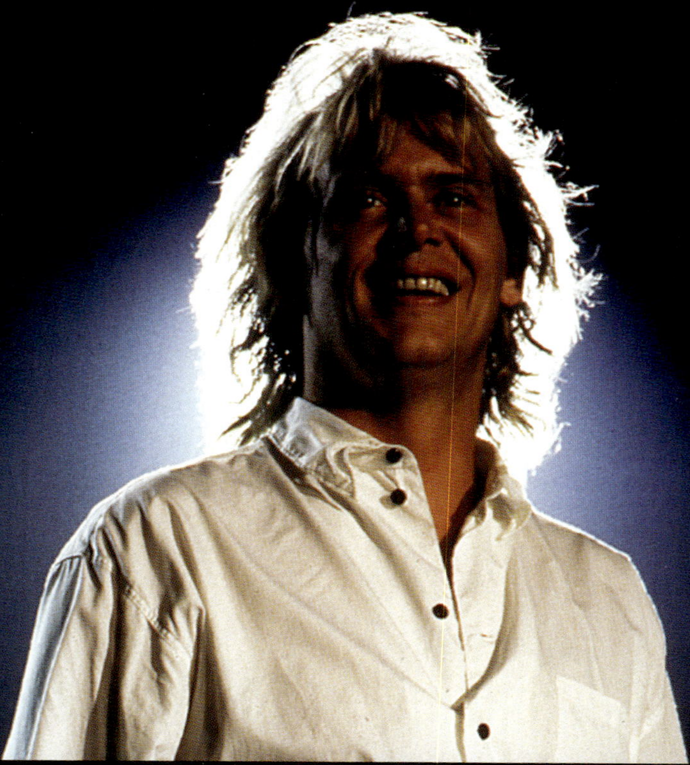

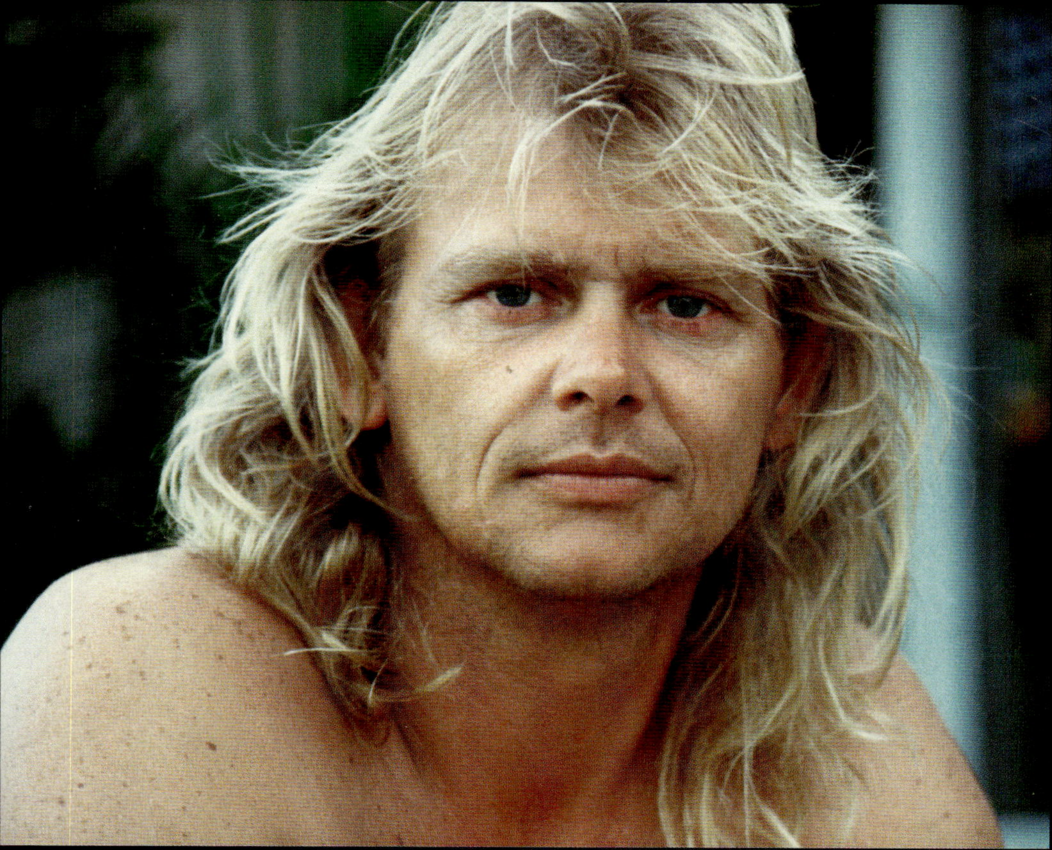

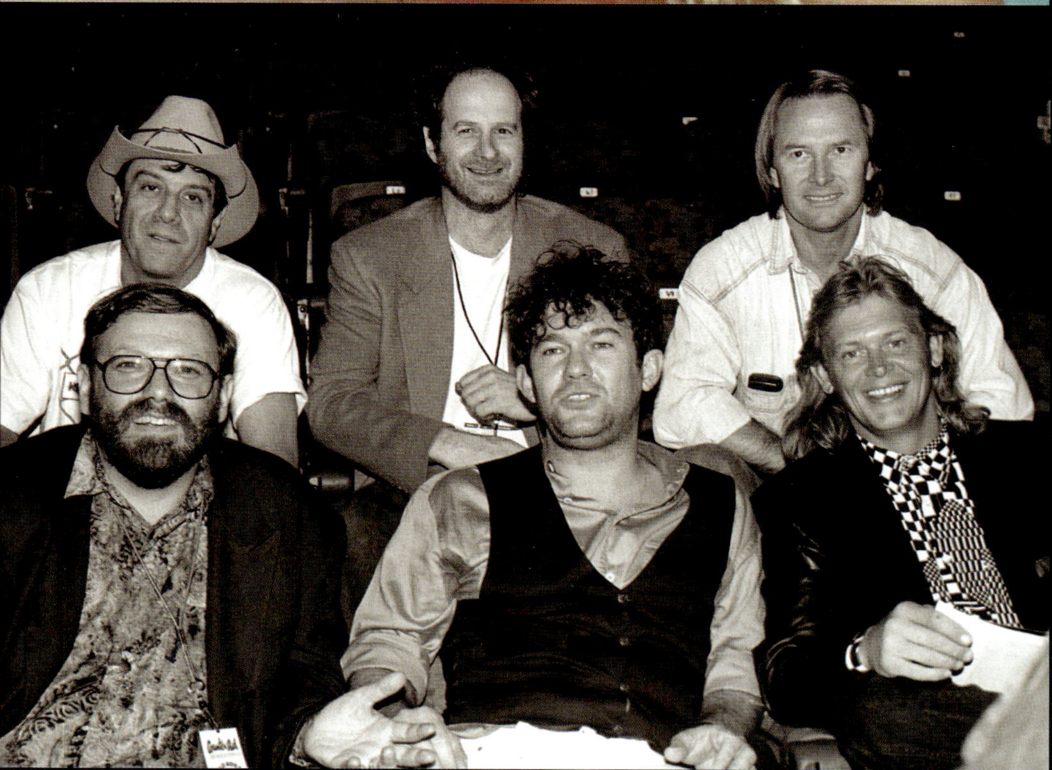

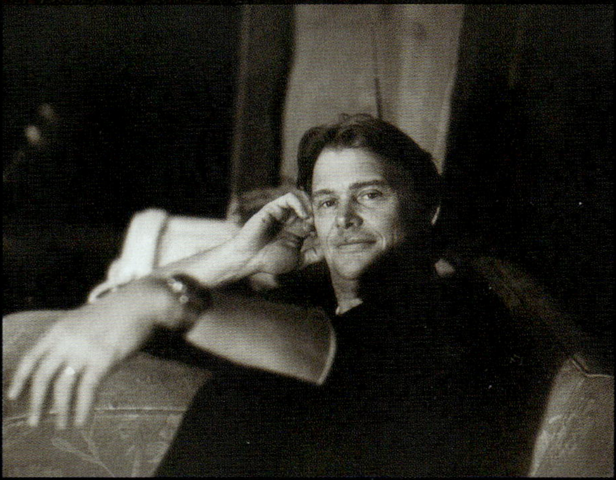

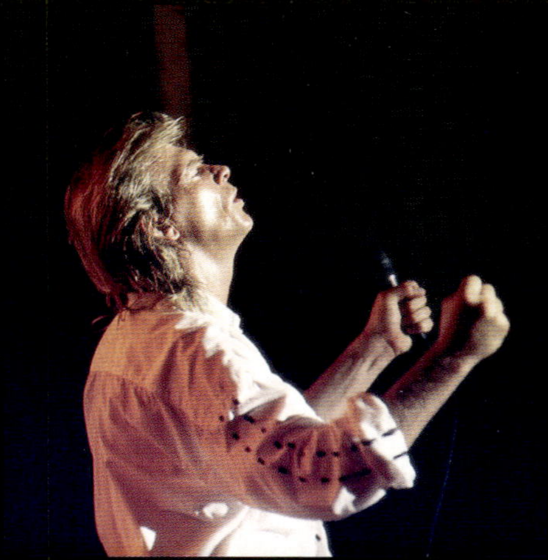

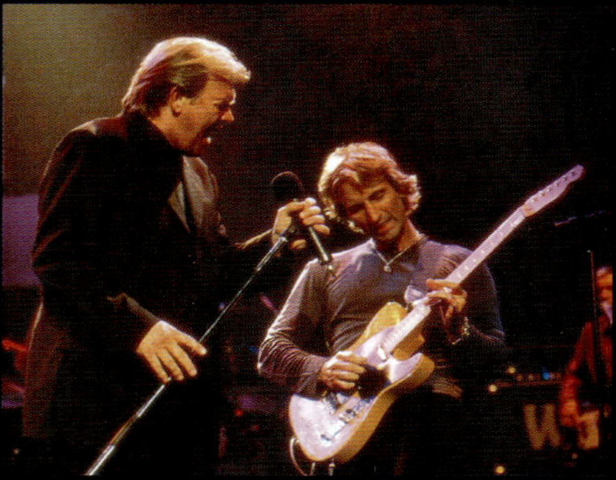

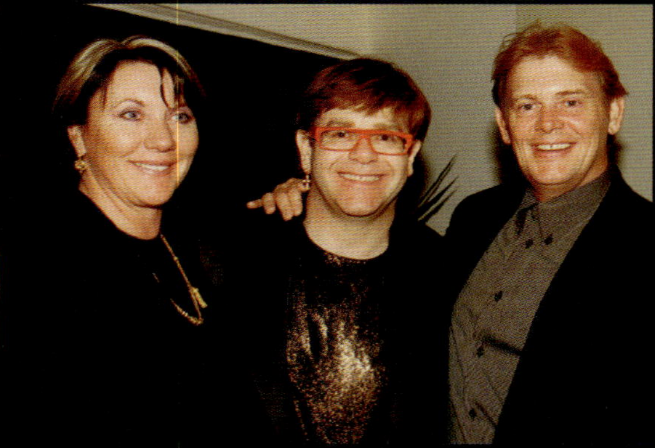

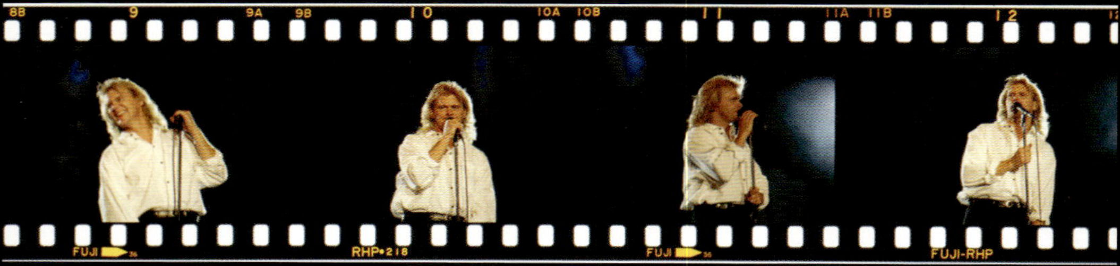
8B
9
9A
9B
10
10A
10B
11
11A
11B
12
FUJI
RHP•218
FUJI
FUJI-RHP

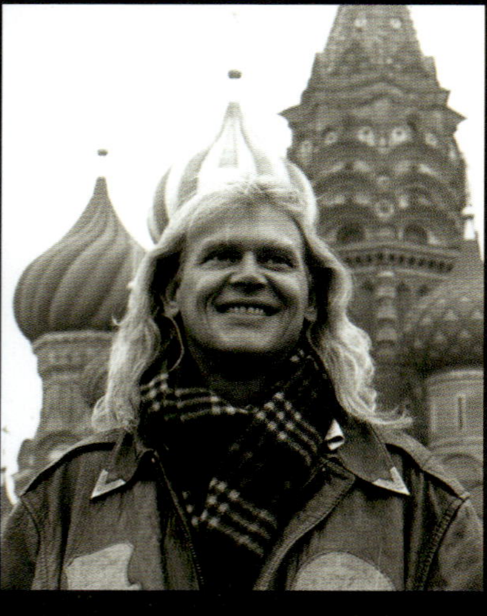

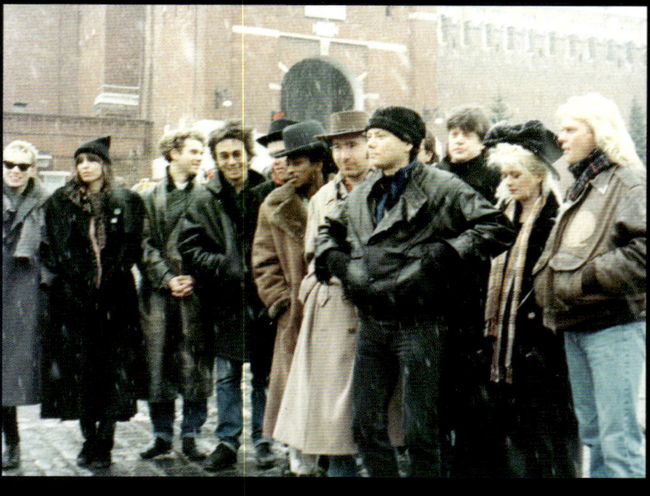

It's true I get by with a little help from my friends.

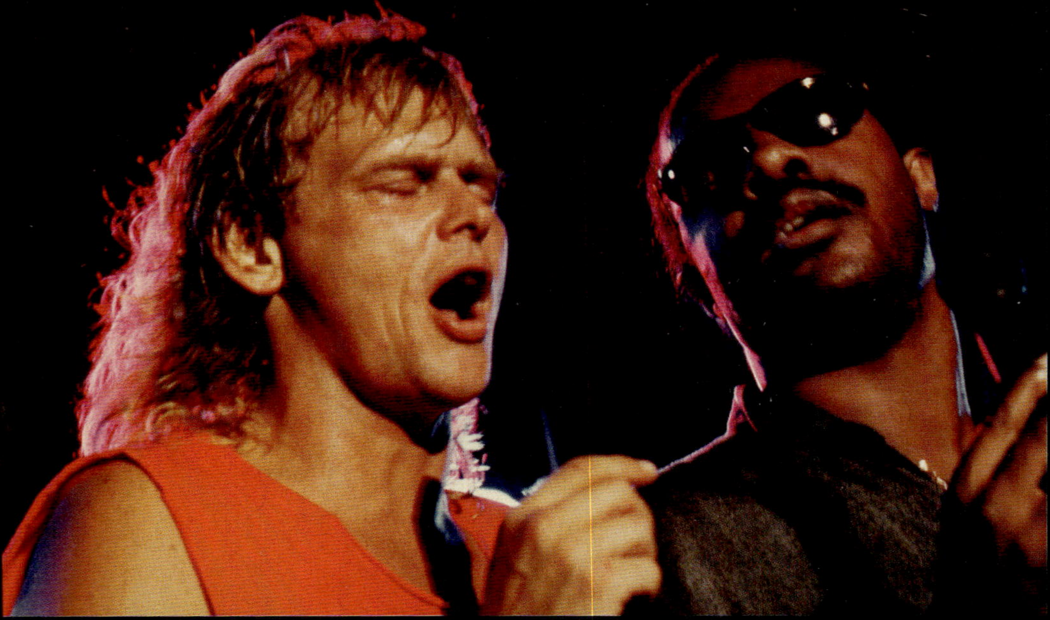

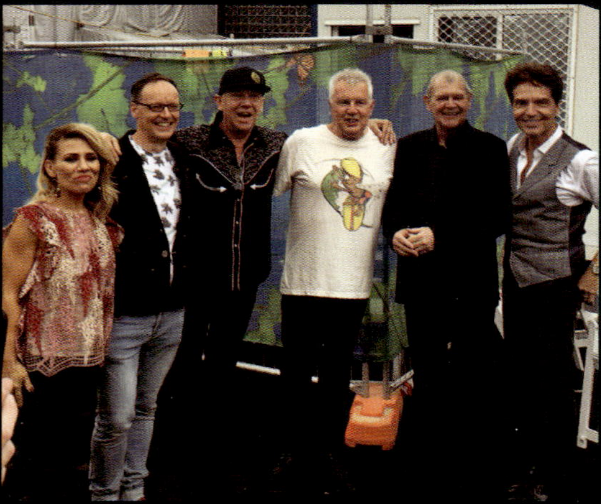

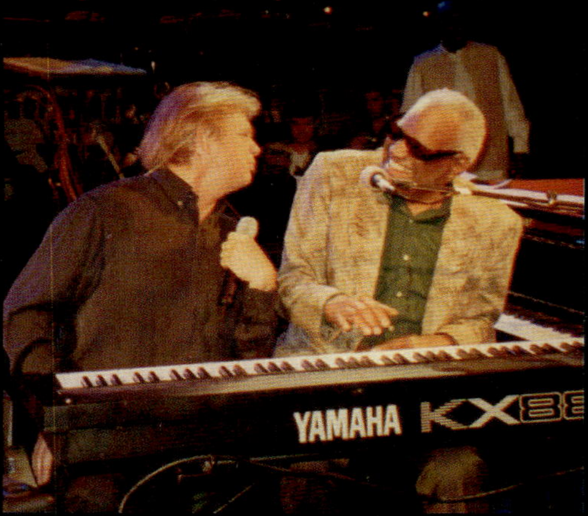
YAMAHA KX8

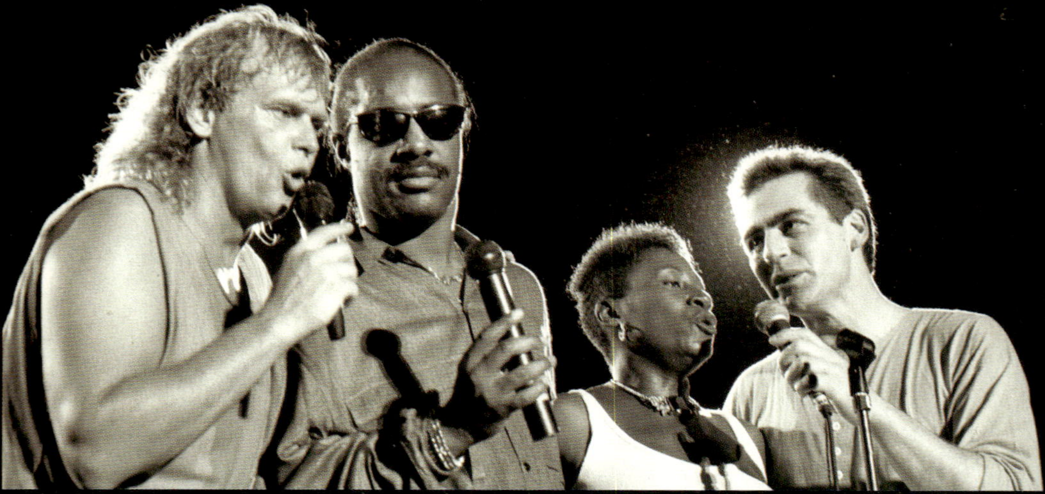

Me with my family and dancing with the woman who is the love of my life.

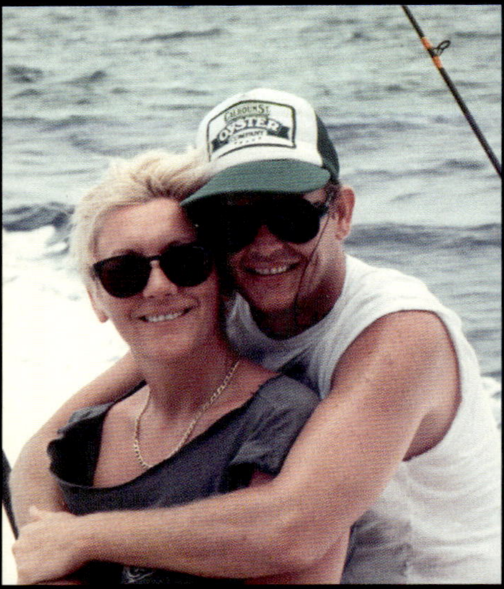
OYSTER

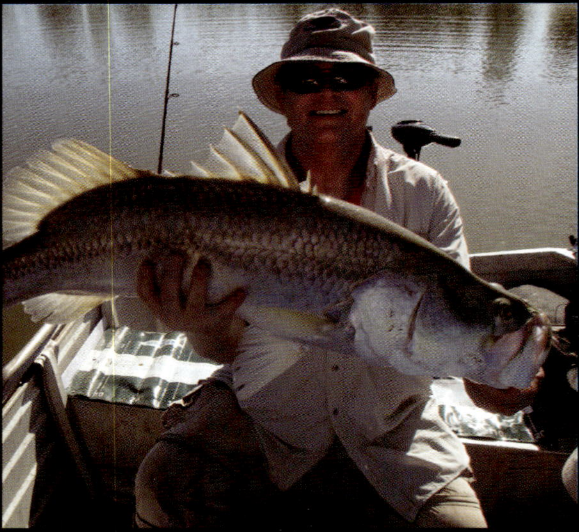

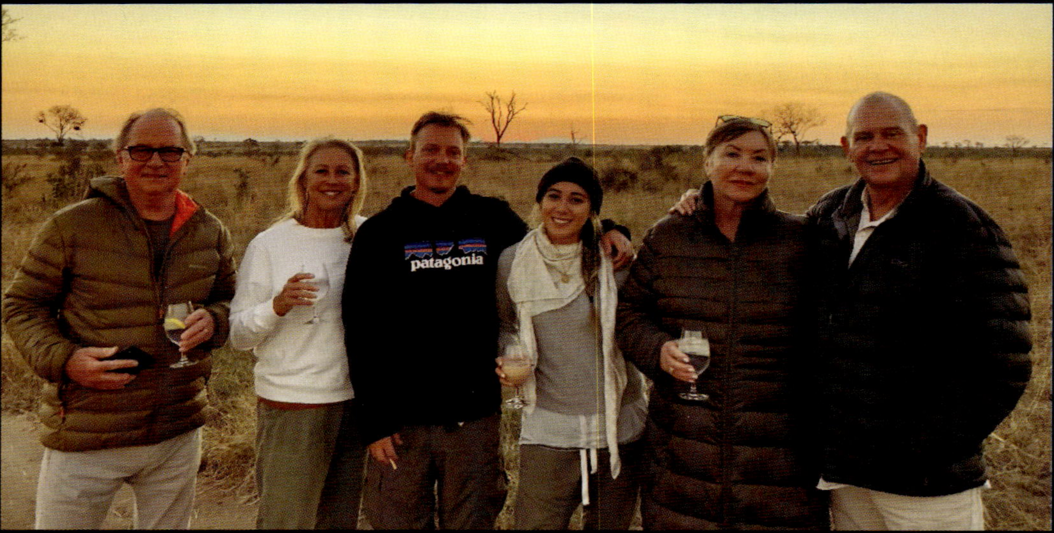
patagonia

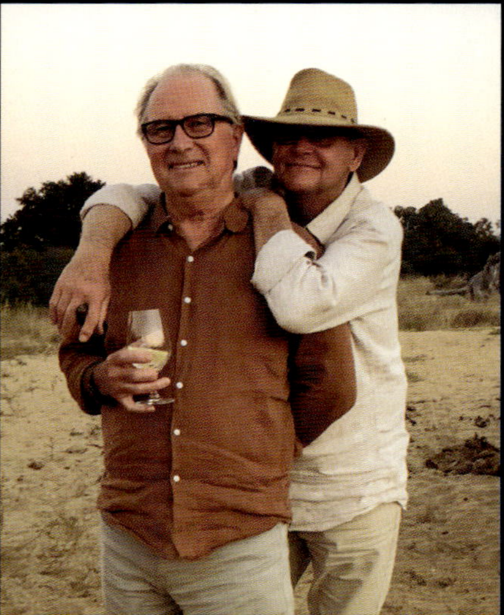

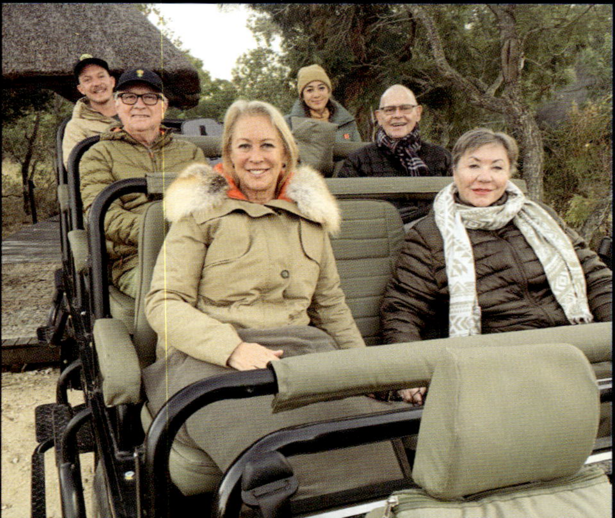

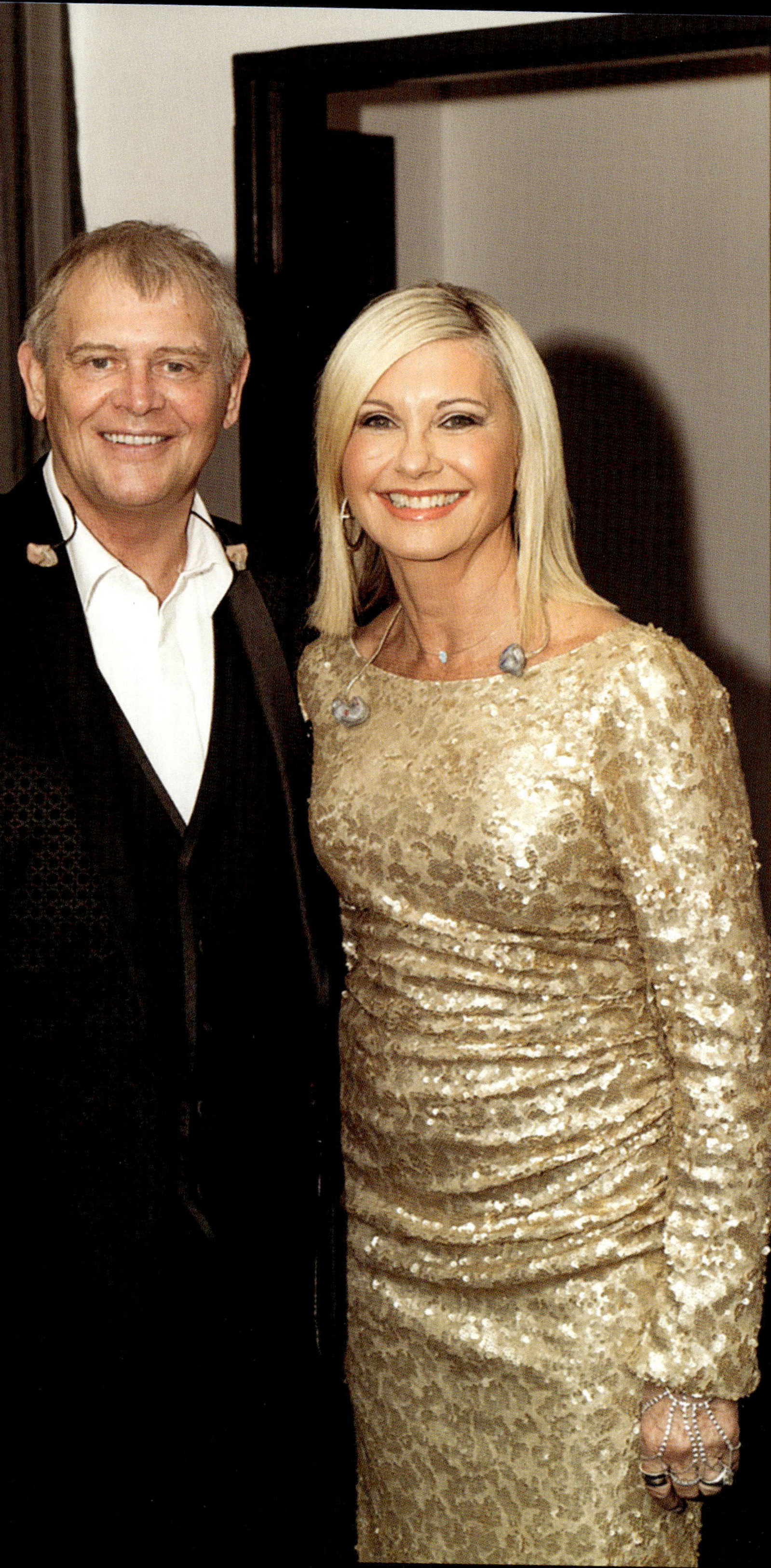

FIRE FIGHT AUSTRALIA

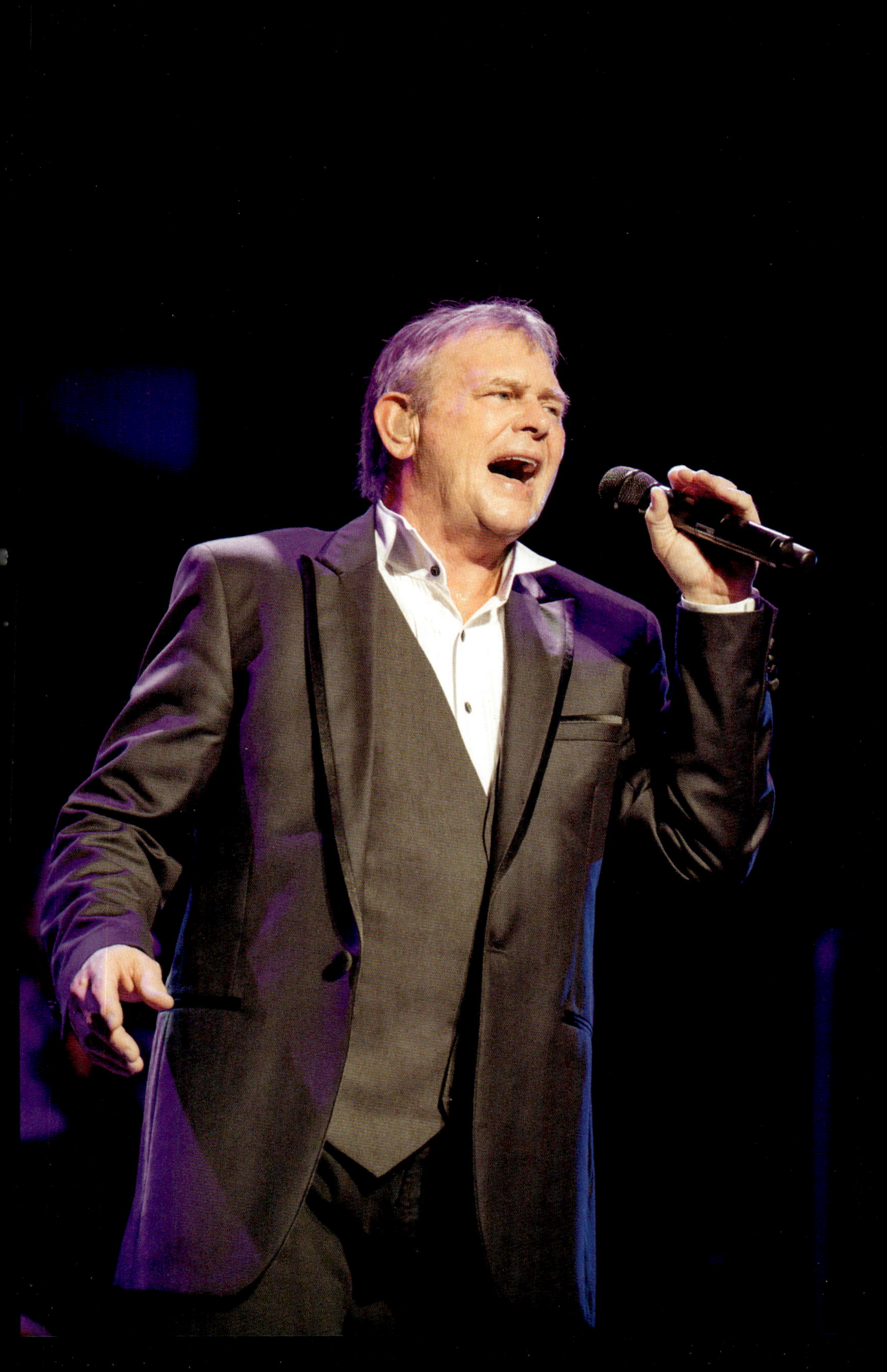

Thanks for it all!

Once John's fans started to get wind that we were dating I became a target. Mum and Dad would get prank phone calls and one day a girl knocked on our front door. Luckily it was the weekend and Dad was home, because when he opened the door she was standing there with a knife. Another time I was walking into the theatre and there were about ten of John's young fans in the foyer. They saw me and started bullying me about John. After a few minutes I'd had enough and I said to them, 'Yeah, we are dating.' They were so stunned that I'd admitted it they left me alone.

Over the years a small number of John's fans have given me a hard time, because they always thought they'd be the one to marry him. But 99.9999 per cent of them are really cool. As we've all gotten older, they settled down because they realised that I'm here to stay. They had to accept that John is with me and that ain't going to change.

But the fans were never the main threat to our relationship. Darryl Sambell was our major concern. Before we met, John had had affairs with women, but he was never in one place long enough to form a real relationship. Darryl made sure of it. Even being together on *Charlie Girl*, it was hard to find free time to spend together. We did two shows on Saturday, and then on Sundays Darryl would drag John off to Brisbane or Adelaide or somewhere else around the country to do a show.

I found out from friends that Darryl was paying people in the cast to spy on John, and when Darryl found out about us, all hell broke loose.

John invited me to some of the parties that were raging around him, but we soon stopped going because Darryl would say awful things to me constantly. Darryl was like Rasputin, he surrounded himself with like-minded bullies and predators. I couldn't stand many of them.

One day there was a barbecue on the banks of the Yarra River. John was running late and I got there a bit early so I sat next to this guy and we were chatting. We were just sitting on a bench talking when Darryl marched up to me. He was being loud and flamboyant and showing off in front of everybody, and then he tried to embarrass me. He said to me, at the top of his lungs, 'You need to be careful because I will make sure John is never in Melbourne again.'

It took me aback for a minute. I had already seen how Darryl worked John and kept him isolated from his family and friends. I thought, *Bugger this!* So I said to him, 'No, Darryl, you need to be careful because I'll make sure you don't have a job.' I figured I'd better stand up for myself and for John, because no-one else was going to. Darryl was frightened to let go, because he knew if he let go, John would be gone.

HE'S CUTE. VERY CUTE

Speaking up didn't make things any better. Once, Darryl left me stranded on an island in the Whitsundays. Derek Nimmo, his wife Pat, another gentleman by the name of Robin Bowring and his girlfriend at the time, whose name I can't remember, joined Darryl, John and me for a trip to Brampton Island. John and I weren't allowed to share a room because we weren't married, so I was sharing with Robin's girlfriend. A journalist and photographer from *TV Week* were coming and Darryl said to me, 'You need to get out of here because of the press.' He didn't want them to know Johnny had a girlfriend. I agreed, so Darryl put me on a plane to Hamilton Island which, in those days, wasn't as flash as it is now. He'd arranged for me to stay with one of the singers in the chorus, I'm sure she was one of his inhouse spies. Darryl had said, 'Don't worry, it'll only be for a couple of days.'

Five days later, I had no money and I was completely stuck. Eventually I got a call through to John. 'Where are you?' he asked. He'd expected me back, and god knows what Darryl had told him to explain why I wasn't there. I explained that I was stuck on Hamilton Island because Darryl wanted me to stay away.

Well, the shit hit the fan then, and John demanded that I was put on the next plane back to Brampton Island. That was the way Darryl worked – conniving, very conniving.

When the bullying didn't work, Darryl tried to get rid of me by having me fired. Kenn Brodziak, KB, as we called him, was the producer of *Charlie Girl* and hugely influential. He was a very powerful man and although I knew who he was, I'd never spoken with him directly, so when I was called into his office I was very intimidated. Obviously, Darryl had spoken to Kenn and given him an ultimatum: either she goes or I pull John out of the show. KB said to me, 'You need to break off this relationship.'

I was young and quite shocked, I just sat there and looked at him, and when he was finished I got up, walked downstairs and found John. I told him, 'I've just been called to KB's office. They're going to sack me if we keep seeing each other.'

That was it for John. He marched up to KB's office and told him straight, 'If she goes, I go.' KB was an entrepreneur – this is the man who brought the Beatles to Australia, for god's sake – he would have known what it would cost him to lose Johnny Farnham but, more than that, KB respected John for sticking up for himself. It pleased him that John was pushing for what he wanted, and what John wanted was me. Fifty-one years of marriage and we are still together.

CONGRATULATIONS!

to the following **EMI** artists who were **WINNERS** in the 1971 **GO-SET** POP POLL!

BEST AUST. FEMALE ARTIST: ALLISON DURBIN

HAVE YOU GOT ALLISON'S GREAT NEW SINGLE, "PUT YOUR HAND IN THE HAND?"

BEST AUST. MALE ARTIST: JOHNNY FARNHAM

YOU MUST HEAR "ACAPULCO SUN"!

BEST AUST. COMPOSER: RUSSELL MORRIS

HAVE YOU HEARD RUSSELL'S NEW SINGLE, "SWEET, SWEET LOVE"?

WATCH FOR RUSSELL'S NEW ALBUM, "BLOODSTONE" TO BE RELEASED SOON!

Best Australian Bass Guitarist — **GLENN WHEATLEY**

Best Australian Drummer: **COLIN BURGESS**

Best Australian Lead Guitarist: **RICKY SPRINGFIELD**

BEST AUSTRALIAN ALBUM **'CHOICE CUTS'** MASTERS APPRENTICES

BEST AUSTRALIAN SINGLE **'ELEANOR RIGBY'** THE ZOOT

Best International Bass Guitarist & Best Composer: **PAUL McCARTNEY**

Best International Drummer: **RINGO STARR**

BEST INTERNATIONAL ALBUM **'ALL THINGS MUST PASS'**

EMI THE GREATEST RECORDING ORGANISATION IN THE WORLD

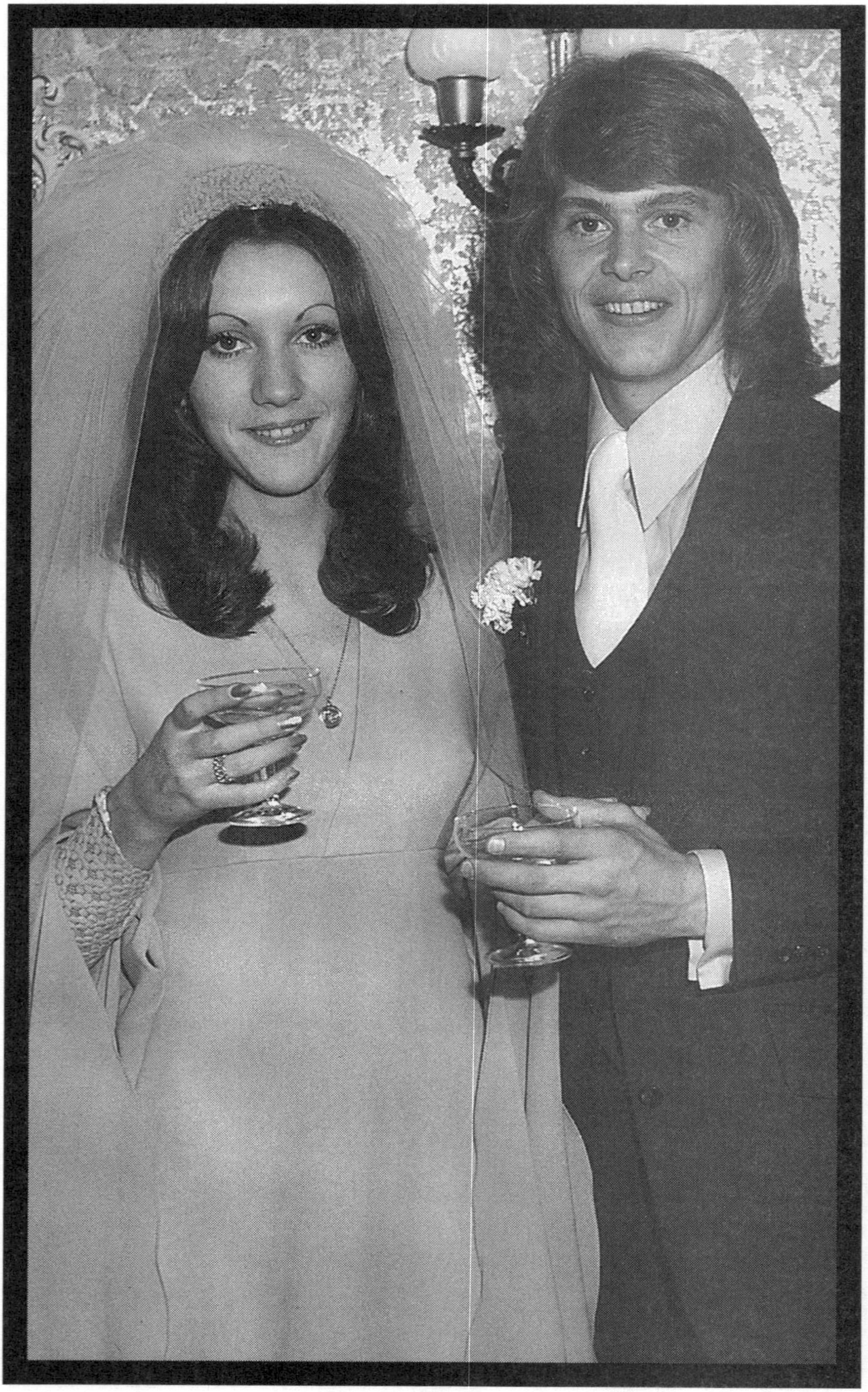

CHAPTER 9

THE HARD WAY

As soon as I got married my career went through the floor. It absolutely tanked and it was really, really hard, but I was too busy being in love to notice or care much at first. The day Jillian Billman became Jillian Farnham would shape my life forever. I'd always wanted to get married. I liked the idea of having someone to come home to, someone I loved and someone who loved me, so I was thrilled to be Jill's husband and thrilled to call her my wife. I still am.

After the madness of our wedding day we escaped it all and went back to the Whitsundays for our honeymoon. Being together on a tropical island was excellent. We felt very lucky. We stayed at the Brampton Island resort so we were away from work and any demands on our time. I knew the owners and staff, as I had been there several times over the years, but being there all alone with Jill made it magic.

When we got back to Melbourne, I moved out of my apartment in South Yarra and Jillian officially moved out of her childhood home in Glenroy. Together, we moved into an apartment on Tintern Avenue in Toorak. Like any young, married couple, we had to work each other out and fit around each other. I liked settling into marriage. But of course, there were things that we had to sort out. Small things and some pretty big ones.

Jill was a rotten cook when we first got together, terrible. To be fair, I wasn't any better. But cooking was something Jill wanted to learn (and I didn't). Over the years she's almost turned into a chef, she's really, really good. She spoils me. Her soups kept me alive during my cancer recovery, they really did. At the moment I am still struggling a bit, because since my surgery I can't open my mouth wide enough to eat anything larger than a slice of cheese, plus I'm still missing my bottom teeth, but last night Jill cooked me an incredible steak and it was fantastic.

Even though she was young, Jill understood the entertainment industry because she was in it. She was a great dancer who'd been dancing professionally since the age of fifteen, and she absolutely loved performing. And yet, when we married, she gave up her career for me. After *Charlie Girl*, Jillian never danced again. I could have happily closed the curtains and bunkered down with my bride, but I desperately needed to earn some cash to set us up. Jill knew I had to keep building my career, and to do that, I needed to go away for work. I still had no clarity over my finances, and now that Jill and I were a team it was clear things had to be sorted.

The way Darryl worked, I didn't have a set amount of money every week to live on, and he never set up a bank account that I had access to. That worked at the beginning, when I was so naive and he was managing everything, but, once I was married, whenever Jill and I had to pay rent or buy groceries, Jill had to walk down to his office and ask for the money. Darryl would give her just enough to pay the bills. We were forever scraping by to make ends meet, and had no ability to save for ourselves.

Charlie Girl had run for well over a year in Melbourne, which was a triumph as far as anybody was concerned, but I hardly saw any of the money I'd earned. On top of that, people weren't falling over themselves to ask me to do more theatre. That was okay at first, because I was always more focused on singing, but my singing career wasn't faring much better. Darryl had warned me my pop star career would be over as soon as I married, and I was starting to believe he might have been right.

The music scene was changing before my eyes. Over the long weekend in January 1973, a couple of months before we were married, the second-ever Sunbury Pop Festival was held on a private farm just north of Melbourne. When the event was first conceived, it was promoted as Australia's version of Woodstock but, with the rising popularity of pub rock, the energy of the festival was edgier than the cliched laid-back, brown rice and hairy legs of the hippie scene. My old friend JOK played at Sunbury the year I was married. The following year Mississippi, a soft rock band that included Graeham Goble, Beeb Birtles and Derek Pellicci, who would go on to form the Little River Band, was on the line-up alongside Sherbet, Skyhooks and the British band Queen. Jim Keays from the Masters Apprentices was the emcee for the 1974 event, and there's a story that Queen were booed off the stage because the cheeky emcee riled up the crowd by asking if they wanted 'these Pommy bastards or some Aussie rock'. I wasn't considered Sunbury material so I wasn't ever invited to join the bill but I would have loved to perform on that stage.

I *was* invited to Tokyo to compete in the World Popular Song Festival though. In November 1972 I travelled to the contest, which was unofficially known as the Oriental Eurovision, as the Australian representative. Thankfully, Darryl stayed at home and I went with singer/songwriter Brian Cadd. We were there to perform Caddie's song 'Don't You Know It's Magic'. I loved the song and loved Caddie, he was very talented and a terrific guy. I had hardly travelled outside of Australia and I'd certainly never been to Japan, so we felt like two kids let loose in a wonderland. There were about 130 singers from thirty-seven countries and we were all competing for the grand first prize, but there were also other prizes, including 'Most Outstanding Composition'. There was a duo from Sweden there called Björn & Benny, who had backing vocals from their partners Agnetha and Anni-Frid. After the competition, Björn and Benny would go on to include these two talented women in the band's regular line-up and change their name to . . . ABBA.

For our song, I had the resident sixty-piece orchestra backing me, but I wanted Caddie to play the piano because I was nervous and certain I would forget the lyrics. When it was our turn, Caddie did indeed play the piano while I sang, and I still stuffed up the words. It didn't seem to matter though, because we won the Outstanding Composition Prize! Afterward, we tried to drink the value of the prize money in sake. We went to this little Japanese bar and we got absolutely rat-faced. Rat, rat, rat-faced. This beautiful Japanese woman took a liking to either me or Caddie – we were so drunk we couldn't work out which of us she actually liked. She was hanging around and I was saying to Brian, 'Go on, Caddie, buy her a drink.' And Caddie was saying, 'No, no, you go and buy her one.'

'You go.'

'No, you go.'

I ended up being the one who bought her a drink but nothing more happened. I was too pissed to make any moves and even if I was sober I wouldn't have, because have I told you about my Jilly? To this day I still can't drink sake.

———

By early 1974, I needed to make a living and I wasn't sure what to do next. I wanted to sing, but the right songs and the avenues to perform them were eluding me. I had recorded several songs with Howard Gable, David Mackay's replacement at EMI, but since my number one with 'Raindrops Keep Falling on My Head', I hadn't found any chart or commercial success.

Thankfully, just as things were seeming quite bleak, I was offered the lead in *Pippin*, another musical produced by Kenn Brodziak that was going to open at Her Majesty's Theatre. I took the job. Most of the male dancers and a few of the female dancers had been in *Charlie Girl*, so I already knew a lot of the cast before the show even began. There are some heavy sex scenes in *Pippin*, and the male dancers loved them. They thought it was hilarious that clean-cut Johnny Farnham was in these scenes and were forever teasing me about it. It was wonderful to be back among the camaraderie of the company, but it was strange being there without Jill.

Jillian and I wanted a family and so we were trying to make a baby. But that could have ended before it had even really begun. Just after we got married, Jill asked me if we could get a cat and I said, 'Yeah, of course.' I didn't ever say no to her, even though I've never liked cats. She got this Siamese cat and called her Sarah. So there we were, naked in the bedroom, getting romantic, and her bloody cat took umbrage at my appendage and bit me on the penis. Little bugger! I was excited and my enthusiasm must have shocked the cat because she nipped me. Because there was no real damage, it was really quite funny even then. There was no blood or anything. It was like the cat just went, 'Jesus, what's that?'

On the night of the *Pippin* dress rehearsal, our flat was burgled. Jill had come to watch, so the robbers must have known we were out. They took everything we had, which wasn't much – some jewellery and anything else they could find. It's horrible to come home to a robbed apartment, an awful feeling. And to make it worse, Sarah the Siamese and her kittens were missing. Not long before, she had mated with a local tomcat and given birth to four kittens. It turned out the night we were robbed the cats had either jumped or, more horrific, were thrown from our second-storey flat. Luckily, they must have all landed on their feet, because the next day we got them all back and none of them were harmed. I grew to like cats, but I will never like thieves.

Pippin did reasonable business in Melbourne, but it didn't match the success of *Charlie Girl*, not even close. Musical theatre legends Ronne Arnold and Nancye Hayes were leads, and one of Australia's singing stars, Colleen Hewett, was my co-star and love interest in the show. When the run was over, Colleen and I joined forces to co-host a television variety show called *It's Magic* for Channel 10. It was a bit of fun – we goofed around, sang, and did some sketch comedy, including a skit called 'The Kids' in which we played a couple of naughty kids to a live studio audience. We did a run of thirteen episodes and then the network called it a day and they axed the show.

After that, I was back to considering what my options were. The hype around the launch of the music show *Countdown* was being felt across the entire music community. We didn't know it would become the most popular music program in Australian television history, but the fact that a program focused on music, and specifically pop music, was going to be broadcast nationally on the ABC every week was a big deal for all of us. I was thrilled to be asked to perform on the very first show. After my experience on *Bandstand*, I knew I wanted to sing live, and that wasn't a problem for the crew at the ABC.

On *Countdown*'s first episode I sang 'One Minute Every Hour'. The host of the show that night was DJ Grant Goldman, and the other acts that appeared were Sherbet, Daryl Braithwaite, Linda George, Paper Lace and Skyhooks. Sadly, the early episodes of *Countdown* were taped over, so I'm pretty sure there's no footage of the first eight episodes, which is a shame, because Skyhooks were one of the huge bands at that time, and they gave an incredible performance.

Their lead singer, Shirley Strachan, was a funny man, he was a laugh a minute. I remember chatting to him backstage and he was going on and on about not caring about commercial success. He looked me up and down then said, 'Honestly, we're just not interested in having "hits".'

He was saying this to me, someone who'd had hits and who knew what it was like to be at the top and also what it felt like to not have commercial success. And so I said to him, 'Shirl, you are full of shit. Get over yourself, get on with it and just do it.'

Seriously, you're only bullshitting yourself if you're in this business and you say you don't want hits. I mean, come on.

To Shirley's credit, he heard what I had to say, and he had a chuckle. There I was, the teenage pop star who was now a married man on his way down, and there he was, a fresh face in a hot new band that everyone wanted a piece of. Of course he wanted hits!

I went on to compere the first colour episode of *Countdown*, which aired on 1 March 1975. Up until that point, the program, like almost everything else on Australian television, was broadcast in black and white. It was lovely to be a part of the historic moment, but strange to be there and not singing. To be honest, at the time I didn't have any songs to sing. I was always looking for songs, because if you're not looking you're not going to find them, but they just weren't coming my way. I certainly wasn't writing. I hadn't written a song pretty much since 'In My Room', and it would be a few more years before I would sit down to write another.

I was still happy for the exposure of being on a national program. All of us musicians were very happy for the gig, which was probably the reason we all did it for nothing. I don't think anyone got paid for doing *Countdown*; I certainly didn't. Same as *Hey Hey It's Saturday*, the variety show on Channel 9. But *Hey Hey* was commercial so they should have paid, whereas *Countdown* was on the public broadcaster so they had some excuse.

Interestingly, Ian 'Molly' Meldrum, Darryl's mate, was one of the originators of the program. He started as the talent coordinator, then was an intermittent reporter, then presented his 'Humdrum' segment before becoming the face of the show. The general public would end up seeing Molly as the champion of Aussie music. It was a massive coup for him.

So while an Australian music show was taking off, I had no songs to sing and EMI pretty much dropped me. To be fair, they didn't *actually* drop me, there was no formal ejection from the label, they just didn't re-sign me. That added to the financial hardship I was facing, but selling records is what the business is all about, and if I wasn't doing that then of course they weren't going to keep me. I knew I had been pretty lucky up until that point. Success in the music industry is very hard to come by, and up until then things had mostly fallen into place for me. Audiences and listeners accepted and enjoyed what I was trying to do. But when EMI and I parted ways it was very disheartening. All I could think was, *Okay, now what am I going to do?* I hoped my manager had some ideas.

Darryl's answer was advertising. With live performance spots drying up, Jilly and I were broke, so I had to do something. I ended up relying on ads on and off for years. I sold soft drink, airlines, cassette tapes and even shopping malls. One time I did an ad for Vaseline. It was a photograph of me in a terry-towelling robe holding a baby with the baby's bare bum pointing to the camera. That bum belonged to my baby boy, Robert. I've always felt guilty about doing that to him, but I needed the money so badly, and there was no other way to earn it. No-one was interested in booking me for gigs.

Kandiah Kamalesvaran, better known by his stage name Kamahl, was really big in the early 1970s and was packing out Her Majesty's Theatre night after night, and getting paid particularly well for it, too. I saw Kamahl after one of his shows and we got chatting. We didn't know each other terribly well but he was a reasonable sort of bloke, and he asked me how I was doing. I mumbled a throwaway response, then acknowledged how well he was doing. He leant in and told me about the money he was making. He revealed he was getting eighty per cent of the profits instead of the standard twenty per cent. This was a revelation to me, because it was usually the other way around – artists got the smaller percentage and everybody else took the rest. This was the first time since Glenn Wheatley had raised it years before, that I'd heard an artist question the system. That's when the penny really started to drop for me. *What the fuck was going on?*

My career wasn't going anywhere, and I was really worried about how I was going to support Jill. We were desperate to have children and had been trying, unsuccessfully, since we were married, but if I didn't have any money coming in, how would I ever support a family? All these thoughts ran through my head and the stress was building. For years I had shut it all out and just sung, because singing was what I did best, but even that wasn't working for me now. All those years of working my arse off and I had nothing to show for it. But it wasn't just the money that was troubling me. The catalyst that finally ended my relationship with Darryl was his behaviour toward Jill.

I knew he'd tried to break us up early on, but I forgave him that at first. But then Darryl was very, very unkind to Jill. He did not want her in the picture at all; he wanted complete control of me. Jill stopped him from having that. And she helped me see my worth, something Darryl had diminished.

At times, in the early years, he was aggressively sexual toward me. He would try it on and I would say, 'Darryl, no. Just leave me alone,' or, 'It's not going to happen.' I said it often enough that I can see now that this rejection turned his attraction into jealousy, hatred and a desire for control. For years Darryl controlled where and when I worked, what I sang, what I wore, what I ate. He isolated me from friends and family, he tried to keep me away from Jill, he drugged me, and he made me believe that all my success, everything I had, was because of him.

When we started out I didn't realise that Darryl had no experience as a manager and that, like me, he was learning as he went. He wasn't honest about that, and I trusted him, which perpetuated the problem. It is the classic cliched artist/manipulative manager story. All the artist wants to do is paint a picture. The manager is responsible for getting the payment for the picture, leaving the artist to concentrate on the art and not have to worry about that other stuff. Of course, too often, that singular focus gets taken advantage of time and time again. And quick money lures quick money takers.

When Jill arrived on the scene, she showed Darryl up for what he was. Even though she was younger than me, she was far wiser to the ways of the world than I was, and she wasn't scared of anyone. Jill knew how important my career was to me and she knew how much trust I placed in Darryl so, at first, she didn't want to rock the boat. She didn't know about the drugs and the sexual advances, otherwise she would have spoken up earlier. But when she realised the extent of his backstabbing, conniving and nastiness, she called him out, both to his face and to me. Jill called Darryl evil and I heard her.

On 12 January 1976, I went into Darryl's office and told him he was fired. I just said, 'I don't want you as my manager anymore.' Immediately I felt a sense of relief. Huge relief. I was finally free from what I can now see was an abusive relationship that had lasted almost a decade.

Many years have passed since then and, up until now, I've found it very hard to unpick what happened to me. But now that I've confronted it, I look back on that time with sorrow. I'm annoyed at myself for being so gullible and trusting. I gave away control of my career, my direction and my life. I was a young bloke and I needed a manager. If I was trying to look after the business and all the finer details as well as sing and perform, I wouldn't have been able to do any of it properly. I didn't know how malicious Darryl would turn out to be. What I wanted to do was focus on singing, performing and entertaining, I wanted to 'paint the picture', so I had to find someone I could trust to take care of the business. I just picked the wrong person. But I would never again give complete control to anyone else. I'd learned my lesson – the hard way.

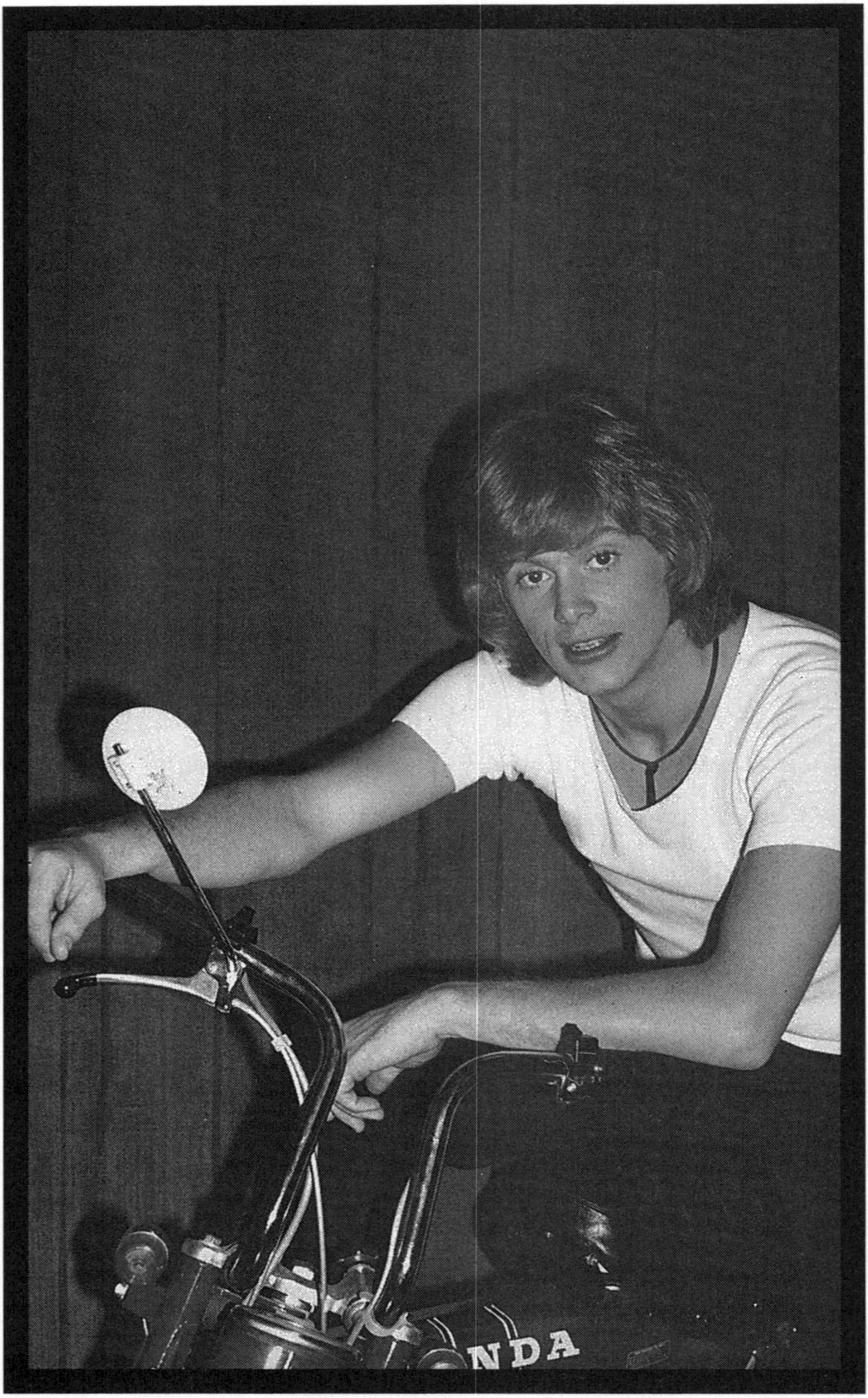
NDA

CHAPTER 10

JOHNNY TO JOHN

I wanted to work. I wanted to perform, and I knew that to survive in this business, I needed a professional manager. One I could trust. So, I went and saw Kenn Brodziak, and asked him if he would help me out. Kenn was lovely and funny, and he was also an experienced impresario. The guy knew how to do business. He agreed to take me on and the first thing he said was, 'I think you should change your name from Johnny to John.' So I did.

I trusted Kenn. He was an honest man, damn good at what he did and, unlike Darryl, he was into detail and respect.

On top of my name change, Kenn had a couple of rules. He banned me from doing commercials – he argued that that kind of work wasn't for stars. He never accepted a booking without discussing it with me, he did all the negotiations and, at last, the money would come to me. That's if I earned any.

He loved a success, old Kenn. Remember, he brought the Beatles to Australia, that was his biggest claim to fame, and it was a pretty solid claim, but he had lots of other lesser-known notches on his belt too. I loved hearing all about them. Once, he toured the American singer/songwriter Don McLean, the man responsible for the eight-and-a-half-minute classic 'American Pie'. Kenn reckoned that touring Don was the best business deal he ever did because all Don needed to draw a crowd was a microphone. Just Don and a microphone meant it was all cream. Ah, Kenn, he loved making money, and his stories gave me a window into the wider world beyond the pubs and clubs of Australia.

But more than all that, Kenn was on my side. I felt supported by someone who knew what he was doing and he became a kind of mentor. It was KB who told me, no matter what reaction you get from an audience it's better than no reaction. If they are cheering you, or even booing you, they are reacting to you. What you don't want is an audience sitting on their hands. I took that to heart, and I always try to get a reaction, no matter how hard I have to work. Though I much prefer cheering!

Another change for the better was that Jill started to come on the road with me. We didn't want to be apart and she didn't have to stay home with kids because we still didn't have any. Why should she sit around at home alone?

I was offered the role of Huckleberry Haines in the romantic comedy musical *Roberta*, which was being put on in a leagues club in Sydney. It was written in the 1930s and set in Paris, and Jacki Weaver was the lead. Not wanting to leave Jill in Melbourne alone, I wasn't keen on taking the role. Kenn went back to the producers and asked for a huge fee and a role for Jill. The producers accepted both and my response was, 'Good on you, Kenn, I'm in.'

Jacki, Jill and I became really close friends. I love Jacki, we've spent a lot of time with her over the years, and I asked her to be in the video clip for 'You're the Voice' . . . but we're not up to that yet. Jill's part in *Roberta* was a small walk-on role as a French maid. It was fun, and we loved being in a production together again. At the end of the run I asked Jill to keep the outfit; I told her I needed someone at home to serve me my coffee. Hah! Yeah right! Have you ever met Jillian?

Kenn also negotiated a role for me on a new sitcom called *Bobby Dazzler*, which was impressive because, as you well know by now, I can't act. I'm terrible, I tried it and I can't do it, otherwise I might have been a film star. No, not really. I was to play the lead role of Bobby Farrell, a young pop singer estranged from his father who ends up with a number-one hit and his estranged father sleeping on his couch.

Maurie Fields was a highly respected vaudevillian performer, actor and comic, and he played my father, Fred, in the series. Maurie starred in lots of Australian television shows, including *Bellbird*, *Division 4* and *The Flying Doctors*, and he also starred in the soapie *Skyways* opposite a young Australian actress called Gaynor Martin, who I would get to know when she started dating Glenn Wheatley. Talk to any Australian actor or comedian of a certain age and they would all consider themselves lucky to have worked with Maurie. Well, I was lucky too, because Maurie was a gem. He was a very funny man and his character in the show had a penchant for the drink. Nearly every time Maurie's character opened his mouth he would either be having a beer or talking about beer. Maurie decided that we should be using real beer, not 'prop' beer. He said to me, 'Now listen, we've got to talk about this, son.' He always called me son. 'We've got to talk about this, son, they are going to want to give us prop beer. Prop beer doesn't taste very good. Let's you and me stand up against it.' I said, 'Okay, yeah, no worries.' By the time we broke for lunch on the first day of filming, I was shit-faced. I was a nervous actor anyway, and those nerves combined with alcohol meant I could barely talk.

There was Maurie, at the start of a take he'd give me a wink then screw up his lines in order to redo the scene and get a refill. He was hysterical. Sigrid Thornton had a role in the first episode of the show as an obsessed fan, and Maurie even gave a rendition of 'Knees Up Mother Brown' in the same episode. Unfortunately, the series was cancelled after one season, but working with the cast and crew was a blast.

Slowly but surely, with Kenn's help, I started making some money. Not an enormous amount, but it was consistent, and with that money, Jill and I were able to buy a house on Chester Street in Surrey Hills, a suburb in Melbourne. It wasn't a big house, but we loved it because it was ours.

Earning money was a great thing, but a recording contract still eluded me. No record company wanted me. I told myself that was okay but in truth, it hurt. Kenn was in the twilight of his career when he took me on, and so we both knew the partnership wouldn't last forever. I respected Kenn enormously, he had a huge effect on me professionally and he taught me a lot. But peddling show tunes to the theatre crowd was making me bored, fat and lazy. I needed someone or something to shake me up and get me back out there doing what I loved most – singing!

CHAPTER 11

BOOM-TISH

I think I told you earlier that I would have loved to be a drummer. I love mucking around on the drums, but that's not why I asked Danny Finley to be my manager. Danny was the drummer in MPD Limited, who had mesmerised me all those years ago at the Dandenong Town Hall, but by the time I got to know him really well he was managing his wife, my co-star in *Pippin*, Colleen Hewett. He was still playing in bands, too. They were a dynamic duo, Danny and Colleen. Danny had a wonderful sense of humour. We used to call him Neddy Morgan, that was the name of his alter ego, a zany nutcase who was always telling jokes. Danny was a hugely positive force to be around, which is one of the reasons I asked him to manage me when Kenn and I called it a day. The other was that he knew rock'n'roll.

When Danny first started managing me there wasn't a plan. We didn't say, 'Let's have a shot at America!' or a shot at England or Brisbane or whatever. It was more, 'Keep playing and keep going.' I just covered the work that was coming in and Danny sold me to get more work. Danny also managed the backing band, and when he was able, he played drums for me. And boy could he play. He got into the habit of scoring every move I made onstage. If I raised my hand, the cymbals would go. If I took a step forward he would hit the tom to the beat of my walk. If I made a joke, 'boom-tish'. It was silly and good fun.

I had done the odd spot on television, but Danny really encouraged me to pursue TV appearances to keep upping my profile. Graham Kennedy, Don Lane, Mike Walsh, they were all good to me and I was regularly invited to be on their variety shows. Don, the lanky Yank, was particularly kind to me, he had me on his show as often as he could. I'd sing a song then have a chat with him in the chairs afterward. I met Sammy Davis Jr when we were both appearing on Don's show. Sammy was very kind and complimented me on my singing, but I was too nervous to relax into the chat with the American legend. The truth was, no matter how many appearances I did, I was always a nervous wreck. Singing live on TV used to frighten the bloody life out of me, but all the musical directors and band leaders knew that despite the nerves, I was always going to sing live and they respected me for that. Appearing on *The Don Lane Show*, and all the other variety shows, meant I was perfectly targeting the leagues club audiences, and those appearances encouraged people to spend the time and money to come along and see me. And that's exactly what I did – I set out with my dwindling reputation to get a crowd.

Wearing my suit and a bow tie, I'd hit the stage of St George Leagues Club in Sydney or Souths Leagues Club in Brisbane with my repertoire of 'Friday Kind of Monday', 'One', 'Underneath the *bloody* Arches' and, of course, 'Sadie'. Because I had been doing these songs for more than a decade, most of the audience, many of whom had blue or pink hair, knew every word to every song. A singalong is a great compliment to an artist. If the audience joins in it's lovely, you feel like you are reaching out and connecting with people. My aim was to make the people who didn't come regret that decision when their friends said, 'The show was alright, it wasn't too bad, you should have come.'

But playing those clubs could be demoralising. Sometimes there would be more people on the stage than in the audience, which was always a bit disheartening. I didn't always have my own band, and working with some of the local backing bands was interesting. Many of them didn't know my songs, so if Danny wasn't there, I'd have to give them chord sheets and even then they'd still get the music completely wrong, or play at the wrong tempo. A couple of times I'd have to stop mid-performance and count them back in. I'd say, 'Okay, go, one, two, three . . .' Sometimes I would even stop the band completely because they were so bad. I'd end up saying, 'It's okay guys, I'll sing this one on my own.'

'Friday Kind of Monday' had a solo section in there and some bands couldn't help themselves, they'd play that section twice as fast. It really annoyed me. I'd turn to them and say, 'No, no, no, no. Stop. Stop!' Despite a band's inexperience or interest, I always gave every performance the best I had at the time. My dad always said, 'If you're going to do anything, do it right, do it properly. Walk away knowing you've done it properly, or to the best of your ability.' That was my basic work tenet then, and still is.

The entertainment rooms in the leagues clubs around Sydney became a staple for a lot of us musicians. I'd generally do three spots a week, and those gigs became my bread and butter. It was a grind, there's no doubt about it, but all that performing put me in good stead. You had to be able to perform live, you had to be able to sing, there was no autotune, there was no hiding. Often there was literally nowhere to hide because a lot of these places didn't even have a stage; we'd set up and perform on the dance floor. The tables and chairs would be pushed back and we'd play right in front of the crowd at the same level as the punters.

I used to sing 'Yesterday' by the Beatles, which I loved to do. This one place, we were performing on the dance floor and just as I put the microphone on the stand and started to sing, this guy walked up and stood right in front of me. *Don't stop, never stop, just keep going* was running through my mind, so I continued to sing 'Yesterday' almost directly to this guy's face.

I had a quick glance around to try to work out what was going on, and as I did he tried to roundhouse me. I ducked his punch and tickled him in the kidneys. As he doubled over, I got him in a headlock. The crowd were going nuts. Then the manager or the security guard, I don't exactly know who he was, but this big burly bloke bolted over to us. He grabbed the guy from behind and had his arms behind his back. This guy didn't like being restrained very much so he threw his head back and headbutted the burly bloke and the bloke's nose just exploded. It splattered all over his face like a ripe tomato. All hell broke loose then, and everyone got involved. I think the guy was part of a football team on a night out. Somehow we got out of there, but it was frightening.

Danny and I didn't just restrict ourselves to the leagues clubs and pubs. I worked wherever they would have me, sometimes in backyards and granny flats and all sorts of odd places. But wherever I played, I gave energy out no matter where we were, and if the audience gave it back it made me want to give even more. I loved performing and I was happy to be singing for my supper, because that's all I ever wanted to do.

Things were looking up. Jill and I had bought a small farm and we still had the Chester Street house, too. And now we were actually saving. We thought we should do something with the money we'd saved, and so Danny and Colleen, Jillian and I, all decided to go into partnership in a restaurant. We called it Backstage and had high hopes for success, but it was doomed from the start. Jillian and I went all in on it financially, we were so enthusiastic and we bought the building and got ripped off something shocking. Then we got the restaurant up and running and we got ripped off in the kitchen. We didn't know anything about the restaurant game and were told later there was a classic restaurant swindle we should have watched out for. The scam would see some staff buy twice as much stock, meat, vegetables or booze as was needed and they'd take the rest home. We weren't there to keep an eye on things and so we had people ripping us off all over the place. It was a disaster. Danny tried to get a handle on the day-to-day administration of the restaurant but he was also managing my career, managing his wife's career and playing drums.

Late one night I got a call from one of the waiters who said a 'high' profile actor from a popular soap opera had come in with four people and was refusing to pay their bill. They told me he'd said he was famous and that he should eat for free – in fact, he said we should be paying *him* for eating at our restaurant. My answer was 'Make him pay and if he doesn't, call the cops.' Thankfully, he decided to pay up.

Unfortunately, there were plenty more incidents like that, and plenty of people who didn't pay. We soon realised that hospitality is one of the worst investments you can make, especially if you know nothing about owning and running a restaurant. The failure of that restaurant took everything we had. We had to sell our farm and any money we had saved was sucked up into the restaurant. Eventually, we had to sell our house on Chester Street to pay for the mess, which was very hard. Jill and I loved that house. It wasn't particularly beautiful but it was the first house we ever owned and so having to sell it to pay bills was really tough. But at least we could do that to clear our debt. Or that's what they told me.

We actually drove past that house on Chester Street the other day. Interestingly, it looked more or less the same. I didn't want to get out of the car, but as I sat there looking, the memory of learning about John Lennon's assassination came to me. On 9 December 1980, standing at that front gate, my hand was in the letterbox getting the mail when I heard about Lennon's murder over the radio. He'd been shot the night before in New York. The memory gave me shivers all over. I asked Jill to keep driving.

In the aftermath of the ruin that was the restaurant, we found out that I hadn't filed a tax return for nine years. I don't want to sound like one of those people who always blames others when things go wrong, but I did think Darryl and then the accountant had that covered off. I was in financial trouble and became really fearful. It was horrible. I didn't know which way to turn or how to help myself. I got quite down about the whole thing, and wanted to stick my fingers in my ears and sing *la la la*, but Jill wouldn't let me. Jill was incredible, she picked me up and said to me, 'We've made a mistake, we can't sit around and wallow in our own tears. We need to get up, move on and carry on.' Jill pulled me out of denial. We were broke, but we were still young, resilient and in love. She made me realise that everyone makes mistakes in life, but if you let them, those mistakes will beat you down, so you have to move onward and upward. I just had to work out how I was going to do that.

CHAPTER 12

PLEASE, PLEASE HELP ME

Jill bought me a pianola. I've still got it. The old thing is covered in cobwebs and dust, possibly rotting in the shed out the back. I've treated it poorly considering how pivotal it was for me and my career. As a kid I never learned how to play the piano, not as an adult either. I can play a little bit by ear, but unfortunately my grandad's knack for the pianoforte wasn't passed on to me. Either way, I was thrilled when Jill gifted me the instrument. I'd sit there for hours playing the three-finger C chord, *dang, dang, dang, dang*. The repetition of that single chord drove Jill mad, she nicknamed my piano hands 'The Claw', but playing those notes over and over was soothing for me. Then, one day out of the blue, I started to sing along slowly. The combination of chord and voice pleased me. I progressed the chords and I sang a bit more. And so on and so forth until finally I played what I had, in its entirety, to Jill. She gasped and said, 'That's great!' That's how I came to create my arrangement of the Beatles classic 'Help'.

Why did I pick 'Help' by the Beatles? I loved their music, I got great pleasure listening to them as a kid and also performing their songs with Strings Unlimited. Someone once told me years later that Paul McCartney heard my version of 'Help' and said he liked it. I never heard definitively whether this was true or not, but I hope he liked it. It was meant as an homage, that's what I intended. People always talk about 'Whispering Jack' and 'You're the Voice' as being my comeback songs, but I think what changed things was the single 'Help' and the subsequent album, *Uncovered*. That's what really got me started again. And it's ironic because at that time, what I needed more than anything was help.

As the restaurant slid into the abyss, taking our meagre life savings with it, I did the only thing I knew how to do, and that was to sing. Glenn Wheatley, my friend from years ago, came down to the Gold Coast to watch me perform. He was back in Australia visiting his parents in Brisbane, after yet another stadium-stacked American tour with the Little River Band (LRB). After the Masters Apprentices had parted ways, Glenn had transitioned into full-time music management and he'd successfully cracked the American market with LRB. I was playing a standard leagues club gig, no different from the hundreds of other leagues club gigs I'd done. There weren't that many people in the audience, but that wasn't unusual. I was singing my usual set, which consisted of 'Raindrops' and 'Sadie'. The band weren't great, but I was used to less than great. Over the years I had gotten used to a lot of less than great.

At the end of my performance Glenn came backstage and I could see it all in his eyes. He was horrified. 'I can't believe you're doing this,' he said to me. 'No, it's okay,' I said. He shook his head. I was changing out of my suit and bow tie and Glenn stood there staring at me. 'It's work. And I need the work,' I said to him. As an artist, the entertainment industry was, by my reasoning, all about getting people involved with what you've got to offer them. At that stage, those songs were all I had to offer them. I was still drawing a crowd – not always a huge crowd, but a crowd nonetheless. But Glenn didn't see it that way. He saw better in me. He saw potential, potential that I wasn't fulfilling. He saw a brighter future at a time when I wasn't daring to dream, I was just trying to survive. He grabbed my suit and bow tie and tossed them in the bin. 'You're better than this, John. You are, and I know it.'

I admit it took me a long time to grow up. My whole career had been engineered by other people. Some of them I remember fondly, others I don't. But Glenn was right. I wasn't happy. It had reached the point where I wasn't enjoying performing. I do what I do because I love singing live, but I had gotten to the point where I wasn't enjoying the material that I was singing. I had a chat with Danny about how I felt and he said, 'Why don't we try to crack America?'

Danny and Colleen knew America, they had lived and worked there for a couple of years before they came back to Australia and Danny started managing me. 'Better still, why don't we all go? You and Jill, Colleen and me. We can get you some meetings and have a holiday as well.' Jill and I had never been to America. We thought it would be fun, and if I had a chance to meet with some people over there that could spark something, even better.

Once the idea was raised, I was all for it. I wanted to go to America and give it a try. I got together a cassette tape of demos and a résumé. The demo tape had a couple of tracks on it, including 'In My Room' and my version of 'Help'. 'Sadie, the Cleaning Lady' was *not* on the tape. The résumé just listed a few of my achievements. Armed with those two things, we arrived in the United States of America, optimistic and ready for anything.

Los Angeles was an interesting place. Olivia Newton-John was based there and she invited us up to her house in Malibu for beer and pizza. When we got there, Olivia was all shook up. Her boyfriend, Matt Lattanzi, had been robbed at gunpoint downtown. He was naturally pretty freaked out by it, but nowhere near as much as we were. For us Australians, the gun culture of America was foreign and very heavy.

I lined up a meeting with an American-based Australian manager, Roger Davies. Roger was having huge success. He was managing artists and bands including Olivia and also Daryl Braithwaite and Sherbet. I wanted to talk to him about possibly taking on my management. When I walked into his office he took one look at me, put his boots up on the desk, got out a toothpick, and then started cleaning his teeth. I played him my demo tape, including my version of 'Help'. Afterward he said, 'Now, what can we do about making you a star?' He made me feel even smaller than I already felt. I looked at him, thought about his question for a moment then responded, 'Nah, nothing. I don't think you can help me. Thanks.' Then I got up and walked out.

Tina Turner ended up recording 'Help'. Roger Davies was her manager at the time, he started working with her not that long after she broke up with Ike. I heard she was interviewed on radio and asked whether she got her inspiration from my version. She denied ever hearing it.

All in all, I met with a lot of record executives and industry people while I was in the States. I did the rounds, but my heart wasn't in it. To be successful in America you need to be based there, and during that trip I decided I never wanted to live in the US, it wasn't me. Jill and I were still hopeful of becoming parents. We had been trying to conceive, unsuccessfully, for years and had recently started to explore the adoption process. We couldn't imagine raising children in America. We loved our home in Australia and wanted to raise a family there.

After all the industry meetings were done and dusted, Colleen, Danny, Jill and I did a road trip to Las Vegas. We set out across the 'Mo'jave' desert, as I called it, in Danny's old Volkswagen. The car had a few quirks. If you were sitting in the front passenger seat you had to keep your foot over a hole in the floor otherwise the whole carload would get gassed to death by the engine fumes.

We arrived in Las Vegas and, amazingly, the Little River Band were playing at the Aladdin Casino. Glenn invited us to the show and I couldn't believe it, people were going nuts over an Australian band. It was just crazy. I'd never seen a show like it before. I'd never been to a big stadium gig. The closest thing

I'd experienced was the Beatles back in 1964, and Festival Hall didn't hold all that many people, whereas the Aladdin Casino was huge. There were 10,000 people in the place and the sound and the energy of the crowd blew me away. I knew the Little River Band were huge in America – I had no idea just how big.

Glenn and I met after the show for a couple of beers. He asked me what I was doing, I told him I was there to see if anyone was interested in signing me. I admitted I'd been without a record contract for a few years, so the trip was a last-ditch effort to drum up some interest. I wanted to record an album and I told him so. Glenn agreed that I needed to change direction and promised to make an album with me, but he needed to finish the tour with the Little River Band first. He said, 'Look, can I give you a call when I get back to Australia?' I replied, 'Yeah, that'd be fantastic.' But I was used to people saying that to me, the old, 'I'll give you a call', then I'd never hear from them again. So I took Glenn's words with a grain of salt. I certainly didn't get my hopes up.

But then he called. I was surprised and thrilled. We met up and Glenn told me about his vision for me. He believed in me, he thought I could be a huge international star. I wasn't sure about that, but I did know that I wanted out of the leagues clubs. I wanted out of cabaret and into rock'n'roll. Glenn said, 'I'll be your manager, but are you up for that?' I wanted to say, 'Yes sir, I'm in,' but in truth I deliberated for six months before I answered. I felt loyal to Danny. It was hard letting go of my partnership with him. We were great mates and he had been a great supporter of mine. He came through the leagues clubs with me, did a great job and I was grateful for all he'd done. Unfortunately, the restaurant failure had strained our professional relationship a bit. We all regretted it and it was a very difficult time, and yet I valued his friendship and didn't want to mess that up. Eventually I sat down with Danny and explained that Glenn wanted to manage me. Danny understood Glenn had connections and a lot more influence than he did, so he was okay with it. It wasn't his favourite decision, but he understood. And so began my partnership with Glenn Wheatley, the man who would help me put my whole career back together and, in doing so, help me regain some of the credibility I had lost as a singer.

CHAPTER 13

THE FARNHAMS AND THE WHEATLEYS

The Royal Charity Concert at the Sydney Opera House on Tuesday, 27 May 1980 was a big historical moment. It was Australia's first Royal Charity Concert and it was an extremely big deal to perform in front of Queen Elizabeth II and her husband, the Duke of Edinburgh. Some huge stars and incredible Australian performers were part of the line-up, including Olivia Newton-John, Paul Hogan, Peter Allen and Helen Reddy, and the whole show was going to be aired simultaneously on Channel 9. Bert Newton was hosting. At the time, I was an unsigned has-been. I hadn't released a record in years, I hadn't been doing much at all, so when the call came asking me to sing at the concert, it was completely out of the blue. I was gobsmacked. To be considered a peer to those performers was an honour for me and I delightedly accepted. Until, that is, I found out what they wanted me to sing.

The concert was going to be broadcast live around the nation and the producer and director, Peter Faiman, was the golden boy of television. He would go on to direct *Crocodile Dundee*, which became the highest-grossing Australian film of all time. Peter was also the producer and director of *The Don Lane Show*, and there's no doubt in my mind that it was this connection that got me the gig. On Don's show I would pretty much sing whatever they wanted me to sing so they probably weren't expecting that to change, but when Peter asked me to sing 'Tie a Yellow Ribbon Round the Ole Oak Tree' for the Royal Charity Concert, I wasn't happy. I didn't want to sing that song. I was grateful for the opportunity, but in my mind 'Tie a Yellow Ribbon' wasn't going to help me reclaim my credibility and I told Peter that. I said, 'I've got a version of the Beatles' "Help" that I'd like to sing instead.' Peter and the other producers weren't convinced. I knew in my heart that my version of 'Help' was as good as I could do at that time. I knew I could sing it in tune, I knew I could sing it strongly.

It's a great song, a great lyric and for once I was presenting my idea firmly and I believed in it. Peter doubled down and said, 'No, we want you to do "Tie a Yellow Ribbon".' So I said, 'Fair enough, I won't do the show.' I held my ground. To Peter's credit, he was terrific – he compromised and said, 'Okay, do both songs.' And I agreed.

At the first rehearsal I went out there and sang his song first, but I kept forgetting the lyrics. I didn't do it on purpose, I promise, the words just wouldn't come to me. I sang, 'Oh tie your yellow ribbon . . . yell-ow ribbon, oh yellow ribbon, yellow ribbon, ribbon . . .' for the entire song, with Tommy Tycho and a sixty-piece orchestra backing me.

Then it was time for me to perform 'Help'. I remembered the words and I sang it as best as I could. People liked it, they let me know they got what I was trying to do. And, at the end of the rehearsal, Peter Faiman came up to me and said, 'You were right, I was wrong.'

So, on the big night I went out there and I sang my arrangement of 'Help'. The reaction to my performance was wonderful. It felt good to have backed myself and my instinct, something I hadn't done for a long time. I met the Queen and the Duke of Edinburgh after the show and yet Peter's words, his acknowledgement that I was right, were just as memorable. So few people had ever said those words to me in a professional context and I couldn't have been more grateful. That was the cherry on top of an amazing night.

A record-breaking six million people tuned in to the concert broadcast that screened live around Australia. It was repeated not long after and drew in even more viewers. So doing that song helped show people that I was capable of more than singing ditties and show tunes. It was early days, but it felt like things might be changing.

And then Glenn Wheatley came good on his promise to do an album with me. From that moment, things really started to change for the better. I was ready to be guided, and Glenn was a great guide. We got on really well, we were friends first and so we understood each other. But Glenn had an understanding of the music business that I didn't have. He also had a handle on the demands of business in general, whereas I didn't know anything about finances. I've got no idea, that's why I have accountants and lawyers and various people to help me. Most did, though some, like Darryl, helped themselves. In this business, money can come very quickly and it can go away just as quickly. Once Glenn was managing me, he made sure I had the people I needed to support me and start afresh.

Glenn introduced me to Liam Hayes, who was LRB's accountant. I spoke to him a few times and I liked the man, I trusted him and we got on really well, so I hired him. We still get on, and he is still my accountant today. It was the same with lawyer Ken Starke. I chatted with Ken and trusted him, so he took over all the legal work I needed done. He's still my lawyer today. It's been a long partnership now, over forty years or so, and Liam and Ken often work as a team on my behalf. I hear from Liam, I hear from Ken, then, between the three of us, we work things through. I have a lot of respect and love for both of them, they are terrific blokes and they've helped me very much.

To do my first album in five years, Glenn connected me with Graeham Goble. Graeham was one of the founders and main songwriters of the Little River Band and he was very keen to produce an album with me. Graeham really liked the way I sang, which was very nice to hear. He also had huge international recognition for his work, because he wrote many of LRB's hits. What I didn't realise at the time was that Graeham liked to be in complete control. To me, it seemed that he was a sculptor and I was to be his clay.

Over the years, people had sent me songs. I collected them all, listened to them and marked the ones I liked. I played my picks to Graeham as potential tracks for the album. Graeham rejected all of them. I had tried many times to sit down and write my own songs, and what came from that were absolute turds. One song idea I had was to use all the derogatory terms for unscrupulous people I had met in my career, terms like 'crooked as a dog's hind leg', 'full as a boot' and so on, then string them together to create a song. I've still got that creation somewhere, and yes, it is as bad as it sounds. One song I wrote that I *was* proud of was 'Jillie's Song'. I was sitting at that old pianola Jill had given me, tinkering away thinking about loving her and the song came out of me.

> *Just a little song to say how much I really love my lady,*
>   *pretty lady*
> *It's my little song to say I love, I really do, I love my lady,*
>   *pretty lady*
> *I feel so good when she holds me*
> *It feels so good to know she needs me*
> *Knowing that she's there, knowing that she cares*
> *And I want this song to be just for my Jillie*
>
> *Each and every time we're apart, you know I miss you lady,*
>   *Jillie lady*
> *It's a love that comes right from the heart, the world can*
>   *see I'm crazy, 'bout my lady*

It's the same almost every day

To say her name is the thing to say

Knowing that she cares, to know that she'll be there

Makes me want this song to be just for my Jillie

I'll always be your slave and now you know it

My heart's as strong as it can be

I could never show it enough to make me happy

Oh I love you

So I wrote just a little song to say how much I really love you baby, pretty lady

Just a lover's song to let you know, you're really quite a lady, pretty lady

And I want this song to be just for my Jillie

I love you Jillie

I only ever tried to sing 'Jillie's Song' onstage once. During one of the early *Whispering Jack* concerts I put it on the setlist, but I burst into tears halfway through and couldn't finish it. I never tried to sing it onstage again. I sang it for Graeham, to see whether we should include it on the album. He liked it and got a co-writing credit for giving it the thumbs up. I also played Graeham my arrangement of 'Help'. He liked that too, and it was included on the album, but he didn't seek a co-writing credit for that one. The rest of the songs on the album were Graeham's songs. In the end Graeham ended up writing or co-writing nine of the ten tracks on the album. He convinced me his songs were better and, to be fair, some of them were, but what that meant was I was essentially singing someone else's album and that someone was Graeham.

We recorded the album in three weeks, and for the first time in my career I was a part of the whole process. A lot of the guys who played in LRB came into the studio and played on the album. It was nice to get to know them. I was more comfortable being in the studio than I had ever been before, because I largely liked the material I was recording. I was finally recording music that was contemporary. I laid down my vocals in three days and it was a learning experience. But despite being comfortable in the studio, I still felt paranoid about being in the recording booth, and recording the *Uncovered* album pushed that paranoia to the next level.

I fell into that old trap once again, I didn't back myself. I should have told Graeham, 'I'm not singing these songs for you, I'm singing them for me and I'm going to sing them my way.' But I didn't. When I realised most of the songs were in a key that was too high for me, I didn't say anything. I kept quiet and I sang the songs the way Graeham wanted me to. He had the experience, and the runs on the board, so I accepted he knew best. I had a good time making the record and was happy to put it out into the world. It was only later that I could see I should have backed myself and been more assertive.

The album was done but none of the record labels would sign me. Glenn shopped it around and no-one was interested, so he finally decided to release the album on his own label, Wheatley Records. Eventually, Glenn did a deal with RCA to distribute the album and it did okay. It eventually went gold, which was awarded after 20,000 album sales but, more importantly, it gave me an opportunity to perform new music live.

Glenn helped me put together the Farnham band to tour *Uncovered*. It was a good band, a fucking good band, but I know a couple of the musicians felt a bit sorry for themselves at first because they were working with me – a lead singer who didn't have any credibility. I was determined to prove them and all the naysayers wrong. The first couple of gigs tanked. The old audience didn't know how to take the new material, and the new audience didn't know how to take the new me. It didn't help that in one of those very early gigs I worked hungover. I had the worst hangover. I think the stress, strain and enormity of the situation got the better of me, because I got shockingly pissed the night before. I was throwing up before the concert and I'd never in my career done that before. I reckon I was still drunk when I went onstage.

My mate Jimmy McCormack was at that show and he came backstage with his girlfriend after the gig. He was a funny guy, Jimmy, he used to go out with Jeanie Jam Roll and even when they stopped going out, Jimmy and I remained friends. That night he looked at me, grabbed my hand, pumped my fist and said, 'We're rich, Budders!' He always called me Budders. It was his way of telling me he liked the show. He was a lovely man, and to have a friend like Jimmy's approval was a big relief. I guess the hangover didn't impact my performance too much, but I never overdid the booze before a show ever again.

I still wasn't getting any radio airplay. Even though I wasn't singing 'Sadie' and 'Raindrops' or 'Underneath the Arches' anymore, I couldn't shake the stigma of those songs. Despite all that, I was ten steps ahead of where I'd been and what I'd been doing in the leagues clubs, so that was a positive. I had nothing to lose, so we kept going.

Prior to touring *Uncovered*, the technology available at my gigs meant whatever I sang was amplified over the PA. You heard what you heard and that was that. I mean, they didn't even mic the pianos, it was crazy. But in this tour, for the first time in my career, I had my own sound box, my own wedge right in front of me. (A wedge is a speaker monitor that's onstage so performers can hear themselves and how they sound.) I could hear myself sing. I couldn't believe it, the roadies put this stuff onstage just for me, it was amazing.

That tour made me appreciate the effort and input of the roadies. They do all the hard work and the musicians get all the glory. Before that tour I'd never thought much about that. I'd look up at the stage and all the gear was there and everything was under lights, but I didn't appreciate the effort that goes into preparing it all. It's impossible to do an impressive show without them, can you imagine? The big, big shows would never happen without them. No way. It's incredible all the work they do. After that run of shows I finally understood what the roadies go through and valued that work much more. The band and I, we all mucked in and helped each other, the loading in and the loading out. We all pulled our weight, but I have to 'dip me lid' to all the roadies out there.

Slowly, word spread. People started coming to gigs and I started enjoying myself. I was loving playing with a good band and I felt really supported to get out there and sing. We had some great times on that tour. In Perth, I bumped into the Australian men's cricket team. This was the era when the Aussie cricketers were idolised, everyone thought of them as gods. We were staying at the same hotel and one night we were all having a drink together. Everyone started getting pretty raucous. Rod Marsh, the Australian wicketkeeper, was a short bloke but he was built like a brick shithouse and as the night went on he picked me up with one hand, put me on a table and said 'Sing!' So I did what I was told. I sang 'Help' and all the cricketers sang along with me, which was really, really nice. After that night, I got to know Marshy and legendary fast-bowler Dennis Lillee pretty well. They were great guys and absolute heroes, and it was fantastic to spend time with them. I really have been very lucky in meeting the people I have and getting to know people with some incredible talent, at the top of their field in whatever they do.

Speaking about the best of the best, with respect to every other singer on the planet, I think Stevie Wonder is the greatest singer who has ever lived, for all different reasons. The facility in his voice is scary. Seriously scary. I love the way he sings, the way he plays, the way he moves around a song. 'Melisma' is the technical term for tricky singing and it's everywhere now, everyone and his dog are trying to do it, perhaps a little too much, but in my mind Stevie was the first person to make it really popular.

I was still promoting the *Uncovered* album when Glenn called me and said, 'Do you want to tour with Stevie Wonder?' Um . . . YES!!!! Obviously I jumped at the chance to tour with my favourite singer of all time. I would have *paid* money to have been on that tour, though I didn't tell Glenn that.

Stevie and I toured Australia together. It was a huge boost when he told me he liked my voice and my singing. The man has the best sense of humour. At one point on the tour, he was walking behind one of his guides with his hand on the guide's shoulder, and I was behind Stevie with my hand on his shoulder. We were being led around to the stage. When we were in place, the first song started up. I sang a little bit and then I went to hand the microphone to Stevie so he could take over. He completely ignored it. We all stopped and I said to him, 'I tried to hand you the microphone, did you see it?' The whole crowd went deadly silent, you could have heard a pin drop. Stevie took his time responding. Finally, he turned around and said, 'Oh sorry, I wasn't looking that way,' which absolutely killed the audience. They loved it, everyone cracked up laughing – including me.

Stevie's crew were also very kind, and were very vocal in their admiration for me and the band. They used to stand at the side of the stage and watch my set, which was lovely because usually, ninety per cent of the time, the other bands and crews on a line-up don't hang around and watch. They usually go about their own business or take a quick rest before their own set, but not Stevie's people. They were always watching from the side of the stage, and I was honoured they took the time.

Apart from being the most incredible singer in the universe, Stevie was a lovely man, and an absolute gentleman. Jillian was pregnant at the time with Robert, quite pregnant. The first time they met, Stevie said, 'May I?' Jill said, 'Of course.' And he got down on his knees and rubbed her belly, and then he sang 'My Cherie Amour' to her bump. It was beautiful. I would be very surprised if there's a singer on the planet who doesn't admire what Stevie Wonder does. A musician of any kind, actually – you can't knock talent like that. And because Stevie was so kind to me and because his team were so kind also, it really gave me a bit more credibility in people's eyes, which I still desperately needed.

It took Jillian and me a long time to have kids. We started trying for children as soon as we got married but, for whatever reason (and nothing to do with that cat!), it didn't happen. Jill is tough, she's strong, and yet every Christmas I'd find her sitting on the couch quietly crying. I'd say, 'What's wrong?' And she'd sob and say, 'I just want a baby.' It was heartbreaking.

Jill desperately wanted to be a mum and I desperately wanted to be a dad. After so long with nothing happening it seemed our dreams of a family weren't going to happen easily, so we decided to adopt. The adoption process in Australia back then was very difficult, and we were told that if we took in a child and then Jill got pregnant, they would take the adopted child away from us. We knew that giving away a baby we loved would have devastated us both, so we went with an agency that helped Australian families adopt Indian children. We got ninety-nine per cent of the way through the adoption paperwork and were close to having a child placed with us when Jill found out she was pregnant. It was a wonderful moment, but we then had to decide whether we should continue with the adoption process as well. It was something we really agonised over, but in the end we decided not to proceed, and Jill focused on looking after herself during her pregnancy. In 1981, after so long wanting and dreaming of having children, it was finally happening.

It was September when Jill went into labour. She said to me, 'John, we've got to go to the hospital now.' I was ready, because in the weeks leading up to the big day she'd had me practise driving to the hospital and back with her in the passenger seat. She was worried about my non-existent sense of direction! I didn't want to blow it and of course, I did.

I was panicking, and Jill was giving me directions while having contractions.

Anyway, we got there safely, fortunately, and the nurses were fantastic, although possibly they were as worried about me as they were about her. I was an absolute mess. I was beside myself, sobbing.

And the nurses said, 'Now, John, be aware that some women swear when they're having a baby.' And Jill can be descriptive sometimes, she has a marvellous vocabulary, particularly when it comes to expletives, so I was expecting all the colourful language but Jill didn't say boo. She gave birth to our beautiful baby boy and didn't say boo. She was unbelievable. And I was nearly fainting, with adoration, with joy, with every conceivable reaction you can have to watching the love of your life give birth. We named our firstborn Robert.

Eight years later, we were blessed again when Jill fell pregnant and we gave Robert a little brother. We named him James. It's just amazing and we are very lucky, they are both great blokes. I'm very proud of both of them. We all have our foibles and we all make mistakes (sorry about the bare bum Vaseline ad, Robert!), but they are good lads and I like them a lot as people. My family is everything to me.

As I've said, meeting and marrying Jill was the best thing that ever happened to me, and so I was really happy when one night Glenn Wheatley raced over to me, grabbed my arm and said, 'I think I've found the one.'

Glenn was my manager, but first and foremost we were mates. I loved the man like a brother, so when he told me he thought he'd found the one for him, I took notice. The Farnham band and I were working at the opening of Billboard nightclub in Melbourne, which Glenn part owned. It was packed, absolutely packed, and after the show when Glenn raced over I looked to where he was pointing and said, 'Oh yeah, you found the one alright. She's lovely. She's gorgeous. She's absolutely beautiful.'

Glenn was pointing at Gaynor Martin, who was a successful actor on the hugely popular soap opera *Skyways*. Glenn was right, she was *the* one! Glenn and Gaynor got married in the Collins Street Uniting Church in Melbourne. The wedding featured in the *Australian Women's Weekly* – remember, Gaynor was a TV star – and I was the best man, alongside Glenn's brother Paul, and Glenn Shorrock, the lead singer of LRB.

Since that fateful night at Billboard, Glenn, Gaynor, Jill and I have always been close. The four of us have spent a lot of time together. We travelled together fairly regularly when we didn't have the kids, and when our kids came along we kept on travelling together. The Farnhams and the Wheatleys are family. I loved us being all together, bringing up our kids together. Glenn and Gaynor had a holiday house next door to us in Port Douglas. We'd all go up there for holidays and I would teach all the kids to ride bikes and fly kites while Glenn was pacing around doing million-dollar deals as an entrepreneur. It was really funny, he'd come out into the sunshine after being on the phone and tied to the fax machine for hours and he'd say, 'Where are the kids?' I'd have them down on the beach flying a kite.

CHAPTER 14

I SAW YOU IN RED ROCKS

Since I left Strings Unlimited, I'd been a solo artist. The idea of joining another band had never occurred to me. Then, out of the blue, Glenn Wheatley suggested I take on the gig as lead singer in the Little River Band, replacing Glenn Shorrock. The idea was put to Glenn by the band, and I was surprised and flattered when I heard about it.

Glenn had been managing LRB since its inception, and together he and the band members had experienced phenomenal success, first in Australia and then in the much bigger American market. I knew Glenn Shorrock from his performances on television shows like *Kommotion* and *Uptight*. We were from the same era, but to my mind the Little River Band were true pop stars, not ditty singers, as I had seen myself up to that point. It might have given me an ego boost to be asked, but I wasn't sure if it was the right direction for me. Making the *Uncovered* album had given me a kick along, and I wanted to keep going to try and find my own voice. The moderate success of the record and the growing crowds at my shows were firing me up. When we were discussing it, Glenn said, 'You know, LRB have a tour of America lined up.' I'd never worked in America and so I thought, 'Bugger it, I'll give it a shot.'

What I didn't know was that Glenn Shorrock hadn't chosen to leave the band, though he admitted later that he hadn't been as committed as he once was. I didn't know the politics of the band, but it turned out that Graeham Goble's relationship with Glenn Shorrock had seriously eroded. It was so bad I think Graeham would have been happy with anyone other than Shorrock as the lead singer. I also didn't know that LRB's star power was starting to fade as their popularity declined. Glenn Wheatley was a good manager, so he had to pass on the offer even though he had some reservations. And, like any good manager, he wanted to get the LRB show on the road. Boosting the band with an injection of new talent and enthusiasm – me – might just be what was needed, and it would do no harm to my profile either. Unfortunately for us all, that tour and subsequent tours didn't sell as well as Glenn and the band had hoped. The album sales were even worse. The band had spent a lot of money recording albums, so they were in significant debt. The way the music industry works, when I joined the band, I took on some of that record company debt. That was another liability on top of the debt I had already racked up with the failed restaurant and the previous mishandling of my financial affairs. I didn't know any of that at the time, though. I thought, *I'm contracted to sing so that's what I'll do, I'll sing.*

I learned quickly that Graeham had a very controlling influence on the band and performances. I'd seen a bit of that during the making of *Uncovered*, but that was only a small taste of what was to come. Later, it would seem to me that he wanted a puppet out the front of the band, not a true entertaining front man. He liked the way I sang, he told me that, and perhaps he also liked how malleable I'd been in the production of *Uncovered* and that's why he wanted me in LRB. We certainly weren't mates when I joined, and we didn't become friends – Graeham and I didn't gel that way.

When I agreed to join the line-up, I told them all that I didn't sing like Glenn Shorrock. He has an amazing voice, he did a great job with LRB and he'd written some great songs, but I didn't want to sing like him or any other singer. I was upfront about that, but I still don't think they were ready for the fact that I wanted to interpret the songs my way, not replicate what had been done before. A song has its lyrics and its melody. I didn't mess with the lyrics, but I did play around with the melody, for no other reason than to make it mine. Early in the piece Graeham would come and say to me, 'That's not how Shorrock sang it.' I had joined one of the biggest bands on the planet, but once again I was singing other people's choice of songs. They were mostly good songs, but they weren't the songs I had chosen and they weren't sung the way I wanted to sing them, so that pressure to bend myself grated.

Singing the way I wanted to sing and putting on a good show were my objectives despite Glenn Shorrock's legacy. I was more interested in being me and getting my point across rather than trying to be Glenn. After a few words in my ear I said, 'I don't do impersonations. I sing a song the way I sing it or not at all.' I also let Graeham know that I was going to engage the audience in every possible way I could.

Over the years, I'd learned lots of tricks to get the crowd involved. I planned to use all of them and hopefully make the audience feel like they'd experienced something special. Before I joined LRB, I'd be working the clubs and pubs and there'd only be seven people in the audience but I'd still give it my all. Seven people or seven thousand people, I'd go out there and

I'd work my arse off. Those people had paid their $20 or $50 or whatever it was, so I always gave them the best that I had. That work ethic stood me in good stead, and it taught me to be able to move on to the next job. I would leave it all on the stage and then it would be done. I don't think the members of LRB were ready for me to do that either.

But it was all still a buzz to be on a tour of that scale. There were three tour buses, with one for Graeham and Beeb, one for the band and the crew in the other one. I ended up seeing a lot of America. We'd do a gig, often at college campuses, then get on the bus and into our bunks and try to get a few hours' sleep. Then we'd arrive at some motel in mid-town America somewhere and try to get a bit more sleep before getting up and doing it all over again, night after night after night after night after night. It was a hard slog, there was no mucking around, it was industrial, bloody full-on rock'n'roll.

Derek Pellicci, the drummer, and I got on really well. It was the same with the bass player, Wayne Nelson, we were good mates. Whereas Graeham Goble and Beeb Birtles and I, we didn't get on well at all. Beeb and I irritated each other – he's not my cup of tea and I wasn't his. Graeham was heavily into new-age spiritualism, numerology and astrology. He was forever doing his astrology chart and, now that I think about it, I believe he was searching for something, though for what,

I'm not sure. As it stands, I haven't spoken to Graeham for over thirty years.

Back then Graeham would ask for his part of the rider in cash, which is absolutely ridiculous. We'd have maybe a bottle of Scotch and a few beers and a pizza on the rider, which was just for the band's consumption after the show, and Graeham would say, 'I don't eat that or drink that, so I want the money for it instead.' When you're endlessly touring, that sort of behaviour really irritated me. Over time, everybody's little idiosyncrasies become magnified. You start getting annoyed with someone for doing something really specific, like the way they scratch their bum, or the way they itch their left ear. All those kinds of irritations grow as a tour wears on.

Graeham came to me after one particular show and said, 'They are all looking at you when I'm playing a solo. So, will you leave the stage when it's my solo?' I said, 'Yeah, no problem.' I figured it didn't cost me anything, so I did it. After the show that night Graeham came to me and said, 'We have to change that because when you walked off, the audience just kept looking at where you went offstage, waiting for you to come back on.' I said, 'Okay, how about I just stand next to whoever is playing the solo?'

Then, they taped me down. They quite literally gaffer-taped my mic stand and mic to the floor so I couldn't roam the stage.

Containing me like this was something I never thought anyone would do deliberately, so when I first saw the gaffer tape on my mic cord I thought to myself, *The silly bastards, obviously they messed up!* It never occurred to me that they knew *exactly* what they were doing. And then, all of a sudden, the penny dropped. I said to Graeham Goble, 'What's going on? I want to perform.' Graeham said, 'No, we just want a singer.' Beeb Birtles backed him up. I respected their musicianship, I really did, I respected the songwriting, some of it, some of the songs were great songs, but they wouldn't let me be me. I can't help myself, I've got to jump around while I'm onstage. I can't stand still. I wasn't doing it for the attention, I was doing it to give energy to the audience. Perhaps it came from dodging apples and tomatoes in those early days? Either way, I didn't feel I needed to defend myself. If they wanted a cardboard cut-out, they should have got a cardboard cut-out. I told them exactly what I thought of the gaffer tape and made it clear that I wasn't going to be restrained.

Despite the monumental challenges and personality clashes, touring with LRB was the greatest onstage experience I could have had. I'd never worked crowds that big. We did that tour of America, and there were some 10,000 seaters and some 15,000-seat venues. Playing to audiences of that size night after night taught me how to work a big audience. The majority didn't know I wasn't Glenn Shorrock, they didn't care, they just wanted to hear the songs. I'd have people coming up to me after the shows and they'd say, 'I saw you guys in Red Rocks' and I'd reply, 'No, I've never been to Colorado.' They thought I was Glenn Shorrock, and that was fine. I just smiled. But all those dates, criss-crossing America, really gave me a good background in the rigours of touring. Touring is a slog, and I learned that you need to get a lot of rest. I also learned about patience and humility. I think I got a bit up myself for a little while there, and some may say I still am. But I defend that by saying you've got to have an ego to do what I do, or to be in show business in general. Ego, in the words of Greg Macainsh, so eloquently delivered by Shirley Strachan, is not a dirty word. What I didn't learn was the danger my ears were in. I did a fair bit of damage to my hearing over the years, right from day one, and now I can barely hear. Industrial deafness, if you like. It's shocking.

Being in LRB was sometimes interesting and sometimes uncomfortable, but the one thing we all had in common was playing music together. Even though we weren't friends, we got the job done well and it was good. The singing was beautiful. A lot of the songs were written for harmonies. And those guys hit their notes every time. It was like a laser focus, bang. To me that felt like Christmas. I would fly off with it, and it was a real pleasure to sing with them, it was just a joy.

But the soaring harmonies couldn't overcome the personality clashes in the band, so it was never going to last. It didn't help that these guys were already millionaires. Graeham Goble, Beeb Birtles and Glenn Shorrock had written some of the biggest hits in the world and they'd sold millions of records so, as the writers, they were getting massive royalties. Whereas as a performer in a band trying to recoup the advances paid to make the albums, I was going backward. I was a long way from home and putting everything I had into the performances, but money was a major worry. Jillian was back in Melbourne looking after Robert and the reality was we had a tab at the local butcher and a tab at the local grocer. It felt like my wife and my newborn son were living off the kindness of local small business owners while I toured America.

One day I was in the studio and Beeb was reading the *Age* newspaper. He was casually perusing the high-end property section when he called me over to ask, 'John, what do you think about this one?' He was pointing at a three-million-dollar property. 'Do you think I should buy it or not?' he said. I felt like he was rubbing his money in my face and it was an attempt at a kick in the nuts. Just an attempt. Good luck to you, Beeb. I mean, you weren't my friend, which is fine. I'm sure he'll agree with that. It all flew off like water off a duck's back. Well, almost.

Night after night I'd go out there and sing my arse off, I was bleeding for the audience, and I'd turn around and wouldn't feel the same energy from Graeham. I'd look at Beeb and didn't feel he matched my energy either. If I stand up in front of ten people and sing them a song, I'm asking for the criticism. If you make any kind of art and you put it in front of someone, you're asking to be judged. Some people thrive on that, and other people don't. It's just the way it is. As Kenn Brodziak said, 'If they're not booing you or cheering you, they're sitting on their hands and you've had no effect.' You have to affect people or move them in some way, whether it be positively or negatively, that's our job as artists. I want to get a reaction.

I tried to talk to Graeham and Beeb about it. I told them I understood it was difficult, and I knew the band was in debt. I said, 'I know it's hard because we're slogging away.' But I was trying to entertain people. I needed them to respect that. Of course, they didn't like that. I was still hungry and was playing to win, and they were playing like they'd already won the game.

I'm not much of a guitar player, never have been, but for one of the endless LRB tours of America, I took a guitar on the road. I started doing this six/eight-time signature on the guitar, with the two strings moving up and down and harmonising with the other. It caught my imagination. I must have a muse somewhere, because then I started to think about the situation I was in – the debt, the animosity. By that stage I was no longer concerned about whether my bandmates were happy. They definitely had a problem with me – it seemed they thought I was trying to take the band away from them. I didn't want to do that, I just wanted to perform and put on a show. I'm sure they'll disagree, which is fine, but I just wanted to get it done and move on. I channelled all of those feelings and wrote 'Playing to Win'.

I've written a few songs, not a great many, but 'Playing to Win' is absolutely one of my favourites. Usually, whenever people ask me about the meaning of a song I ask what it means to them. Because that's what music is all about, it's supposed to take you somewhere and everyone will take something different from it. 'Playing to Win' is one of the few songs I've ever actually explained, and what I've said is that I wanted to get out of the chains I felt I was in. You can hear my frustration when I sing this song. You want me, you come and get me. That's really the essence of the song for me.

I had ninety per cent of the song written and then I showed it to the band. Graeham Goble wrote the bridge and we recorded it. The royalties got split up among everybody, which felt unfair to me. I lost a big percentage. It was pretty disheartening.

My time in LRB taught me an awful lot about all sorts of things. It was great singing with those guys, they had beautiful tone and beautiful pitch, and those harmonies soared. They were great musicians, it was a great band to be involved with on that side of things, but there were undercurrents of animosity, jealousy and petty peeves that played out during my time in the band. When you put a group of people together, particularly musicians, that can happen. You've got to have a fairly thick skin in this business. I thought I did, but it wasn't thick enough.

I don't regret it. It was worth a try. I mean, the Little River Band were the shiny penny in the pile and if it had happened, it would have happened big. But the truth is, I didn't make any money in LRB; in fact, I went backward. However, I walked away knowing that I'd left it all on the stage.

I know this about myself. I don't want to leave a drink undrunk. I am tenacious and I'll battle on if I know I'm right. If I know I'm going the right way, then I'll go full steam that way. My time in LRB showed me exactly what I wanted to do. I wanted to be responsible for recording what I wanted to record. I did not want to have to sit down with five or six other guys and say, 'I like this one' and then be outvoted because they didn't. I was done with compromising. Finally, I realised what I really needed to do was to get on with it. I wanted to stand or fall on my own decisions. I wanted to go solo, that was my whole thing, so it was all up to me to make that happen.

You're the voice.. try and understand it...
Make a noise and make it clear...
  Ooh oooh etc.
We're not gonna sit in silence,
We're not gonna live with fear...
  Ooh oooh etc.

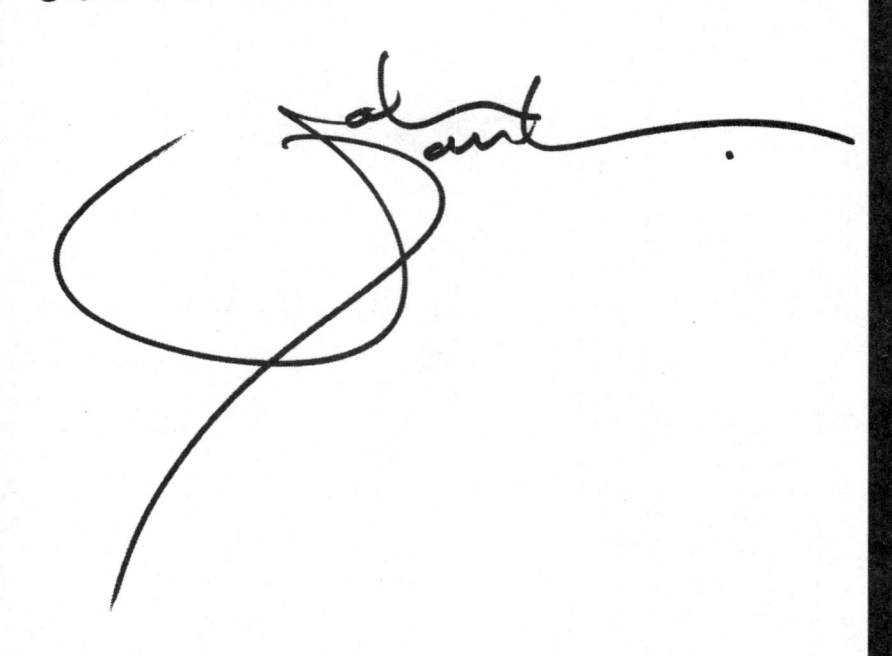

CHAPTER 15

WHISPERING JACK PHANTOM

I'm not ashamed or afraid to hash over those early days. I'm not ashamed of 'Sadie' and the years that followed. But, as I've said, a lot of the work I did meant I wasn't taken seriously, I was treated like a pretty-boy puppet. That was hard to cope with because all I've ever wanted was to be a professional singer with credibility.

I knew my time with LRB had ended well before it was over. I finally went to Glenn and said, 'I want to leave the band.' When I spoke those words I instantly felt relieved. Finally, the pressure of being a part of someone else's band would be lifted. But I still had the pressure of having to earn a living. I needed to go out and work and make money to support my family and pay back my debts, but I still wanted to try and be at least honest about what I do. I needed to feel comfortable and happy about where I was going, what I was doing and how I was going to do it.

Glenn was a very entrepreneurial man, he couldn't help himself, he was always busy, busy with lots of irons in the fire. He gave me a chance with *Uncovered* and then another with the Little River Band. When that was all over, he agreed to back me again. He said, 'Let's make another album, I'll support you.' But before he did, he wanted to know that I was committed. He had a lot to lose because records weren't cheap to make. They're still not cheap, you are spending hundreds of thousands of dollars on a whim, on a bet, it's almost like gambling. In his business dealings Glenn had already taken on some extensive debts, so he needed to know I was committed and ready to do the work. In turn, I needed to know that he was committed because I was in my own little piece of horror. We promised each other to make it work the best we could. The trials of LRB, and everything I had ever done professionally, strengthened me to make what I considered was probably a last-ditch effort, my final chance to do it on my own.

But before I could put my heart into another album, I needed to get myself together. All that time away from home in America and the tension in LRB had taken a toll. And so had the financial pressure I was under. I don't think of myself as a down sort of person, but sometimes I do get a bit blue. Jill knows me back to front and she's always there for me. She could see my head wasn't in a good place and so she sat me down and we had a chat. She helped pick me up. She said, 'You've got to do this. Go ahead and do it.' My response was, 'I am not sure I can.' And Jill said, 'Yes, you can.' I didn't argue; instead, I set about getting my head on straight. I was doing this.

In preparing to record, Glenn shopped around some of the big-name producers in the business. He had some interest from the American superstar producer Quincy Jones. This is the guy who produced Michael Jackson's *Thriller*, the bestselling album of all time. Glenn was talking to Quincy, but, because of the dates available, Quincy could only give the project a small amount of his time. It wasn't enough. To be honest, the thought of working with such a big name got me worried. I felt that I was going to be right back in the same situation I had always been in, where the producer would call all the shots. With someone like Quincy Jones, how could I disagree if he wanted to do something a different way to me? He had the experience and the runs on the board, all I had was my instincts and too often, in the past, I doubted myself. I'd think *Okay* and do what I was asked even if it didn't sit right. I respect people's talent, I respect their judgement and their criticisms, I'm happy to take it, but for this album I needed to be the one who decided what I was singing and how I sang. For this to work, I needed to do that for myself.

I knew Ross Fraser, he'd been doing the front-of-stage sound for LRB. At some point he was also a guitar techie. When Glenn recommended Ross as the producer for this new album I thought he was an interesting choice. Ross hadn't done a great deal of producing before, but he felt like the right choice. He's dry as a bone, Ross. When we started rehearsing and then recording the album I'd bleed from every orifice trying to sing a song. I'd say, 'Do you want me to sing it again?' and he'd go, 'Meh.' I used to want to kill him. It became a bit of a joke, actually. I'd do a take and then I'd say, 'Rub that out, I'll do another one just for Ross.' It became a backward and forward thing, which was fun and it kicked me on, he made me work and make decisions.

Putting musicians together for a record is really important but I needed something even more for this record. I needed collaborators and people who would inspire me, listen to me and work with me. We needed a keyboard player. And with David Hirschfelder I got that and so much more. David played keyboards in LRB when I was in the band and we got on well. If Hirschy had a solo on the piano, he would get up and work it. He and I were showmen rather than just performers, and even when that was frowned upon by others that didn't stop either of us. On top of being a bit of a show-off, David is the best, he's just so clever. He isn't just a piano player, he is an arranger, composer and musical savant. He was inspired by what I was trying to do, too, and I think he did himself proud as well.

Dougie Brady ended up being the engineer when we finally got into the studio at Armstrong's. Doug is a lovely guy. His older brother is Mike Brady, who was the M in the band MPD Limited. Dougie was, and still is, an incredible engineer. He really knew his way around the studio and he helped me enormously. Dougie Brady is right inside the album too.

Ross, David and I wanted to work together and so we needed somewhere to get started. Jill and I had already sold our Chester Street house to pay all our debts, so we were renting a house on Manningham Road in Bulleen. The house was on a main road and it was nothing like our dear little house on Chester Street, but money was tight so it was where we needed to be. I was comfortable there and it cost us nothing more, so we decided to set up pre-production in the garage.

David came over and set up his Fairlight CMI (computer machine instrument) Series II. This was basically a digital synthesiser, sampler and digital audio workstation. An Australian invention, that machine was part of the early digital music revolution. The first time I had seen and heard a Fairlight was when I supported Stevie Wonder's Australian tour. Stevie was one of the first people in the world to own and work with one and the sound, combined with his voice, blew me away.

I had a few bits and pieces of equipment, Ross had a drum machine and Doug Brady borrowed an eight-track machine for us to muck around with in the garage, but it was David and all his amazing musical instruments that would really set the tone for the album. David was only young but he loved his technology and he was incredibly clever, really, really, really clever.

I wanted to try something different, and I wanted to try something new. The Fairlight was an expensive piece of equipment and David knew how to work it. You could take a sample of your voice, or of anything, and plug it into the Fairlight and it sounded amazing. One of the guys at the recording studio owned a Porsche and had driven it over to my place, and we wondered what it would sound like if we sampled it. So we recorded the Porsche door being closed and then being slammed. I can't remember if we used it in the album or not, but it sounded great. The Fairlight gave the sample depth, guts and shape. It was amazing.

David was a genius and his enthusiasm was unrestrained. We'd be in the garage working, David would be tinkering on his Fairlight and I'd be tinkering around on a keyboard and, quick as a flash, he'd pick up on something. I'd look up and I'd be shunted onto the couch. His excitement at embellishing an idea would take over and he'd manoeuvre me off the keys to continue exploring it. It was hilarious, and his ideas were wonderful.

We were in a cabal, Ross, David and I, doing what we were doing in secret. Jill was upstairs with baby Robert. She'd occasionally pop down with a tray of tea and some biscuits but, generally, she left us alone to do what we did. It wasn't a piss-up or anything like that, we treated it like a full-time job. Ross and David were both coming into the garage each day, not at eight o'clock in the morning, more like ten or eleven o'clock; musicians' time. We never had a set time, it wasn't work between ten and seven or anything like that. We worked until we thought we'd reached a limit or until one of us had had enough for the day. That's the way I still work. If I'm doing anything with the band, rehearsing or anything, and someone's over it or tired I'll say, 'Let's finish,' and we'll take it up again the next day. We drank a lot of tea and I smoked a lot of cigarettes. I had a cigarette in my mouth ninety per cent of the time I was awake. Crazy. Glenn would occasionally come in and have a bit of a listen.

Just because we had drum machines, a Fairlight and sequencers and all sorts of stuff didn't mean I wanted to make a techno pop album. I squashed that idea from the beginning and said, 'We're not making disco music here.' Not that there is anything wrong with disco! It's just not me. We set about using the technology wisely but I was starting to get stressed. I couldn't stop worrying. What if this album failed? What would I do?

Despite those worries, I believed in the process and, frankly, I was fortunate that I was able to surround myself with the best people I could. Without David's input, without Dougie's input, without Ross's input, without Glenn and all the musicians who worked with me on that album, it would never have come together.

But we had to find the songs. I had hundreds of songs, hundreds of them on cassettes from all over the place. Some of them had already been recorded by other people, so they were out. It was difficult to get hot songs, like the really, really great songs from the top writers. They weren't going to give me their best songs because I wasn't selling albums. I mean, if you've written a song and you get a chance to give it to Madonna or Tina Turner or Shania Twain or me at that point, who are you going to give it to? Fucking not me. That's just the way it runs and I understood that.

I was looking for something that grabbed me. A lot of the time, people press play on a song and if it doesn't grab them in the first four or eight bars they turn it off. I decided that the least I could do, as a courtesy to the writer, was to listen to the song the whole way through. By doing this, I also figured that if I found a part of the song that I liked – I might have loved the chorus or the bridge or I might have loved the first verse – my thinking was I could always talk to the writer and say, 'Hey, I love what you've done here. Can you get further into that part of it?' So yeah, I'd listened to them all the way through, and it was very time-consuming but it was worth doing it that way, it really was.

One song I vividly recall rejecting was the Bernie Taupin and Martin Page song 'We Built This City', which was recorded by Starship. The demo was amazing and it definitely grabbed Ross and David, but it wasn't one for me. Thankfully, Ross and David respected my opinion. If your heart's not in it, then you're not going to do it properly, and after a career of forcing myself to sing songs that weren't really me, I didn't want to do that anymore.

The album started to take shape. We wrote a couple of songs – I was kicking myself that I didn't save 'Playing to Win' for myself, but there you go. There was a bit of album fodder in there. 'No One Comes Close' and 'Pressure Down' were among the best that we had available to us at the time. 'Pressure Down' and 'Reasons' were both really good songs, I love singing those kinds of songs and the bass line that David devised for 'Pressure Down' was great.

Harry Bogdanovs or the publisher, I can't quite remember which, played us the demo to 'Pressure Down' and it was such a quirky little song. I liked the lyrics, I liked the melody and after David Hirschfelder worked on it through his Fairlight and sequencer, I loved it! In my opinion up to that point, 'Pressure Down' was the strongest song we had. The album could have been called 'Pressure Down', and as far as radio fodder went we felt it was a strong contender, which was exciting because it had been years since the radio stations had played any of my songs.

Ross Wilson from Mondo Rock gave us 'A Touch of Paradise'. They had already released it so ours was a cover, but Ross was gracious and said he liked our version, which is always very gratifying to hear from a songwriter.

Sitting in that garage with Ross and David, for the first time in my career I got to sing and be me in the way I wanted to sing and be me. I tried to put my heart into every beat of every bar of every song. I don't want to sound pompous, but you'll find that most artists do the best they can in the time they have to do it. I tried. And Glenn backed me, he never interfered artistically, he just backed us to get it all together. In that garage we did the work and recorded all the tracks as demos to take into the studio. Come to think of it, those demos are probably still around somewhere. I've probably got them in a box in a cupboard somewhere at home . . .

Then, about two weeks before we were due to go into the studio, I got a tape. It came from the publishers through Glenn's office and it had 'You're the Voice' on it. I put it in the tape deck and pressed play. Jesus! It was so me. It says power. Power to the people. It's a very powerful song, if you look at it. I never really looked at it as a political song but if you look at it that way, it plants, fair dinkum, right there in your heart. I just felt I could sing it. And I said, 'Yeah, this is me, I want this song now. I want it. This is mine. Please let it happen.'

I don't often think about sliding-door moments, but this song changed so many lives in such positive ways and that kills me. It just kills me. It helped Glenn through all his monetary problems, it helped me through mine, it put our kids through school. All sorts of wonderful things happened because of that song.

No singer wants to be defined by one song, but that particular song had everything I could wish for as a singer. It had great lyrics. A great melody line. I loved the chord progression. It means a lot to me and as soon as I heard the first little beats, which David eventually turned into the famous *clap, clap, clap, clap, clap, clap, clap-clap, clap, clap,* I got goosebumps. And it's real hard to forget the *Whoa, whoa, whoa, whoa, whoa.* But seriously, it means a lot to me for all different reasons and I still get emotional when I sing it.

When I heard the demo that first time, I heard bagpipes for the solo section in my head. I told Ross and David and they both went, 'Fucking bagpipes?' I said, 'Yeah, bagpipes.' I've always loved the Beatles but as far as Australian bands go, AC/DC are phenomenal. Bon Scott was a great singer, I loved Bon. I read something yesterday, there was a bit of press saying that the original singer, Dave Evans, the one before Bon, was the best singer that the band had. I beg to differ, mate! Bon Scott was amazing. I only met him very briefly, I didn't know the guy, but I admired his talent. He had a great, great voice. AC/DC are so good. And Bon was able to cap it off. I'd love to have seen Bon live. I loved his version of 'It's a Long Way to the Top (If You Wanna Rock'n'Roll)'. I love that song, it's an absolute Aussie classic and the bagpipes in it really work for me. Later, I'd often sing it in my sets when I was touring.

We'd already have the bagpipes out for 'You're the Voice', so I figured we may as well use them again, it's a two for one!

'Fucking bagpipes?' David saw I was serious. He said, 'Bagpipes? Wow. Okay.' And Hirschfelder is a bloody genius, he had to redo the whole arrangement of the song so that the bagpipes would sit perfectly in it.

No-one said no to us recording 'You're the Voice' at the time. Chris Thompson, one of the writers of the song, said some things that felt pretty mean to me early in the piece and apparently he didn't want me to record the song because he had doubts about my credibility. I never heard from the other songwriters. Chris's comments upset me, but they didn't stop me.

We went out of our way to pick the best songs that we possibly could out of the thousands of songs that we got. And as I said earlier, none of the big songwriters were forthcoming with their finest songs because I wasn't selling millions of albums.

We finished pre-production in the garage and then moved into the studio for production. I don't like having people in the studio when I'm singing. As I've told you, it's my thing, I get paranoid when I'm in the booth doing my vocals. Getting over that red light fever is something every recording artist has to get through. It can really restrict you if you're not willing to really give it a shot and fall off or hold back. If you do that, it's never going to work. Generally, you'll sing a song about fifteen to twenty times to warm up and then you really get going. Like I said earlier, I'd be bleeding from every orifice and I'd go, 'How was that?' and Ross would just go, '*Mmmm*, meh.' I'd think *What more could I give it?* Laying down vocals can get a bit taxing, you have this insane pressure to get it done properly.

With this album I wanted to push myself. I had recorded the vocals to 'You're the Voice' and, as far as I was concerned, it was finished. But I took it home to see how it felt to live with it for a few days, just in case. After those couple of days, I wasn't happy with my vocals on the song. I needed to do it again. Glenn and Gaynor had been out at some fancy dinner and they were all frocked up when they came into the studio. They'd listened to the latest production version and weren't totally hooked. Them being there gave me the kick in the arse that I needed. I went into the booth and really put some blood in it, and it worked, it felt amazing. I sang 'You're the Voice' at full voice rather than falsetto, because being a smoker my falsetto was terrible anyway. Now that I've quit smoking my falsetto is back, which makes me happy. It's no good to me at the moment, but it's back.

I guess this is the time to tell the truth about how the album got the name *Whispering Jack*. My nickname among some is Jack Phantom. I got the name on that trip to America with

Danny Finley and Colleen Hewett. Our mutual friend Loretta took us all to this African-American soul club in Los Angeles, and we were the only white folks there. Loretta knew Alex Love, the singer hosting the evening, and she went up to him and whispered in his ear that her friend, the singer Johnny Farnham, was in the audience. And then Alex announced over the PA, 'Ladies and gentlemen, this evening we have in the audience the great Australian singer, Johnny Phantom!' Alex got me up onstage. I was too nervous to sing, but we laughed our bloody heads off. The mix-up was silly, and very funny. Over time, Johnny became Jack, like my grandfather, but Phantom stuck, so I was called Jack Phantom by Danny and Colleen and some others as the years went on.

But there's more. Ted Lowe was an English snooker commentator for the BBC and because of his husky, hushed tones, he was given the nickname 'Whispering Ted'. I had a little Walkman, remember those portable cassette decks? Well, during the *Uncovered* tour to pass the time between gigs, I would narrate things into the Walkman in the same style as Whispering Ted, only I would narrate really mundane things, like the guys eating breakfast or shaving or someone walking toward me. I narrated every bloody thing I could. If we were in a pub somewhere I'd narrate what was happening around me with earnest seriousness and I'd sign off, 'That's all from Whispering Jack Phantom.' I ditched the Phantom part but decided to call the album *Whispering Jack*.

When Glenn and I started working together, from the start, I always called him 'Boss'. I'd say, 'Hey Boss, what's happening?' It was a term of endearment. Throughout the production of the album, Glenn was a source of inspiration. He'd come in, have a listen and be blown away by what he heard. It was exactly the kind of encouragement we needed, and it helped me a lot. When the album was finished, we ran off some dubs from the big twelve-inch tapes to cassettes and handwrote the track listing on them. Glenn tossed me a cassette and asked me to sign it, which I did.

I love ya Boss – Thanks for giving me the chance to do this. Glenn you're the best. John x

It was done. The album was finished, it had a name and so it was time for a listening party for everyone who'd worked on the album, plus a small selection of industry colleagues. I was freaking out and terrified. I didn't want to go. Jill and I drove to the studio in this little Mazda that we'd bought for three hundred bucks off a friend. The whole way there I was curled up into a ball under the dashboard on the passenger side, sobbing. I was completely forlorn and saying to Jill, 'I can't do this, I really don't want to do this, I can't go in. I can't.' I didn't want to face anyone. I had no idea what people would think of the album and how it would be received more widely, and it mattered so much to me.

For so many years I had tried to be strong, I had tried to keep it together, but Jill and I were broke, we had a young son and we were surviving on the goodness of others. In that car on the way to the studio it all came to a head. It was either going to be yes or no, for me there was no middle ground – everything was riding on this album. The thought of failure, that people wouldn't like it or wouldn't respond to it, was too much for me. That fear was paralysing.

As always, Jill was right there beside me. She was willing me along. She kept her eyes on the road and said, 'Come on now, let's go and we'll see what happens. We'll just go along and accept what will be.'

JOHN FARNHAM

DARYL BRAITHWAITE
RICHARD MARX
RUSSELL MORRIS
BACHELOR GIRL

ARTIST

CHAPTER 16

JOHNNY PETER FARNHAM

It's such a personal feeling, putting out an album. I don't think anyone who hasn't done it could understand the pressure. Having said that, everybody must go through these sorts of things, big or small, all the time in life. You want to get your point across but the minute you put yourself out there you're asking for criticism. When you put an album out you know you are going to cop it from some, but whatever they think or say, you can't let it beat you. Tall poppy syndrome definitely exists, but Australians love a battler and I'm nothing if not a trier. Onward and upward, fight on, that's me.

But I still remember the physical terror of that day. My heart was pounding. Everyone was crammed into the studio – record executives, Ross Fraser, David Hirschfelder, Doug Brady, as well as all the musicians who played on the album. Glenn and Gaynor were there, everyone was drinking glasses of champagne or beer. During the recording and mixing sessions, we'd had a few visitors popping in so there was already a bit of a buzz around the project, and now the energy in the room was electric. Everyone was there to hear *Whispering Jack*. Once the music started, my heart didn't stop pounding until well after it was over. They liked it. They loved it, I was very grateful that everyone enjoyed it, which was great. It was a good feeling and a huge relief, especially after spending a bloody hour driving in under the front passenger seat crying. I'm a silly old fart.

That was the first hurdle. Then it was Glenn's turn. His job was to shop *Whispering Jack* around, trying to get a distribution deal for the Wheatley Records album. He worked hard but he couldn't get one. No-one wanted *Whispering Jack,* which was hugely disheartening. It was awful, and yet we knew we had a reasonable product. Finally Brian Smith, the managing director of RCA, listened to the demo of 'You're the Voice' and agreed to distribute the Wheatley Records album through RCA. RCA Records was fully acquired by Bertelsmann in 1987, making it a part of Bertelsmann Music Group (BMG). Because BMG was German, I ended up going to Germany a number of times for promotional tours, television shows and radio interviews. It's funny, I've always disliked doing interviews, I never really enjoyed them and it's such a big part of the game. And yet being interviewed in Germany and hearing their reactions, hearing them say good things about me and my work was unusual. They took me and the album on face value, they didn't compare it to my past, they didn't have preconceived notions about who I was or, more importantly, who I wasn't. I desperately wanted this album to be judged on its own merit, and it stood up. It stood up on its own and made its own place. And in Germany, *Whispering Jack* and John Farnham was all they knew. No Johnny–Sadie in their memory banks.

I've never been more excited to get out there and tour an album. Let's go. Let's fucking go. So we had to get a band together.

We found a guitarist, Brett Garsed – actually, Glenn found him. Brett had sent Glenn a cassette of his guitar playing, purely on spec. Glenn was blown away by what he heard and he said to me, 'You've got to hear this guy play.' Ross and I listened and he blew us away too. Brett had recorded himself playing on a small cassette player. He had hacked a cassette player to use it as an amp then recorded himself, and we discovered that he's a very, very fine player. Interestingly, years later when

Stuart 'Chet' Fraser joined the band, he had a totally different playing method from Brett. Chet was physically this skinny loaf of bread and he used bloody barbed wire as guitar strings – not quite, but they could have been. And then there was Brett, who played a guitar strung with spider webs and he was built like a brick shithouse. Brett did the Rambo thing, huge muscles and tank tops. Totally different styles and both incredible players.

Angus Burchall was just a kid when we got him in to play drums on a couple of tracks. We were all impressed with him. Gus is a great bloke, a funny little bugger, he's quick-witted and deadly on the drums. Lindsay Field and Venetta Fields came on pretty early in the piece. I had some younger backup singers, Nikki Nicholls and Kimmy Collins, and they were fantastic, but Ross had the idea to get two older voices. Venetta was a gem, she was an absolute professional and a veteran – she had already toured with Ray Charles, Pink Floyd, Barbra Streisand, and Ike and Tina Turner. Venetta was funny and she kept us all in line, me included. I can't help myself onstage, I have to tell jokes, or talk and talk and talk and talk and talk to the audience. I'd be chatting away and from behind me I'd hear, 'Sing, motherfucker! Sing!' It'd be Venetta putting the boot up my arse. When I tried to get my own back, she'd never flinch. We'd do 'A Touch of Paradise' and during the saxophone solo I'd turn my back on the audience and look at her and mouth something cheeky. She never batted an eyelid. I'd seen and done a lot in my career but Venetta had seen and done a whole lot more.

What a band it was! I still have deep respect for all of them because I know how talented they are and they never let me down. They always gave me everything they had, they gave me one hundred per cent every time. I never demanded or insisted they did – I'll admit that I wanted and expected it, but I didn't insist on it. They were free to play somewhere else if they didn't want to play. But if they did, then I encouraged them to look at each other, to use each other and to work with each other. We all got on really well, it was one of the best bands in the world. You won't find any better, you'll only find different. They're great players with good ethics and I appreciated every single one of them. I paid them well and I treated them well and that matters a great deal to me, because if you get on with your workmates, work is going to go better.

We started in small venues because none of the big venues would book me. I went out and gave it my all, I performed so that the people who came would go home at the end of the night and tell their friends what they'd missed. The crowd were a lot younger than my normal crowd, and I think half of them had no idea who I was anyway, so I took them along for the ride.

For those early shows, my old friend Frank Thring recorded an introduction for me, which was a bit of a laugh. I got Frank to say, *'Ladies and gentlemen, would you please welcome to the stage Whispering Jack. Who the fuck is Whispering Jack?'* We'd play that over the PA before we came on, it was good fun. Frank also did the introduction for the video clip to 'Pressure Down'. The clip starts full frame on Frank's face and he looks down the barrel of the camera lens and says, 'There's only one step left to overcome in your quest for success ... PRESSURE.'

The *Whispering Jack* artwork was Ross's idea. He had it all sketched out and he pitched it to me along the lines that there would be a photo on the front of me whispering into a woman's ear, then on the inside sleeve there'd be another photo of her slapping me. I said, 'Aren't people going to be wondering what I'm saying in her ear?'

Ross looked at me and replied, 'Yes John, that's the point.' And if you're wondering what I said to that woman on the cover, I didn't say anything. We shot the photo of her slapping me first, and she hit me pretty hard the first take. She toned it down on subsequent slaps. I think we used the photo of the first slap. Ross did a great job with that album cover, it worked well.

I pulled in another dear friend, Jacki Weaver, for the video clip of 'You're the Voice'. I love Jacki with all my heart and when she started going out with Derryn Hinch, who was a journalist at the time, I said, 'You're not going out with that dickhead are you?' And she said, 'Yeah.' And I said, 'Well, don't dare bring him around to my house!' Of course, then Jacki couldn't wait to bring him around and I fell in love with the guy. In the media he was being terribly controversial but he actually turned out to be a reasonable sort of a bloke. In the clip, the two of them played a married couple who were having a blue over the kitchen table. They were good sports. Remembering all this makes me realise I haven't talked to Jacki for a long time, about eighteen months at least. It's been wonderful to see her career take off in America. She's always loved acting and she's good at it. I think I've pretty much seen everything she's done and she's always terrific. And she was great in that 'You're the Voice' video clip.

We started the tour and we were sleeping on the bloody amps in the vans at first, but then the tour got bigger and bigger and bigger. We started to get full houses and a couple of weeks in Glenn said, 'We're going to have to go to bigger venues.' Alright by me, Boss!

I very rarely read reviews. Even now I don't google myself, I'm not on Facebook or social media, it's not something I've ever really done because, from the early years, I learned that it can be quite hard to rise back up after a bagging. It can be too easy to lose yourself in other people's opinions. But I'm not completely removed from it all, I like to know what's going on, so Glenn would give me a summary of the write-ups. But I could gauge the crowds myself, and the feedback from audiences was amazing. Touring is always hard work but our hard work was being repaid. The band was also inspired by what was happening, they were getting off on the buzz and excitement of the crowd. We were all getting a kick out of it and we were enjoying each other's work. It was good, really good.

The single was released in September 1986, but no-one would play it on the radio. Glenn actually owned a stake in Triple M at the time, and he still couldn't get it played on air, so he took it around to all the other radio stations. Cherie Romaro at 2Day FM, one of the few women working in radio at the time, who's now a legendary programmer, was largely responsible for the success of 'You're the Voice' and *Whispering Jack* in Australia. She heard it, she liked it and she gave it a shot. Unlike the other radio managers and disc jockeys, she didn't get hung up on my back catalogue, she didn't let her preconceptions about me or my work stop her from listening to the song. Cherie listened and she liked what she heard, so she played it on her station and from there it took off. I'm forever grateful to Cherie. Because of her, *Whispering Jack* was played on radio and because of her, it all took off.

We were driving somewhere in Glenn's little blue Porsche when we found out it had gone to number one. I was in the passenger seat and he was talking on the phone so I wasn't paying attention. He put the phone down then turned to me and told me we were number one.

The album took off, and I didn't know which way to turn. All of a sudden we were booked to play in stadiums. I couldn't believe it, we did nine sold-out shows in Melbourne, five in Sydney, we had to get a bigger venue in Brisbane. Our tour, *Jack's Back*, ended up outselling both Michael Jackson's and Billy Joel's Australian tours that year. I have to say, my time in LRB, love it or hate it, helped prepare me for the rigours of big stadium concerts. And this time I wasn't restricted onstage, because the microphone was mine, all mine. It was amazing and also overwhelming. So much was going on around me but I had to concentrate on singing, I had to perform, so I couldn't really take it in. The only time I had outside of performing was directly after each show. We'd all have a couple of beers back at the hotel to wind down. I'd go to bed in the early hours of the morning, then I'd sleep all day and then Glenn would wake me in the afternoon for another sound check. Poor Glenn, it was tough for him because he'd stay up having a few drinks with me then have to get up at eight in the morning to manage all the logistics. But if I didn't sleep, I couldn't sing. Sleep became a real focus for me because it rested my voice. I had to have plenty of sleep.

I can remember saying to Glenn one time, 'No wonder so many people in our business get into drugs!' It would have been easy to use drugs to calm down after a gig, then more drugs to help you sleep and then different drugs to wake you up to perform. I don't know whether I was ignorant, stupid, smart or what, but I didn't do any of that shit. I would have the occasional toke of a joint, but not really, because I hated being out of control. Perhaps all those years of Darryl slipping drugs into my drinks cured me of the attraction of any serious drug use forever.

Different bands have their different warm-up routines. Some bands say a prayer, some hold hands and sing 'Kumbaya', some get in a rugby huddle and cheer each other on. When we were working on this book, Poppy told me it's rumoured that the Foo Fighters dance and sing to Michael Jackson songs while drinking shots of Jägermeister. We didn't do any of that. But we did have a ritual. Brandy is my drink of choice, and a quick slug of brandy before the show became a tradition fairly early in the piece. I think it was the first stadium we did, the band all stood in a circle and everyone had a shot of fighting brandy. We could have drunk a thousand-dollar bottle of brandy but it wasn't to be enjoyed, it was a tool to be used. So we drank a shot of cheap brandy, shouted 'Kick my fucking arse' then went onstage and gave it our all. We played to over 120,000 people on the *Jack's Back* tour. It was amazing, just amazing.

The first Australian Record Industry Awards (ARIAs) were held in 1987 at the Sheraton Wentworth Hotel in Sydney. Elton John hosted the evening, and artists who had released music between 1 January 1986 and 31 December 1986 were eligible for awards. Many of them were there – INXS, Jenny Morris, John Williamson, Slim Dusty and me, to name a few. This was before the event was televised, which is the only reason Elton agreed to host it, and it was a pretty loose affair, though I did wear a dinner suit and a bow tie. I had actually met Elton at Molly's house way back in 1971. I think initially he thought I was brought in to 'make friends', if you know what I mean, but we cleared up that misconception pretty quickly and enjoyed a chat. He had a good sense of humour; the album he had out at the time was *Madman Across the Water* but he called it *Madam Across the Water*. He was alright, old Reggie, and without question an amazing songwriter and terrific singer.

Jill and Gaynor came to the ARIAs night with Glenn and me and frankly, I can't remember much about it because I was in such a spin. After I won the first award I spent the rest of the time in a daze muttering, 'What the fuck is going on?' It was so awesome. Enormous. I put my heart and soul into *Whispering Jack*, I gave it the best shot I could give it and fortunately, the record was a smash. I was dizzy with all the wonderful accolades and the acceptance by the industry, it meant a great deal to me. I had to go up onstage over and over again to receive awards. I ran out of people to thank and things to say. I do remember thanking Glenn. I said, 'Most of all I would like to thank my manager and very close friend, Glenn Wheatley. He put his money where my mouth is. I thank him very much for that.' We ended up winning six awards that night: Album of the Year, Single of the Year, Best Male Artist, Best Adult Contemporary Album, Highest-Selling Single and Highest-Selling Album. *Whispering Jack* is still the highest-selling Australian album in Australia, selling over 1.6 million copies. On the night, Glenn turned to me and said, 'This will never happen again in our lifetime.' And he was right. No Australian artist has come close to beating that record in Australia. Well, he was half right. I'm still alive so who knows what could happen.

It wasn't only industry perception that had changed. The money started to come in, too. I was able to pay off my debts. I don't want to shove my good luck down everybody else's throat, but in a couple of years I went from being constantly stressed about money to being able to buy our forever home, which Jill and I are still in today. It was amazing. We were also able to afford someone to come in and help Jill. We employed a woman called Deanna, who helped with Robert and the cooking and cleaning. Deanna was great and she was also a lovely companion for Jill because I was away working a lot. She became a good friend to us both.

When *Whispering Jack* went to number one, Jill splashed out and bought me a Porsche. I had always admired Glenn's 911 Carrera, so Jill surprised me with a 1981 burgundy Carrera. It's beautiful. I don't drive anymore but I've still got it, it's wrapped in plastic and sitting in the garage. My boys won't let me sell it, but if I did, my friend Louis Guthrie, from *Charlie Girl* days, has been working as a luxury car dealer for years so he could get me a good price. It hasn't even got dust or 50,000 clicks on it. It was a beautiful gift and I love it.

Being seen as a credible singer by my peers meant the world to me. Daryl Braithwaite, who was crowned King of Pop after me, in 1975, 1976 and 1977, was making an album and he gave me a call and asked if I could sing backup vocals on it. There was a bit going on at the time and I didn't know him terribly well, but I figured it was only a little effort on my part, and I was flattered to be asked, so I said yes. In the studio, I didn't know how far to push my notes so I asked the producer, Simon Hussey, 'Do you want me to try a few things or have you got something you want me to do?' And Simon said, 'Go ahead and try a few things.' So I did and they liked it and used it. In the end I sang backup on three tracks on Daryl's album, including 'As the Days Go By'. It was a lot of fun.

I'd been touring constantly and covered a lot of Australia, and before I knew it, it was January 1988. That year marked two hundred years since the arrival in Botany Bay of the First Fleet. There were huge bicentennial celebrations and also protests planned around the country. It was mooted by some that I was going to be named the Australian of the Year, which is an award that recognises outstanding achievement and contribution to the Australian community and nation. Entrepreneur and philanthropist Dick Smith had won it the year before, and actor Paul Hogan the year before Dick. Glenn called me and said, 'Mate, you know, they want to make you the Australian of the Year.' And I said, 'Well, did you tell them that I'm not an Australian citizen?' He hadn't, so he had to do that quick smart otherwise it was going to complicate the whole affair.

The powers that be were really lovely about it, I was able to get naturalised and get an Australian citizenship pretty much overnight. I went into Glenn's office and I swore on the holy book and officially became an Aussie. Jill was heavily pregnant with our second child, and I was worried that the timing of the event was going to interfere with me being at the baby's birth, but everything worked out and it was a beautiful day. The ceremony was held at Kirribilli House, the official Sydney residence of the Prime Minister, who at the time was Bob Hawke. I'm not a great public speaker, I'm not a speech maker but I had thought about what I wanted to say. I wanted to thank everyone, and tell them how blown away I was, how lucky we are to live in Australia and that I thought, if handled well by our politicians, Australia as a society and a nation could get better and better. I stumbled through it and got my point across, hopefully, but I did cry like a baby. The moment overwhelmed me. Funnily enough, it turned out that the Honourable

Robert James Lee Hawke was also a weeper – he bawled his eyes out, too.

Politics aside, Bob Hawke was a funny guy. I liked him, he was easy to get along with and he was a bit of a rogue. While he was in office, Bob invited Glenn and Gaynor and Jill and me to Canberra. We were having this meeting because people were bootlegging albums and mine were being bootlegged a lot. We were having dinner and a drink, Hazel was there, and we're having a lovely time and it was all going really well and then Bob noticed Glenn's watch. Glenn loved his luxury watches and that night he was wearing his Rolex. Hawkie noticed it and said, 'That's a nice watch, Glenn.' Glenn said, 'Thanks, I really love this watch, it's my favourite.' At that, Bob stood up and walked out of the room. A moment later he returned wearing a suit jacket and he said, 'You want to buy a watch?' He undid his jacket and there's dozens of watches pinned to the inside of it. I thought he was joking and I said, 'I like that Timex one, that's a beauty.' Bob said, 'You can have it.' I objected and told him I couldn't take his watch and he said, 'Take it. It cost me twenty-five bucks, it's a knock-off.' We were there to talk about stopping knock-offs and there was the prime minister wearing a jacket full of bloody knock-off watches. Bob kept insisting I take the watch and I kept saying I couldn't. Gaynor growled at me, 'Take it!' but I couldn't bring myself to, so I left Canberra without that Timex. I'm a fool, it would have been a great keepsake. Bob was a funny man. We saw him two or three other times, and we always had a good laugh together. It was amazing the doors that were opening and the people we were rubbing shoulders with.

Businessman Christopher Skase approached Glenn, wanting me to perform at the opening of his Mirage Resort in Port Douglas. At the time Skase was well regarded, this was before people started to realise he was dodgy, so Glenn was of course open to a paid gig. The proposed payment was a substantial sum of money, as well as two of the condominiums in the resort. We said yes, which is how the Farnhams and the Wheatleys came to own holiday houses in Queensland. Anyway, Skase's party was just outrageous. Completely outrageous – champagne, booze, bikinis everywhere. The next night Skase hosted another big party on one of the large patios near the pool. As it got dark, Glenn and I got into the pool in full stealth mode. We swam over to the edges, grabbed people and pushed a few into the pool. It was stupid of us, and we spent the next couple of hours searching the pool for a diamond bracelet that one of the ladies had lost in the chaos. We found her jewellery, but Christopher Skase wasn't thrilled with us at all. Before that he was always personable to me, as was his wife, Pixie, but he did the wrong thing by his investors and many Australian people and that is disgusting, there's no doubt about it.

I worked several parties over the years. The band and I played at prominent Melbourne businessman Richard Pratt's house. I played at tennis player Lleyton Hewitt's wedding to actress Rebecca Cartwright. Lleyton had won the US Open in 2001 and Wimbledon in 2002 and I was thrilled to be asked, so I waived my fee. I said, 'Pay the band and I'll just turn up and sing.' We worked at Gretel Packer's twenty-first; Gretel is media tycoon Kerry Packer's daughter. It's interesting doing those gigs. I mean, it's pretty decadent to buy a pop star for your birthday party. If you'd told me and my family back when I was a kid in Noble Park that I'd be at these types of parties and being paid to perform, we would have thought you were bonkers.

Sometimes at those gigs they used to go a bit too far in what they thought you would do. It was like they thought they had unlimited access. There'd be an expectation that I'd play at their party then meet everyone there and then mow their lawns and pack their suitcase for their next holiday. My answer to that was, 'You didn't buy me, you bought the music.' I wasn't being paid for all the other ancillary stuff.

Every so often the requests from famous people were downright weird. I worked for the Prince and Princess of Wales,

Charles and Diana, once. I sang 'You're the Voice' and afterward Diana came up and I was introduced to her. 'This, Your Highness, is John Farnham.' Diana looked at me and she said, 'Oh, I like your leather pants!' I didn't know what to say. She seemed to be a sweetheart. At that same function, one of Princess Diana's ladies-in-waiting came over to Jill and said, 'Princess Diana needs to go to the ladies' room, would you accompany her, please?' Jilly absolutely freaked out and said, 'No, I'm not doing that, I can't.' When the lady-in-waiting moved off to ask someone else, Jill whispered to me, 'I couldn't do it! What am I going to chat to her about and what if I say the wrong thing? Or have to curtsy when she's washing her hands?' So somebody else had to make small talk with Diana, Princess of Wales in the bathroom that night.

I had been in the public eye for a long time, but the exposure that came with the success of *Whispering Jack* was like nothing else. People were always after my autograph and I signed some interesting things, from boobs to bags. It's a bit disconcerting when a young lady comes up to you, flashes one of her boobs and says, 'Here, sign it, please.' It's awkward, because usually you've got to hold on to something in order to sign it, but a bare breast made that problematic. I was always very careful where my hands went on those occasions, but I did always sign my full name: Johnny Peter Farnham.

Most people were cool, but sometimes someone would take it too far. Jill's dad Bob was a real Aussie larrikin. I loved the man, and was completely distraught when he had a stroke. He lasted for a few years in a wheelchair but then his health took a turn for the worse. We'd been called into the hospital with Jill's sisters and Phyllis, her mum. Bob was in his bed and he was on the way out; it was a really fraught and emotional time. This nurse came into the room, ignored everyone else and walked right up to me and said, 'Can I have your autograph, please?' I was quite taken aback. I mean, she could see what was going on, she was a nurse on the ward for heaven's sake. I was stunned but managed to politely refuse. I said, 'I might do it later on, but we're busy right now.' I couldn't believe it. Like I said, most people are pretty reasonable and I'm sure she didn't mean to be offensive. Some people don't see the human being, they only see the figure or the star or walking newspaper headlines. I hope she didn't want to be unkind but, in reality, she was.

And the roller-coaster ride didn't stop. 'You're the Voice' went to number one in Germany and Sweden and we ended up doing several tours in Europe. I loved touring over there and the band loved it, too. One minute we'd be in Denmark, the next minute we'd be in Rome, then a quick trip over to Sweden – it was wonderful. We did some of the huge German music festivals and played alongside the Eurythmics, Joe Cocker and Tina Turner. It was fantastic performing in front of 90,000 or 100,000 people and having a large number of them knowing all the words to my songs. I've got a great chunk of the Berlin wall at home, which was given to me in Germany by a fan. That great big lump of concrete still has graffiti on it. Pretty amazing to hold on to a piece of history.

Actually, it was in Germany, in a hotel bar, where we had a run-in with a baby grand piano. Well, not exactly a run-in. We were staying in this beautiful hotel enjoying a few drinks at the bar after a show and everyone, the band and the crew, was singing and drinking. Then five of the road crew disappeared. They were big boys these lads, and it didn't take long to find out what they were up to. They picked up this piano that was on the mezzanine level of the hotel lobby and carried it down the stairs toward the bar. Every step they took the piano went *fung, fung, fung*. But when they got to the bar, they couldn't get the baby grand through the doors. That didn't deter them. They pushed it as close as they could against the door so that David Hirschfelder could play the piano and still be in the bar. And so David sat down at the keys and all hell broke loose. Everyone went wild, singing and carrying on until the hotel management arrived and closed us down. They shut us up pretty quick. It ended up costing me five thousand Deutsche marks to have the piano tuned and put back where it should be. It was a lot of fun while it lasted.

At the height of *Whispering Jack* fame, I was getting letters from all over the world, and a lot from England and Germany. People often just addressed the mail to: *John Farnham, Australia.* It was a big thrill and a nice stroke of the old ego. They wrote to tell me they liked the music, they'd ask me what Australia was like. Sometimes they'd include phone numbers and, like the old days in Noble Park, I would ring a few of them just to say thank you. They always got a kick out of that, and I got a kick out of it, too.

Europeans took to 'You're the Voice' really, really well, but I was a one-hit wonder in most of those countries. Nothing much ever happened again, nothing more than a little bit of a tickle here and there. I still get a few royalty cheques every now and then, small ones, so it's a very nice reminder of that time.

People kept saying America was the place I had to be, and I would love to have found success there, but I would have had to tour constantly there, live there and bring my children up there and, with respect to America, I would rather live in Australia thank you very much. That was a no-brainer for me. I wasn't going to uproot Jill, Robbie and James to chase a dream. The American record company liked the song, but they wanted to remix it their way, and the very famous record producer who remixed it to their liking did an awful job in my opinion. It was so awful that I wouldn't let it be released. It was missing the magic of Ross's mix. The Yank executives just didn't get it.

I was able, very luckily, to make up my own mind and say, 'I don't necessarily want world domination, I'm quite happy with where I am.' I could barely keep up with the work I had in Australia, so anything else was too much. I was so happy that *Whispering Jack* worked. I mean, that album changed my whole life in so many ways. I turned forty a couple of years after it was released and it completely changed the trajectory of my life and was pivotal in creating my present existence. I am so grateful for it all.

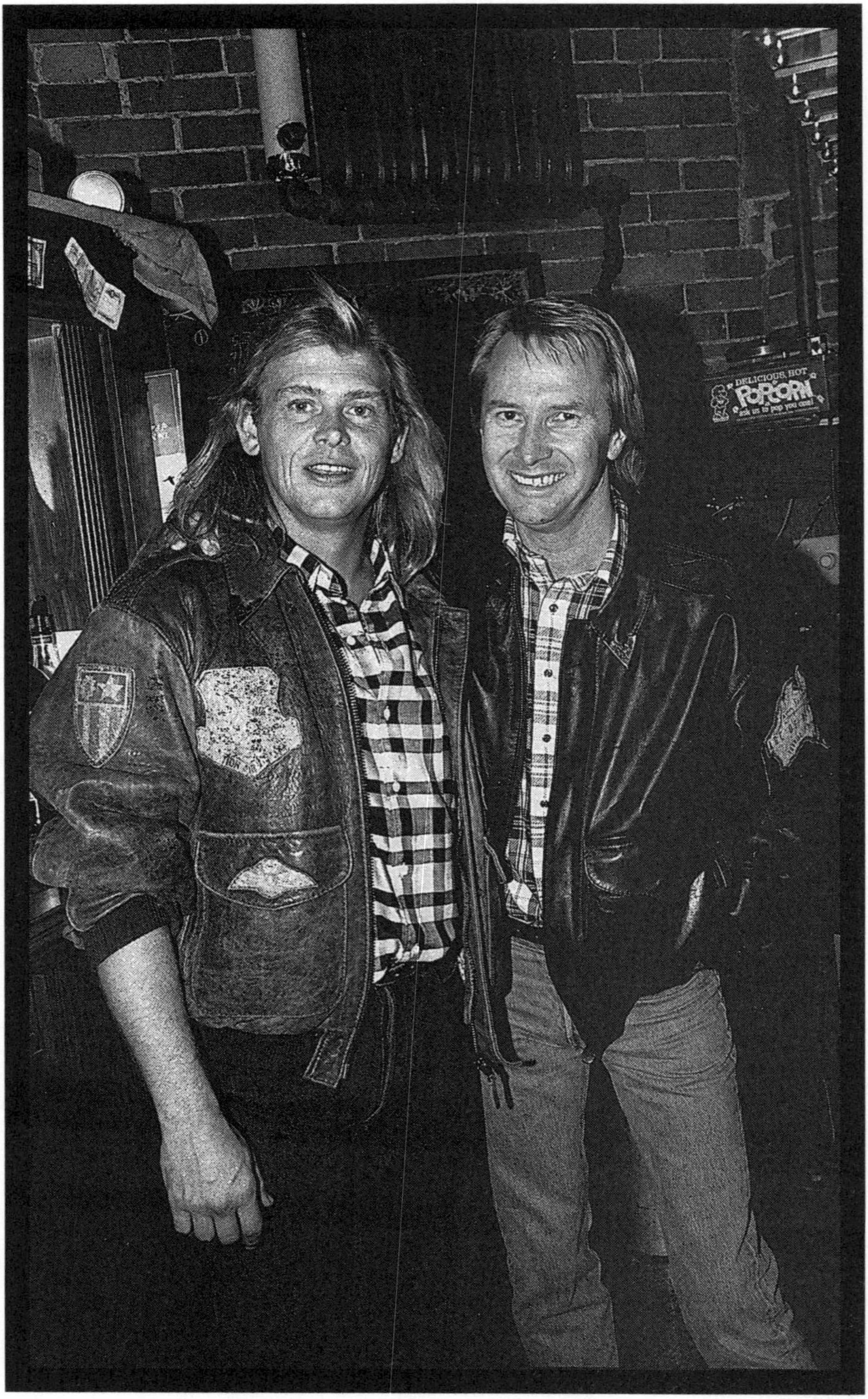
DELICIOUS, HOT
POPCORN
ask us to pop you one!

CHAPTER 17

BURN FOR YOU

It's notoriously difficult to follow an album like *Whispering Jack*. Something *that* big that hit all the right notes is rare. It was the highest-charting album of the 1980s in Australia and it was the first Australian-made album to be released on CD. As of today, it is still the highest-selling album of all time by an Australian artist. It succeeded beyond my wildest imagination. I wanted the follow-up album to be accepted and have it build on what I had already done, to confirm my credibility as a singer and a musician. That kind of pressure is tantamount to trying to get away with murder.

And I didn't want to just replicate 'You're the Voice'; I was never going to be able to match that. Making new music that did all I wanted it to do was always going to be a Herculean task. I needed a single and an album that were going to stand beside 'You're the Voice' and *Whispering Jack*. I knew people would compare them, so I wanted to record something that had people saying, '"You're the Voice" was good, but this next one is good too.' In choosing the direction and style, I wanted to show people that I don't just make one kind of music, I can make a variety of songs.

I think it says a lot that the team from *Whispering Jack* wanted to continue working together and supporting each other. Ross Fraser, David Hirschfelder, Doug Brady, the band, Glenn Wheatley – everyone was up for doing it all over again. So, as soon as we came off the road, we got started on the next album. I went back to my process of selecting songs, listening to them all the way through, but this time it was different. Before *Whispering Jack* I hadn't been selling any records so I was lucky to get any songs. Now, I was being sent the best of the best from here and overseas. And, even better, I was also being sent songs that had been written specifically for me.

Todd Hunter, who was a founding member of Dragon, and Johanna Pigott, a musician who formed XL Capris and Scribble, were a songwriting duo (and married couple) who co-wrote

Dragon's 1983 comeback single 'Rain' alongside Todd's younger brother and Dragon vocalist Marc. Todd and Johanna teamed up to write a song for me and when I heard the demo, I was knocked out. I loved it. I was very flattered and very grateful for 'Age of Reason' because it just fitted exactly where I wanted to go at that time. I liked the lyrics, I liked the music, I liked the way it was done, and when David Hirschfelder got his hands on it I loved it even more.

One of my favourite pieces of music is the piano solo in 'Age of Reason'. It was Hirschfelder's brilliant work and I love it. David actually played two devastating solos for that song and we ended up cutting the front half of one into the second half of the other. When we dropped it into the arrangement it fitted perfectly. That solo is still one of my favourite things to listen to, it's so powerful. Before a show David used to spend more time on his hair than he did limbering up his fingers, but then again, so did I, when I had hair. I've said it before, David is a genius and also a fantastic performer . . . and by all accounts, he still has great hair.

When I recorded the final studio version of 'You're the Voice' I had nothing to lose so I was able to give every little bit of grit that I had. I went balls out and it worked. When I listen to 'Age of Reason' now, I think I played it a bit too safe. I'm annoyed with myself because I could have done better. When

I sing the lyrics, 'What about the world around us', you can hear this awful falsetto. I don't have a very strong falsetto, or I didn't then. It's stronger now because I've stopped smoking, but when I recorded 'Age of Reason' my falsetto was pretty bad. I could have sung in full voice, only quieter, and it would have done the same thing – in fact, it would have sounded better. But, hey, I learn a bit more about my voice every time I sing.

Other songs on the follow-up album included a song from writer, producer and musician Dave Stewart, from the Eurythmics. It came through the publisher, but he wrote 'Blow by Blow' specifically for me, which was nice. Jon Stevens, the lead singer of the band Noiseworks, co-wrote 'Listen to the Wind', and a couple more of Chris Thompson's songs also made it onto the album. Despite my reservations, knowing that Chris had initially been against me recording 'You're the Voice' because he didn't rate me or my voice, I decided his songs 'The Fire' and 'Don't Tell Me It Can't Be Done' were the best out of the selection we had. After the album was released, Chris called to tell me he didn't like the way I sang 'Don't Tell Me It Can't Be Done'. I picked up the phone and without much lead-in he said, 'You didn't sing it very well.' I was taken aback and angry, and I replied with, 'Fuck off, never ring this number again.' Chris's songs weren't bad but with hindsight, we could probably have chosen better.

We put two bonus tracks on the CD, covers of AC/DC's 'It's a Long Way to the Top (If You Wanna Rock'n'Roll), written by Angus Young, Malcolm Young and Bon Scott; and Cold Chisel's 'When the War Is Over', which was written by Steve Prestwich. They are two of my absolute favourite songs and I used to love singing them. Both of them, lyrically and musically, are right up my alley. Jimmy Barnes, who originally sang 'When the War Is Over' with Ian Moss, is a good sport in regard to my singing it. Jimmy has a very impressive range and he's a great bloke. We've sung that song together a few times over the years and each time it's been great fun. Our versions are chalk and cheese, but he says he likes mine, which is generous of him. I think it would have been better to replace a couple of the average songs on the album with those two covers. You live and learn.

Unlike the limited funds we had for the 'You're the Voice' video clip, we had a substantial budget to shoot the video for 'Age of Reason'. The director, Steve Hopkins, asked me, 'Do you have any problems with helicopters?' I replied, 'No . . .' and before I could say anything else Steve said, 'Good, we're going to fly you to the top of a mountain range and then we're going to drop you off and film you.' Umm . . . I was thinking, *Okay, how hard can that be?* Turns out, *How wrong could I be?*

The Cathedral Range, known as Nanadhong by the traditional owners, the Taungurung people, has some spectacularly sharp ridges. They are part of the Great Dividing Range in Victoria. I got in the helicopter and, before we took off, the pilot said, 'Okay, John, what I'm going to do is, we're going to go to the very tip of this thing and I'll put one skid on a rock there and when I say go, you step out of the chopper and stand on the rock. You got that? You step out onto the rock. Okay?' And I thought, *Fuck! That sounds scary!* But, of course, I didn't say that out loud. I didn't want to disappoint the film crew or the pilot so I said, 'Yeah, I can do that.'

We flew up to the top of the Cathedral Range and then the pilot slowly lowered down and lay one of the landing skids on the top of a rock, which was at the peak of the range. The rest of the helicopter was hovering and when I looked down it was a sheer drop of about a kilometre. I came very close to embarrassing myself – my bowels felt like they went to water. It was bloody high! I stood on that skid and willed myself to step out onto the peak. I made it and, as soon as I did, the pilot pulled away and flew off. I was left up there on this mountain in my red lumberjack coat and my lumberjack boots, all alone in the wilderness. Before I could take it all in properly, seemingly out of nowhere I heard, 'Hello. Hello.' What the . . . ? 'Over here,' the voice said. I looked over and there were two people climbing up the peak toward me. They were out for a day of adventuring. I thought to myself at the time that I would've much preferred climbing up the mountain to stepping off a helicopter skid, but actually, who am I kidding, I wouldn't choose to do either.

Once the climbers were out of shot, the chopper circled around me as I sang along to the song; someone had been up there before me and hidden a speaker in the scrub. After a few takes, it was time for me to step back on the skid and get back in the chopper. I felt pretty brave after all that, but I'm really glad I didn't fall, it would have been *very* nasty. The things you do for art!

My heroics on the mountain were rewarded – the 'Age of Reason' video clip won a Logie for Most Popular Music Video in 1989. American actor Raquel Welch was a guest, and she was seated at the same table as Jilly and me. Raquel was a stunner. I was in the middle, Jilly was seated on one side of me and Raquel was seated on the other. As the night wore on, Raquel took quite a shine to me. She let me know in no uncertain terms that she wanted to become friends. And I mean . . . nudge, nudge, wink, wink . . . *friends*. I was bemused and I said to her, 'Just a minute, Raquel, let me ask Jill.' I swivelled a little to look directly at Jill then turned back to Raquel and said, 'Sorry, my wife said no.' Raquel laughed her arse off, she thought that was hysterical. We all had a few drinks together, it was a fun night. Later, I told my father that Raquel Welch had been keen on me and he said with a laugh, 'You silly bugger, I'll never forgive you for turning her down.' That's fine, Dad, but you wouldn't have had to live with my Jilly if I did!

If I thought filming the 'Age of Reason' video clip was scary, it was nothing compared to the album launch. Glenn organised for it to be a part of the World Expo '88 in Brisbane. It was estimated that 25,000 people would attend, but millions more would tune in to the Channel 7 live broadcast and local radio stations were going to simulcast it across the country. Expo '88, as it was known, was a huge cultural event to promote Queensland as a tourist destination. It was a huge success, but thinking about that concert, particularly the pressure of the live broadcast, still makes me feel nervous almost forty years on. Leading up to the night I was really suffering from pre-performance nerves, and to combat them, I spoke to a professional. She suggested I get in one of those float-tank things. So I did. I took my trousers off and put bathers on, and I got into this float tank. I was lying in this thing, and I must have nodded off because I woke up about an hour later and I felt terrific. I felt calm, I felt composed, I felt really, really good, if not a little salty. I still got nervous before going onstage, but everything came together and the crowd was so giving, it was a wonderful night. Come to think of it, I'm not sure why I didn't incorporate a float-tank session into my ongoing pre-show routine. That would look great on a rider.

The album, which we named after the single, debuted at number one, the single went to number one too, and it became the highest-selling album in Australia in 1988. It would go on to sell eight times platinum. My goal to put out music that would complement *Whispering Jack* was achieved.

Given it was a new album and we wanted to do something a little bit different, Glenn had the idea to get the Melbourne Symphony Orchestra (MSO) to join the tour. It was a great idea. Touring with the orchestra was just awesome, awesome, awesome. I got goosebumps every night. The emotion created by performing with a sixty-piece orchestra is devastatingly wonderful. I'd be singing and the sound of the orchestra would go *whack*, it would hit me in the guts each and every night. In turn, the members of the orchestra let me know that they enjoyed touring with us. It was an incredible experience for everyone.

I hadn't sung 'Sadie, the Cleaning Lady' as a part of my set for a long time. When I toured *Whispering Jack*, someone in the audience would always shout out, 'Sing Sadie!' I used to pretend to argue with them and I'd shout back, 'No!' Someone else would shout back, 'Yes!' And I'd respond again with, 'No.'

There would be this backward and forward between me and the audience. Sometimes, occasionally, we'd hop into it for a few bars just for fun, the same with 'Raindrops' and 'Friday Kind of Monday', but we'd never play the whole song. Then David Hirschfelder had the idea to incorporate 'Sadie', all of it, into the *Age of Reason* tour setlist. I was *very* reluctant, but then he wrote an arrangement for the orchestra. For years I had avoided singing 'Sadie' for fear of losing any credibility I'd gained, but after David suggested including it in the show, I felt that I needed to let people know I wasn't ashamed of it. I'm still not ashamed of it. As I said before, as I've said one hundred times, it's not the best song I've ever recorded, but it's a huge part of the reason that I'm still around and it's been a nice hill to climb. So, I agreed to include 'Sadie, the Cleaning Lady' and, after all those years, I sang it backed by my band and the MSO sixty-piece orchestra. I felt good and in control. Singing 'Sadie' also gave me a chance to thank the people in the audience who had supported me since those early years so long ago.

Age of Reason was only moderately successful in Europe. It peaked at number four on the Swedish charts and went gold in album sales there, but it failed to reach the top ten in other countries, apart from New Zealand and Norway, where it went to number six and nine respectively. It wasn't a patch on the success of *Whispering Jack*, but it held its own. On the strength of it and my career, I was invited, along with some of the most famous musicians in the world, to launch Greenpeace's *Rainbow Warriors* album in Moscow, in the then Soviet Union.

To raise awareness and funds for their environmental campaigns, Greenpeace had put together a compilation of singles from some of the world's best-known artists. My invitation to the album launch came by way of producer and promoter Ian Flooks. Ian had successfully promoted *Whispering Jack* in Europe and obviously thought I could hold my own among some of the best musicians in the world. I nearly blew it. We all gathered in Red Square in Moscow and all we had to do was introduce ourselves. Peter Gabriel kicked us off, then Annie Lennox said, 'Hi, I'm Annie Lennox and I'm with Eurythmics.' Next it was, 'I'm Chrissie Hynde and I'm with the Pretenders,' then, 'I'm The Edge and I'm with U2.' When it was my turn I said, 'I'm John Farnham and I'm from Australia.' Everyone laughed their arses off. I still to this day don't know why they laughed. I mean, what's so funny about that?

Things went from embarrassing to downright scary when I started drinking brandy out of the bottle. Not vodka, which might have made sense given I was in the Soviet Union, but brandy. I got terribly drunk and I don't know what I was thinking but I started goosestepping up and down the square like a Soviet soldier – well, actually, more like a complete idiot. Four real Soviet soldiers saw me and marched over. They were livid, and I was too drunk to talk. Thankfully Glenn Wheatley was with me and he called Ian over, who in turn got the interpreters involved, and they managed to talk down the soldiers. It was a really frightening experience, I honestly thought they were going to take me around the back and shoot me. Huge thanks to those interpreters – if it wasn't for them I might be dead or rotting in a Siberian gulag. To this day I have no idea why I got so drunk. The only reason I can think of is that I really liked the Russian brandy. It went down too easily.

Recording *Chain Reaction* was a lot of fun. It was the third album Ross Fraser, David Hirschfelder, Doug Brady, the band, Glenn Wheatley and I did as a team. We worked hard. Recording is not a cheap process so we didn't lark about, but we enjoyed ourselves. I ended up co-writing eight of the twelve tracks on the album, which was unusual for me. I don't do a great deal of writing but at that time I was enjoying the rush and the collaboration. We thought, why can't we express ourselves by writing all these different songs, so we did. The track 'Burn for You', co-written by Phil Buckle, Ross Fraser and myself, was definitely the stand-out song on the album. Phil had written the line 'I got myself into some trouble tonight, I guess I'm just feeling blue,' and the three of us started working on it from there. Together we came up with the rest of the song and it really worked.

I love singing 'Burn for You' so much. The guitar work on the song is amazing, and some of the best guitarists in the world, including Tommy Emmanuel, have played that song with me. I'm very lucky.

Around the time we were releasing *Chain Reaction*, Glenn asked me to lend him some money. Of course I lent it to him. He still had his finger in so many different pies – he had the radio station EON FM, he was working in sports management, he was floating his company on the stock exchange, and he had a whole lot of other projects, many of which I had no idea about, on the go. Glenn loved the entrepreneurial side of business, he thrived on it, whereas I'd had my entrepreneurial dabble with the restaurant and got burnt big-time. It wasn't my thing. In my mind, I had tried it, it didn't work, so I didn't want to get involved with any of that again. Ever since the restaurant disaster, I've played it safe. I feel very lucky that I was able to get out from under that debt, and from then on,

I wanted to keep it all straight and risk-free. Glenn was the complete opposite and I loved him for it. Without him taking a risk on me, *Whispering Jack* may not have happened. I don't regret lending Glenn money, and he repaid me with interest, but I wish he hadn't kept his financial problems from me, because maybe I could have helped a little more.

In 1992 another huge opportunity came my way. I was offered the role of Jesus in a new musical production of *Jesus Christ Superstar*. Given that I met Jill while we were both working in a musical, the theatre has a very, very special place in my heart. I was very interested, but I was hesitant because I'm no actor. But when I looked harder at what I'd have to do I thought this role was less of a stretch than what I'd faced in *Pippin* and *Charlie Girl*. All I had to do was sing and emote. Sure, there was movement and stage awareness involved, as the role required the performer to be in specific places at exact parts of a song, but that didn't faze me because I'd done that when working on TV shows in the old days. It was the same, they'd get you to walk over to the left then walk over to the right and, after that, walk to the middle. The choreography wasn't too hard and the songs in *Superstar* were great. An added bonus was that David Hirschfelder was the musical director and also played keys, so I said, 'I'm in.'

All in all, *Superstar* was a fabulous experience; it was a great cast and I loved singing those songs. Apparently Lord Lloyd Webber, aka Andrew Lloyd Webber, is notoriously pedantic about how his songs are sung, which is funny because, as my experience in LRB showed, I'm the wrong person to pick if you want your songs sung in a particular way. I was well and truly done with being told how to sing; I do my versions and I add my own phrasing and notes. Richard Wherrett, our director, didn't try to control or restrict me at all, and he allowed my interpretations onto the album as well. *Superstar* was a massive, massive hit. I felt great. It was a rock opera in the round and the energy and stagecraft were awesome. I worked with an incredible cast, people like Kate Ceberano, Jon Stevens, John Waters, Angry Anderson and Russell Morris, they were all wonderful. I did good work on that production and my performance was well received. I just remember being continually motivated by the audience's reaction, they really liked it.

The producer of *Jesus Christ Superstar* was Harry M Miller. Harry was a colourful character who'd been in the game a long time. He had brought the musical *Hair* to Australia in 1970 and toured the Rolling Stones to Australia in the sixties. When the production of *Superstar* was on, Harry invited Jill and me and Glenn and Gaynor to his house in Sydney for lunch. Then another time we went out to his farm, where he owned all these beautiful polo ponies. Harry could ride really well, as he used to play polo. I was admiring the horses and he said, 'Do you want to have a ride?' I said, 'Yeah, I'll have a go,' so I hopped on and rode this polo pony through the bush. I'd never sat on a polo horse before, it was a beautiful horse, very responsive and I managed to have a long canter. It was a great, unexpected day and is now a lovely memory.

I don't ride horses anymore. We still own horses, but I haven't ridden for a few years now. I miss it. Jill got me into riding. When we moved to where we live now, Jill asked me if she could buy a horse. She grew up with horses, her sisters all had them as kids, plus we are on some acres so it made sense. Our property is right next to a bush track that goes down to the Yarra River and so it is perfect for riding. I could never say no to Jill, not that she needed my permission, so of course I said, 'Sure you can.' Jill bought this horse called Cisco. I'd never ridden before and about a year after she bought Cisco, she bought me a horse called Sonny, which was a cutting horse. Riding a cutting horse is like riding a bucking horse sideways. It's great fun and I got really into it and started competing. Cutting horses are trained to cut, or isolate, livestock from herds, they are incredible animals with amazing speed, intelligence and an ability to gallop in two strides then stop. It's unbelievable. I really enjoyed it and, with Jill, we developed this hobby together, me on my cutting horse and Jill in her Western dressage. Jill's a theatre girl, she's always loved dressing up, so she's got the girly chaps and pretty hat. But the best thing of all about having the horses was when we grabbed a bottle of wine and a round of cheese and rode off into the bush together. We'd spend the day or the afternoon riding, then find a spot for a picnic. It was a great escape for the two of us. Being with Jill is always a good thing.

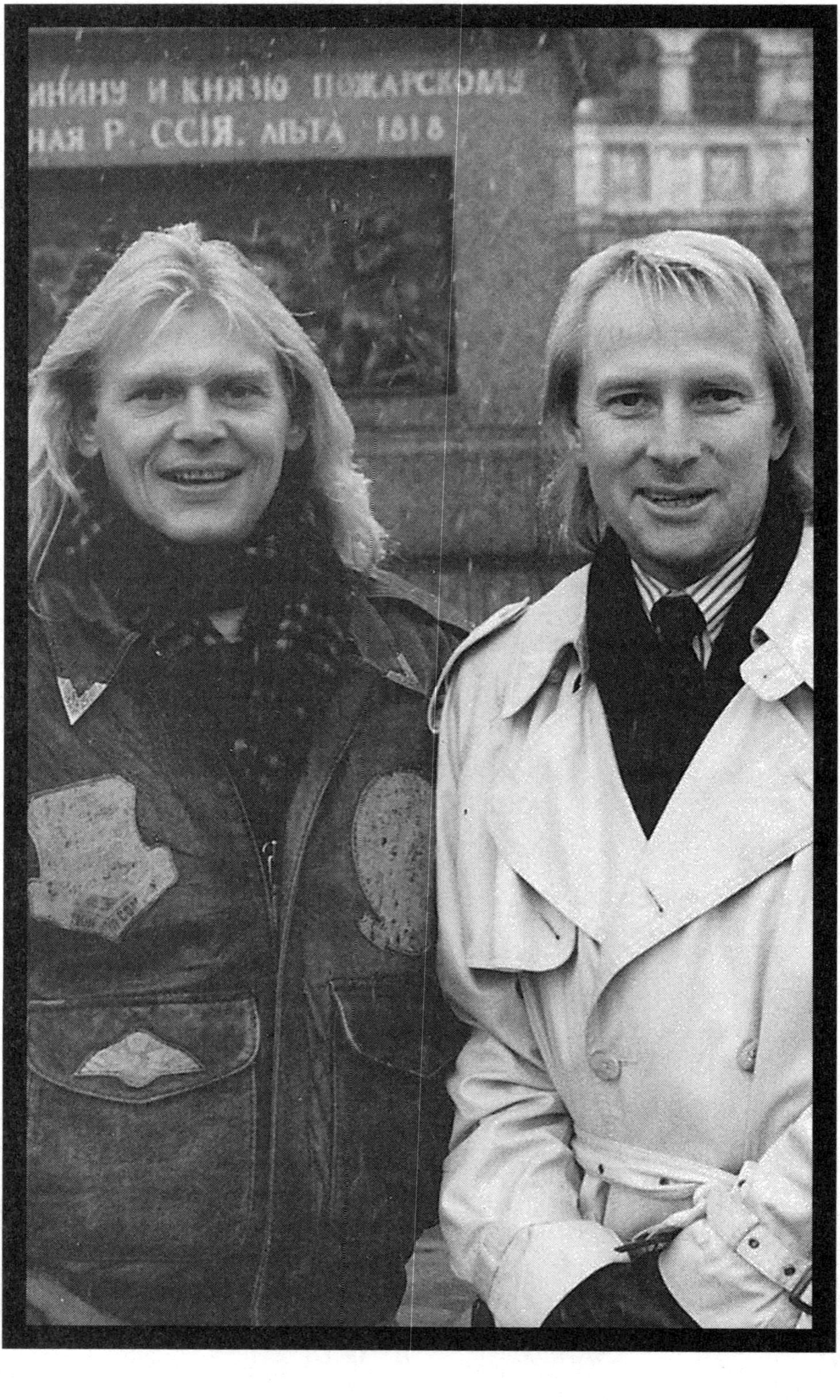
ИНИНУ И КНЯЗЮ ПОЖАРСКОМУ
НАЯ Р. ССIЯ. ЛѢТА 1818

CHAPTER 18

THE GOOD, THE BAD AND GOODBYES

Lately people don't recognise me much because I don't have the mullet, or even much hair, and the facial surgery and the disfigurement throw people too, but after *Whispering Jack* and the subsequent albums and projects, Jill and I couldn't go anywhere because it'd be mayhem. Even if Jill was out somewhere by herself and used her credit card, it was like, 'Oh, any relation to . . . ?' It became really difficult to go to public places. I am using the word 'difficult', but I'm so thankful for what happened and grateful that so many people cared about me and liked my work. But sometimes the attention was hard. Especially when we were out as a family.

When Robert and James were young kids, they didn't understand it. And as they got older, my fame could be a problem. For them. One time Rob got into trouble for something at school and when the teacher caught him he said, 'I don't like your father's music.' It was ridiculous, it's not Rob's fault I'm his father and his teacher's taste in music had nothing to do with him. I went and had a word with the teacher. I said, 'You just teach. I don't care whether you like my music or not, but you don't take it out on my son.'

I am really proud of my sons. It can't have been easy having a dad in the limelight and often away touring or performing. Jilly was always there for them and I was there when I could be. I always wanted to be, and it's all worked out in the long run. Both of my boys ended up finding their way into music. Rob had a great band and played at a couple of my gigs, and James was always interested in live audio engineering. He got a foothold into the game by helping Robert's band. Then, when he'd learned a bit there, he started working with my audio crew. My crew are very good, they gave him the nickname Lucky Diamond Jim and took him under their wing. James started at the bottom, he got the drinks first, then slowly he worked his way up. He fitted in really well, learned a lot and the crew love him. Now he has the skills and the experience to do it all himself and he is ready for that. James was recently offered a job, but he ended up having an operation so he couldn't take it, which is a shame. I know other opportunities will come along for him soon.

Jill, Robert, James and I would spend a lot of time in Port Douglas, sometimes with the Wheatleys. Sometimes I'd take three or four days off and we'd go camping. We'd pack the tent and some bread rolls and go and sleep by the river. We always made sure we camped upstream because there are no crocodiles upstream. There might be a couple of freshwater crocodiles, but no salties. Saltwater crocs frighten the bloody life out of me, I've seen a lot of them and they really are dangerous. Over the years we've also made some very good friends up there. Gary 'Spike' Ashcroft and his wife, Julie, are wonderful people. Spike takes me fishing a lot. We go out in a tinny looking for barramundi and sometimes we charter a boat and go out to the reef. We'll catch a coral trout, knock the sides off, cook it and eat it. It's beautiful being out on the water away from it all.

Australia is a big and amazing country. I haven't seen it all, but I am lucky to have seen a good bit of it. Back in the sixties and early seventies, Col Joye, the first Australian pop performer to reach number one on the local charts, and his band the Joy Boys, used to tour across Australia on a train incessantly. Col was a lovely man, and back when I was starting out I did some work with him and the Joy Boys on one of their train tours. I loved it. Travelling with Col was what inspired the *Jack of Hearts* tour that we put together to promote the album *Romeo's Heart*. Logistically the tour was a bit of work, but the plan was to travel by train for most of it and play at some of the outback towns whose communities often miss out on big live music acts. These were places we'd never toured before. I was lucky that I got a cabin to myself on the train because everyone else had to share. Despite that, the band were all on board with the plan. We had a bar car, and the audiences at the shows were great. A crowd would meet us at the train station and then they'd be there the next day to wave goodbye when we left. That tour strengthened my view that I didn't need to chase work in America or Europe – we had enough work to do here in Australia, and it was such fun doing it.

That train tour was one of the highlights of my career, but there have been so many great moments that I know when I finish this book I will kick myself for forgetting one or ten things I could have shared. And every step of the way Glenn Wheatley was there, backing me and cheering me on. But then my manager and dear friend made a big mistake that cost him dearly.

Glenn was caught up in a scam by a British businessman who targeted some of Australia's rich and famous. People like Paul Hogan and John 'Strop' Cornell were also lured in by the bloke. The trouble was, Glenn wasn't rich. He had hit some tough times financially when his nightclub business failed, and so the offer to help him with his financial difficulties and minimise his tax sounded good. But it wasn't good. Glenn was investigated by the Australian Tax Office and it took a few years, but he finally went to court in 2007 and pled guilty to tax evasion. The judge sentenced him to two-and-a-half years' imprisonment with a minimum of fifteen months to serve. We were all devastated. It was crushing for Gaynor and their kids and soul-destroying for Glenn but, as Gaynor says, he did the wrong thing, took it on the chin and did his time.

I loved that man deeply. I loved him very much and he was a good friend. He was always honest with me and, yes, we could argue and disagree, but he usually won most arguments because he would eventually have me see reason. I run on emotion. But, other times, I would win, because I would argue from an artistic point of view and he could understand that, because he was a musician too, at one point. Glenn knew he made a very bad error of judgement and it cost him ten months in prison and damaged his reputation. He survived the ordeal, though he got a bit of a stirring while he was inside – he told me he had a fair few threats from the other inmates because of who he was. He spent a bit of time in solitary confinement because of those threats so it was definitely tough going. I went to visit him while he was in there, I wanted to show him my support. He knew I was there for him. And Jill and I were there for Gaynor and the kids.

While Glenn was in prison, I stopped working. I took almost two years off. I spent time with Jill and the kids, I rode the horses a lot. Not working gave me a moment to sit back and count my chickens. It made me reflect on the important things in life and, for me, they are most certainly Jill, James and Rob. They are everything. But every father is going to say that about his family.

When Glenn was released from prison on 19 May 2008 he had to serve five months of home detention, but he was ready to get back to work and redeem himself. It didn't take him long to say to me, 'I think we can do this auditorium and that venue.' And I said, 'I'm in.' There was no game plan as such, it was more a case of keep on keeping on. I was ready to get back on the horse, so to speak.

Looking back over all these years I sometimes have to pinch myself because I was able to work with some amazing people. Sometimes I think, *Did I really work with him or her? Wow!* I can't list them all because that would almost be another book, but there are a few real stand-outs.

Ray Charles was incredible. He was just a lovely, lovely guy and he's one of my favourite singers. We were booked to perform at the opening of Crown Casino in Melbourne on 8 May 1997. Anthony Warlow and Kylie Minogue were also on the bill. It was a bit difficult organising a time to meet and rehearse with Ray. I tried. It got to two days out from the performance and I still hadn't met him, and his manager was being a little tricky. When I finally met Ray I said, 'Hi mate, I'm so pleased to meet you, I'm such a big fan, I love what you do,' and then I added, 'Your manager has been very difficult to deal with.' He replied, 'John, the artist has to do the figuring.' I was a bit puzzled and I said, 'Okay,' and then Ray said, 'Whatever you want to do, we'll do.' The manager was fine after that and Ray started calling me Jack, which I absolutely loved: 'Hey Jack.' The show was fantastic and I was honoured to share a stage with such a legend.

About a year later, Robert came into the lounge room and said, 'Dad, there's some guy on the phone who's saying he's Ray Charles.' And it was *the* Ray Charles, he had called to see if I could come to his concert. I was so taken aback by his offer I said, 'Oh, oh I can't Ray, I can't because I've got uh, an appointment with my wife.' I felt such a fool, but I couldn't have stood it, I was beside myself with nerves. I mean, Ray Charles was personally inviting me to his show and I didn't have the courage to accept his invitation. Maybe he might have asked me to get up onstage and perform with him, and that would have been okay. I can cope with being onstage. In all honesty, I couldn't go because I feel a bit funny in crowds. I can get up onstage in front of 100,000 people and I'm fine. I'll get nervous beforehand, but the nerves go when I sing. But offstage, as an audience member, I'm beside myself standing among a crowd of people. I am so uncomfortable and I can't stay there.

Talking about big crowds, I did the AFL grand finals three or four times and I waived a fee the first couple of times. I thought *Oh, what a pleasure. What an absolute honour!* Then I found out how much they were paying the other singers and entertainers. I'm pretty sure I was never paid anything like that. One year Michael Gudinski asked me to perform at the grand final and I said no. Nobody turns down performing at a grand final but having done it a couple of times already, I knew all too well that it's a tough gig. Firstly, it's in broad fucking daylight, you're on this tiny little stage and there's a football field between you and the thousands of people in the audience you're trying to rev up. It's hard to make it special in any other way than noise. I said, 'Michael, I'm not doing it. I don't want to do it.' True to form, Michael wouldn't take 'no' for an answer. I held my ground and then Michael started pleading with me. 'Please John, please do it.' No, I just didn't want to do it. But Gudinski got me anyway. I ended up doing it only because he had already made the announcement. The stage was set up in one of the stadium races, which meant I sang with my back to lots of people. Sorry folks, I hated that. Otherwise, it wasn't too bad. When we performed 'You're the Voice', a troupe of bagpipe players marched out underneath us, which was a bit of fun. For the last couple of choruses, Jimmy Barnes and Mark Seymour, from Hunters & Collectors, joined me and the band onstage.

That reminds me of another Gudinski story. Years ago, Michael and Sue and Jill and I were on holidays in Queensland and each night we'd play Scrabble for hours and hours and drink red wine while we did. It was fantastic. One night we were chatting and playing Scrabble and quaffing red. Michael had recently signed Kylie Minogue and we were talking about that. I said to him, 'Michael, can I just say something that I think would really work for Kylie?'

And he said, 'Yeah, of course'.

'Okay. Look, Kylie is so pretty and so gorgeous and so tiny, I reckon you should get her to dress up as a showgirl. Get her in feathers and high heels, you know, the whole outfit.' Of course I was referencing Jilly and her showgirl days.

Michael listened to what I said that night and we didn't speak about it again. The next thing I know Kylie is touring *Showgirl: The Greatest Hits Tour*. I never managed to ask Michael if that idea came from our Scrabble chat and now I never will have the chance. We miss you, Gudinski.

Back to tricky managers, Whitney Houston's was also a challenge. We all got the message from him that if we came across Whitney in the corridors at the Entertainment Centre, we had to look away. Under no circumstances were we to look directly at Whitney. Of course, I couldn't wait to come across her. I left my dressing-room door open and I was constantly looking out to see if she was coming, then as soon as I saw her, I yelled out, 'G'day Whitney, how are you going?' Whitney was fine about it. She was a fucking awesome singer. To that manager's credit, at the end of the concert he told me I was a good singer, he said, 'I like your voice.' To which I said, 'Thank you.'

Working with Olivia Newton-John was like being with an angel most of the time, she was just gorgeous. She used to tell me that I was her favourite singer, and to hear that coming from her was lovely. I loved Olivia, I'd loved her since I watched her on *Bandstand* and *The Go!! Show*, before I was a professional singer, so to be able to spend any time at all with her was a blessing. Olivia cared about everybody and she was very natural. When we did the opening of the Sydney Olympics, 'Dare to Dream' was the song. I had to give her my hand because she had this long dress on, which was difficult to walk in. So I gave her my hand and we walked down some stairs with the crowd on either side, the main stage was down the front. We made it down the stairs okay and when we were walking through the crowd some girls caught my eye, they were singing out, 'We love you.' I ran over to say hello and in doing so, let go of Olivia's hand. Without me to steady her, Olivia almost lost her balance and went over. This was live television – 3.7 billion people were watching and I nearly caused Olivia Newton-John to fall down in front of them. She steadied herself and kept singing, but I felt like a bit of a dick.

When Olivia, Anthony Warlow and I toured *The Main Event* in 1998, Anthony would often mess with me by holding a note a little longer than was necessary. He was a classically trained singer, he wasn't a smoker and if I had to do a harmony with him, sometimes, not always, he'd hold the note just that little bit longer so I'd have to stop and take a breath. I don't know whether he knows I know, but he got a kick out of it, which was fine, I can live with that. We all had a good time together but Olivia was special. She was a very gentle, genuine person. She had a wicked sense of humour, too. I'd say something filthy and she'd crack up, not to encourage me but just because she couldn't help herself. She was a lovable person and there wasn't a bad bone in her body. Olivia was an inspiration to the end.

That reminds me of the time I sang with another of Australia's favourites, Kylie Minogue. I've sung with her a couple of times, she's gorgeous, but the show we did in East Timor was ... interesting. Alongside Bernard 'Doc' Neeson, Glenn and I were a big part of organising the *Tour of Duty – Concert for the Troops* that happened on 21 December 1999. The concert was to show support for the Australian soldiers leading the United Nations–backed International Force East Timor (INTERFET), after a very violent referendum that overwhelmingly voted for independence. The concert was going to be broadcast in Australia live from Dili Stadium. Kylie was on the bill and so were the Angels (with Doc upfront), James Blundell, Gina Jeffreys, The Living End, the Dili Allstars and the RMC Army Band and army performers. Roy Slaven and HG Nelson hosted (aka John Doyle and Greig Pickhaver).

Doc is not with us anymore to chat about this, but when we were discussing the details, I suggested not including 'Am I Ever Gonna See Your Face Again' in their set, because the audience response to that song and that lyric is 'No way, get fucked, fuck off.' I said, 'Mate, we're going to be live on Australian TV so please don't do that song.' Doc spat the dummy and said, 'How dare you tell me what to sing?' I understood because it was one of their biggest songs, but I was worried they'd stop the broadcast back in Australia. I bargained with him and said, 'If you hold it back until after the live cross, then I'll come onstage and I'll bring Kylie and we can all sing it together.' Fortunately, Doc saw reason. When the live television recording finished, true to my word, I got Kylie up onstage with me and Doc, and we all sang together as the rain fell. When we'd sung the words asking am I ever gonna see your face again, I put the microphone up to Kylie's mouth and she sang, 'No way, get fucked, fuck off' along with the 4000-strong crowd in front of Major General Peter Cosgrove, José Ramos-Horta and Xanana Gusmão. It was fantastic! Kylie did it and I loved her for it. She's got a good sense of humour and it's wonderful seeing her career going so well. She is a champion.

Working with Tom Jones was mind-blowing. We did a ten-show concert tour of Perth, Sydney, Melbourne and Brisbane in 2005 called *Together in Concert*. Tom is a gentleman and a pleasure to be around. I was so affected by his voice, even as a kid growing up I loved him. At the age of eighty-four the man can still sing his arse off. He'd go on and do his set, then I'd go on and do mine. Then we'd both sing together. When the show was over, he'd put his arms around me and say, 'Come on, let's go and have a drink and a cigar.' Most nights after the show Tom and I would go to a restaurant to drink and eat and smoke and he'd tell me all these lovely stories. He told me one time he was sitting in the bathroom chatting to Elvis while Elvis was having a shower after he'd performed. Elvis was a big Tom Jones fan too, and there he was singing in the shower, doing his Elvis thing, while Tom listened. I was amazed that Tom got to meet Elvis, let alone hear him sing so up-close and naturally. The King apparently asked Tom what he thought and Tom said, 'Great song, Elvis.' I asked Tom what song it was and he said, 'I can't remember!' I mean, Elvis Presley was singing to you from the shower and you can't remember the song? I think that would be an unforgettable experience, but after hearing some of Tom's stories, it's clear he's had a lot of those.

Talking about Tom Jones, I got a lovely phone call the other day. It was a video message from Jimmy Barnes and Tom Jones telling me to get well and kick arse. They told me that they love and miss me. It was wonderful, and then the next day,

Jill got a message from Tom asking me to give him a ring. So I did, and Tom and I spent half an hour chatting. He asked me how I was and what was going on. Tom is an absolute total and utter professional. I got to tell him I love him, which I do. The other day I read a critic's review of his gig in Perth, and the guy raved about it, he said it was fantastic. Apparently he didn't miss a note, which doesn't surprise me at all. The man may be in his mid-eighties, but he is still the best.

Sometimes the magic doesn't happen on a tour and there is nothing much you can do about it. Stevie Nicks and I toured together for a few shows in Australia and New Zealand in 2006 but it wasn't quite the right billing. I never got to sing with Stevie. The show opened with Vanessa Carlton, I was on next and then it was Stevie's turn. Someone told me that at the Brisbane show a few people left halfway through Stevie's set and she wasn't impressed. There was no communication between 'her people' and 'my people' at all. I sent her a humungous bunch of flowers and I never heard back, so they may never have reached her. Years later there was a bit of a media beat-up to promote a book, saying I was sacked from the tour. Glenn put paid to that. I wasn't sacked. But apparently Stevie did say, 'Nobody told me I was working with Australia's Frank Sinatra!' I've never been sure whether I should be flattered by that comment or not. Anyway, Frank's dead, I'm not, but I'm closer than I'd like, I'll get there.

One time, Jill and I were on our way to Canada, we were going there to ski. We were standing at the airport check-in getting our boarding passes and, out of the blue, this woman runs straight at me and wraps her arms around me. She said 'John Farnham!' and I said, 'Hello.' Then realised who she was. The woman said, 'I'm Celine, I love your voice.' It was Celine Dion! All I could say was, 'Shouldn't I be saying that to you?' I really am a big fan of Celine's. That day in the airport we didn't have time to chat because she had to get on her flight, so I got that hug and then she was off on her way.

When she was doing some shows here in Melbourne in 2018, she asked me to get up onstage and sing 'You're the Voice' with her and I did. It was amazing. She even had the bagpipes ready. Before I left the stage Celine was so gracious and she told the crowd that 'You're the Voice' is one of her favourite songs and that I was one of her favourite singers. Wow! Being told that by one of the world's best singers is so very flattering. When her documentary, *I Am Celine Dion*, came out, I was flattered all over again. That show in Melbourne was a very special night, and what a beautiful voice Celine has. The pitch, range, strength and power of it is amazing. Celine is a great singer. I know she's had some health battles too, and I send her all my love.

I've got up onstage with various people over the years. It really is an honour to do that. Coldplay is one of the bands who I've sung with. Coldplay are good guys and their lead singer, Chris Martin, is a very nice man. Like I've said, you've got to have an ego to do what we do but I haven't had any trouble with anyone, everyone has been lovely.

I did these shows with Lionel Richie in 2014. It was billed as 'One Stage, Two Music Legends – All the Hits – All Night Long'. For a few people the night was far too long, because the turnaround between my set and Lionel's dragged on. Lionel was a reasonable bloke and after one of the shows Paul Dainty, the promoter who brought him to Australia, took me, Lionel, Glenn and Gaynor out to dinner. Jill wasn't there that night. It was pretty late by the time we'd eaten and when Lionel left the restaurant I could see him out the window. He turned back and beckoned to me. I said to Glenn, 'I've been beckoned, I'd better go.' I went out to chat to Lionel and he started talking about the show and said, 'People are leaving before I come on, so I think if you drop a couple of songs that'd help and I'd have time to get on.' I said, 'I'm sorry, I can't do that. This is a double bill, we've each been allocated ninety minutes.' He mentioned again that people were leaving the concert before he started and I told him why. I said, 'Look, you guys are doing a forty-minute turnaround, that's forty minutes between me going off and you coming on. That's why people are going home. If your guys are having trouble getting set up, my boys will help you if you like.' Long story cut short, Lionel got his guys to do the turnaround quicker and everything worked out. Apparently Lionel said to Glenn, 'I'm a crooner, John's a singer.' I don't know about that, but you can't make an audience wait. Just get on with it. The oldest trick in the book is to dawdle as long as possible if the act before you is any good, to put some distance between you, and I was lucky because the audience were really good, so my sets were firing.

I've been so very lucky, I've had some amazing audiences. And when they are reacting to what you're doing, it kicks you on. It spurs you to be better. My audiences gave so much back, it made me want to bleed for them. Every night I wanted to go out and give everything I had for them, I wanted to leave everything on the stage.

The Fire Fight Australia fundraising concert held in Sydney in February 2020 was a good one. The audience were terrific. The line-up was impressive with Olivia, Queen and Adam Lambert, Daryl Braithwaite, Hilltop Hoods, k.d. lang and Amy Shark just some of the performers who'd donated their time. Comedian Celeste Barber emceed the event. It was the best possible cause I could think of after so much of the country had been burnt by bushfires and so many people had lost their homes. Singer Mitch Tambo got in touch not long before and asked if I'd mind if he sang 'You're the Voice' at his shows. And I said, 'No! I don't mind at all, I think it's great.' Then I added, 'Why don't you come and do it with us at the Fire Fight concert?' Mitch jumped at the opportunity. Then I got a call from Queen guitarist Brian May, I don't know where he got my number from, and he said, 'Can I play "You're the Voice" with you at the Fire concert?' No-one would hesitate . . . 'Absolutely, yes!' He asked if I still did it in the same key and when I told him I did he said, 'Great, I'll be there.' On the night, he knew the song inside out, back to front and upside down.

It blew me away when Mitch sang in the Gamilaraay language. It really worked for me. It sounded great and the audience got into it as well, which was fantastic. I enjoyed that he wanted to do it. Anyone can sing that song if they want to, that's fine. I don't have any control of it, but to use my recording of it commercially, as an ad or something like that, I won't let that happen. The only time I allowed it to be used like that was for the Indigenous Voice to Parliament referendum. When I was approached I said yes immediately, because in my mind really, what's it going to hurt? How does letting a group of Aboriginal and Torres Strait Islander representatives offering advice on government laws and policies that directly affect them hurt non-Indigenous people? I mean, it's not going to cost anybody anything. I only wish more people had voted yes.

Olivia sang with me at the Fire Fight concert. That was really special. We sang 'Two Strong Hearts' and I couldn't help teasing her about her recent damehood. I introduced her as Dame Olivia Newton-John and Her Highness, but more importantly, as my friend. Olivia came back at the end of the show and sang with me, Brian May and Mitch Tambo on 'You're the Voice'. I think that was the last time Olivia sang or performed onstage, and probably the last time I did too. A month later the Covid pandemic shut everything down.

Mum and Dad always came to my gigs. Same with Jeanie Jam Roll, Uncle Alan, Jackie and Stephen, they always came to any opening night in Melbourne. I always made sure to get them a private box up the top at Rod Laver Arena, or wherever I was working, so they could sit down and relax and enjoy the show. They always loved it, and it was really lovely to have them in the audience. Having them there meant a lot. From when I was a kid, family has been everything and, no matter what, the support my family gave me never wavered.

Losing my mum was devastating. Fairly soon after we bought our house, we bought the house behind us and moved Mum and Dad in there. We were lucky to have the money to be able to look after them, but it ended all too quickly. Rose was very, very sick for a long time before she died. She came up to Port Douglas to holiday with us and she got sick while she was up there, but she didn't say anything to anybody at first, because she didn't want to ruin the trip. She'd been living with bad emphysema for a long time, but she got sicker and then it turned into pneumonia while we were holidaying. Her condition deteriorated, and she had to go in an ambulance to Cairns. She stayed in hospital in Cairns for over six months, she was too sick to move. We rented a flat for Dad just up the road from the hospital so he could visit her, and we flew back and forth all the time around work. Eventually Mum recovered and came home, but she was never really right after that. She really suffered in her last few years. Mum was always a shallow breather, she had terrible lungs, and then to top it all off she got shingles. She was real sparkly in her youth, my mum, but she was never robust in her later years. I miss dear Rosie. She was always on my side, and I loved her so very much.

Dad had a stroke before Mum was really sick and he was in a wheelchair. He was okay, he was still able to talk and tell jokes. I take after my dad in lots of ways, not just whistling, and neither of us ever shut up. He was a very funny guy with a great sense of humour. I still come out with the occasional dad joke. When he had the stroke, he spoke to the doctor and said, 'Will I be able to play the piano after this?' And the doctor said, 'Probably not.' Dad said to him, 'That's alright, I couldn't play it before either.' Boom-tish!

That was typical of my old man, he was the king of dad jokes. I said a similar thing when I had my cancer operation. It was a twelve-hour operation and I had to sign a form so that they could give me a blood transfusion if I needed it. I said to the bloke with the form, 'Can you go and find a piano player and take their blood, because I've always wanted to play the piano.' The guy laughed his arse off.

We lost Jeanie a few years back. Jeanie Jam Roll and I were still very close, I loved her with all my heart. I really do regret being unkind to my little sister when we were young – it was normal brother/sister stuff, but I miss her now she's gone. When my father had his stroke, Jeanie took on caring for him unflinchingly, she was very brave, and it was hard work but she was equal to the task. Old Jam Roll had worked as a florist and she loved it, but when my father had his stroke she quit floristry to look after him. Then Mum got sick and, for a while until Mum died, she was caring for both of them, which really restricted her. It was around that time that she developed agoraphobia. Then she got a melanoma, but she neglected it. I called up my doctor, Doctor Morris, and even though he wasn't doing any house calls I begged him to see her because she wouldn't leave the house. He did, and he diagnosed the sore on her leg as a skin cancer. We managed to talk Jeanie into going into hospital but then she refused any of the treatment. The cancer grew and grew and finally it entered her bloodstream. If she had dealt with it earlier, she would still be with us today. Saying goodbye to people you love is the hardest thing anyone can ever do. I've said too many of those goodbyes lately.

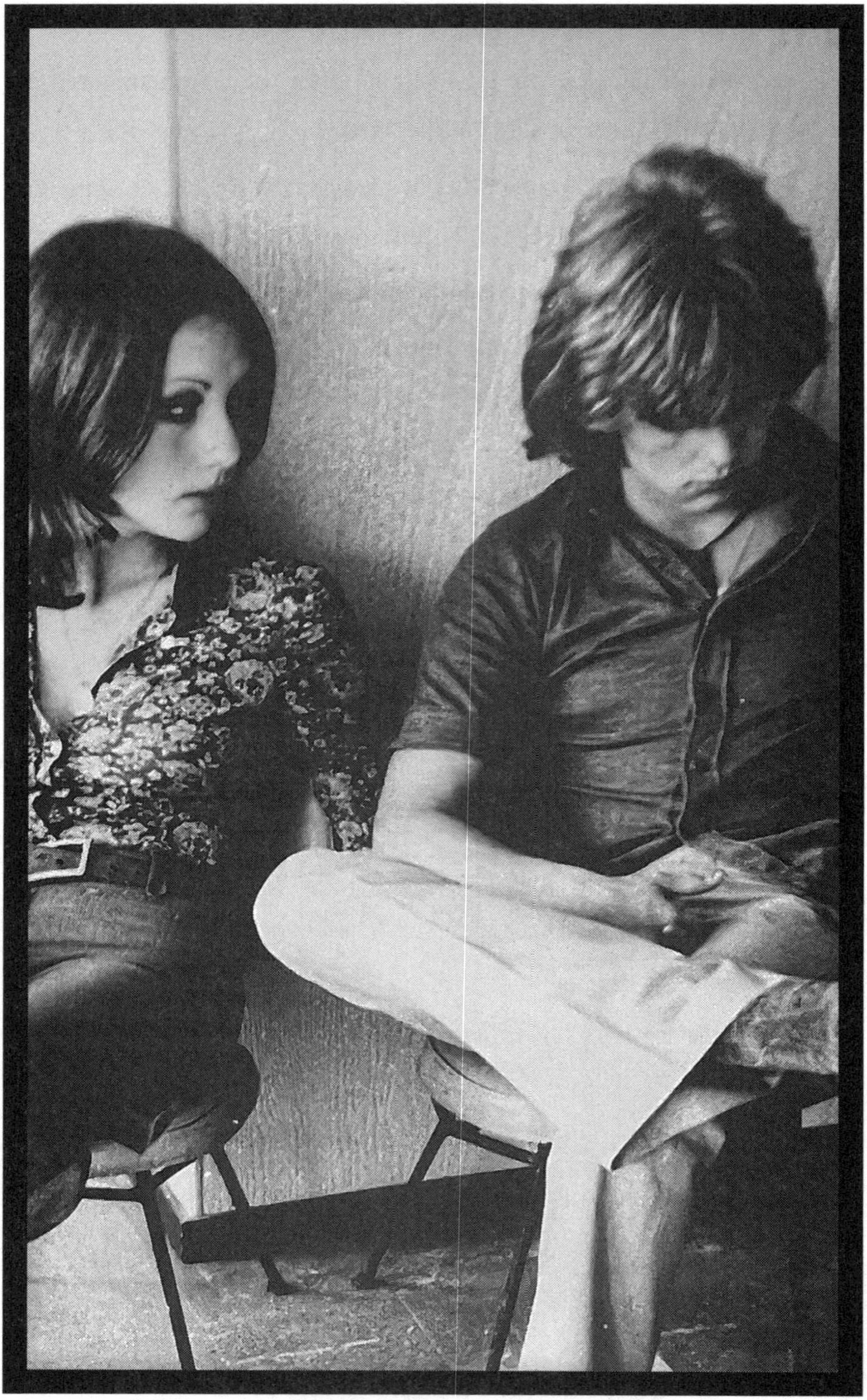

CHAPTER 19

YOU ONLY LIVE ONCE
A WORD FROM JILL

Loving and living with John has been an interesting life, and mostly a whole lot of fun. Yes, there's been some highs and lows, but all marriages go through those patches, anyone telling you different isn't telling you the truth. We'd have lots of fun, though, John and I.

I think the eighties were my favourite era. We were a bit naughty, but fun naughty, if you know what I mean. We did a lot of travelling in that period, too, which was great. John did go through a cocky stage. Years and years and years ago, he got too big for his boots. For a brief time he was a bit full of himself, a bit 'Aren't I fabulous!' That was an interesting period and I had to pull him down a few pegs there. That wasn't the John I know well, but it's not surprising it happened. If people tell you long enough and often enough that you're absolutely fabulous, you start to believe it. And, then, if you believe the hype, you get big-headed, cocksure.

At that time John had been on the road for months touring and everyone would do everything for him, he didn't have to think about anything other than singing. I was at home with Robert and James for a lot of it, keeping the family home going and doing all the small things you have to do every day when you have two kids and pets and a life. When John would come home from a big tour, I'd give him a few days to settle down and then I'd say, 'Can you please put the rubbish out? Oh, and while you're out there, pick up the dog shit in the yard, please.' You know, just standard home life. 'You want a cup of tea? Yeah, great, kettle is over there.' And, 'Please put your dirty washing in the laundry and then go and clean the toilet.' I've had to be like that, otherwise he would have been hopeless to live with. He was bad enough sometimes, anyhow.

So there's been things that were hard, sometimes it was a struggle but we got through it. Mostly we've had fun, enjoyed ourselves, travelled and experienced a lot together. We both adore our boys and have loved watching them find partners.

I suppose, like most parents, all you want and hope for is that your children are happy. It's strange talking about the boys. We have been so protective of them. We just wanted to make sure they had a normal childhood but now they are men. Of course, as a mother I am ferociously protective like a lioness and always will be, but I am so happy that Robert and Melissa found each other and to see Rob so happy is wonderful.

Tessa and James have been together for sixteen years. Tessa is like a daughter to me and John adores her with his whole heart. Tessa has been such a source of strength for James and us too. With John in hospital and throughout this ordeal, Rob, Mel, James and Tessa have been there for us both and I will never be able to thank them enough.

John and I have made the most of things. You only live once, and that's what we'd always tell each other. I hope my boys do the same.

It's a good life and we've made great friendships. John and I, Glenn and Gaynor, the four of us were a great team. We were like peas in a pod. We used to laugh a lot, we had a lot of fun. And when the boys were busy working, Gaynor and I used to go off together and get into trouble. A lot of trouble. We certainly made the most of things.

When John isn't working, sometimes he can get a little bit depressed. Before he was diagnosed with cancer, it had been two years since he had performed. The last time was at that Fire Fight Australia concert in 2020, which was wonderful. But once he gets a bit down, he doesn't want to do anything. I can't go there with him, I have to give out a bit of tough love. Over the years I've had to be strong. I've had to be a wife, a mother, a psychiatrist, a doctor, I've had to be all those things in one. I've had to be strong and bossy to keep the family together, to keep moving forward, and I have done that because I love John and I love my family. John is a classic Cancerian, he likes to walk sideways and go around everything, rather than face any issues head-on. To this day he acts like that when he's faced with a tough decision or situation. He always beats around the bush rather than deal with it and then, of course, that just makes a situation worse for him.

John knew there was something wrong. He had a big white mass on the inside of his cheek and you could physically see it. For several months I was saying to him, 'Let's go see about that thing in your mouth,' and he'd say, 'No, it's alright, it's alright, it's alright.' He kept putting if off and putting it off.

I pleaded with him to go see a doctor and finally he did. In August 2022 he was diagnosed with oral cancer. The doctor took one look at it and said, 'It's cancer. We're going to have to take it out.' My natural inclination was to not waste any time. I figured the sooner it was out, the better. John would have put it off, but we'd just watched his sister die from untreated cancer, so I wasn't going to mess around waiting. He had to get it done right away and I pushed him to act quickly.

Of course, John was scared going in for surgery. I was scared too, but I had work to do, I had to plan as much as possible for whatever outcome we were faced with. It was difficult, and a few times there I was really frightened because his surgeon at the Royal Melbourne Hospital thought they were going to lose him. He got through the surgery okay but then, when he was recovering, he fell over and broke his back. It was the worst time because he had to go back into hospital and they had him on such strong painkillers that he totally freaked out and had delusions. He was so distraught, several times we had to reassure him that he was in hospital and that they were looking after him and not harming him.

John got through that and then he had some trouble with his blood work and then, just after Christmas, he started a course of radiotherapy and he didn't want to eat. He had no interest in food and no appetite, so the body weight fell off him. He got down to sixty-three kilograms, which is very small for him. Because of the treatment, he lost his bottom teeth, they had to take them out. And, just for the record, they didn't take his jaw. I know lots of people think that's what happened, but in the end they removed the cancer from his cheek and they also scraped his jaw to make sure it hadn't gotten into his bones. Thankfully the cancer wasn't in his bones, which was great news, and so he's still got his bottom jaw, even though the radiation has messed that up a little bit. In hospital they were feeding him through a tube in his stomach, which was pretty grim. I started taking in my home cooking. Things I knew John would like. He would eat a couple of mouthfuls and that would be it, he wouldn't be able to manage any more. For a while there, it felt like one thing on top of another for John. It was a traumatic time for all of us, but we got through it. Now he's back to eating, which is a good sign, but he can't open his mouth very far, so it's hard.

After that bad run with John, James, our youngest son, got sick with diverticular disease, which is an inflammation in the large intestine that can become a medical emergency. James was really sick and ended up having part of his large intestine removed. After the surgery he had a colostomy bag for a few months. When the doctors went in to do the reversal surgery, they opened James up and discovered a lot of scarring in his gut. They decided they had to give his digestive system time to rest and recover, so they gave him another colostomy bag but this time in his lower intestine. It wasn't the news James wanted to hear, and having two members of the family battling ill heath was stressful. The doctors are hoping they'll be able to take James off the bag later this year. And I am hoping his health issues back off and he can get back to living his life.

For a period there I was thinking to myself, *I'm going to wake up one of these days and it's all going to be roses and sunshine and wonderful again. I'll wake up and all our worries will be over.* It was bad enough to see John go through cancer, but to see James going through his health issues was almost worse, because James is our son and your kids aren't meant to get sick like that when they are young and just starting out.

Earlier this year there was light in all the darkness. In February, Robert, our eldest son, married his partner, Mel. Mel and Robert are a great couple and Mel is a wonderful daughter-in-law. The wedding day was fantastic. It was also John's first public outing after his surgery, which I'll admit was a bit daunting for him. John doesn't look bad. He definitely looks different, but he doesn't look bad. After getting over that hurdle of venturing out, he's gained a bit of confidence in his appearance but he still doesn't like going out. Although, let's face it, that's nothing new, he never did like going out. But being seen by everyone at the wedding was a big step forward for him, mentally and physically. It was a beautiful wedding, despite being freezing cold and rainy, it was a lot of fun and everyone looked great.

When John was going through cancer, there was quite a bit of media attention about his diagnosis and treatment, and the interest shocked him. He was really overawed by the public's outpouring of good wishes. It surprised him, in a lovely way. John's still very modest about his success and he's felt that way for a long time now. He can't believe that people care so much about him.

I don't know if John will sing again. It just depends. Because of the radiation, that whole side of his face is rock hard. The flesh, the muscle, the tendons, none of it is supple. The surgeons need to work out how to loosen it all, so we have to be patient. He's disappointed, naturally, because he may not be up on a stage again and he loved that. He absolutely loved performing, but we'll just have to wait and see. Having said that, the doctors have given him exercises to do. The exercises are to loosen his mouth, and he does them . . . intermittently. It's hard for me to not nag – I mean, it's not strenuous, it's not like he has to go out and run a bloody marathon or even a hundred yards. If it means he'll be able to sing again or even eat food like a normal person again, then do the bloody exercises! But that's not John. Like I said, he's a Cancerian, so he'll pretend it'll fix itself rather than tackling it head-on. And to be fair, the exercises hurt. The faces he pulls when he does them make me realise how much pain he's in when he opens his mouth too far. But I think the desire to sing will push him to keep trying.

At the end of the day, it is what it is. John is very lucky that they got onto the cancer early enough. A lot of people aren't so lucky. John Blackman, who we knew from *Hey Hey It's Saturday*, wasn't so lucky. He ultimately died from a heart attack only recently, but he really suffered through his battle with oral cancer.

There's always someone worse off. That's the way you've got to think about it and it's what we tell each other. We are lucky. You've got to keep going forward, otherwise you're going backward. Besides, I'm crossing my fingers for grandbabies – soon, I hope, before we get too bloody old and we can't get down and play with them. I love kids and so does John. Aside from that, which we have absolutely no control over, I'd love to travel again and maybe go back to Africa.

We've loved going to Africa over the years. We first went to Africa on our twenty-fifth wedding anniversary and travelling there has given us so many wonderful memories, it's such an amazing continent. We want to take the whole family on holiday there. James and his partner, Tessa, have come with us before, but Rob and Mel never have.

It sounds tough, but I really think John needs to get off his arse and do things. Booking a holiday will give him something to look forward to. Something to work toward. There are a lot of things that John is missing. Because he hasn't been working, that means his band aren't working with him, so that's made him feel guilty. There were a lot of people on the road with him, so he employed a lot of people and he feels responsible for them. But it's hard because, after losing Glenn, he's lost a lot of his inspiration. Glenn was a massive motivator. He was a very positive source for John in getting him out there and performing. The two of them were hilarious. Glenn always insisted on walking John to the stage but his sense of direction wasn't much better than John's. It didn't matter which venue, somehow they'd get lost walking from John's dressing-room to the stage, causing everyone to panic. And the squabbling. They were like a pair of bickering biddies. They didn't actually *argue*, they never yelled at each other, but they used to have 'words'. And whenever they were having 'words', Gaynor and I would sit there, roll our eyes and say, 'Here we go again!'

There are things John needs to do and things we both want to do. Like I said, we'd often say to each other, 'You only live once' as we seized a moment or went on an adventure. Now, more than ever, we have to embrace that. John is lucky. He's alive. And I am lucky because he is still here. After fifty-one years of marriage, we've still got life to live.

CHAPTER 20

THANK YOU

There's nothing like getting out there, onstage. Whether it be in front of ten people or 10,000 people or 100,000 people, it's always the same for me. I get toey, I get nervous and then when I start singing and I get feedback, it's like a drug. It's like life's blood, it's incredible. I've been so lucky with my audiences, there are people out there who know every lick, every split, every spit of every note of every song. I'm terrible, I forget lyrics, even lyrics of songs that I've been singing for years. I'd need a teleprompter down the front these days because if I stuff up one breath, I'll get grief from the audience. Deservedly so.

My audiences are normally with me all the way, and if they aren't, I'll fight to win them over. If I am performing to 100 people and ninety-nine of them are on their feet but one of them is sitting, that's the one I work to get involved. You've got to win them over. It's not an ego thing, it's a performer's thing. I don't think there's a performer on the planet who doesn't try to win over that one person who's sitting on their hands. And when you succeed in engaging that person, it's absolutely fantastic. Like I said at the start of this book, there's no doubt I have an ego. My ego is obese and over the years I've been satisfactorily fed. I love being a singer and a performer and so now, after surviving mouth cancer, I might have to learn how to tap dance, because I don't know how to do anything else but sing.

I was diagnosed with cancer in August 2022. Like Jill said, I had this thing that was on the inside of my cheek and Jill pushed me to get it checked out. It was a tumour and it was cancerous. Cancer doesn't discriminate, but as soon as I was told the results, I couldn't help thinking it was my own fault. I smoked very heavily all my life and then when I quit cigarettes, I took up cigars. If I was awake, I had a cigar or cigarette in my mouth ninety-nine per cent of the time. People told me to give up but I didn't listen. I started smoking when I was about fourteen, much to my parents' disgust. They were very heavy smokers but they didn't want me to smoke. After Dad caught me a couple of times, I smoked in secret.

A smoking addiction makes you antsy. The only way I can describe it is, it's like if you're a bit thirsty and you're told you're not allowed to have a drink, you instantly want one even more than you did before. If I ran out of cigarettes, I immediately wanted one. I had pneumonia when I was a kid and I've still got residual lung damage from that. Then, after years of smoking, I developed emphysema. That exacerbated my breathing problems, which is not great for a singer. If you can't breathe, you can't sing. Actually, if you can't breathe, you can't do anything because then you're dead aren't you? Finally, that breathlessness caught up with me and I decided I was going to do something about my addiction. I went cold turkey and stopped smoking completely.

I didn't smoke for ten years. Before that, my dad and I would often have a cigar together at Christmas. We stopped doing that. Then, one Christmas, my boys mentioned that Grandad and I used to have a cigar together and they wanted to do that with me. So I went and bought a box of Cuban cigars. It would have been cheaper to buy a car, or maybe half a car, but on Christmas Day I busted out these cigars for me, Robert and James. I cut and lit them and we all had a puff. My boys smoked about an inch of these five-inch cigars before they put them down and then out. I kept going and then the next day I looked at this box of Cuban cigars and said to myself, 'Well, I'm not going to throw them out!' That impulse kickstarted a renewed smoking habit. It was such a crazy waste of money and there I was, smoking again.

Now I know everyone is vaping, but they are just as bad, apparently. Crazy. I tried chewing tobacco once. We were in Texas at a horse show and I was riding a horse in the competition. One of the blokes came up and said, 'Hey John, you want to try some tabacky?' I declined, but he still gave me a wad of the stuff so I tried it. It was disgusting. Awful. Whichever way you are getting that nicotine hit, just don't.

But smoking wasn't my only vice. I've always enjoyed a few drinks after a concert and it was never a problem until work slowed down during the Covid lockdowns. I guess I got bored. I'd be sitting in my chair watching TV drinking every night and, little by little, it crept up. I was drinking two bottles a night, and then there were nights I noticed I drank three bottles.

I've always been one to stick my fingers in my ears and go *la, la, la, la*. Early in my career I let things slide that I should have addressed, I know that. You'd think I should be able to cope more than I can because I'm seventy-five years old, I've lived a life and have experience to draw on, but I still try and avoid the tough things. The excessive drinking allowed me to shut things out. We were living in an uncertain time, live music was on hold and so smoking and drinking were welcome distractions. And then, on 1 February 2022, my friend Glenn Wheatley died. The man was like a brother to me. Covid scared the shit out me, I think it scared the shit out of everyone, but watching it take my friend was terrifying. I don't think I've really processed the loss of Glenn. Even now it doesn't seem real. I still find it very hard to talk about because I can't find the words to sum up all that man meant to me and the way our families were joined. Glenn, Gaynor, Tim, Samantha and Kara are family to me, Jilly, Robert and James. It was devastating to me, to Jilly and to my boys and I just wanted it not to be true.

The months after Glenn died were tough. And then in August that same year Jill hassled me to go to the doctor. I had that lump in my mouth that didn't go away. I thought it was an ulcer but Jilly wanted it checked out. And we all know I listen to Jill and do what my wife asks. I was referred to a maxillofacial surgeon, she took a biopsy and it came back positive. The lump in my mouth was a tumour, the tumour was cancerous and they wanted to operate immediately. So they did. The operation lasted twelve hours. I was told later that someone from the medical team called Jillian a couple of times while I was in theatre, apparently I was very close to dying.

Spoiler: As we all know, I survived the surgery.

I woke up in ICU with the most intense feelings of paranoia. I had no idea where I was and I was convinced I had been kidnapped. I was so drugged up on whatever they were giving me I couldn't get out of the bed, even though I tried. I had a catheter in, so they strapped me down but being restricted and drugged terrified me even more. Eventually, Jill, Robert and James came in and seeing them put me at ease. They assured me that I was okay but, oh geez, the feeling was awful and even talking about it now gives me a bad feeling. I don't think I've ever been so scared in my life.

Then, the week after the surgery, I started to have some dark thoughts. I've never felt so low in all my life. The thoughts were so dark, I don't want to share them on this page. But they were very bleak and I wasn't sure how to get beyond them. The cancer diagnosis had gutted me. I was lucky, I had the best possible doctors, they were amazing, but the surgery left me with a fair amount of facial disfigurement and pain. All that had built up to a point where the thoughts nearly got the better of me.

I was in ICU and then I was moved into a general ward, and I was going to spend some time in a rehabilitation hospital after that. It was intense and gruelling. And then, one morning I was being taken to have scans and all sorts of tests. I looked across and an ambulance had just arrived at the hospital. This young girl came out of the back of this ambulance, she would have only been about twelve or thirteen years old. She was completely bald, and when I saw her she was slumped in a wheelchair, eyes down, head down, hunched over. There were tubes coming out of her all over the place, and two defeated-looking people were standing next to her, I assumed they were her mum and dad. I watched this young girl, who had her whole life in front of her, and yet she looked so sick and frail. She had a whole life to live and there I was, a man who had lived a good life, feeling sorry for myself.

Seeing that girl also made me realise that I'd frightened myself with those dark thoughts. I had to do something about them. It was up to me to pull my socks up a little bit. I said to myself, 'Cancer got me but it hasn't killed me.' I also realised I needed to talk openly with my doctors about my fears, so I told them about the thoughts I was having. They were great and said, 'You're going to be okay. Let's move on, onward and upward.' They were fantastic and helped me deal with my fears and the emotional impact of it all. And Jilly was there. She was never going to let me go. With help, it only took about a week for me to overcome those thoughts. I'd never felt that way before, I'd never had those thoughts, and talking about them was the only thing that made me feel better. It didn't take long for them to fade away. So, if anyone does feel like that, if you're having dark thoughts, go and talk to someone. Get it out, confront it, get help to deal with them. I was down, very down, but now, most times, I'm fine and I feel a lot of gratitude. The truth is, there's always some poor bugger worse off, and you have to remember that and find a way to get through the bad times.

Getting rid of that tumour and having all that treatment saved my life, there's no doubt about that. But one of the things that contributed to my dark thoughts was thinking I'd never be able to sing again in public. Now, almost two years later, I am still not sure that I ever will. My facial disfigurement from the surgery means that I can't open my mouth wide enough for a strip of spaghetti, let alone to sing a top C. At this stage I can't get the movement to make the sounds I want to make, and that's where the vibrations and my voice come from. It's still a very disconcerting thing. And trying hurts. The good news is my vocal cords haven't been affected by the radiation treatment I've had. Yet. Apparently the effects can continue after you finish receiving the dosage, it just keeps going and going and going, which is a good thing when you are trying to hold the cancer back. But the doctors have checked my voice box a couple of times now, and so far there haven't been any adverse effects, so I'm glad about that.

THANK YOU

It's really strange, I haven't had any personal contact with the band or crew since going through cancer treatment. At first I was too sick, and now it is almost too hard for me to reach out. They are amazing people and they are on my side, they've sent messages of strength and best wishes, but I can't help feeling I let them down. I'm sure they are all doing fine, they're the best there is so I'm sure they are all gainfully employed, but I feel like I let them down because I can't take them on the road anymore. I can't do the tours. As people they are wonderful, and as musicians they are even more wonderful. It was a joy to sing with them all.

Over the years I've tried to look after the band and the people who tour with me. It was a pretty steady team, though I've had a few member changes over time. Joe Creighton left and then Craig Newman joined. Craig is an incredible bass player and I used to love working with him. Lisa Edwards joined Venetta and Lindsay and I've been spoilt having those backup singers behind me. Lisa is a wonderful singer and her voice is matched by her big heart and kindness. When David Hirschfelder left, Chong Lim joined and became my musical director. Chong is wonderful; his work ethic and resilience to my bad jokes and teasing is like no other. My brief to everyone was, 'You don't have to play the same thing every night, you can do your fiddly bits wherever you like. As long as we get through the song with the right chords, I'm happy.' It was lovely to be inspired by those guys while I was onstage. You won't get better than my band, you'll just get different. They are as good as it gets. And they never let me down. My crew, too, they were unbelievable. They were there for me every step of the way and I am so thankful to them. I just wish we could do it all again tomorrow.

And then there are the people who supported me. I don't like saying 'my fans', I think that's a bit much. What I mean is the people who came to the concerts, the people who bought the albums. Because of them I was given the chance to do what I like to do, under the best possible circumstances. I'm so grateful and I feel like I've let them down a little bit too, because I never got a chance to say goodbye properly. Singing and relating to the audience, with the band, was incredible. It was, as I said, my life's blood. I'm disappointed that maybe I won't get another chance to feel that. I loved it. Loved, loved, loved it.

I still sing at home, though. I can barely open my mouth but I still wail in the shower. I love to make noises with my throat. Since I was a kid I've loved to whistle, I've loved to sing. I was given a gift and to be able to get out there and affect people in some way was a special thing. I would like to continue doing that. So, though I am not putting all my hopes into it, we'll see. I still haven't got my bottom teeth, they are putting them back in soon, I hope, then maybe. Who knows? I will give it a crack when I can. I'll go into the studio, Chong and Dougie will be there, and we'll see if I can sing in tune.

After all that I have been through recently maybe I am learning what is good for me (sometimes the doctors don't agree on that). I'm proud to say I haven't had a glass of wine for three years. Not one. I do have a couple of beers at night and I don't mind the occasional bourbon on ice, that's a treat. I talked to one of the professors who's been helping me through this, he's the one coordinating my operations and he told me recently that I am completely cancer free and everything is going nicely. I told him I was having a couple of beers at night and he said, 'Well, don't.' I'm sorry, Professor, but I'm not going to give that up. I know I have a little bit of liver damage, and that's why he wants me to stay off the booze. I guess the damage happened over the years but, bugger it, even though I have to drink my beer with a straw I am not giving it up. Weirdly, I'm enjoying it more with a straw, and I don't mind getting a light buzz up, otherwise why would you drink alcohol? If I didn't want a buzz I would be drinking kombucha. So I am doing what I am told, most of the time.

And I am still here. Here to love my wife. Hug my sons. Watch my boys and their partners build their own lives. I was able to be there when Rob got married earlier this year. And we were all together holidaying recently. I am here for all of it, I am so grateful.

I can't believe we are at the end of the book. I've been asked to sit down and write my story many times over the years and I've never wanted to do it. I've actually dreaded it. I didn't expect people to be interested in me or my life. I've been around forever, most of my music audience now are forty or fifty years younger than me. I didn't want my story to be boring or show I'm not the brightest penny in the till, but to be honest it hasn't been as bad as I thought it would be. For the most part I've enjoyed sitting down with Poppy. Yes, going through this process has been challenging at times – I have all these wonderful memories, but I have a lot of painful memories as well. Talking about losing people I love is hard. Talking about some of the choices I made was difficult. I wanted to be honest, but I didn't want to bash people either. I'd rather say nothing if I can't be positive. But here it is in my own words.

THANK YOU

I've been very, very lucky with all these hit songs, accolades, album sales, fabulous collaborators and, most importantly, fantastic audiences. What I hope you'll take away from my story, if you can, is to stay positive. No matter what comes at you, just stay positive. I hope that is what my life shows, that it can always get better. I know that's a bit of pressure right there, but if I have learned anything in my life, it's that no matter how tough things seem, they can turn around for the better. My life absolutely shows you that.

So thank you for being there. Thank you for being there for me. I am so very grateful. I'm getting teary, don't you fucking start getting teary on me. Onward and upward.

Love,

John

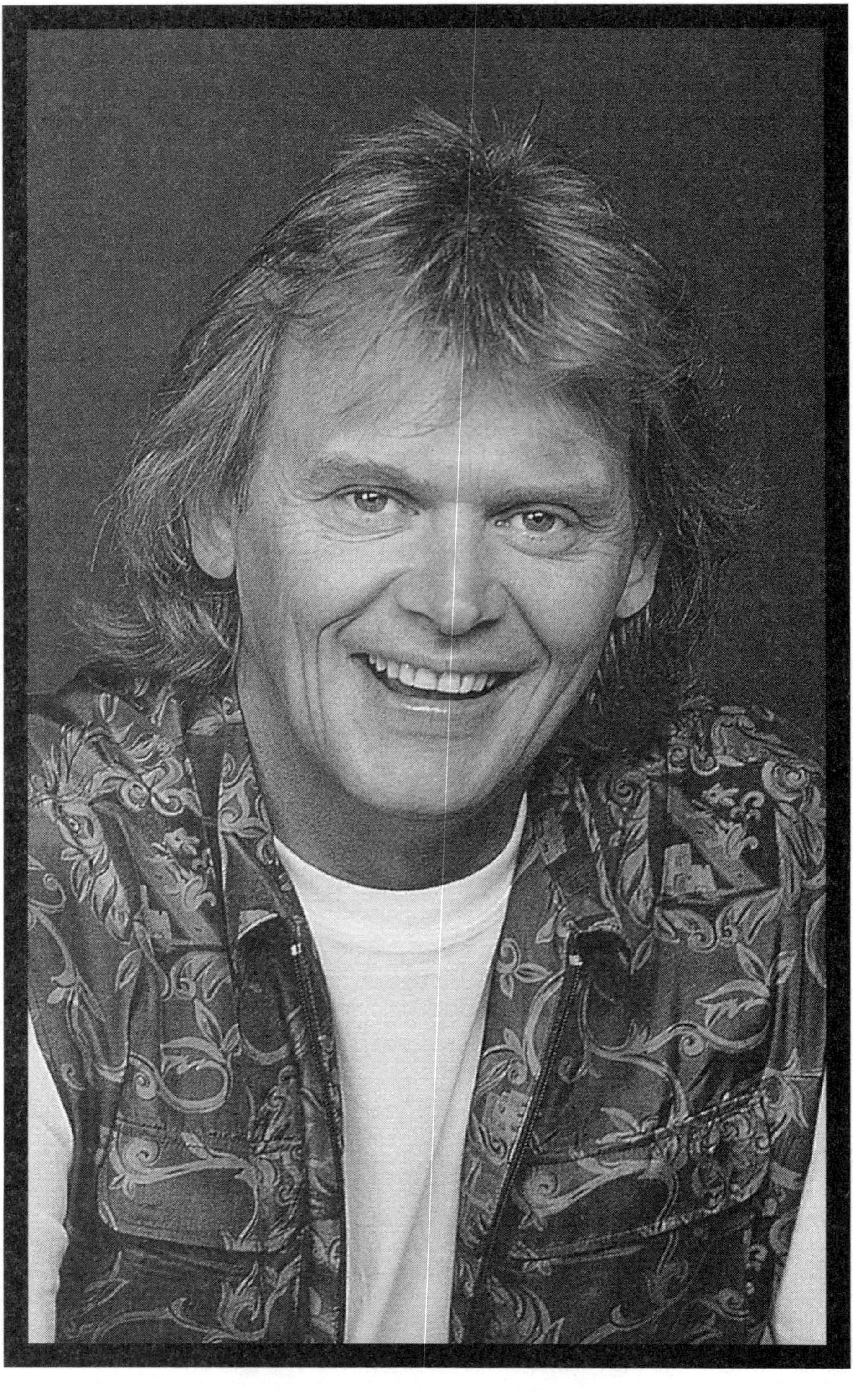

ACKNOWLEDGEMENTS

Thank you.

The John Farnham Band: Lindsay Field, Lisa Edwards, Craig Newman, Chong Lim, Angus Burchall, Brett Garsed, Susie Ahern, Rod Davies.

Past band members: Joe Creighton, David Hirschfelder, Wayne (Wiz) Nelson, Stuart (Chet) Fraser, Steve Williams, Venetta Fields, Dannielle Gaha, Chuck McKinney, Phil Buckle, Jack Jones, Bob Coassin, Lex Tier, Stephen Housden, James Roche, Kevin Dubber, Mark Dennison, Geoff Wells, Tommy Emmanuel, Nikki Nicholls, Kimmy Collins, David Glyde, Peter (Bones) Lothian, Jordan Murray, Lachlan Davidson, Joe Petrolo, Greg Macainsh, Roger McLachlan, Michelle Argue, Donna McConville, John Clarke,

Sam See, Margot Moir, Bruno Di Stanislo, Sam McNally, Barry Sullivan, Michael Clarke, Gerry Pantazis.

All the bagpipers and those who pretended to be.

John Farnham crew: Adrian Smith, Chris Newman, Grant Walsh, Lee Anne Meyer, Frank Iskra, Catherine Poynter, Adam Alderucci, and James Farnham.

Past crew: Michelle Dundon, John Henderson, Gary Radbourn, Peter Lothian, Barry Woods, Michael Wickow, Denis Murphy, Simon Gregg, Shelley Maine, David Sneddon, Tom Kehoe, Jim Brewster, Grant Jennings (GJ), Mick Wilkinson, Matthew English.

And to all the other wonderful crew who came and worked on my tours.

To the producers, engineers, assistant engineers and in fact everyone who worked on my albums, but in particular Ernie Rose, Doug Brady, Roger Savage, Aaron Humphries and, of course, Ross Fraser. Thank you.

To all my record companies over the years and the great folk who work there ... THANK YOU ONE AND ALL.

EMI

Wheatley Records

RCA

BMG

SMEA

Gotham

ACKNOWLEDGEMENTS

Thanks to all the promoters and my longtime agent Frank Stivala.

My thanks to Greg O'Connor, Serge Thomann, Dave Anderson, Jimmy Pozarik, Matt Deller, Bob King and all the creatives and photographers along the way.

To the Fan Club: Sue Smith, Lyn Albury and Maree Illingworth . . . thanks girls for all your help and support over the years.

Ken Starke, Liam Hayes and Mick Hall: my thanks to you all for your expertise and guidance.

To all the surgeons, doctors, nurses and medical staff: my heartfelt thanks for your excellent care.

In particular, these rockstars: Mr Timothy Wong, Professor Joseph Torresi, Mr Jeremy Wilson.

And everyone at: The Royal Melbourne Hospital, Peter Mac Cancer Centre.

David Wilson: thank you for being there for the family and me through thick and thin over many years.

To my management teams over my career: thank you.

To my dear friend Glenn Wheatley, your unwavering support and belief in me has meant more than words can express.

And to Gaynor and Poppy who guided me through the journey of writing this book, thank you . . . I think.

John

POPPY'S ACKNOWLEDGEMENTS

I would like to express my heartfelt thanks to the following people who made the creation of this book possible:

Annie, thank you for your unwavering love and support and to my daughter Tilda, for your constant encouragement.

Thanks to Gaye Stockell for meticulously reading every draft. Thanks to Cecilia Ritchie for your generosity. Thanks to Dad, Julia, Chloe, Tom, Shiraz, Saoirse, Tighe, Cam and Sunny.

Thanks to my cavalry – Tania Lambert, Roslyn Durnford, Zoe Taylor, Denise Wright, Melitta Firth, Sarah Hill, Sara Zucchiatti, Kosta Bakis, Eloise King, Jo Chichester, Liza Bahamondes, Kim Ison, Anna Whiting, Tracey Paul, Morgan Richards, Kat Franks, Kalita Corrigan, Eliza Collett-Burns, Jerry Mai, Sam Loi, Erynn Binns, Mitch Hatten, Samantha Dinning, Emma Watts, Fiona Dobbrick, Amy Rudder, Jason Last, Chris Frith, Drew Smith, Elissa Baillie, Andrew 'Fuzz' Purchas OAM, Clayton Noble, Julia Kalceff, Zac Grant, Tessa Meyrick, Courtney Gibson, Joseph McMahon, Jonathan Messer, Robb Innes, Emma Partridge, Ann Marsh, Hayley Conway, Sarah Maddison, Steph Frith, David Frith, Mark Sterrantino, Toni Barton, Sam Simmons and Caroline Barnett. Thanks to Jane Gazzo, Jeff Apter, Clarke Forbes and Jeff Jenkins. Thanks to Mitch Spooner and Studio Grabowski. Thanks to

ACKNOWLEDGEMENTS

Caroline Verge, Albert Chan and Charlie Winn. Thanks to Lisa Millar, Alley Pascoe, Michael Robotham and Marc Fennell. Thanks to Sue and Maree for your assistance and speed-dial cross-references.

Thanks to David Hirschfelder, Ross Fraser, Angus Burchall, Cherie Romaro, David Mackay, Peter Foggie, Howard Gable, Lindsay Field, Lisa Edwards, Venetta Fields, Chong Lim, Joe Creighton, Tommy Emmanuel, Tom Kehoe, Graeham Goble, Chris Thompson, Bev Harrell, Kate Ceberano, Richard Marx, Robbie Williams, Celine Dion, Olivia Newton-John and everyone who shared their Farnham memories.

Thank you to Olivia Hoopmann, Steven Robinson, Aaron Smith, Miriam Kenter, Siobhan Dee, Georgia Blake and Jarrod Otten for your contributions and support. A huge thanks to Vanessa Radnidge and all the team at Hachette: Kirstin Corcoran, Karen Ward, Lillian Kovats, Alysha Farry, Isabel Staas, Madison Garratt, Kate Taperell, Louise Stark, Chris Sims, Tonile Wortley, Gemma Shaw, Vanessa Lanaway, Pam Dunne, Simon Paterson, Samantha Collins and Christa Moffitt to name only a few for all your work and support.

Thanks to Robert and James Farnham.

A sincere thank you to Gaynor Wheatley for believing in me.

Lastly, a massive thanks to John and Jill Farnham. Thank you for trusting me with your incredible story.

THE STORY OF *THE VOICE INSIDE*

For years, John refused any suggestion of sitting down to write an autobiography or memoir. Poppy had never written a book before. But when the documentary *John Farnham: Finding the Voice* was released, everything changed. John watched the film and felt that the writer director got him. He felt like he could potentially trust Poppy with his story. With Jill and Gaynor's encouragement, John agreed to sit down and write his story with the help of Poppy.

The two of them sat down over the course of months to chart and process the stories of John's extraordinary life. Poppy approached the project with dedication and respect, immersing herself in John's world, listening intently to his stories, asking thoughtful questions and capturing the essence of his journey. John, in turn, gradually opened up, sharing not just the public highs and lows but the private moments that shaped him.

Their collaboration was a dance of trust and understanding. Poppy often found herself inspired by John's resilience, creativity and humour, while John was moved by Poppy's genuine interest and empathy. Together, they laughed and shed tears, sifting through memories and piecing together a narrative that was both honest and reflective. Jill also sat down to share her perspective and story, adding depth and richness to the narrative.

Throughout this journey, Poppy and John developed a deep bond. Poppy's fresh perspective and John's wealth of experience complemented each other perfectly. Jill and Gaynor provided constant support, ensuring that the process remained smooth and focused. The result was not just a book, but a testament to a life well lived, full of passion, struggle and triumph – capturing the heart and soul of an extraordinary Australian icon.

Poppy Stockell is an award-winning writer, director and producer with a penchant for stories exploring human identity, humour and the inherent contradictions of existence. She has written and directed for all the major networks and her independent projects have played to big audiences at the world's most prestigious festivals including SXSW, Hot Docs, Sheffield DocFest, New Orleans Film Festival and the Sydney Film Festival. Her work has been recognised by an AACTA and a Walkley Award, a UN Media Peace Prize, two Logie nominations and the Audience Award at the Sydney Film Festival. Poppy's Logie-winning feature, *John Farnham: Finding the Voice*, recently became the highest box-office grossing Australian documentary of all time and her scripted comedy series *Triple Oh!* won the coveted Luna de València Grand Jury Prize.

SELECT DISCOGRAPHY

CDS = Compact Disc Single, EP = Extended Play, LP = Long Play, LRB = Little River Band, P/C = Picture Cover

RELEASE DATE	TYPE	TITLE	CHART POSITION
23 Nov 1967	Single	Sadie / In My Room (Also USA/ Argentina) (France/Denmark P/C)	1
1967	Single	Sadie / Friday Kind of Monday (UK) (Germany P/C)	
1967	Single	Half Heaven, Half Heartache (Demo, not released)	
1968	EP	Sadie / In My Room / Friday Kind of Monday / I Don't Want to Love You (P/C)	

RELEASE DATE	TYPE	TITLE	CHART POSITION
Mar 1968	Single	Underneath the Arches / Friday Kind of Monday (P/C)	2
Apr 1968	LP	Sadie	1
Jul 1968	Single	Jamie / I Don't Want to Love You	8
Nov 1968	Single	Rose Coloured Glasses / Scratchin' Ma Head	19
Nov 1968	LP	Everybody Oughta Sing a Song	
Dec 1968	Single	I Saw Mommy Kissing Santa Claus / The Little Boy that Santa Claus Forgot	
Jul 1969	Single	One / Mr Whippy	1
21 Nov 1969	Single	Raindrops Keep Falling on My Head / Two (Germany P/C)	1
May 1970	EP	One / Underneath the Arches / Rose Coloured Glasses / Jamie (P/C)	
Jul 1970	LP	Looking Through a Tear	11
Jul 1970	Single	Mirror of My Mind / What Can I Do? (NZ Release)	11
17 Sep 1970	Single	Comic Conversation / Pretty Things	10
Dec 1970	Single	Christmas Happy / The Ringing Reindeer	
Dec 1970	LP	Christmas is . . . Johnny Farnham	
1971	LP	For the Love of Man (Proceeds to UNICEF) (Give a Little Love)	
Mar 1971	LP	The Best of Johnny Farnham	
May 1971	Single	Acapulco Sun / As Long as Life Goes On	21
Aug 1971	LP	Johnny	24
Sep 1971	LP	Together (with Allison Durbin)	20
Nov 1971	Single	Walking the Floor on My Hands / My Favourite Occupation	25
1972	Single	Give Me Tomorrow (Demo, not released)	

SELECT DISCOGRAPHY

RELEASE DATE	TYPE	TITLE	CHART POSITION
Mar 1972	Single	For Christ's Sake Help the Kids / Hey Rev (Robin Jolley) (Proceeds to Project Childcare)	4
May 1972	LP	Charlie Girl (with Anna Neagle and Derek Nimmo) (soundtrack)	
Jun 1972	LP	Johnny Farnham Sings the Shows	
Sep 1972	Single	Rock Me Baby / Nobody's Fool	4
Nov 1972	Single	Baby Without You / That's Old Fashioned (with Allison Durbin)	16
Dec 1972	Single	Don't You Know it's Magic / Sweet Cherry Wine (Also Japan P/C)	12
Mar 1973	Single	Everything is Out of Season / It's Up to You	8
1973	EP	Diana /Blueberry Hill / Johnny B Goode (NZ)	
Jun 1973	LP	Johnny Farnham Sings . . . Hits Magic & Rock'n'Roll	
Jul 1973	Single	I Can't Dance to Your Music / Beautiful City	12
Oct 1973	LP	Johnny Farnham Sings the Big Hits of '73 Live	45
Nov 1973	Single	Shake a Hand / If You Would Stay	24
May 1974	Single	Corner of the Sky / Morning Glow	
Jul 1974	LP	Pippin (with Colleen Hewett) (soundtrack)	
Sep 1974	Single	One Minute Every Hour / Baby Don't Get Hooked on Me	91
6 Sep 1974	LP	Johnny Farnham Sings Hits from the Movies	
Jan 1975	Single	Things to Do / To Be or Not To Be	88

THE VOICE INSIDE

RELEASE DATE	TYPE	TITLE	CHART POSITION
Jul 1975	LP	J.P. Farnham Sings	
Jul 1975	Single	Don't Rock the Boat / Running to the Sea	
Jul 1976	LP	Johnny Farnham's Greatest Hits	
Sep 1976	Single	You Love Me Back to Life Again / Call Me Back	
Nov 1977	Single	Rock and Roll Hall of Fame / Monkey See, Monkey Do	
1980	LP	The Best of Johnny Farnham	
Jul 1980	LP	Uncovered	20
Jul 1980	Single	Help / Back to the Backwoods (Also Spain P/C)	8
Oct 1980	Single	She's Everywhere / On My Own	90
1980	Single	She Says to Me / I Never Did Get Through (The Netherlands P/C)	
Jan 1981	Single	Please Don't Ask Me / I Never Did Get Through Please Don't Ask Me / Back to the Backwoods (USA)	67
Apr 1981	Single	Too Much Too Soon / Jillie's Song	82
1981	Single	Too Much Too Soon / Jillie's Song (The Netherlands P/C)	
Sep 1981	Single	That's No Way to Love Someone / Blame It on the Weather	52
1982	LP	Greatest Hits Vol. 2 (LRB)	
1982	Single	Down on the Border / No More Tears (LRB)	7
1982	Single	St. Louis / Easy Money (LRB)	
1983	LP	The Net (LRB)	

SELECT DISCOGRAPHY

RELEASE DATE	TYPE	TITLE	CHART POSITION
1983	Single	The Other Guy / Take it Easy on Me The Other Guy / No More Tears (USA P/C) (LRB)	18
1983	Single	We Two / Falling (LRB)	
1983	Single	You're Driving Me Out of My Mind / Falling (USA/Ger/UK/Spain) (LRB)	
1983	Single	You're Driving Me Out of My Mind / Mr Socialite (USA/Japan P/C) (LRB)	
1984	Single	Nothing's Gonna Stand in Our Way (12" marbled disc P/C) Nothing's Gonna Stand in Our Way (7" P/C) (from *Savage Streets* soundtrack)	
1984	Single	Justice for One / The Quiet Ones You Gotta Watch (7" P/C) Justice for One / Innocent Hearts (12") Justice for One / Nothing's Gonna Stand in our Way (7" French P/C) (from *Savage Streets* soundtrack)	
1984	LP	Playing to Win (LRB)	
1984	Single	Playing to Win Extended Rock Mix / Playing to Win / Through Her Eyes (12") (LRB)	
1984	Single	Playing to Win / Through Her Eyes (NZ/Canada/Philippines/SA) (LRB)	
1984	Single	Playing to Win / When the War is Over (Alternate B Sides) (LRB)	
1985	Single	Blind Eyes / The Butterfly (Live at the Pier) (Also with alternate B Side) (LRB)	
1985	Single	Incredible Penguins (Happy Xmas – War is Over) (12") (vocals)	

RELEASE DATE	TYPE	TITLE	CHART POSITION
1985	Single	Love (It's Just the Way it Goes) (with Sarah M. Taylor) (from *The Slugger's Wife* soundtrack)	
1986	Single	Break the Ice / With You (Germany and Scandinavia) Break the Ice / Thunder in Your Heart (7" P/C USA) (from *Rad* soundtrack)	
1986	Single	Break the Ice / The Quiet Ones You Gotta Watch / Nothing's Gonna Stand in Our Way (12" Marbled disc) (Also a 7") (from various soundtracks)	
1986	LP	No Reins (LRB)	
1986	Single	No Reins on Me / Paper Paradise (LRB)	
1986	Single	Face in the Crowd / Thin Ice (LRB)	
1986	Single	Time for Us / It Was the Night (LRB)	
15 Sep 1986	Single	You're the Voice / Going, Going, Gone (P/C)	1
20 Oct 1986	LP/CD	Whispering Jack	1
Dec 1986	Single	Pressure Down / Let Me Out (P/C)	4
2 Feb 1987	Single	A Touch of Paradise / Help (Live) (without and with P/C)	24
May 1987	LP	The John Farnham Phenomenon	44
May 1987	CD	Whispering Jack / Limited Edition Silver Disc (first Australian-made CD)	
May 1987	CD	Whispering Jack / Collector's edition, made with Kalgoorlie gold	
Sep 1987	Single	Reasons / One Step Away (P/C)	60
1987	Single	You're the Voice / Going, Going Gone / Help (Live) (Maxi)	

SELECT DISCOGRAPHY

RELEASE DATE	TYPE	TITLE	CHART POSITION
1987	Single	Pressure Down (12 inch mix) / Pressure Down / Let Me Out (Maxi)	
1987	Single	A Touch of Paradise / Love to Shine / No One Comes Close (Maxi)	
1987	LP/CD	Another Side of John Farnham	44
1987	Single	When the War is Over / How Many Nights? (LRB)	
1988	LP	Too Late to Load (LRB)	
1988	LP	The Farnham Years (LRB)	
4 Jul 1988	Single/CD	Age of Reason / When the War is Over (P/C, Picture CD)	1
25 Jul 1988	LP/CD	Age of Reason (Also released in a 2 pack with Chain Reaction)	1
1988	Single/CD	Age of Reason (extended mix) / Age of Reason / When the War is Over (Maxi single)	
1988	Single/ CDS	Two Strong Hearts (Extended mix) / Two Strong Hearts / It's a Long Way to the Top (Maxi)	
Sep 1988	Single	Two Strong Hearts / It's a Long Way to the Top	3
1988	Single/ CDS	Beyond the Call / Blow by Blow / Blow by Blow (Quake mix) (Maxi)	
Nov 1988	Single	Beyond the Call / Blow by Blow (P/C)	41
1988	Single/ CDS	That's Freedom (Club mix) / That's Freedom / In Your Hands (Maxi)	
1988	LP/CD	Time Brings Change	
1989	LP/CD	Greenpeace – Rainbow Warriors (You're the Voice)	
May 1989	Single	We're No Angels / Listen to the Wind	87

RELEASE DATE	TYPE	TITLE	CHART POSITION
14 Aug 1989	Single	Communication (with Dannielle Gaha) / Attitude (Question Time) For Get Real Project (P/C and Booklet included)	13
Aug 1989	Single/ CDS	Chain Reaction / In Your Hands (P/C)	
Sep 1990	Single	That's Freedom / New Day (P/C)	3
Sep 1990	CDS	Burn for You (Special Commemorative Disc)	
24 Sep 1990	LP LP CD	Chain Reaction Track by Track Interview Disc Pop up cover and Jewel case (Also released in a 2 pack with Age of Reason)	1
26 Nov 1990	Single/ CDS CDS	Burn for You / Chains Around the Heart (P/C) Burn for You / The Time Has Come / Chains Around the Heart	5
Mar 1991	Single	In Days to Come / Reasons (Live) (P/C)	49
4 Nov 1991	CD	Full House (Jewel case and foldout digipak)	2
Nov 1991	CDS	When Something is Wrong With My Baby (with Jimmy Barnes)	2
Nov 1991	Maxi CD	Please Don't Ask Me (Live) / Chain Reaction (Live)	22
Jul 1992	CDS	Everything's Alright / Overture from JCS)	4
1992	CD	Jesus Christ Superstar (with Kate Ceberano and Jon Stevens) (soundtrack)	1
1992	CDS	Full House Mega Mix (Extended Version) / Full House Mega Mix	
1993	CDS	Seemed Like a Good Idea / Rolling Home	16

SELECT DISCOGRAPHY

RELEASE DATE	TYPE	TITLE	CHART POSITION
1993	CDS	Angels (Single edit) / Full House Mega Mix (Ext) / Angels (Ext)	36
7 Feb 1993	CDS	4 Track Collectors CD Talk of the Town / When All Else Fails (European mix) / Don't You Give Up (live at Gotham) / Playing to Win (Acapella Gotham)	36
18 Oct 1993	CD	Then Again ...	1
1994	CDS	The Reason Why / Only Women Bleed (two different covers)	
8 Aug 1994	CDS	Fight for Survival (Proceeds to Care Australia, Rwanda Appeal) Always the Same / It's a Long Way to the Top / Angels / Chain Reaction / Age of Reason (Recorded live at the Concert for Rwanda)	
6 Nov 1995	CD	The Classic Gold Collection (also released in a 2 pack with Where Do I Begin)	
1995	CD	Where Do I Begin (also released in a 2 pack with Classic Gold)	
13 Nov 1995	CD	Memories of Christmas (same tracks as Christmas Is ...)	
1995	CD	Johnny Farnham (same tracks as Classic Gold)	
1996	CDS	Don't Let it End / All Kinds of People (Extended mix) Don't Let it End (duet with Chiu)	
1996	CDS	Have a Little Faith (Radio edit) / Have a Little Faith (Acoustic) / Cool Water (with Smoky Dawson)	3

RELEASE DATE	TYPE	TITLE	CHART POSITION
1996	CDS	A Simple Life / Second Skin / Ten Year Anniversary Mega Mix (Brahms 4)	29
3 Jun 1996	CDS	Heart's on Fire / Over My Head	
3 Jun 1996	CD	Romeo's Heart with bonus tour disc with bonus interview disc	2
Oct 1996	CD	Whispering Jack (10th Anniversary Edition)	
1997	CDS	All Kinds of People / All Kinds of People (Extended version)	
1997	CDS	Every Time You Cry (with Human Nature) / Everything is Out of Season (Live) / You're the Voice (Swing version) (with MSO live)	3
29 Sep 1997	CD	Anthology 1 (Also available as a boxed set)	1
29 Sep 1997	CD	Anthology 2 (Also available as a boxed set)	12
29 Sep 1997	CD	Anthology 3 (Also available as a boxed set)	20
1998	CD	Philharmania (Various Artists) (John sings A Whiter Shade of Pale)	
14 Dec 1998	CD	Highlights From The Main Event	1
30 Aug 1999	CD	Live at the Regent Theatre	7
2000	CD	Uncovered (digitally remastered)	
2000	CDS	You're the Only One / I've Been Lonely for So Long	
7 Jul 2000	CD	33⅓	1
17 Jul 2000	CDS	Trying to Live My Life Without You / I Thank You (Live Studio)	

SELECT DISCOGRAPHY

RELEASE DATE	TYPE	TITLE	CHART POSITION
Oct 2000	CDS	Man of the Hour / Man of the Hour (Live in Studio) / You Don't Know Like I Know (Live in Studio)	
Oct 2000	CDS	Dare to Dream (with Olivia Newton-John)	
13 May 2002	CD	Love Songs	
7 Oct 2002	CD	The Last Time	1
	CD	Special Limited Edition includes a CD-ROM of John's Photographic Record of the making of The Last Time	
13 Jan 2003	CDS	Keep Talking (Redball Remix) / The Last Time (Brahms 4 Remix) Keep Talking (Album Version)	
Sep 2003	CDS	We Will Rock You (with Queen) (Media release) (Also on One Voice)	
20 Oct 2003	CD	One Voice – the Greatest Hits	2
20 Mar 2005	CD	John Farnham & Tom Jones Together in Concert	3
6 Nov 2005	CD	I Remember When I Was Young (Jewel case and digipak)	2
2006	CD	Whispering Jack (20th Anniversary Edition)	
12 Oct 2008	CD	Collections	
31 Jan 2009	CD	Essential	
27 Jul 2009	CD	Greatest Hits	1
21 Aug 2009	3 CD	The Essential John Farnham	
15 Oct 2010	CD	Jack	2
30 Sep 2011	CD	The Acoustic Chapel Sessions	2

RELEASE DATE	TYPE	TITLE	CHART POSITION
Mar 2014	2 CD	Greatest Hits NZ Tour Edition	10
18 Jul 2014	4 CD	John Farnham: The Box Set Series	
25 Jun 2015	CD	Two Strong Hearts Live (with Olivia Newton-John)	1
11 Nov 2016	CD	Friends for Christmas (with Olivia Newton-John)	1
27 Nov 2016	Vinyl/CD/ DVD/ Box Set	The Complete Whispering Jack (30th Anniversary)	
2017		Friends for Christmas Deluxe Edition (3 bonus tracks)	
2023	LP	Age of Reason (35th anniversary green vinyl)	
19 May 2023	CD	Finding the Voice: music from the feature documentary	2
21 Jul 2023	LP	Greatest Hits (green vinyl, 2LP)	
17 Nov 2023	LP	Whispering Jack (numbered limited edition, black and white marbled vinyl)	
24 Nov 2023	LP	Friends for Christmas (with Olivia Newton-John) (red vinyl)	

This select discography does not include all repackages, overseas releases, reissues, remastered versions, videos, DVDs, or tracks on compilations.

Thanks to Lyn Albury and her website www.johnfarnham.info and to Maree Illingworth and Sue Smith of the John Farnham official fan club, who were of invaluable assistance in this compilation and for the list of gigs, tours and events.

GIGS, TOURS AND EVENTS

Note: This list is indicative but not comprehensive. There were many hotel/club gigs and shows at shopping centres and other events in the early days, as well as tours of every state and New Zealand. The venues post-release of *Whispering Jack* were smaller to begin with but increased in size as momentum gathered.

COHUNA SHIRE SOLDIERS MEMORIAL HALL
Cohuna, Vic, 29 April 1967 (with Strings Unlimited)

SUPPORT ACT FOR COL JOYE SPECTACULAR
Memorial Hall, Bourke, NSW, 4 March 1968

WOODVILLE INDUSFAIR
Woodville, SA, April 1968

ST MARY'S HALL
Dandenong, Vic, 23 May 1968

MYERS IN-GEAR SHOP
Entertaining lunchtime crowds, 23, 24 and 25 May 1968

FIRST MAJOR TOUR
Blast-off '68 Pop Spectacular with Larry's Rebels
Founders Theatre, Hamilton, NZ, 20 June 1968

THE TWILIGHTS FINAL CONCERT
Trocadero, Sydney, February 1969

PENTHOUSE
Ormond, Vic, 15 March 1969

PICCADILLY
Ringwood Town Hall, Vic, 15 March 1969

OPUS
South Yarra, Vic, 8 June 1969

HMAS CERBERUS
'Charlie Brown's Closet', June 1969

OPERATION STARLIFT
An all-Australian concert series with the Masters Apprentices and others, August 1969

MUSIC IS CHRISTMAS
A Christmas Pantomime, Adelaide, December 1969

DICK WHITTINGTON PANTOMIME
Sydney, Brisbane, Melbourne, Adelaide, December 1969 to January 1970

TUNARAMA FESTIVAL
Port Lincoln, SA, 26 January 1970

FESTIVAL OF PERTH
2 February 1970

GIGS, TOURS AND EVENTS

JOHNNY O'KEEFE SHOW
Albert Hall, Canberra, 18 February 1970 and Albury, 19 February 1970

CHEVRON HOTEL
Gold Coast, Qld, 14 June 1970

CAROLS BY CANDLELIGHT
Sidney Myer Music Bowl, Melbourne, 24 December 1970

MUSIC FOR THE PEOPLE
Sidney Myer Music Bowl, Melbourne, 28 March 1971

SAVE THE TRADES HALL
Charity Concert, Adelaide, 14 May 1971

ICELAND
Moorabbin, Vic, 12 June 1971

CHARLIE GIRL PREMIERE
Her Majesty's Theatre, Melbourne, 25 September 1971

MUSIC FOR THE PEOPLE
Sidney Myer Music Bowl, Melbourne, 19 December 1971

BUSTER FIDDESS BENEFIT CONCERT
State Theatre, Sydney, 6 February 1972

STARRY NIGHT BALL
25 March 1972 (70th Anniversary of Jewish National Fund)

FESTIVAL HALL
Melbourne, 9 August 1972

THE PRODIGAL SON: A ROCK OPERA
St Paul's Cathedral, Melbourne, 6 to 9 September 1972

MATTHEW FLINDERS HOTEL
Melbourne, 29 October 1972

DORSET GARDENS HOTEL-MOTEL
24 November 1972

CAROLS BY CANDLELIGHT
Sidney Myer Music Bowl, Melbourne, 24 December 1972

MUSIC FOR THE PEOPLE
Sidney Myer Music Bowl, Melbourne, 11 March 1973

MATTHEW FLINDERS HOTEL
Melbourne, 11 March 1973

CARIBBEAN GARDENS 'FUN DAY'
Scoresby, Vic, 8 April 1973

DONCASTER SHOPPINGTOWN
27 April 1973

DORSET GARDENS HOTEL-MOTEL
10 June 1973

CANOPUS DANCE
Box Hill City Hall, Vic, 4 August 1973

PARKMORE/KEYSBOROUGH SHOPPING CENTRE OPENING
27 November 1973

SUNDAY NIGHT AT THE OPERA HOUSE
9 December 1973

CAROLS BY CANDLELIGHT
Sidney Myer Music Bowl, Melbourne, 24 December 1973

PIPPIN PREMIERE
Her Majesty's Theatre, Melbourne, February 1974

MUSIC FOR THE PEOPLE
Sidney Myer Music Bowl, Melbourne, 10 March 1974

GIGS, TOURS AND EVENTS

OPENING OF OUTDOOR AMPHITHEATRE
Festival Centre, Adelaide, 27 October 1974

CAROLS BY CANDLELIGHT
Elder Park, Adelaide, 15 December 1974

PINOCCHIOS
Perth, 20 December 1974

CAROLS BY CANDLELIGHT
Sidney Myer Music Bowl, Melbourne, 24 December 1974

SUMMER IN THE CITY MUSIC FESTIVAL
Sidney Myer Music Bowl, Melbourne, 22, 23, 24, 25 and 27 January 1975

CANBERRA THEATRE
8 February 1975

MOOMBA OPENING CONCERT
Dallas Brooks Hall, 1 March 1975

MARCH TO THE STARS
Camberwell Civic Centre, Vic, 2 March 1975

MUSIC FOR THE PEOPLE
Sidney Myer Music Bowl, Melbourne, 9 March 1975

NIGHT OF THE STARS
Festival Theatre, Adelaide, 1 July 1975

ABERDEEN CHATEAU (FOR GEELONG FOOTBALL CLUB)
6 September 1975

SUNDAY STAR NIGHT
Her Majesty's Theatre, Melbourne, 26 October 1975

BATMAN PARK, MELBOURNE
(For Vic. Assoc. for Deserted Children), 6 December 1975

SANDOWN PARK HOTEL
Noble Park, Vic, 31 December 1975

MUSIC FOR THE PEOPLE
Sidney Myer Music Bowl, Melbourne, 1 February 1976

EARTHQUAKE RELIEF CONCERT
(For victims of the Italian Earthquake)
Melbourne Town Hall, May 1976

ROBERTA
Musical staged in Sydney
Premiered June 1976 and ran for 8 weeks

QUEANBEYAN LEAGUES CLUB
19 September 1976

MUSIC FOR THE PEOPLE
Sidney Myer Music Bowl, Melbourne, 19 February 1978

VFL GRAND FINAL
MCG, 29 September 1979

FESTIVAL OF SYDNEY
Forecourt of the Opera House, December 1979

ROYAL CHARITY CONCERT
Sydney Opera House, 27 May 1980

FARNHAM AND FRIENDS
Pub tour, 16 to 24 September 1980

QUEANBEYAN LEAGUES CLUB
7 March 1981

SUPPORT ACT FOR STEVIE WONDER AUSTRALIAN TOUR
April 1981

GIGS, TOURS AND EVENTS

THE SHOW
Festival Theatre, Adelaide, 1 July 1981

COMMODORE HOTEL
Melbourne, 18 September 1981

CAROLS BY CANDLELIGHT
Sidney Myer Music Bowl, Melbourne, 24 December 1982

MELBOURNE CONCERT HALL (LRB)
7 and 8 February 1983 (Filmed for an HBO Special)

THE FOX THEATRE (LRB)
Missouri, USA, 19 and 20 July 1983

THE STANLEY THEATRE (LRB)
Pittsburgh, USA, August 1983

JAPAN TOUR 1983 (LRB)
9 to 13 September 1983

BAYFRONT ARENA (LRB)
St Petersburg, Florida, USA, 26 April 1985

SPOKANE OPERA HOUSE (LRB)
Washington, USA, 22 May 1985

GRAINSTORE TAVERN
Melbourne, 28 and 29 October 1986 (First two gigs following the release of *Whispering Jack*)

POWERHOUSE
Ballarat, Vic, 30 October 1986

LE ROX
Adelaide, 31 October 1986

THE PALACE
Melbourne, 3 November 1986

THE FLIGHT DECK
Melbourne, 5 November 1986

RITCHIES
Preston, Vic, 6 November 1986

HYATT HOTEL
Melbourne, 7 November 1986

WEST GIPPSLAND PERFORMING ARTS CENTRE
Vic, 11 and 12 November 1986

SANDOWN PARK HOTEL
Noble Park, Vic, 13 November 1986

SYDNEY ENTERTAINMENT CENTRE
16, 17 and 18 November 1986

TIVOLI
Sydney, 19 November 1986

CANBERRA ROYALS RUGBY UNION CLUB
ACT, 20 November 1986

SHELLHARBOUR WORKERS CLUB
NSW, 21 November 1986

NEWCASTLE WORKERS CLUB
NSW, 23 November 1986

BRISBANE
26, 27 and 28 November 1986

PLAYROOM
Gold Coast, Qld, 29 November 1986

BILLBOARD
Melbourne, 3 and 4 December 1986

EXCELSIOR HOTEL
Thomastown, Vic, 5 December 1986

GOULBURN VALLEY HOTEL
Shepparton, Vic, 7 December 1986

JOHN FARNHAM IN CONCERT
30 January to 10 March 1987

MONTREAL
Canada, 1 May 1987

MONTREUX GOLDEN ROSE ROCK FESTIVAL
Switzerland, 15 May 1987

ROCKPOP IN CONCERT 1987
Galopprennbahn Riem, Munich, Germany, 27 June 1987

GRONA LUND AMUSEMENT PARK
Stockholm, Sweden, 28 June 1987

VOLKSPARKSTADION
Hamburg, Germany, 3 July 1987

JACK'S BACK
2 November 1987 to 2 January 1988

WORLD EXPO '88
24 and 25 July 1988

AGE OF REASON
29 September to 23 December 1988 (September/October in Europe)

SUMMER TOUR
18 November to 10 December 1989

CHAIN REACTION
11 November 1990 to 26 January 1991

TIVOLIVREDENBURG
Utrecht, Netherlands, 25 June 1991

JOHN FARNHAM SINGS WITH MLC CHOIR
15 December 1991

JESUS CHRIST SUPERSTAR
August to October 1992

TALK OF THE TOWN
February to April 1994

CONCERT FOR RWANDA
Flinders Park, Melbourne, 7 August 1994

AUSTRALIA'S BEST FOR THE BUSH CONCERT 1994
Rod Laver Arena, Melbourne, 7 September 1994

AUSTRALIA REMEMBERS – GALA TRIBUTE
50th Anniversary of end of World War 2, 13 August 1995

JACK OF HEARTS TOUR
23 September to 26 November 1996

LANGELANDS FESTIVAL
Rudkøbing, Denmark, 25 July 1998

SHEPHERDS BUSH EMPIRE
London, UK, 27 July 1998

THE MAIN EVENT
(With Olivia Newton-John and Anthony Warlow)
26 October to 11 December 1998

SPECIAL AIRBORNE SERVICES RESOURCES TRUST FUND
Perth, 15 February 1999

I CAN'T BELIEVE HE'S 50 TOUR
11 June to 8 July 1999

GIGS, TOURS AND EVENTS

TOUR OF DUTY — CONCERT FOR THE TROOPS
Dili Stadium, East Timor, 21 December 1999

OPENING CEREMONY OF THE 2000 OLYMPIC GAMES
With Olivia Newton-John, 15 September 2000

MAN OF THE HOUR
2 November to 3 December 2000

LEEUWIN ESTATE WINERY
Margaret River, WA, 16 and 17 February 2002

THE ESPY
Esplanade Hotel, St Kilda, Vic, *The Last Time* Album Launch, 5 October 2002

COHUNA
Vic, 12 October 2002

THE LAST TIME
6 November 2002 to 15 June 2003

TWIN TOWNS
Tweed Heads, NSW, 15, 16 and 17 December 2003

PENRITH PANTHERS
Evan Theatre, Penrith, NSW, 19 and 20 December 2003

MISSION ESTATE WINERY
Hawke's Bay, New Zealand, 28 February 2004

TEMPUS TWO WINERY
Pokolbin, NSW, 6 March 2004

BAROSSA UNDER THE STARS
Tanunda Pines Golf Club, SA, 13 and 14 March 2004

STARS AT SIRROMET
Sirromet Winery, Mt Cotton, Qld, 15 May 2004

JOHN FARNHAM AND TOM JONES TOGETHER IN CONCERT
9 to 20 February 2005

TSUNAMI BENEFIT CONCERT
Sidney Myer Music Bowl, Melbourne, 27 February 2005

GREASE ARENA SPECTACULAR
6 May to 10 June 2005

WITH THE SYDNEY SYMPHONY ORCHESTRA
Sydney Opera House, 7, 8, 10 and 11 February 2006

WITH THE MELBOURNE SYMPHONY ORCHESTRA
Hamer Hall, Melbourne, 14, 15 and 16 February 2006

WOLLONGONG WIN ENTERTAINMENT CENTRE
Wollongong, NSW, 18 February 2006

JOHN FARNHAM AND STEVIE NICKS
20 February to 7 March 2006

COMMONWEALTH GAMES CLOSING CEREMONY
MCG, Melbourne, 26 March 2006

THE SPIRIT OF THE NORTH
Cairns Convention Centre, Qld, 16 June 2006

SOUND RELIEF
With Coldplay, Sydney Cricket Ground, 14 March 2009

LIVE BY DEMAND
3 September to 31 October 2009

KIMBERLEY MOON EXPERIENCE
Kununurra, WA, 29 May 2010

LUNA PARK 75TH ANNIVERSARY CONCERT
Big Top, Luna Park, Sydney, 4 October 2010

GIGS, TOURS AND EVENTS

JOHN FARNHAM LIVE
23 October to 27 November 2010

WHISPERING JACK – 25 YEARS ON
4 October to 26 November 2011

V8 SUPERCAR CHAMPIONSHIPS CONCERT
Sydney Olympic Park, NSW, 3 December 2011

STAR CITY EVENT CENTRE OPENING
Sydney, 24 and 25 January 2013

JOHN FARNHAM & LIONEL RICHIE
ANZ Tour, 2 to 23 March 2014

DECADES FESTIVAL
Pine Rivers Park, Strathpine, Qld, 18 October 2014

TWO STRONG HEARTS TOUR WITH OLIVIA NEWTON-JOHN
4 to 19 April 2015

RIVER4WARD
Crown Riverwalk, Melbourne, 23 April 2015
River4Ward raises funds for Sony Foundation's youth cancer program, 'You Can'.

THE AGE MUSIC VICTORIA AWARDS HALL OF FAME CONCERT
Palais Theatre, Melbourne, 20 November 2015
John inducted into The Victorian Hall of Fame

A DAY ON THE GREEN
21 November to 12 December 2015

ONE ELECTRIC DAY
Werribee, Vic, 29 November 2015 and Elder Park, SA, 6 December 2015

QANTAS CREDIT UNION ARENA
Sydney, 16 December 2015

THE VOICE IN THE VALLEY — V8 SUPERCARS AFTER CONCERT
Hidden Valley, Darwin, 19 June 2016

CRUISE N GROOVE
Aboard *Radiance of the Seas*, 15 and 16 October 2016

RED HOT SUMMER TOUR 2017
14 January to 9 April 2017

A DAY ON THE GREEN
Mitchelton Wines, Nagambie, Vic, 18 February 2017

JUPITERS CASINO
Gold Coast, Qld, 22 and 23 February 2017

A WEEKEND IN THE GARDENS
Royal Botanic Gardens, Melbourne, 10 March 2017

HOTEL ROTTNEST
Rottnest Island, WA, 12 March 2017

HOBART
Derwent Entertainment Centre, Hobart, 26 March 2017

HOPE ROCKS
Hope Estate, Pokolbin, NSW, 8 April 2017

PLAYING IT FORWARD
Hisense Arena, Melbourne, 28 June 2017
Benefit concert for former John Farnham Band guitarist Stuart Fraser

A DAY ON THE GREEN
Peter Lehmann Wines, Barossa Valley, SA, 25 November 2017

ONE ELECTRIC DAY
Werribee, Vic, 26 November 2017

GIGS, TOURS AND EVENTS

WOLLONGONG WIN ENTERTAINMENT CENTRE
Wollongong, NSW, 1 and 2 December 2017

A DAY ON THE GREEN
Kings Park, Perth, 4 February 2018

BY THE C
Seafront Oval, Hervey Bay, Qld, 10 February 2018

RED HOT SUMMER TOUR
17 February to 24 March 2018

WATPAC V8 RACE CONCERT
Townsville, Qld, 7 July 2018

BIG RED BASH
Birdsville, Qld, 12 July 2018

ONE TROPICAL DAY
Darwin Amphitheatre, 14 July 2018

SINGAPORE
Gardens by The Bay, 1 October 2018

HAY MATE – A CONCERT FOR THE FARMERS
Scully Park, Tamworth, NSW, 27 October 2018

ANTHEMS
National Arboretum, Canberra, 17 November 2018

A DAY ON THE GREEN 2018
24 November, 1, 2 and 8 December 2018

RED HOT SUMMER TOUR
23 March to 27 April 2019

MT ISA MINES RODEO
Mt Isa, Qld, 11 August 2019

TOOWOOMBA CARNIVAL OF FLOWERS
Toowoomba, Qld, 22 September 2019

SINGAPORE
Gardens by The Bay, 25 and 26 October 2019

ONE ELECTRIC DAY
2 November to 7 December 2019

NEW ZEALAND
Villa Maria Winery, Auckland, 30 November 2019 and Michael Fowler Centre, Wellington, 1 December 2019

LIVE IN THE VINES
Sandalford Wines, Swan Valley, WA, 8 December 2019

HAY MATE: A BUSH CHRISTMAS CONCERT
Mornington Racecourse, Vic, 15 December 2019

FALLS FESTIVAL
Lorne, Vic, 28 December 2019
Marion Bay, Tas, 29 December 2019
Byron Bay, NSW, 31 December 2019
Fremantle, WA, 4 January 2020

FIRE FIGHT AUSTRALIA – CONCERT FOR NATIONAL BUSHFIRE RELIEF
ANZ Stadium, Sydney, 16 February 2020

PHOTO CAPTIONS

PAGE 1
I was just shy of my tenth birthday when we arrived in Melbourne. I'd grown up with music and songs in my life, my family were always singing, but I had no idea of the adventures to come. But I left school and took an apprenticeship as a plumber. The top right photo is of the crew from Caulfield Heating and Cooling at our Christmas Party in 1966. I am the young lad in the back right and my boss Stan Foster is opposite me on the left. The photo was sent to me by Bob Morrison, so thanks for the memory Bob.
Bottom left and right: These are early publicity shots of me.

PAGE 2
'Sadie, the Cleaning Lady' was released in November 1967 and the rollercoaster of promoting, performing and watching that record hit number one was nuts. I had a lot of fun but I was flat out like a lizard drinking. That song would bring me so many opportunities.
Bottom: Me with my brother Stephen.

PAGE 3

The moment I first saw Jillian Billman my heart leapt. To this day when I look at Jill I see the gorgeous woman she is and the young dancer she was. She was an absolute knockout! We have had some great adventures and Jill is my rock. These are some photos of Jill rehearsing, in costume, an early candid shot of us together and Jilly riding pillion on my motorbike in Darwin.

PAGE 4

Top: Parkinson in Australia interview, 1980.
Middle right: With Glenn Wheatley, the man was like a brother to me.
Bottom right: The first ever ARIA Awards in 1987. It wasn't televised so was a pretty loose affair. I couldn't believe it when we won six awards that night. A platinum-haired Elton John presented that night and he had a great sense of humour.

PAGE 5

Top: Six million people tuned in to watch the Royal Charity Concert beamed out live from the Sydney Opera House on 27 May 1980. At the time I was an unsigned, former pop idol so when I got the call asking for me to perform I was gobsmacked. I shared the stage with some incredible performers like Peter Allen, Paul Hogan, Julie Anthony and my friend, Olivia Newton-John
Middle: Receiving my Australian of the Year Award. Bob Hawke presented the award – and we both ended up crying.
Bottom: With the Little River Band. From left to right: Graeham Goble, Stephen Housden, me, Beeb Birtles, Wayne Nelson, Derek Pellicci.

PAGE 6

Top: Contact sheet of candid shots in the studio, recording *Whispering Jack* and playing ping pong between takes. As well as me, there's David Hirschfelder at the piano. (Photos on this page courtesy Serge Thomann)

PHOTO CAPTIONS

PAGE 7

Bottom: Molly Meldrum, Michael Gudinski, Glenn Wheatley, Glenn A. Baker, Jimmy Barnes and me at the ARIA Awards, Melbourne, November 1991. (©Bob King Photography, bobking.com.au)

PAGE 8

Top right and middle left: Photos courtesy Serge Thomann.

Bottom left and right: I was invited, along with some of the most famous musicians in the world, to launch Greenpeace's *Rainbow Warriors* album in Moscow. It was very cool to be in the company of Annie Lennox, Chrissie Hynde, The Edge, Peter Gabriel, Jerry Harrison from Talking Heads, Karl Wallinger from World Party and others in Red Square. But the brandy was deadly!

PAGE 9

Top left: Heading out to perform at the AFL Grand Final with Venetta Fields.

Top right: Me with Kate Ceberano. Kate and I were in *Superstar* together and it was a fabulous experience; it was a great cast and I loved singing those songs.

Middle: Belting it out with the incomparable Jimmy Barnes. He is a good man, Jimmy! (Photo courtesy Serge Thomann)

Bottom: The crew for *Tour of Duty – Concert for the Troops* on 21 December 1999. The concert was to show support for the Australian soldiers leading the United Nations-backed International Force East Timor (INTERFET). Kylie was on the bill and so were the Angels (with Doc upfront), James Blundell, Gina Jeffreys, The Living End, the Dili Allstars and the RMC Army Band and army performers. Roy Slaven and HG Nelson (aka John Doyle and Greig Pickhaver) hosted. (Photo courtesy Serge Thomann)

PAGE 10

Top: Performing with my favourite singer of all time, Stevie Wonder. (Photo courtesy Serge Thomann)

Middle left: Backstage at *A Day on the Green* in 2018 with Tania Doko and James Roche (Bachelor Girl), Russell Morris, Daryl Braithwaite and Richard Marx.

Middle right: Performing with Ray Charles. (Photo courtesy Serge Thomann)

Bottom: Performing with Stevie Wonder, Venetta Fields and Lindsay Field at the Thebarton Theatre in Adelaide, 1987.

PAGE 11

Top: With family, who mean everything. (Photo courtesy Serge Thomann)
Bottom left: With Jill, Rob and James.
Bottom right: Dancing with my Jilly at Ripponlea.

PAGE 12

Top left and right: Me and Jill and my other love . . . fishing!
Middle and bottom left and right: The Farnhams and the Wheatleys. Africa, 2018.

PAGE 13

With my good friend and absolute legend Olivia Newton-John, taken backstage at our *Two Strong Hearts* tour in 2015.

PAGE 14

The Fire Fight Australia concert in 2020 saw musicians come together for the best possible cause, after so much of the country had been burnt by bushfires and so many people lost their homes. I think that was the last time Olivia sang or performed onstage, and could be the last time I did too. (Photos courtesy David Anderson)